Fantastic Alice

Fantastic Alice

EDITED WITH
AN INTRODUCTION BY

Margaret Weis

ACE BOOKS, NEW YORK

This book is an Ace original edition,
and has never been previously published.

FANTASTIC ALICE

An Ace Book / published by arrangement with
the editors

PRINTING HISTORY
Ace edition / December 1995

ISBN: 0-441-00253-6

ACE®
Ace Books are published by The Berkley Publishing Group,
200 Madison Avenue, New York, NY 10016.
ACE and the "A" design are trademarks
belonging to Charter Communications, Inc.

PRINTED IN THE UNITED STATES OF AMERICA

10   9   8   7   6   5   4   3   2   1

Contents

Introduction

Charles Lutwidge Dodgson was born on January 27, 1832, in the parsonage of Daresbury, Cheshire, England. A mathematician, teacher at Oxford University, noted photographer, Dodgson was the author of such scholarly tomes as *Euclid and His Modern Rivals* and *Symbolic Logic*. He was the epitome of the proper Victorian gentleman. And he was also (although he would always deny it) Lewis Carroll, the man who created one of the most whimsical, fantastical, humorous, horror-laced children's novels in the English language: *Alice in Wonderland*.

This might seem out of character, but Dodgson had been writing whimsy and humorous material for years prior to *Alice*. He entertained his seven little sisters with plays, puppet shows, and satires on the stern and doleful children's literature of the Victorian era. A shy man with a severe stammer, Dodgson lived a relatively lonely lifestyle, with only a very small circle of close friends. His outlet was in inventing games and puzzles, playing with words and language, all of which appear in *Alice.* The *nom de plume* Lewis Carroll is an anagram based on the letters of Dodgson's name.

Alice in Wonderland was, according to one of Carroll's friends, Reverend Robinson Duckworth, conceived during a boat trip down the Isis (one of the headwaters of the Thames River) in Oxford in 1856. Carroll and Duckworth had taken the three children of Henry George Liddell, dean of Oxford University, for a ride in a rowboat. One of these children was ten-year-old Alice Liddell. To keep the children entertained, Carroll made up a story of the adventures of a girl named Alice.

Alice was so enthralled by the tale that she asked Carroll to write the adventures of Alice down for her. He promised he would and the work was completed in February 1863. The famous illustrator John Tenniel read it and consented to draw illustrations for it. As Carroll searched for a publisher for the manuscript, various titles were chosen and discarded: *Alice's Hour in Elf-Land*, *Alice Among the Elves*. Macmillan, the publishers for Oxford University, agreed to publish the book under its final title, *Alice's Adventures in Wonderland*.

Alice was an immediate success. Not surprising, considering the staid, moral, humorless books being given to children of the time. Children in the Victorian era were considered to be smaller versions of adults and were expected to act as such. This was the era of children working in factories, of children being trained to be thieves and pickpockets, and not far removed from a time when children could be hanged for committing crimes. Children were given books that lectured them on the virtues of being obedient, responsible, and reasonable. "Bad" children came to sad ends. "Good" children were rewarded with gingerbread and angel wings.

Carroll points out the absurdity of such notions by having Alice enter a world that is *not* responsible, a world that is *not* reasonable—in other words, the real world. A world of adults. He points out the absurdity of adult behavior and he celebrates the fact that Alice *is* a child. She remains a child, even when she grows to the size of an adult, and, as a child, with a child's common sense, she finds her way through the unreal, delightful, frightening world. Most importantly, she is filled with a child's wonder at the nonsensical world around her. And so are all of us who visit and revisit this Wonderland.

In *Fantastic Alice* are many modern-day fantasy writers who have tumbled down the rabbit hole and would like to share their wonder with you. The Contents reads like a list of fabulous treats at a literary tea party. Roger Zelazny, Janet Asimov, Esther M. Friesner, Jody Lynn Nye, and Mickey Zucker Reichert are just a few of the adventurers traveling through Wonderland. We hope you will enjoy our tribute to Lewis Carroll, as we further explore his wonderful world.

—MARGARET WEIS

Fantastic Alice

Something to Grin About

Lawrence Watt-Evans

∞ ∞

When the doorbell rang Melody dropped the phone, tossed the stack of bills on the table, and ran to answer it, expecting to see Todd there in the hallway with some new argument. She'd had the last word before he stormed out—she already regretted that, and he wasn't likely to let it stand. Sooner or later he'd be back to shout at her some more.

But it wasn't Todd; it was a uniformed deliveryman, not UPS or FedEx or any she'd seen before, but some courier service with a fancy, unreadable red-and-blue logo that was blazoned across the man's breast pocket and the back of his clipboard. On the floor by the deliveryman's feet was a large plastic box.

"Melody Duke?" he asked. Before Melody could reply, he held out the clipboard. "Line 8," he said.

She signed, and while she did he lifted the plastic box by a handle on the top and set it inside her door. When she was done she handed the clipboard back and looked down at the box.

"Where's it from?" she asked, but he had already turned away and gotten halfway down the stairs.

She shrugged, started to bend down for a look at the tag wired to the handle, then remembered the phone. She gasped, ran back to the kitchen, snatched up the receiver, and said, "Mother?"

The line was dead; her mother had hung up.

"Oh, *poop*," she said. Not that the discussion had been going anywhere; her mother still didn't like Todd and still didn't think she was safe living there, and Melody had been through all that with her parents any number of times without any minds changing.

She glared at the phone for a moment, then hung it up. Then she realized she had left the apartment door standing open with the mysterious package just inside, and despite what she told her parents, this was not *really* a completely safe neighborhood, especially with Todd gone for the moment. . . .

She dashed back to the living room, hauled the plastic crate inside, and slammed the door. For good measure she threw the deadbolt, then flopped down cross-legged on the floor to look over her new acquisition, whatever it was.

The tag on the handle had her name and address in the TO portion; the FROM read, "Abigail Duke, 7 Little Moreton Lane, Chester CH6 E11, ENGLAND."

Her British grandmother.

Her grandmother who had just gone into the nursing home.

Her grandmother who owned a cat Melody had promised to look after, a promise that Melody, eight thousand miles away, had not until this moment taken seriously. Now, however, she looked at the plastic crate and realized that yes, this was a pet carrier.

"Ohmigod," she said. She turned the crate around, and yes, there was the door, with rows of little airholes punched in it. She bent down and peered through the holes.

The crate was empty.

Melody blinked and sat up.

Had her grandmother's cat *escaped* somehow? How could it

have? The door was still latched. Had someone stolen it? She'd heard about people who stole cats and sold them to testing laboratories. Or had Grandma Duke maybe gotten confused and sent the crate empty? She'd always been a little dotty, as Melody's father put it, and now she was so old . . .

Melody had only met her grandmother three or four times, but the old lady had never seemed *that* dotty.

Of course, Todd would never stand for a cat around the place, so it would be just as well if there *was* no cat, but maybe the cat had just found some corner to hide in. Maybe if she took a closer look . . .

Melody untwisted the wire from around the latch and popped the door open—and out stepped the cat.

It was a very *large* cat, with splendid stripes and a long graceful tail that swayed elegantly as it strolled daintily away from the pet carrier. It was rather plump, but not actually *fat*. Dark tufts projected from the tip of either ear, and it moved in utter silence, its broad and well-furred paws soundless on the well-worn carpet. When it was well clear of its prison it turned, settled to the floor, wrapped its tail about itself, and grinned up at Melody.

She blinked at it in surprise. She'd never seen a cat grin before, and how in the world could a cat that size have hidden from her in that carrier? She looked from the cat to the carrier, then back again, and the cat simply grinned at her.

It was unquestionably a magnificent animal, but still . . .

"I can't keep a cat!" she said, to no one in particular.

The cat tipped its head and looked at her. "Whyever not?" it asked.

Melody blinked again. The cat's expression had been so easy to read, she told herself, that she almost thought she'd heard it speak.

"It's not allowed," she said, not sure why she was saying this aloud. "My lease says no pets. And anyway, Todd's allergic to cats and he hates animals. And my mother would complain about how much it would cost to *feed* a cat. She thinks I'm wasting my money trying to live here instead of staying home with her, and if I were feeding a cat . . ."

"And how is it your mother's business?"

"Well, that's what *I* keep saying," Melody agreed. "It's my money, and I can spend it any way I like, can't I?"

"I don't know," said the cat. "Can you? You certainly *may*, for all of me, but I wouldn't be sure you *can.*"

It was at that point that Melody realized she was holding an actual conversation with a cat.

"You can *talk!*" she said.

"So can you." The cat had a pleasant voice, either a tenor or a low alto, Melody couldn't decide which, with the same lovely British accent as her grandmother.

Which made sense, in a way, if you admitted a cat could talk in the first place. She stared at the cat for a moment, and it grinned placidly back.

"I must be mad," she said at last.

"Oh, we're all mad here," the cat replied.

"I know that line," Melody said, staring at the cat. "I know *all* of this . . . a talking, grinning cat? A Cheshire Cat?"

The cat licked the tip of its tail thoughtfully, then remarked, "Your grandmother *does* live in Chester, after all; what *other* sort of cat ought she to have?"

"You can disappear," Melody said accusingly. "That's why the box looked empty!"

The cat did not deign to reply to that.

"This is crazy," Melody said. "That was in a story, it wasn't true. I *must* be mad!"

"Oh," the cat said, "is *nothing* one reads in stories true, then? How curious."

"I didn't mean *that*," Melody said. She stared at the cat.

It wasn't disappearing. It did talk, and it did grin, though.

"This is crazy," Melody said again.

The cat did not bother to reply to that.

"Listen, I really can't keep you here!" Melody said. "The landlord won't stand for it. No pets, it says so in the lease. It's right there in . . . what are you doing?"

The cat's tail had gotten shorter, she was sure of it—and as she watched, more of it vanished, followed by the animal's hindquarters, and then the rest of it, until nothing was left but the grin.

Melody was not a calm person. She had been known to lose her composure over a misplaced can of soup or a crooked shower curtain. Ordinary catastrophes such as a missed train or broken heel could reduce her to hysterics. Todd's tantrums and invective had brought on tears for *months* before she had gotten used to them. Even so, watching a cat disappear inch by inch, until nothing remained but the grin, when a cat had no business grinning in the first place, was beyond question the single most unsettling thing she had ever seen in her life. It was all she could do to keep from screaming, and a small, strangled squeak did escape, despite her best efforts.

The cat's head reappeared.

"I don't think your landlord would notice me, should I prefer that he not do so," the cat said.

"I guess not," she said weakly.

"I don't suppose you'd have such a thing as a piece of liver about?" the cat asked. "I spent a very long time in that box. I'm hungry." As he spoke, the rest of him abruptly reappeared.

Melody stared at the cat for a moment, then resigned herself to it—the Cheshire Cat was real, it was here, it was hungry, and it was her responsibility, at least for the moment. "I'll see," she said.

She stumbled to the kitchen and opened the refrigerator, and then, for no reason she was aware of, glanced up.

The Cheshire Cat was sitting on top of the refrigerator, curled up with its head on its forepaws, watching her.

Melody screamed.

5

The cat blinked lazily and continued to stare at her as she caught her breath and, hand on her heart, tried to calm down; then it grinned.

"Did I startle you?" it asked.

"You scared me half to death!" she said. "I left you back in the living room!"

The cat didn't reply to that, but instead looked down and asked, "Is there any liver?"

"No," Melody said as she rummaged through the refrigerator's drawers and compartments. "There's some hamburger—would that do?"

"That would certainly be better than nothing," the cat said. It vanished.

Melody stared at the spot where it had sat for a moment, then turned and cautiously looked around.

The cat was standing on the counter, just under the phone, the tip of its tail brushing the receiver.

That seemed as good a place to feed it as any, Melody decided; she pulled out the tray with its leftover lump of ground beef, peeled off the plastic wrap, and put it on the counter.

"Thank you," the cat said. Then it began eating.

By the time Melody had closed the refrigerator and turned back, the hamburger was gone.

"Is there any more?" the cat asked wistfully.

"No," Melody said, very definitely. "No, there isn't. And you can't stay here. Even if you *can* hide from the landlord. My mother would nag me about wasting money, and Todd would be sneezing all the time—if he came in at all! If I kept a cat he might not come back!"

"Who's Todd?"

"My boyfriend. Sort of. I mean, he is, but we fight a lot, or sometimes, when he gets mad about something or I get mad, so he keeps leaving me, but he doesn't really, I mean we don't really break up, because then he always comes back, sooner or later, after he's over being mad or if he gets mad at his new girlfriend, if he has one, which he did twice, the rat, and I apologize and promise not to do whatever it was again, if I can figure out what it was I did. And I make him dinner and we'll be back together until he gets mad again."

The cat stared at her for a moment, then said, "Would you care to reconstruct that statement so that it makes sense, or shall I simply accept the intelligible portions as they stand and ignore the rest?"

"Oh, shut up. I don't know why I'm talking to a *cat*, anyway."

"Perhaps because *I'm* speaking to *you*," the cat suggested.

"Which you have no business doing! Cats can't talk!"

"I can. And I'm quite certain I'm a cat."

"Well, you're not *my* cat. You can't stay here!"

"And where am I to go, then? Your grandmother sent me here because she believed you had promised to take care of me when she could no longer do so; it wasn't *my* idea."

Melody frowned, and looked about helplessly. She could hardly take her grandmother's cat to the pound; she would have to find it a new home.

"Maybe one of my friends could take you," she said.

The cat considered that.

"I'll ask around," she said.

"And for now?"

"You can stay for now, I guess," Melody reluctantly conceded.

"In that case, might I trouble you for some more food? Fish, perhaps, if there's no liver to be had?"

Melody shuddered. "I hate seafood," she said. "Look, I'll go down to the market and buy some cat food, okay? Liver flavor, if they have it."

"Being a cat, I can't honestly say I would be grateful, but I would very much enjoy being properly fed."

"All right, then," Melody said.

When she returned to the living room, Melody noticed the

now-empty cat carrier and took a moment to tuck it away out of sight in the coat closet before she prepared to go out. She didn't want Todd seeing it when he came back; he hated pets. He might hit her again; he hadn't lately, but if he found out she had a cat, he might.

As she put on her jacket and collected her purse she had the distinct feeling that she had lost her debate with the cat—but that was hardly new; she lost arguments with Todd and with her mother all the time, and she'd probably have lost arguments with her boss and her coworkers at the shop if she'd ever had the nerve to argue with any of them in the first place.

Losing to a cat seemed somehow a bit worse, though, and in retaliation she slammed the door on her way out, which did not trouble the cat at all. It watched her go, then washed itself and settled to sleep on the kitchen counter.

It was awakened a moment later by a loud ring from the telephone. Annoyed, the cat uncurled and glared up at the device.

It rang again.

The cat got to its feet, stretched up a paw, and knocked the receiver from its hook. It fell rattling to the counter, then lay still, the receiver directly in front of the cat.

"Hello?" a voice said. "Melody?"

"I'm afraid Melody isn't here," the cat said into the mouthpiece.

For a moment there was silence, and the cat considered resuming its nap; then the voice said, "Who am I talking to? That's not Todd's voice. Who are you?"

"I'm Melody's new boarder," the cat replied. "Most people just call me Cat."

"Boarder? You mean a roommate? Melody didn't tell me!"

"I've just arrived," the cat said.

"Oh! Well, I . . . well, that's wonderful. I'm Melody's mother, and I've been telling her for *months* that it wasn't safe living there alone, that it was too expensive . . . Are you splitting the rent?"

"I expect to do my share, Mrs. Duke," the cat answered.

"And . . . well, what about Todd? I know Melody denied it, but I thought he was living with her, and there isn't *room* for three, is there? *Todd* never paid any rent, of course—I think that's why he kept coming back."

"I haven't met Todd, Mrs. Duke. I believe he's left."

"For good, I hope. I know I shouldn't say such things, but really, Melody can do better, I'm sure, if she'd once get rid of him!"

"I wouldn't know. I do know Todd isn't here, and I am."

"Well, that's wonderful. You have such a lovely accent—is it English?"

"I'm from England, yes. From Cheshire."

"What an interesting coincidence—my mother-in-law lives in Cheshire!"

"Yes, I believe Melody mentioned that."

"You said your name is Catherine?"

"Just Cat will suit me fine, Mrs. Duke."

"Melody isn't there?"

"She stepped out to the market just now."

"Oh. Well, when she gets back, you tell her that I called, okay?"

"I'll do that, Mrs. Duke."

"All right, then. Good-bye!"

"Good-bye." The cat reached up with one paw and pressed down the hook.

Unfortunately, it had no way to hang the receiver back up—that was more than mere paws could handle. The result was a dial tone that was not particularly to the cat's liking, even before it changed to the phone-left-off-the-hook warning. The cat eyed the noisy receiver with distaste. It decided a nap was no longer practical; it hopped down from the counter and ambled into the living room.

The doorbell rang. The cat stopped, midway across the living room, and glared at it.

"Melody?" a male voice called.

At this new intrusion on its privacy the cat wondered whether perhaps this place was insufficiently peaceful to be a suitable residence—but it was, as yet, unfamiliar with any better alternative in the area. With a flick of its tail, it vanished.

A key scraped in the lock, and the apartment door opened; a young man stepped in.

"Melody? It's me—I came back for my stuff!"

The cat watched, unseen.

"Come on, bitch, I know you're here!" the young man shouted.

The cat considered that. It did not much like this loud, ill-mannered person. Furthermore, if this was Todd, he was an obstacle to the cat's remaining comfortably settled here.

Something would have to be done about that. Ordinarily, the cat preferred to simply watch humans going about their foolish little lives, but in this case intervention seemed appropriate.

"Is that anything to call her?" the cat asked.

The young man—Todd, the cat supposed him to be—looked about, but was unable to locate a source for the words he had just heard, and concluded that he had just imagined them, or perhaps overheard something from another apartment.

"Damn," he said. He marched in, leaving the door standing wide open, and peered into the kitchen.

No Melody.

He tried the bedroom—also vacant. The bathroom was dark and empty.

He returned to the bedroom and began collecting his belongings from the nightstand and dresser into a laundry bag—and incidentally pocketing a few dollars Melody had left in the bedside drawer.

"Is that money yours?" the cat asked; its head had appeared, floating in midair just behind Todd's ear.

He whirled, but the cat's head had vanished again.

"So you're a thief, as well as an exploitive scoundrel?" the cat asked from the other side.

"The bitch owes me!" Todd protested.

"Oh? For what? For putting up with months of abuse? For apologizing when you demand it? For cooking your supper and paying your rent?"

"What is this?" Todd demanded. "Is this place haunted or something? Is this someone's idea of a joke?"

"I suppose it would be too much to suggest this is the voice of your conscience," the cat said musingly.

"I don't have a goddamn conscience, Jiminy Cricket," Todd said sneeringly. "Who *are* you?"

Then he sneezed messily.

"Damn," he said, as he groped for the box of tissues on the dresser.

The cat chose that moment to rematerialize, back on the floor just behind Todd's right leg. It stretched out one large, well-furred paw, extended its claws as far as it could, and then dug them firmly through Todd's sweat sock into his ankle.

"Aaaaugh!" he screamed into the tissue he had been using to wipe his nose.

The cat retracted its claws and vanished.

"What the . . ." Todd's sentence was interrupted by another sneeze. As he bent over, the cat applied a pawful of claws to Todd's left ankle.

The noise Todd produced in response was a fascinating combination of scream, sneeze, cough, and choke. He staggered back and sat down heavily on the bed, both fists clenched, a soggy tissue dangling from one of them.

"*Who did that?*" he demanded, looking about wildly.

The cat, of course, had vanished again; now its head reappeared behind Todd's right shoulder and spoke.

"I did it," the cat said. "And I'll do more of the same as long as you're here, or if you ever set foot in this apartment again."

11

"Fine!" Todd said, flinging down the tissue. "That's just god-damn fine, whoever you are! The bitch isn't worth it. Hey, Melody, you hear me? You ain't worth it. I can find another girl who'll treat me better!" He looked down at his ankles and saw blood seeping through his socks.

"Oh, Jesus, I'm bleeding," he said. "Damn it, look at that! Look what you did! Jesus!" He dabbed at the blood and only succeeded in spreading it further. He snatched a handful of tissues from the box and stuffed them into his socks as makeshift dressings, and was interrupted several times by sneezes as he did so.

"Doesn't she ever dust in here?" he grumbled. "What the hell am I sneezing at?"

The cat considered the sight of Todd, sitting on the edge of the bed and bent down to stuff tissues in his socks, and was unable to resist.

Todd felt a sudden weight on his back, and the mysterious needles that had gouged his ankles suddenly scraped across the back of his neck.

"*All right!*" he said, jumping up. He whirled, but saw no sign of his attacker. "All right, I'm going! Jesus, give me a minute!"

"No," the cat said.

"Oh, crap," Todd said, grabbing a final clump of tissues with one hand and his nose with the other as he fought back a fresh attack of sneezing. He snatched up his laundry bag and fled, hobbling.

The cat watched him go.

When Todd was out of sight, and his footsteps had faded to inaudibility, the cat pushed the apartment door closed.

The phone was still making its annoying buzzing noise, but the bedroom was reasonably quiet; the cat jumped up on the bed, curled up, and went to sleep.

Several minutes later Melody returned, and discovered, as she fumbled for her key, that the door was unlocked. Worried, she opened it.

"Todd?" she called.

No one answered. She stepped in and looked around.

Nothing was out of place, so far as she could see. The phone was buzzing, though; she went to the kitchen, put her bag of groceries on the counter, and hung the receiver up.

She didn't remember leaving it off the hook. "Todd?" she called.

"He isn't here," the cat replied. "He was, though. He collected a few things, and then left."

"He did?" Melody frowned. Todd almost always left a few things behind; that was one reason she always expected him to come back eventually.

"And your mother called," the cat said.

"She did? How do you know?"

"I knocked the phone off the hook," the cat admitted.

"Oh, she's probably furious!" Melody snatched at the receiver and dialed.

A moment later, as Melody was making frantic apologies, her mother said, "Oh, that's all right—but why didn't you *tell* me about that lovely Cat?"

"Cat?" Melody said, horrified.

"Your new roommate! She sounds wonderful; I'll have to meet her sometime."

Melody glanced at the cat, which stood in the kitchen door, grinning at her. "Roommate," she said weakly. "Right."

Five minutes later Melody hung up the phone and glared at the cat.

"I don't know how you did that," she said.

"Your mother doesn't seem to object to my presence here," the cat remarked.

"No, she doesn't," Melody agreed. "You said Todd was here?"

"Well, a young man who had a key was here."

"That was Todd. Did he see you?"

"No, I don't believe he did."

"Well, *that's* something, anyway."

"Did you buy food for me?"

"Oh, yeah." Melody fished a can of cat food out of the bag of groceries and slapped it into the electric can opener.

She watched thoughtfully as the cat ate.

"All right," she said at last, as it licked its paws after finishing, "you can stay until Todd comes back. But the minute he's back, out you go."

The cat curled up and began to purr. "That," it said, "will suit me just fine."

The Rabbit Within

Gary A. Braunbeck

⤬

By homely gift and hindered Words
The Human heart is told
Of Nothing—
"Nothing" is the force
That renovates the World . . .

—*Emily Dickinson (#1536)*

*A*t the very end of the dream, the same dream he's been having for quite some time now, he finds himself standing at the end of a long, lonely road and singing a nonsense song as if he were a child again—"Fal-de-ral-dal-riddle-dee-rum"—then a pair of voices begin shouting from far away: "I see Nobody on the road!" says the first voice, and the second replies, "I only wish *I* had such eyes! To be able to see Nobody! And at that distance too!" Then, even though he can't see them, he begins jumping up and down, waving his arms to attract their attention, crying, "I'm right here, waiting! Come on, I'm right here!"

But the only reply is an echo that sings the second part of his childish nonsense song: ". . . with a rim-dim-diddy and a rum-dum-dum. . . ."

Then Matthew wakes in the dim light of dawn to the sound of the dog scratching at the kitchen door. The bed feels cold, despite the layers of blankets piled on top of his body. He sits up and leans against the headboard, then reaches over and fumbles a book of matches off the antique nightstand. It takes a moment for his hands to stop their shaking but he waits patiently, then strikes one of the matches and touches flame to the wick of an oil lamp. The room glows warmly from the light but Matthew himself feels no sense of home. He hopes that he's not getting sick. He has only himself to depend on.

He feels a draft coming from the window over the bed and turns to pull back the curtain. The window seems like an ice sculpture to his tired eyes, covered as it is in patterns of frost, but the center of the glass is clear, allowing him to easily see the two graves at the top of the hill behind the farmhouse.

His wife, Rebecca, rests in the grave on the left, her slumber just as deep now as it had been six years ago on the morning he'd buried her; his daughter, Sarah, rests in the right-hand grave, her slumber entering only its second year on this morning. Between them is a third and much smaller grave, but he chooses not to think about it right now because the dog is barking its raspy, insistent bark. Matthew releases the curtain and swings his legs over the side of the bed. The touch of the cold, cracked wooden floor against his bare feet reminds him of how cold his life and heart are, how barren the house feels now that he's alone. He sighs, runs a hand through his thinning gray hair, and coughs. There are chores to be done, chickens to be fed, cows to be milked.

Another winter's day to be gotten through.

He pulls on his tattered bathrobe, then makes his way toward the kitchen. The dog runs over to meet him, its nails clicking against the linoleum floor, and Matthew shambles to the back door and opens it; he sees the silver layer of frost covering the storm door and the fresh coat of snow that covers the ground beyond the porch and he thinks, *You would have loved a morning like this*—but whether the thought is directed toward the ghost of his wife or his daughter he cannot tell. He pushes open the door and the dog shoots past him, leaping from the porch and landing in the snow which comes almost to its belly. The dog whirls in a circle, creating a cloud of snow-fog, then bounds across the white-blanketed field to some secret place whose true worth only a dog can appreciate.

Matthew watches the dog disappear into an icy cluster of bare and frozen branches that have taken the place of the rosebushes that were there in the summer. He looks once more at the graves, and notes with a workman's eyes that the crosses need mending. *Have to go through the firewood and find some proper sticks*, he thinks, then goes to his tool drawer to see if the small coil of chicken wire is still there.

Mornings have never been easy for him but this morning weighs particularly heavy on his shoulders. December 15. Rebecca had died on this day six years ago. Sarah had only been two at the time and hadn't understood where Mommy had gone. Matthew did his best to comfort her, to explain to her about death, but she hadn't understood, not until much later.

He feels like an old man of seventy even though the calendars, the clocks, the dates and names and events he remembers and, though they're private and not all that reliable on their own, his memories themselves tell him that he's only fifty-two, not an old man yet, not this early in the game.

Still, the loneliness ages him.

He starts a pot of coffee, then opens one of the cupboards over the sink and pulls out the first mug he touches—which turns out to be Sarah's bunny rabbit mug, and suddenly Matthew finds himself being spun backward in time, to a morning not unlike this one two years ago when Sarah, who'd just turned six, insisted that she come along with him on the morning chores.

He sets the cup down on the counter, takes a deep breath, and whispers, "The owl would never have been so gentle," to the chilly, silent house.

The only response is the sound of the dog barking from somewhere in the snow outside.

"You're still sick," he told Sarah. "It's only twenty degrees outside, hon. You stay in here and fix us some hot chocolate. I won't be long."

"Please, Daddy? I want to go with you so we can put those flowers on Mommy's grave."

He bit his lower lip and tried to think up another good reason for her to stay put. From the day she'd been born Sarah had been a sickly child, too thin, too pale, too weak. The doctors hadn't thought she'd live to her first birthday but she'd shown them, all right. Physically she was and always would be frail, and the recent bout with the flu had only made her look smaller, drawn, and breakable, like a delicate porcelain statue. Maybe he was being too protective, but he couldn't stand the thought of anything happening to her—not only because she looked so much like her mother and was, in a way, the only thing he had left of Rebecca, but because she was so independent, already her own woman and convinced that the farm would fall to ruin without her to keep her father in line and remind him of what's what and who was really in charge. Even with something as simple as stacking the firewood, she had to supervise, always telling him, "That's enough, Daddy, time to start a new row."

Despite his better judgment, Matthew nodded his head and said, "All right, but that's all you're going to do, okay? You and me'll go put the flowers on Mama's grave and then it's right back inside with you. And you'll be dressed warm, understand? Two pairs of socks and your long johns, plus I want you to wear that scarf I got for you and—"

"*And* a sweater on top of my shirt and earmuffs and my coat with the hood. Yes, Daddy."

He shut up then and shrugged his shoulders, a little embarrassed that she'd caught him being a worrier again.

Sarah crossed over to him and put a hand on his unshaven cheek and said, "You're a sweetie."

"No," he replied, "you're the sweetie."

"Nuh-uh, *you* are."

She *tsk*ed at him and put her hands on her hips and smiled and shook her head and looked so much like her mother at that moment that Matthew wanted to cry. Here, in his daughter's smile, was the ghost of Rebecca's own smile the night she'd accepted his proposal of marriage with a "Well, you certainly took your time about it, didn't you?"

"Best be gettin' yourself ready," he said.

She moved so quickly that a casual observer would never have believed she'd been running a temperature of 101 only three days ago.

They made their way outside and up the hill, Sarah cradling the flowers in her arms like a proud mother with her newborn baby, and when they reached Rebecca's grave Matthew noted that the cross had fallen a little to the right and so he knelt down and began to adjust it, unaware that his daughter was crying until he turned to look at her.

"It's all right," he said, smiling as he touched her flushed cheek with one of his gloved hands. "Graves're a place for tears, honey. Your mother misses you, too."

Sarah shook her head, then wiped her nose and pointed to a spot a few yards to the right. Matthew had to squint against the glare of the sun as its light intensified the brightness of the snow, but he was soon able to make out the furry lump that had brought tears to Sarah's eyes.

A small white rabbit lay on its side, back legs splayed apart and dark eyes unblinking, covered in a thin layer of ice and snow. He didn't have to touch it to know that it was quite dead.

"It, uh . . . it must've got lost or hurt or something and froze to death."

"Poor thing," spluttered Sarah. "And it was somebody's pet, too."

"What makes you say that, hon?"

"Lookit the way it's dressed."

Matthew crossed to the frozen rabbit and brushed away the snow, uncovering something bright blue. He squinted once more, then dug his hands in underneath the frozen body and worked it out of the ice.

The rabbit was wearing a small blue vest, complete with two small side pockets and three gold buttons. Someone had gone to a great deal of trouble to make this vest. He wondered if the person who'd done this was the kind who also made their dog wear silly outfits at Christmas or knitted sweaters for their cat.

"Who do you think it belongs to?" asked Sarah, coming up next to him and petting the rabbit's stiff, cold fur.

"Don't rightly know, hon. Probably belongs to someone in town. Rabbits can run pretty far pretty fast, you know. Poor little guy probably got loose and just ran until he got too cold and, well . . ."

"How can God be so cruel, Daddy?"

"Oh, Sarah," he said, putting down the rabbit's body and pulling his daughter close to him. "Freezing to death like this, it's . . . it's supposed to be a peaceful way to die. God wasn't cruel to this bunny."

"I'll bet it was scared. I'll bet it was all scared and lonely, just like Mommy when she died in the hospital and we . . . we weren't there. Poor bunny."

"Shh, hon. Look at its face, okay? It doesn't look like it was scared or lonely, it looks like it . . . like it was in a hurry to get back to business. Maybe it just decided to take itself a bit of a rest before getting on. Maybe it died looking forward to a bunch of things."

"So God wasn't . . . wasn't cruel to it?"

"No. It died peaceful. The owl would not have been so gentle."

"Mommy liked rabbits."

"I know she did."

Sarah wiped her eyes, kissed Matthew on the cheek, then set about the business of arranging the flowers on Rebecca's grave. Once that was done, she said a little prayer, then crossed herself and said, "Can we bury the rabbit up here next to Mommy? She'd like that."

Matthew stroked his daughter's back and nodded his head.

They found a shoe box in the back of one of the closets and used that to bury the rabbit in. Sarah insisted that it have its own little cross as well. Once they were done and she had prayed over the rabbit and the two of them were on their way back to the house, Sarah took Matthew's hand and said, "Remember when you told me that Mommy would live on inside me as long as I remembered her?"

"Yes, hon, I do."

"And that as long as she lived on inside me I'd never feel lonely and sad?"

"Uh-huh."

"Is it okay if I remember the rabbit, too?"

"I don't see why not. It was one of God's creatures, and I'm sure He appreciates somebody remembering them."

Sarah grinned. "I'll remember it the way it was before it died, running along through the snow, hopping over sticks and logs and stuff. I'll remember it like I do Mommy." She touched the middle of her chest. "The rabbit will always be running in my heart, and Mommy'll be there watching it. And laughing. I liked her laugh. It was pretty."

Matthew stopped dead in his tracks right then, so moved was he by his daughter's sudden grasp of death and memory and the abstract connection between the two.

"You okay, Daddy?"

"Yes, Sarah, I'm fine." He turned and looked up at the graves. "I miss Mommy," he said. "Sometimes I think about her and I—" He stopped himself. What good would it do, telling her that he was finding it increasingly more difficult to remember what Rebecca's face looked like? Why did the empty spaces left in death's wake have to keep on taking things away from the living? Wasn't the pain of loss enough?

"You're a sweetie," said Sarah.

"Nuh-uh, *you're* the sweetie."

"Nuh-uh."

"Uh-huh."

"You won't get sick and die, will you, Daddy?"

"No, hon, I won't. Not for a long, long time."

" 'Kay," she said, then went on ahead of him to open the door, calling over her shoulder that she was going to make some hot chocolate for them and was going to use her bunny mug so he'd better hurry.

Matthew waved at her as he approached. For just a moment there, right before she'd run ahead of him, he'd wanted to say, *You have to promise me you won't get sick and die either,* but he hadn't.

That was the first thing that crossed his mind on the night she died, less than four months later.

"It was a hard winter, this last one," the doctor at the hospital told Matthew. "It must've been too much for her system. I know it's not a lot of comfort to you right now, but it was a miracle she lived this long. An immune system as delicate as hers . . . well, she had eight good years, you should try to remember that. She was a happy little girl and she loved you. Remember that."

Matthew nodded his head and said nothing. He wondered if the farmhouse was too old, after all. Maybe he hadn't gotten all of the cracks in the floor and around the windowsills. Maybe he hadn't kept the fires hot enough to keep the place warm. Maybe he should have made her dress warmer than he had.

Maybe he should have said no and made her stay inside, then they wouldn't have had to go out a second time to bury that goddamned rabbit.

He wiped his eyes and took a deep breath, feeling a cold space in his heart where once something had run free.

The dog scratches at the door, wanting back inside. Matthew looks once more at the bunny rabbit mug before shoving it back into the cupboard. He wonders if he was wrong to tell Sarah that God wasn't cruel; this morning it feels like God is very cruel. Too cruel.

When the dog comes trotting into the house it pauses by the door and shakes itself dry—as dry as it can get, anyway—then skitters over next to the wood-burning stove and squats down, dropping something shiny it carries in its mouth.

At first Matthew pays it no mind, but as the dog bats at the thing with one of its paws it slides up against a leg of the stove and makes a short, sharp *ping!*

"What you got there?" says Matthew as he comes over to the dog. "You dragging metal scraps in from that junkyard over by the old steel mill?" He kneels down and experiences a moment of dizziness. God, please don't let me be sick, there's too much to do. He steadies himself, rubs Merle's head, and reaches for whatever it is the dog has brought inside.

At first he thinks he must be mistaken, but as he holds the item up to the light and wipes away the snow and dirt, he sees the tiny winding device and presses down on it, and the front of the thing unlatches and pops open, revealing the Roman numerals.

"Now where in the hell did you manage to dig up a gold pocket watch?" he asks the dog. The dog whines once, then lies flat, resting its head on its front paws. Matthew stands and makes his way to his desk in the adjoining room. He sits down and turns on the lamp and holds the watch under the light.

Even through the dirt and melting snow and ice that cakes it, he can see that it is an exquisite piece of work, the kind of time-piece his own father had always referred to as a turnip watch. The hands are still, the big one pointing down, the little hand up. Twelve-thirty, Matthew thinks as he removes a tissue from a nearby box and begins cleaning the watch. He starts with the cov-erpiece, noting as he cleans that there are figures etched in the gold, odd figures—a man with a horse's head who looks like a chess piece, a large-faced woman wearing a crown, an egg-shaped man wearing a bow tie who is sitting on a wall, a walrus in a jacket and vest, a man with a very small body and very large head wearing a gigantic, lopsided top hat, a sheep with spectacles resting at the end of its nose, and a few soldiers whose bodies seem to be noth-ing more than playing cards. He grins at them all, admiring the de-tails in their features.

Once he is done cleaning the watch, he winds it and holds it near his ear. The soft *ticka-ticka-ticka* makes him smile. He marvels at the craftsmanship that must have gone into making this watch—Heaven only knows how long it must have been buried in the snow, and here it still runs just fine.

He finds a can of polish and an old rag and sets about making the watch shine. It is only after he is finished and the watch has been returned to its original splendor that he notices the second hand is running counterclockwise.

"Well, now, ain't that a shame? A fine-looking watch like this." Then he notices that the Roman numerals are reversed—the VI is at the top and the XII at the bottom. Not only that, not only are the numerals backwards on the face, but they are upside down as well.

"I'll be," he whispers. "Merle," he calls to the dog, "you've found yourself a backward-running watch. 'Course I'd expect nothing less from you, you simple thing."

Merle gives a little *yip!* as if to say, "You're quite welcome."

Matthew stands and turns toward the mirror over the fireplace and holds up the watch, then turns it so that the bottom faces up and the top faces down.

The mirror reflects a raggedy man holding a magnificent watch whose face reads 6:00—just like the clock on his desk.

"Now, isn't that something? Finding a backward-running watch that's got the right time." He smiles at his reflection, then closes the watch and looks over at Merle. "They'd've gotten a real kick out of this, you know?"

Merle lifts his head and cocks his ears.

"You did good, Merle. The morning seems a bit more interesting now, doesn't it?"

Merle yawns, then moves closer to the wood-burning stove.

"You're right," says Matthew, heading toward the bedroom. "It's time I got to the chores. And I'll be sure to bring in some extra firewood, that sound good?"

Merle shrugs, then falls asleep.

"Too much excitement for you, I know, boy." He dresses himself for the day's labors and puts the watch in his pocket. It has the feel of a good-luck charm to it and Matthew likes that a lot. He could use a little good luck these days because mornings are never easy for him.

Buttoning up his coat, he finds himself singing to himself, a simple nonsense song: "Fal-de-ral-dal-riddle-dee-rum . . ."

Which he sings while he journeys toward his dead.

As he reaches the top of the hill he sees that Merle has been digging at the rabbit's grave. Matthew curses under his breath and starts to heave the snow and dirt back in place. Merle has even dug through the top of the shoe box. Matthew can see a patch of blue from the rabbit's vest and shakes his head. This would upset Sarah no end, so he takes care as he fills in the grave. She would want it to be neat. He reaches over to pick up the small cross he'd made for the rabbit's grave and stops when he sees the thin gold chain dangling from it. He removes the chain and looks at it, thinking, *How can this be?* He takes the pocket watch out and holds it next to the chain.

"Oh, my," he whispers as he snaps the chain in place.

Where had this come from?

The wind picks up, and the chill in his bones and chest deepens. He puts the watch and chain back in his pocket and finishes fixing the crosses on Rebecca's and Sarah's graves. His hands are shaking. His breathing is strained. His vision blurs slightly and he can feel the sweat soaking his skin.

"Dammit," he says. Not now, he can't afford to get sick now. He's alone and there's much work to be done.

He goes to the barn and milks the cows, then feeds the chickens, then double-checks the heaters to make sure they're running well and safely. It wouldn't do for him to get careless and burn down the farm. He wipes the sweat from his eyes, gathers the eggs and places them along with the buckets of milk in the industrial-size refrigerator near the entrance. He coughs as he checks the generator to make sure it's putting out plenty of juice, then steps outside and closes the barn door behind him.

He is surprised to find that it has begun snowing again, and heavily at that. Great swirls of blowing snow enfold him. For a moment he stands, hands sunk deep in his pockets, staring toward the house and its makeshift driveway that leads to the road, and he thinks he sees two figures at the far end of the road but then he blinks and they are gone. Sick; he knows he's getting sick and there's still the firewood to deal with. *(That's enough, Daddy, time to start a new row.)* He puts his head down and moves forward, then veers left toward the tool shed. He feels bad at the moment and cold, too damn cold, but there's a little something on a shelf in the shed that should take care of that. He gets to the shed and pulls open the door, then reaches in and pulls something from a shelf beside the door. Turning his back to the wind and blowing snow, he unscrews the cap from the small bottle of vodka, then lifts the bottle to his lips and tips it and drinks. It makes almost no differ-ence—he feels no better or worse for having taken the drink; all he's done is stop himself from feeling as bad as he would have felt without the liquor. Rebecca never approved of his occasional snorts, but she kept it to herself out of respect for a man's privacy. He puts the cap back on the bottle and replaces it on the shelf, then shuts the shed door and resumes his journey back to the house, an arctic explorer plunging deep into the wild snow as he sets out for the North Pole.

It's a lot deeper than expected, six or eight inches already, and he curses himself for not having checked the weather report on the radio before going out this morning and this is what he gets when he's careless, a surprise snowstorm that leaves him plodding through six or eight inches of snow, a lot of it drifting, propelled by a merciless northern wind, a heavy, wet, hard-driving snow that sticks to every surface facing it—trees, the house, the shed, the barn, and now himself. He feels as if he's turning into a living snowman as he trods toward the house that seems so far away, a dark, warm opening in a too-white world, miles and years away from him, and he wonders if he will ever get there, if he will spend years, an entire lifetime, out here in the snow slogging his way to-ward the silent, warm house where the only thing waiting for him is an old dog that can't be too long out of the grave itself, and then he'll be truly alone, but that's the way of all life, isn't it, so he keeps going, slowly, joints aching, chest tightening, and by the time he reaches the woodpile he's completely white, even his face, even though he's pulled his head down into his coat as far as he can and he can barely see through the waves of wind-whipped snow lashing against him but he keeps moving because there's too much to do, so he begins loading wood into his arms, trying to ig-nore the fiery ache in every muscle, then he sees the two figures at the far end of the road again, only now they seem to have been joined by others, three, maybe four, and he wonders if they're lost or maybe if they'd just been passing through these parts and their car had broken down, and as he squints his eyes to get a better look he sees that some of them are oddly shaped, just like the figures on the watch, tall and thin like reeds or squat and egg-shaped, lolling from side to side, and he hears a child's voice singing, "...with a rim-dim-diddy and a rum-dum-dum..." and the heat is consuming him, he's dizzy and can't seem to pull in a breath as the figures come closer, one of them a tall man with a chess-piece horse's head, mist jetting from its nostrils, and Matthew blinks, dropping the firewood and covering his face with cold, gloved hands as something rises up in his gut and sticks in his throat and he blinks again, pulling his hands away just as a sunken figure whose head seems far too big for its body comes up to him and tips its lopsided top hat and says, "Six o'clock now, six o'clock! Tea time! Tea time for the soul!" and then there is only the snow and the icy wind and the pressure in his chest and throat as Matthew tries to ask the odd figures who they are and what they want but it's too late now, he's sick and the ground is coming up to meet him. . . .

What happens over the next few hours—maybe even days, as far as Matthew can tell—takes place in an aching blur of disjointed images and sounds and sensations.

The fever seems to rise and fall, draining his body of life and his spirit of resolve. He knows that he is back inside the house, in his bed, the covers pulled up around his chest. He hears voices, several voices, talking excitedly to one another.

"I've never heard of 'uglification.' What is it?"

"Never heard of uglifying! You know what 'to beautify' is, I suppose?"

"Yes, it means—to—make—anything—prettier."

"Well then, if you don't know what to uglify is, you *are* a simpleton!"

"Quiet!" squalls a harsh-voiced woman. "If the two of you continue to quarrel, I shall have you beheaded!"

"Not at tea time, I must insist! Such unpleasantness has no

place at a splendid table such as I've set for us. Now, sit down before it gets cold!"

A chicken clucked.

"Off with its head!"

Then comes the sound of an ax *chunk*ing down through brittle bone, and the chicken is silent.

Later, the house fills with the sweet aroma of roasted poultry, and a dim figure comes into the room and lifts Matthew's head and spoons delicious chicken soup into his mouth.

He sleeps without dreaming, then wakes to silence.

He rolls over and reaches for the pocket watch that is lying on the nightstand. He pops it open and sees that the numbers seem to have righted themselves. It is still 6:00.

"Six?" he croaks.

"Six o'clock!" shouts a voice from the kitchen. "Tea time, tea time! Everyone take their places before it gets cold! I'll not have you complaining about cold tea and cakes!"

"Off with your head!"

"Oh, do be quiet, my Queen. Your cackling disturbs the dog. Look at the dear beast, will you? It's been ages since he's seen a happy table such as this!"

Merle yips contentedly.

Matthew falls back against the pillow, his chest tight and the sweat drenching his face.

He sleeps without dreaming, then wakes to silence.

He rolls over and reaches for the pocket watch that is lying on the nightstand. He pops it open and sees that the numbers have reversed themselves.

From a corner of the bedroom comes a soft, rhythmic *squeak-squeak-squeak*. Matthew pulls himself up and fumbles a match from the matchbook, then sets flame to the wick of the oil lamp. Its glow reveals a figure sitting in a rocking chair in the corner, knitting, and every now and then leaving off to look at him through a great pair of spectacles. The figure wears an old-fashioned sleeping gown, the kind Matthew's own mother used to wear, and across its lap is a multicolored quilt. A fluffy sleeping cap covers most of its head, but not enough that he can't make out the ears standing straight up.

"Do you wish for a cool drink?" asks the Sheep as it puts the final touches on what it's knitting.

Matthew pulls himself back against the headboard, frightened and confused. He tries to look around to see if there are any other strange figures in the room with him but his muscles are too stiff and sore.

"You may look in front of you, and on both sides if you like," says the Sheep; "but you can't look *all* round you—unless you've got eyes at the back of your head."

"Who are you?" he manages to ask.

"Your soul's nurse, dear sir," says the Sheep. "Such a sad state we found it in." The Sheep rises from the chair and comes over to the bed. "I must say, though, that it looks as if my care has been quite good. You're looking ever so much better.

"Does the rabbit still run within you?" asks the Sheep.

Matthew folds his arms across his chest. Tears fill his eyes.

The Sheep pats his head. "Just as I thought. Such a pity that you've let him die a second time. The owl would have been more gentle. Do you think your dear little girl would approve?"

To his horror Matthew realizes that he can't summon the memory of Sarah's face. Oh, there are snapshots tucked away in photo albums, tucked away with everything else of theirs that he'd stored after their deaths so he need not look at them and be reminded of how much he'd lost, but those photos are only of moments, brief instances of time captured before they passed by, and *those* faces he can remember well enough, but it's the other faces, the faces they wore between the photographs, during those long stretches of life when no one thought to bring a camera, that he cannot remember. Sarah's last birthday, Rebecca's grin when she woke him in the morning, the way the two of them looked at him when he'd broken his leg a while back . . . those faces are lost to him, and he feels a new emptiness blossoming within him where before something had run free.

At that moment a well-dressed walrus sticks its head in the room and says, "The oysters are ready."

"Be right there," says the Sheep. Then it tucks Matthew into bed and says, "You rest, dear sir, and I'll be back with some hot broth."

He falls back into the pillow and into darkness.

He wakes to silence. This time he does not roll over to look at the watch; instead, he pulls himself out of bed, surprised to see he's wearing his father's old sleeping gown, and hobbles over to the closet. He takes a few deep breaths, listening, and hears their voices echoing from the kitchen.

"I do so love tea time!"

"Oh, don't let's start with that again! It's *always* six o'clock now, which means it's always tea time. None of us are so dim that we need to be reminded every time you finish a sip that it's tea time!"

Matthew opens the closet door and reaches in the back and pulls out the shotgun. He checks to make sure it is loaded, then stumbles out of the bedroom and toward the kitchen.

"I want you out of my house," he says, aiming the gun straight in front of him as he blunders around the corner and through the doorway.

They are seated around the table, the Sheep nurse, the man with the horse's head, the man with the lopsided top hat, the walrus, the huge egg-shaped man, the soldiers with cards for bodies, even Merle is sitting in a chair, a derby on his head and a polka-dotted tie around his neck. A silver teapot is on the table, steam puffing from its spout. There is a tray of Sarah's favorite cookies beside a tray of Rebecca's homemade cupcakes, and a plate filled with roast chicken.

"Do put that thing down and join us," says the Sheep. "If

31

you're not careful, you might shoot yourself. And we wouldn't want that, would we?"

Matthew does not answer. His gaze is fixed upon the tall, covered centerpiece on the table.

Merle leans forward and removes the cover.

Matthew falls against the wall, his arms weakening. The shotgun's barrel slowly drops toward the floor.

The centerpiece is a porcelain statue set upon a round wooden base that shines with a hand-rubbed finish. The statue is protected by a glass dome.

It is a statue of himself standing over Sarah's hospital bed. His face is expressionless. He holds one of her hands. She is smiling at him. She looks so small, so very, very fragile. With her other hand she is pointing at her chest.

"Tea time for your soul," says the Sheep.

". . . no . . ." whispers Matthew.

One of the card soldiers comes over and takes the shotgun away from him. "It's best you remember now," it says to him, then proceeds to unload the shells from the chamber.

"Do tell us," says the Queen, "or I shall be forced to have you beheaded."

"Not at tea time," says the man with the top hat.

"Oysters?" asks the walrus, offering up a tray.

Matthew manages to make it into a chair, then turns the statue toward him.

"Such a dear little girl," whispers the Sheep. "She looks like she's telling you something—perhaps *asking* something of you?"

"Yes," replies Matthew, his voice thick with grief.

"You miss her, don't you?" asks the man with the horse's head.

"Yes."

"We have a friend whom we miss, as well," says the Sheep. "His endearing impatience, his prickly whiskers, his pink nose and great, floppy ears. Ran off from us long ago and left us nothing to remember him by. It's difficult, isn't it, finding that your memories of someone are fading more and more with each new day?"

"Yes."

"If only we had something to remember him by," says the Queen, and for the first time there is genuine sorrow in her voice.

Matthew looks at Merle, who nods his dog-head and rises from the table and trots into the bedroom, returning a few moments later with the gold pocket watch. He gives it to the Sheep, who thanks him and gives it to the Queen.

"The time has come," says the walrus, "to talk of missing things, of smiles and faces and laughter, of promises and broken wings—"

"And why," says the huge egg-shaped man, "your soul has grown so cold, and of the nonsense song you sing."

The Sheep stood beside Matthew and touched the back of his neck with great tenderness. "You did promise her, didn't you?"

"S-she told me not to cry, that she would remember me just like she remembered her mother and the rabbit. She pointed to her heart and said, 'The rabbit is running inside me, Daddy.' Then she . . . she asked me if I would remember the rabbit for her after she was gone and I said yes and she said that was good because she'd had the rabbit in her for so long that she and it and her mother had become the same thing, and as long . . . as long . . ."

"As long as the rabbit within you ran free, you would never be alone."

"Yes," says Matthew, unable to look at the statue any longer.

"It's terrible, isn't it," says the egg-shaped man, "when things fall apart?"

"I didn't mean to end up this way," says Matthew. "I tried, I really tried to get over it . . . but I can't. They were so alive and I miss them so much and the house seems so . . . so cold without them. I can't help it, I just . . . I couldn't look at their things anymore. It hurt too much. So I put their things away . . . most of their things . . ." His gaze falls upon Sarah's bunny mug that is on the table, close to him. "I'm scared," he whispers. The words are a prayer, the first he's uttered in years. "I wake up and the house is so dark and cold and I feel like an old man without them. I can't even remember what they looked like. Or the sound of their voices. The way Sarah giggled or how Rebecca sang to herself when she was folding laundry. They're gone and they're not coming back. All that's left are their graves and a few lousy pictures.

"I'm finished and useless. I got no reason to go on living without them but I don't want to kill myself, you know? I don't want to die but I don't want to go on so I just . . . I just go through the motions and hope everything'll stop soon.

"The worst thing, though, is thinking about how things could have been. Would Rebecca still be in love with me when she turned sixty? Would Sarah marry and have kids? Would I have made a real go of this farm?

"Just one moment with them. That's all I want. I just want them back for one moment. I want to pick a minute when we were all together and happy and I want to be able to put it on like a warm shirt and stay there forever."

"You don't believe that can be done," says the Sheep.

"I know. But I like to dream about it. But even then I always wind up alone at the end of the road singing that stupid song that Rebecca used to sing to Sarah when Sarah was a baby. A baby's nonsense song."

The room is blurry, the figures fading as they gather together and move toward the door.

"They're very happy with us," says the Queen.

"Indeed, they are," says the Sheep. "Sarah tells the children wonderful stories in the after-time. She gathers them together and puts a light in their eyes as she speaks of you and this farm. We have felt all your simple sorrows and wished for you many simple joys, but yours is a heart that's frozen, and the rabbit within you is trapped in the ice, dying, and with it dies your memories of those you loved.

"But winter gives way to spring, good sad sir, and now that we can remember our dear, lost friend who's buried upon your hill"— the Sheep gestures toward the Queen, who holds up the pocket watch—"perhaps we will find a way someday to repay you."

"Good-bye, Matthew," say the odd figures.

He places his head on the table and closes his eyes. He listens to the sounds they make as they leave, then lifts his head and watches them move across the snow-covered field, finally disappearing over the hill.

He looks at Merle, who is still wearing the derby and tie.

"Nothing to add?"

Merle yawns, then gives a tired bark.

Matthew rises from the table and takes the glass-covered statue and sets it on the mantel and then stumbles back to bed.

He sleeps without dreaming, and wakes to silence.

He dresses himself slowly and quietly. He is not at all surprised to find that the statue is gone from the mantel, or that Merle no longer wears a hat and tie, or that the silver teapot is missing. The fever, he thinks, the fever.

The house is cold, so he puts on his coat and gloves and goes outside to gather firewood.

He aches everywhere.

Mornings are never easy for him.

He goes to the woodpile and leans over and grabs at a chunk of wood, yanks at it, but it won't come. He brushes aside some snow and tries to pick up another chunk of wood, but it's frozen as well. He curses and kicks at the pile and one piece near the bottom comes loose. He picks it up and uses it as a hammer to loosen the others. He's out of breath and sweating inside his coat. A second log comes loose and he uses it along with the first one to go to work on a third, but this one seems frozen solid. *Come loose, dammit*, he thinks, beating down with the logs, *Come loose!* He eventually gets the third one loose and picks it up and stacks it with the others in his arms, then he kicks at a fourth piece because he's angry and he's tired and sad and lonely and is cursing all wood loudly, but as his foot connects and the fourth piece cracks free he slips against the ice at the base of the pile and loses his balance and falls and the pieces of wood in his arms roll into the snow as the woodpile cracks and shudders and then collapses, scattering sticks and logs all around him. Slowly, on hands and knees, he gathers up a few pieces, then stands, his hip burning in pain where he landed on it, and begins making his way back toward the house when he sees something over his shoulder, an odd patch of sky; where most of it is a depressing slate gray, one patch is summer-bright and moving across the horizon independently of the rest. As it veers toward him he hears voices singing the nonsense song, and he keeps his eyes wide open as he sees himself, many years younger, coming down the hill with Sarah by his side. Her face is glorious, so radiant and smiling, but before he can say anything a sound to his left draws his attention and he turns to see Rebecca and another younger version of himself hanging invisible clothes upon an unseen line. His wife's raven-dark hair billows backward in the wind and Matthew is stunned at how beautiful she is. He hadn't remembered her being so lovely. Another sound, and he looks through a window to see yet another of his younger selves decorating an unseen Christmas tree with his family. He nearly drops the wood as he realizes that some of these memories—for now the property is crowded by them—are of things that never happened—there is Sarah dressing for her high school graduation, looking more stunning than he'd ever imagined she would; here is Rebecca bemoaning yet another patch of gray in her hair and say-ing that turning sixty isn't so bad, after all—forget that she was only forty-two when she died; over there is Sarah and her husband bringing their children to see Grandma and Grandpa on their silver wedding anniversary; now it's back to more familiar memories—him proposing to Rebecca, teaching Sarah how to tie her shoe, then the proud parents watching as their little girl takes her first hesitant steps. Matthew feels a comfort in his center that has been absent for too long, and closes his eyes, praying that they will still be surrounding him when he opens them again, and when he does look the memories are thicker than before and he feels the ice melt and crack and then the rabbit within him is running fast and free and for the first time in many, many lifetimes, Matthew smiles a genuine smile. He wonders what surprises are waiting inside the house, which suddenly seems so full of life, so warm and inviting, and he turns to go inside but realizes he can't leave the woodpile like this, so he sets the three logs aside and proceeds to arrange the pile into neat rows, one piece of wood snugly against the other until he hears Sarah say, "That's enough, Daddy," and he nods his head and grabs a few more pieces and moves down a few steps, the laughter of his daughter ringing in his ears as he stacks one piece evenly atop another, then one more beside it, all snug and tidy and uniform, so very uniform, as the start of a new row should be.

FOR WILLIAM F. NOLAN

Epithalamium

Roger Zelazny

∽ ∾

*I*t rained that night and the old lady made tea, as was generally the case. Sipping it, there at the kitchen table, she looked back over her quiet life. Memories of childhood came to fascinate her, and she wondered again at the quietude that had followed. Though she'd inherited the house and received a small stipend from a trust fund and had traveled considerably she'd never found the right man; or vice versa. The game was about over for her now, though she'd never really been invited to play. There had been nothing of great interest or reminder save for a few visits with the man who hunted people, and the last of these had been years ago. Now . . . Now it was peaceful to drink her tea and listen to the rain, to reflect on the complexity of existence and one's own useless role in most of it. She had done a lot of volunteer work, read a lot of books, remembered the wars. She'd been a nurse in both of them, though the second time had involved luck, expediency, and a need that transcended age. Well, there had been one man, back in the first war, she recalled—a quiet British lieutenant named Colin. They might have been happy together, she mused, but the fields of Flanders had eaten him, along with so many others.

She moved to the other room and stoked the fire, adding a few sticks, as she meant to take a second cup of tea in the parlor.

Halfway through the cup and some old thoughts, the doorbell rang. She glanced at the clock. It was near midnight.

She rose and crossed the room, opening the door partway.

"'Evening, Miss Alice," he said. "Axel J. Beangern at your service. I was wondering whether we might use it tonight."

"Goodness! I don't know whether it's still working," she said, opening the door more widely. "Come in out of the rain."

Beangern, as always, was clad in brown leather. He wore a hunting knife on his belt, a pistol on his right hip, and he carried a shotgun in his hand.

"Why the shotgun?" she asked.

"It slows him down," Beangern said.

With that, he pushed in his prisoner—a tall, slim, dark-eyed, dark-haired fellow clad in black. He was handcuffed and he wore leg irons as well.

"'Evening, Miss Alice," he said. "It's been a long time."

"Indeed it has, Lucer," she responded.

He smiled, raised his hands, and the right one incandesced.

"You cut that out, Lucer," Beangern said to him, and the fire died.

"Just an old flame for an old flame," Lucer said.

"You always were a flirt," she responded, returning his smile. "Will you gentlemen have some tea?"

"Of course," they both replied, "on a night like this. We'll stand, though, if you don't mind. Hate to soil your furniture."

"Nonsense. I insist you sit," she said.

"He is good at guarding people when they're chained and he's standing by them with a shotgun," Lucer said.

"That is not the reason," Beangern stated.

She shrugged and returned to the kitchen. Shortly, she came back with a tray bearing two cups of tea and some biscuits. Both men were now seated.

She served them, then seated herself.

"Same as usual?" she asked.

"Pretty much," Lucer replied. "I escaped prison, came over to here, got a job, and the bounty man came after me."

"Same as usual," Beangern said. "He escaped from prison, injuring a lot of people on his way out, came here and organized a secret society dedicated to revolution and commenced buying weapons and training the members in their use. I caught him just in time."

"So what happens to him now?" Alice asked.

"I take him back," said Beangern.

"You seem the only one able to bring him back when something like this happens," Alice said.

"True. He's quite dangerous, but then so am I," Beangern said.

"This is all a lie," Lucer said. "But I haven't yet seen the truth make any difference."

"I'd listen," Alice said.

"I'm sorry," said Beangern, "but he hasn't the time to tell you all of his lies. We must be departing soon."

"He's like a samurai," Lucer said. "Terribly well-trained and true to his code—whatever it is. If you tried to detain him, he might do you harm."

"I would not," said Beangern. "Alice is an old friend."

"Very old," Alice said.

"Why do you keep escaping if it always comes to this?" she asked Lucer.

"It will not. This is the last time," Lucer replied.

"Oh, why is that?"

"Because the cycle is at an end."

"I don't understand," she said.

"Of course not. But I have eaten the Whitcomb Pie and know that it is so."

"Whatever you say," she said, pouring more tea for them all. "My part in your business ended long ago."

Lucer laughed.

"Callooh! Callooh!" he said. "The story never ends."

Beangern laughed, too.

"It will end very soon," he said.

"In a way, callay! In a way," the other said.

"So long as Beangern holds his fief, the world runs well," Beangern said.

"Well, it runs," Lucer acknowledged, "with the lunatics in charge, as you left them."

Beangern chuckled.

"I find this vastly amusing," he said. "And surely Alice remembers."

"How could I not?" she said. "There were times when it terrified me."

"And there were times when it showed you wonders such as few of your world have ever seen," Lucer added.

"I can't deny it. But they don't balance."

"What of it? It has changed considerably since your visit—and tonight it shall change again."

"From what to what?" she asked.

"It must be seen," Beangern replied.

"At my age it no longer matters."

"On the contrary. It means a great deal that you be present for the enactment and return. There was a reason you were tempted to visit us so long ago, Alice."

Lucer snorted and his chains rattled. Beangern sipped his tea.

"You were brought in to be viewed by your prospective husband," he said.

"Oh, and who might that have been?"

"The real ruler of the place."

"I'm a little old for that part now. If someone like that wanted me, he should have done something about it a long time ago."

"Events," said Beangern, "rose to spoil his plans."

"What events?"

"A small war."

She sipped her tea.

"So you must accompany us on this special occasion."

"Sorry. The story is ended now," she said. "Over. Done with. You've come too late."

"It is never too late," Beangern said, "while I live. And I will not die."

He ate a biscuit. Lucer sipped his tea.

"Will I?" Beangern suddenly asked.

"Whom are you asking?" said Lucer.

"You."

"You fear this night," the other replied, "that it holds your death."

"Well, does it?"

"Even if I knew I wouldn't tell you."

Beangern began to raise his shotgun, glanced at Alice, and lowered it again. He ate another biscuit.

"Quite good," he remarked.

"There is still the enactment," Lucer stated.

"Hush now."

"Of course. It matters not."

"What is this enactment?" Alice asked.

"It is a ritual in which the fallen star Beangern must participate. Else will he be swept away."

"Nonsense!" Beangern roared, spilling tea on his jacket. "I perform the rite for old times' sake. Nothing more."

"What rite?" Alice inquired.

"The ritual of return to the heavens from which he came," said Lucer. "On Yuleki's Day. His place has been vacant too long."

"You make him sound like a god," Alice said.

"He is, like one of the god kings of old in your world."

"I thought that the Red King and Queen—or the White . . ." Alice began.

"There were many lunatics in Wonderland," Lucer responded. "Beangern sent many of them into strong exile or imprisonment and rules now himself."

"Is that true?" Alice asked.

"The man exaggerates," Beangern replied. "The Red King and Queen still rule. I occasionally assist."

"And what is the part you would have me play in all this?" asked Alice.

"A small one," Beangern replied.

"He lies," said Lucer.

"What then?" asked Alice.

"Witness," Beangern replied.

"I am an old lady you have confused considerably," Alice said. "I'll have no more of this rabbit-holing and mirroring. Let us finish our tea and I'll see you off."

"Of course," Beangern stated. "Come, Lucer. Drink up, and we'll be on our way."

The men finished their tea and Lucer took another biscuit. Both men rose then, and Beangern looked toward Alice. "Would you conduct us to the conveyance now?" he said.

"You mean the mirror?"

"Yes."

"Come this way," Alice said.

Rising, she led them to a flight of stairs and took them up it. Pushing back a hatch and throwing a light switch, she illuminated a low-wattage bulb, which revealed a dusty attic filled with the detritus of decades. At the room's far end hung a mirror, its reflective surface facing the wall.

Alice halted and suddenly asked, "Why do you need it? You obviously got here without it."

"The other way is strenuous," Beangern replied, "and subduing this fellow takes a lot out of one. The other reason is convenience."

"Convenience?" Alice said.

"Yes," Beangern replied. "On the night of Yuleki in the place where the kinyon grass grows, and the Ulb who ate a Jabberwock goes forbling forth to vie, with Kibling and Dars Dadisdada, 'tis soon enough to die, Ryanda! Step through, Lucer!"

He nudged the other man with the shotgun barrel. Lucer approached the mirror and vanished.

"I'm not going back to that place," Alice said.

Beangern laughed and stepped through the mirror. Shortly afterwards, Alice felt herself drawn toward it. She tried to resist but the effect was too strong. Step after resisting step, she was forced to advance until she stood before it and, after all these years, entered.

She stood for several moments within the reversed image of her attic. Then she turned, seeking the mirror, but could not find it. She knew then that she must depart the attic. Turning, she crossed the room, switched off the light, and descended the stair.

She made her way to the back door, opened it, and stepped outside.

It was no longer her garden. It had become a glade in the midst of sunset, two roads emerging from the trees to cross at its center. Beangern stood on the crossroad, shotgun still a-smoke. Lucer lay panting at his feet.

"Tried to escape," Beangern said. "I expected it."

"Is he going to be—all right?" Alice asked, moving to the man's side and kneeling, her nursing training returning in a great rush through her mind.

"Of course," Beangern replied. "He's healing already. Practically impervious. And stronger than an ox. Stronger than me, even. Lacks my combat training, though."

"How do you know these things about him?" she asked.

"He used to be my servant, my man-at-arms. We came here together."

"From where?" she said.

He pointed skyward. "Up there. I am of the fallen star they could not return."

"Why not?" she asked.

"Some metaphysical crime for which the others would never release him, should he come into their power," Lucer moaned.

"Nonsense. 'Twas a mere difference of opinion we had," Beangern stated.

Lucer rose slowly to his feet, hand pressed against his side. "That does smart," he remarked.

"Tell her that you lied," Beangern stated.

"I will not. 'Tis true."

"I'll blast you again."

"Go ahead. Waste our time. Callooh."

"Callay. She'll see for herself this day."

"This night, I say. Away. Let's away."

"By the bye, I say. A little rite to light our way."

With that, he commenced a series of arcane hand movements. The air seemed to brighten about him as he did. Finally, he stopped and indicated that the journey was to continue.

"What was that all about?" Alice asked.

"Dars Dadisdada and Rottery Khan will be riding out tonight," Beangern said.

". . . And the Choipery Girl will circle the world on wings like a bat," said Lucer. "The Challkers Rose will rise from the sea and bloom, and the foongli lights dance on bay and slope. A reminiscence of your Halloween, and a ritual protection against it."

"It would seem that things have changed," she said.

"Just the names," said Beangern.

"More than just the names," said Lucer.

"I would like to be returned to my home now," said Alice.

"I am afraid that that is impossible," said Beangern. "You are needed here."

"Why?"

"This will become apparent later."

"I may choose to withhold my cooperation."

"I think not," said Beangern, raising a small whistle which he wore on a chain about his neck. He put it to his lips and blew upon it.

A minute passed.

"I think I am going to go back," Alice said.

"Impossible," Beangern replied, and in the distance a low rumble rose up.

She listened for a moment, then asked, "What is that sound?"

"Motorcycles," he replied. "Members of the royal guard—the Twittikins—are on their way."

"That was an awfully quick response," she remarked as their shapes came into view on the road ahead.

"Actually, I whistled for them before I left. This one is a new request, for later. You must recall that one can run and get nowhere, or stay in place and make progress—or phone to speak with yourself yesterday."

"Well, somewhat."

"It has its fine points. That's all."

The bikers approached, drew near. When they halted before them, Beangern approached their leader, a big-bellied man with arms like tree trunks. He wore blue jeans, a black leather vest, and hordes of tattoos. His scarred face broke into a smile.

"Someone you want done for?" he asked Beangern.

"Just guarded," Beangern said. "Miss Alice here."

"Why, she's just an old bag. Why's she need guardin'?"

"Watch your language, Nik. She's a friend of mine. But we can't let her go until tomorrow. So hang around and keep an eye on her. She's got an odd element of probability calls."

"What's that mean?"

"Funny things used to happen around her. They still could, in this place."

The Twittikins advanced to be near her. Above them, amid the branches of a nearby tree, she thought for a moment that she spied the form of a grinning cat.

"Let's be movin' along now," Beangern said.

"Where to?" asked Lucer.

"Why, the palace, of course. To get a fresh judgment pronounced against you."

"Yes, for they do get stale, I know," Lucer said, "like moldy bread."

Beangern laughed. "We'll find you some fresh words to chew over," he said, "in a fresh cell, where mold and oxidation enter not."

"No, for tonight is a very special night, demon star."

"Lucer, you wrong me."

They began walking.

"If that way be north today, we'll be to the palace shortly after sunset," Lucer remarked.

Alice moved nearer.

"There is something about him," she said, "that seems even more abnormal than usual."

"Oh, he's certifiable material, all right," Lucer said, "like most of us. But he's grown too dangerous to buck. And his powers are at a peak come Yuleki."

"And your own?" she asked. "You do seem to have a few of those yourself."

"True," he said. "One never knows how things will fall out in this place. Callooh!"

"Callay!" she responded, smiling. "Are we both crazy, Lucer?"

"Maybe a little," he replied.

"What about letting the prisoners talk?" Nik hollered.

"Let them," Beangern said. "It doesn't matter."

They trekked into the twilight, away from the setting sun.

"Things are a little different this time," Lucer told Alice. "I think they want everything legal and proper."

"What does that mean—in this place?" she asked.

"He'll get the King and Queen to say that it's okay to send me to the mines, that you must attend the rite of Yuleki, and that Beangern's fief remains secure."

"That makes him the real ruler here, doesn't it?"

"I'd say so."

"Does that mean that he was the one who'd summoned me and observed me years ago, looking for the bride he never married?"

"Yes. I was with him at the time. Hidden, he observed all your adventures."

"Why, for heaven's sake?"

"To see how you responded to such unusual stresses."

"Why that?"

"Should you come to reign here, it would be useful to know how you dealt with the environment."

"And I failed."

"No. There was a war here as well as in your world. It caused such things to be bypassed until too late."

"You're saying I should have been queen."

"Empress."

". . . To Beangern."

"Undoubtedly."

"In that case, I'm glad things fell out as they did."

"And I, also. I don't think you'd really have liked it."

"What now?"

"There seems to be no choice. We go through with it. I've a feeling I'll have a part in this one since it's the ending of a celestial cycle and the beginning of a new one, and spirits may mount or descend."

"I don't understand."

49

"Natural laws in this place. If we ever have an opportunity longer than this, I'll try to explain."

"Why not try it now?"

"Because that bulk up ahead is the castle, and we'll be there before very long. Suffice it to say that Beangern is a stellar spirit who fell to earth at the last major cycle. He saw that this place was a looney bin, and he took it over and set it right."

"Why, then, do you oppose him?"

"He went too far. Now it is a matter of his whim, rather than law or principle, that rules. Perhaps he has gone truly mad. He fears that the Feast of Yuleki, the Yark Angel, may be a time when he could be drawn back to his true realm, never to return."

"You'd think that would make him happy."

"Yes, but it doesn't. He likes it here. He has near fought Yuleki himself over this point."

"This is good?"

"For everyone here there was some good at first."

"Except me," she said.

"Don't say that. You are necessary."

"For what?"

"It must have seemed different to you when you were but a girl, but your adventures then can be viewed in two different ways."

"Oh. I stumbled into a magical kingdom and had some strange experiences. That's how I view it. You have an alternative?"

"Yes. How do you like this one? You were the magical being that entered here. You, as observer, precipitated all the strange experiences you had."

"That is certainly a novel way of regarding it."

"I think you had it, and that you still might."

"What does it mean if I do?"

"You might be able to help to expel him, this time of all times. Everything else will be poised for such a thrust."

"You sure such a thing will work?"

"No, but if we don't try it now it may be eons before another chance occurs. Not all of the royalists will be left. Perhaps not any."

"Let me think about it."

"Better think fast."

They continued their trek to the Castle of Hearts. Beangern told the first person he saw—a short, red-haired gardener—to announce his arrival. The man ran off screaming, "Beangern has come! Beangern has come!"

"I find their enthusiasm touching," Beangern remarked. "Come, let us enter. We shall hunt down their majesties."

Beangern drove the others ahead of him now, lest Lucer free himself and lead Alice astray. He left the Twittikins to guard the gate. He located the King and Queen dressed in rags and hiding beneath the bed in a fourth-floor bedroom.

"Why do we find them so?" Alice asked.

"Guards! Protect us! Off with his head! Beangern! Beangern! Dead! Dead! Dead!" cried the emaciated Queen of Hearts and her diminutive husband.

"They have conceived some ill fancy of me," Beangern replied, his eyes flashing fire, "and compounded it with their tendency to shirk their duties. Come now! Both of you! Out of there! There's a royal decree in need of issuing."

"Why us? Why us?"

"Because you're royal. The decretals need decreting, the world it needs its words, Lord Lucer to the mines again, Beangern to his fiefdom, Alice to her Judgment Chair. Write it down! Write it down! Sign it at the bottom! Circulate the ruddy 'crete to everything alive! And save a ruddy copy for the bloody archive!"

"Scrivener! Scrivener!" cried the Queen.

"Why call only two?" asked the King. "Make it more plural."

" 'S, 's," added the Queen.

"Sounds like a tired serpent," said the King.

"Retired servants claim pensions," said the Queen. "What has

51

this to do with them? And what has become of them? What? What?"

"The mines!" cried Lucer. "To save on pay. Release them, release them, release them, pray!"

"This cannot be," said the Queen. "Who would order such?"

Lucer turned and stared at Beangern.

"You liked them overmuch," said the man.

"Release them!"

"Not today."

"Where are our robes royal?"

"In the laundry."

"You sold them. You're disloyal," said the King.

"And the Jewels of the Crown?" asked the Queen.

"On exhibition in the town."

"Lies! Lies! You've robbed us. Bring them back! Bring them back!"

"I hear the scriveners in the hall," said Beangern. "Let us set them up, and tell them what I say."

"I think we do not need your help. We'll do it our own way."

"In that case friends and favorites will be the ones to pay," Beangern said, as he raised his whistle.

"Stop!" cried the King. "We'll do as you say."

"I thought you'd see the light. It must be done tonight. Now, as a matter of fact."

He opened the door and let them in. There were four.

"You lack tact. But you hold the winning cards," said the Queen.

". . . Lucer Starborn is hereby reassigned to the mines. All other political imprisonments are reconfirmed. Axel J. Beangern is reconfirmed in the possession of his fief—" Beangern said.

"That," Lucer said, "is contingent on your sitting through the Feast of Yuleki in the chapel on your property."

"I know that!"

"Very well. Write it down."

". . . And Alice finally present on this night of all nights of the year."

"I know no fear!" said Beangern.

"None spoke of fear but thee."

"This is not part of the decree!" Beangern shouted. "Add the salutatories and affirmations to what has gone before, and be damned with them!"

"Such language!" said Alice.

"He's not at all a gentleman," said Lucer.

"Execute the order! Return him to the pits!" cried Beangern.

"I claim my right to be present at the service," said Lucer.

"Bring him along, then. We'll send him from there when it's done."

Lucer raised his hand and squeezed one of Alice's. "I am to be myself this night," he said, "and likely he will not."

"This is good?" she asked.

"Rejoice and honest be," Lucer replied, "and we shall make it so, come St. George and Low Heaven."

"I fear that I do not understand."

"You will when the time's at hand."

"But Beangern always seemed the gentleman, and you the criminal—though a very polite one."

"He lies. You've seen how he deals. In fact, he also steals."

"I believe. He does deceive."

"Soon we will leave, for the service. Are you hungry? He would see that you are fed, if you are. Wants you strong."

"I'll come along without the bread. I don't know that I care to brave a meal in this place now."

"Why should that be bad?"

"Because everyone's half-mad."

"Yes, but they're half-sane, too."

"I'm on your side. Enough said. Callooh!"

"Callay!"

"Let's be away!" cried Beangern.

They left the castle and the day. They traveled through the hilly lands, to the realm of Whileaway.

"Sing for me, Alice," said Lucer, and she began "Auld Lang Syne."

The Twittikins roared on ahead and behind, the moon dripped butter and venom, and everywhere she looked, it seemed the cat's grin was upon her. A cool, near chill breeze swept them, and all the shadows became a blanket of black.

The moonlight sparkled on a massive block of ice to the right of the trail. They examined it as they passed, and Alice's voice wavered as she beheld within it—frozen in mid-gesture—a March Hare, a Dormouse, and a demented-looking Hatter.

As they crossed the next hill she heard a great, crystallike shattering, though no one else seemed to.

"Sing more loudly here," Lucer said, and she did. A snuffling, chuffling, snorting followed, as of a laboring walrus climbing a slope. Again, nobody else seemed to notice.

". . . And at this glade you must sing with particular sweetness," he said.

She did, and the chortling roar that near shook the darkness from the night seemed heard by everyone, from the automatic weapon fire that followed from the Twittikins. The rearmost vanished and their weapons grew still as a dark cloud swept across the road, passing over them.

"Lucer," she whispered, seizing his biceps, "what is it you have me doing?"

"Sorry, naught but pure song, m'lady. Think, think back on all you remember from your earliest visits. If there was aught that you loved, sing to that. Remember, remember, Alice, this place as it was."

And Alice's old voice broke, many, many times, as she recalled and reworded old ballads and music hall songs.

"What is that caterwauling?" Beangern cried, his ears now long and silky, his mouth more full of teeth than before.

"Lady Alice would sing," Lucer replied, "as is her right."

Beangern growled and grew silent.

"He must allow it," Lucer said. "You must unscathed be."

"Why?" she asked.

"Your power is sacrosanct," said he. "You are she who came long ago."

"A lifetime wasn't that far back," she said.

"In this place time doth different flow."

"I'll never understand."

"I say you will. Pray, sing on."

And again she sang. This time, the night came alive with bird cries, cricket calls, and the rustling of leaves. Overhead, the stars shone more brightly than Alice had ever seen them glow, and the moon seemed to swell as it made its slow way zenithward.

"Confound!" Beangern cried, his trousers now split to free his jointed tail, eyes still flashing fire.

"Sing on," said Lucer, and she did.

At last, they reached the top of a high hill, overlooking a vale splashed with moonlight like buttermilk. At their back, Alice heard noises. Beangern called a halt and regarded the prospect for a moment. He raised his right arm and extended a claw. "This is the place where music comes to die," he said. "This is the fief of Beangern. My powers increase here."

". . . And your form seems to have shifted," Alice said.

"Tonight 'tis unavoidable," he said, "when the Powers descend and rise to walk the world."

"I thought that Beangern was a god or demigod. Your form seems more demonic."

"These terms are meaningless in this twisted place," said he, "and as for the rest, read your Nietzsche."

"I understand," said she.

"So I have won, you see. I made you wait till your powers waned and drained. A draft of damp air would blow you away."

"You've watched me all these years?"

55

"Indeed, through laughter and tears."

"Not too much laughter."

"Nor many tears. Sorry 'tis such a bland life you've led. But so it had to be."

"All for this night?"

"All for this night."

The crest on his backbone rose to a ridge on his head. His hoofs clattered against rocks as he shifted position.

He pointed again. "And there is the chapel, in yonder valley."

They saw the diminutive building, all alight.

"Come," he finally said. "Tonight is indeed the night."

They followed him down the hillside and through the twisting ways of the valley—Beangern, Alice, Lucer, the King and Queen of Hearts, the Twittikins, unassorted courtiers and nobles. The Twittikins were again diminished, in a firefight with something that had howled from behind a boulder. When they searched the area afterwards, nothing could be found.

Great numbers of dark birds passed overhead as they advanced upon the chapel, and there were rustlings within the high grasses all about them. The earth seemed to tremble on several occasions, and deadwood snapped as heavier footfalls occurred.

Lucer had hold of her arm now and she had a stick in her other hand. She leaned on both.

"Not too much farther to the chapel," Lucer remarked. "You'll be able to rest once we've arrived."

"I'll make it," she said. "I must see the story through."

"I'm sure you will. Your presence is necessary, either way."

"Win or lose? Live or dead?"

"Exactly."

An owl dipped above them. "Who?" it asked.

"Me," she answered.

Beangern growled, and birds fell dead from the sky. The earth shook and the wind grew stronger. At last they reached the chapel and Beangern let them in. The place was filled with candlelight, there was a low altar against the forward wall, and a circular sky-light poured starshine and the glow of the rising moon down upon the pentagram drawn on the floor beneath. Against the chapel's rear wall was a throne all of red stone, and to this Alice was led.

"Pray, rest yourself!" cried Beangern, and the ground shook as he increased in stature. He moved forward then, motioning the others to seat themselves in pews. Lucer and the King and Queen he allowed to remain near Alice. He moved then to the front of the chapel, and, looking upward, addressed some unseen presence beyond the skylight:

"You up there. This is Beangern," he said. "I know you can hear me, tonight. All right. Tonight is the night, but I want you to know that I hold everything in the palm of my hand. You waste your time if you think that you can do much about it. I know you've been waiting to nail me, Yuleki, but it's too damned late. I've been sucking power out of this land down the years. I'm too strong for you now. One touch more, and the world I have set up will endure forever."

"Alice," Lucer said softly, "I am going to break these chains now and fight him. We are of about equal strength but I will lose because his technique is better. When I appear to be going down for the third time, cry out for Yuleki to come to you. And use your name."

"Why are you as strong as that thing he has become?" she asked.

"I forget."

". . . And why is his technique better?"

"Not sure. No matter."

"Then why must you fight?"

"I must hold him till the moon is higher."

"Why?"

"I don't remember. But it will help us against him."

". . . Now, on this night of all nights of the year," Beangern intoned, "we are gathered together in the eyes of Yuleki and anyone else who cares to look, and we will join in matrimony the master and lady of this place."

"Lady?" Alice said. "Where is she?"

"That's you," Lucer answered, raising his hands and spreading them. He drew them taut and beads of perspiration broke out upon his brow. Then the chains snapped and he bent to draw upon those which held his ankles.

Beangern raised his shotgun. Alice moved to stand before Lucer.

"Damn it, lady! Get out of the way!" Beangern cried.

"No," Alice replied. "Something's wrong here and I want to see it right."

"You're going about it wrong!" he roared.

Lucer's chains broke and he rose to his full height. Beangern sighed. "All right. We must settle this yet again," he said.

Lucer advanced to the center of the chapel and Beangern set aside the shotgun and moved to meet him.

A flash of lightning crossed the sky as they met. Then the two were rolling about the pentagram.

The door to the chapel was opened and the figure of a White Rabbit entered. Alice thought that she heard him mutter, "Oh dear!" as he seated himself in a pew near the front. He watched the fray as the two combatants struck, their fists shattering brick, stone, or flagging when they missed each other.

Finally, she felt the rabbit's gaze upon her. He stared for a long while before his eyes widened in recognition. She nodded then.

The Rabbit rose and made his way slowly along the lefthand wall. When he came to the throne he said, "Alice . . ."

"How's the Dormouse?" she asked.

"Still in the teapot. How are you?"

"Oh, time has taken its ticket for the show," she said. "And yourself?"

"You freed me earlier with your singing."

"What? How?"

"You're magic. You must know that by now. I was with the Jabberwock after you sang him loose. He's waiting outside to eat Beangern if he can."

The Rabbit's eyes turned toward the combatants. "Tough pair, those two. Hard to tell which is master or man."

"Not for me. Beangern has ceased to be a man."

"He will always be a mere man-at-arms among the skiey hosts."

"What are you saying? He is a fallen star—a higher being whose contact with this world may have corrupted him."

The Queen of Hearts shrieked as the combatants rolled near to her, Beangern's horns scoring the stone at her feet. Then the combatants rolled away again.

"Lord Lucer is the fallen star," replied the Rabbit, "who must be made this night to remember himself. Beangern was his servant, who usurped his place when the forgetfulness fell upon Lucer."

"What?" cried Alice. "Beangern an imposter?"

"Indeed. Now that you've freed me, I hope to see him pass one way or the other this night."

There came a crash as the two men struck the wall and the building shook.

"Why does Beangern outclass his boss?" Alice asked.

"A man-at-arms has special combat training, for service against the dark legions," replied the rabbit.

It seemed that Beangern and Lucer hammered upon each other forever, as the moon rose higher and higher. Then Beangern's blows began to appear more telling, and finally he knelt upon Lucer, and, catching hold of his head, began to bang it upon the stone floor. Seeing this, Alice cried out, "Yuleki, Yark Angel, help us now! This is Alice calling." Then she moved toward them.

With a flash, a ball of white light appeared above the penta-

gram. Beangern rose and faced it, leaving a panting, bleeding figure upon the floor.

"It is not fair that you should come for me now, Yuleki!" he
cried. "I am tired and cannot face you properly!"

"All the better then," a musical voice rang out. "Transform!
You lose no face by coming along with me without strife."

Beangern glanced at Lucer. "Do you remember?" he called
out.

"Remember what?" Lucer responded.

Beangern looked back at Yuleki. "I maintain my battle mode
and we fight," he said.

"Very well."

He plunged forward. When he made contact with the bright
sphere, it raised him above the ground, spun him round like a
whirlwind, then slammed him down upon the stone. It drifted into
a position above his chest. He attempted to raise his arms and legs
and could not.

"You should have made it last longer," he whispered, "for his
sake. I have been trying to cure him for decades. I thought that
this might do it. I wanted him whole, so that he could be returned."

"My plan was otherwise."

Beangern turned his head toward Lucer. "Master!" he cried.
"Remember! Please!"

"I do, faithful servant," came the response; and Lucer took
Alice's hand in his own. A faint glow suddenly surrounded her.

"Your job here is done," Yuleki said to Beangern. "But his is
not, though he is whole again. He will repair this land, which you
sacrificed in the cause of his healing."

"I could help him!"

"That would not be prudent. Their memories of you are
bad."

There followed a crash of thunder and both Beangern and the
light were gone.

Alice felt the years fall away as her odd aura strengthened.

"What is happening?" she asked.

Lucer drew her to her feet.

"I take you back along the years to your youth, old friend," he said. "By the way, there really should be a wedding tonight. Are you game?"

"Are you serious?"

"Indeed I am. I do want your help as well as your company. After all, you are the true goddess of this place."

"This is too much," she said, staring at the back of her hand as the wrinkles faded. "I'll never understand."

"Come with me."

He walked to the door of the chapel and flung it open. They were all there, Humpty and the grinning Cat, the Dormouse and the Hatter, the March Hare, the Walrus and the Jabberwock. The Choipery Girl passed overhead. A great cry rose up.

"Lucer and Alice! Lucer and Alice!"

"This seems as good a place as any," he said. "Will you have me, Alice?"

She looked out over the multitude of creatures, many still arriving. Then the Queen said, "Do it, Alice. I know we need you. Beangern's fief is yours now, of course. Do it."

Alice looked at Lucer, looked at the crowd, then back at Lucer.

"You're all mad," she said. "But so am I."

Music fell from the skies. Looking up, she saw a small star rising through the spheres to the empyrean.

A Common Night

Bruce Holland Rogers

"So it's another one of her sunset poems," the young woman said, managing to make it sound partly like a question and partly like a bold assertion so that Julian could decide for himself which it was. She gave him a neutral look.

He looked past her, out the second-story window to the bare tree outside. Snowflakes were falling.

"Next to 'Leaping like Leopards,' this one seems obvious," said another student, the one with short-cropped black hair. Randal. Or was it Roger? Five weeks into the semester, Julian would ordinarily have had their names down by now.

"I mean, the spots are a clue," Randal or Roger continued. " 'She died at play, Gambolled away Her lease of spotted hours . . .' When I get to those spots, it reminds me of the one we did last week." He flipped pages and read,

> *Blazing in Gold and quenching in Purple*
> *Leaping like Leopards to the Sky*

Then at the feet of the old Horizon
Laying her spotted Face to die

"That's one thing I like about reading her," Randal said. "Once you've figured out a few of the poems, you sort of have an idea of what she's up to. It's almost fun."

Two or three in the seminar circle laughed at his "almost."

"I just don't see why she has to work death into every other poem," the young woman continued. "She's so *morbid.*"

No one said anything. For an unnaturally long time, the students waited for Julian to stick up for Emily Dickinson.

"Well," he said, but then the next word was very difficult to find. He kept staring at the window, at the falling snow. "Well," he said again.

He had stopped sleeping several nights ago—two or three. He wasn't sure. For weeks, he'd slept fitfully amidst the daily rounds of Home-Hospice-Campus-Dinner-Hospice-with-the-kids. Lately he would lie awake all night, listening to the dark, closing his eyes, but never drifting off.

He blinked and looked away from the window. "Death was rather more present in the nineteenth century," he said. "More ordinary, I mean. We tend to hide it away, but death and thoughts of death were more routine."

"But why dwell on it?" the young woman asked.

He looked at the book in his hands. It was full of words, and it was his job now to summon up some more of them, to use Dickinson to explain Dickinson. He could do it. Even after days without sleep, he could do it, but he noticed what a hollow exercise it had become. Whatever he might say next would sound good and satisfying, but it was just a stream of words.

"Let's look at 675 again," he said, and before they had finished turning their pages he recited the first stanza from memory. ·

Essential Oils—are wrung—
The Attar from the Rose
* Be not expressed by Suns—alone—*
It is the gift of Screws—

"There's a lot packed into the eight lines of this poem," he said, "and we've already talked about how it seems to be about the poems themselves. But you can think about this as a wider metaphor, too. Attar isn't expressed by suns. That is, you don't get essential oils, you don't get the essence of reality by waiting around for it. You have to squeeze it out. Getting the essential oils out is tough on the rose, but it's the only way."

"And thinking a lot about death is a way of squeezing," said Randal.

"I can enjoy life without thinking about death all the time," another student said. "I agree with Chrissie. These poems are such downers. I don't like being depressed."

Julian thought of Von Trepl's dialogue with Death. Don't blame me for the anguish you're feeling, Death told the Plowman of Bohemia. Your anguish is your own fault. If you had restrained your love for your wife, you'd be free of sorrow over her death. The greater the love, while you hold it, the greater your pain in the end. Unpleasure follows pleasure.

Anna was not dead, but she was already lost to Julian. He had sought out the old German text when the tumor had overtaken the speech centers of her brain. She still recognized Julian, but she couldn't speak. The bridge of words between them had burned, and there were things that still needed saying, would always need saying. Holding her hand as she lay watching him was not enough.

But he didn't mention the Plowman of Bohemia to the seminar. Why bother? It was all just words. Dickinson, too, just words from the dead. Empty, empty. The more he had studied dead words, the more dead they had become. It was the words of the living that mattered, and those had run out. He didn't know if the dead words of literature would ever have anything to do with him again.

"There's a poem I read last night," Randal said, "that I think fits. It's 1100." He found it and began to read.

Julian's attention drifted to the window again. Was that a cat in the tree? But it was gone, the round head vanishing almost as soon as Julian had made out the shape.

> *The last Night that She lived*
> *It was a Common Night*
> *Except the Dying—this to Us*
> *Made Nature different*
>
> *We noticed smallest things—*
> *Things overlooked before*
> *By this great light upon our Minds*
> *Italicized—as 'twere.*

The young man's voice droned on as the snow fell outside the window. The words blended and fell in on one another and his voice blended and mixed with the voice of the departmental secretary as she was saying, "Dr. Preston? Excuse me, Dr. Preston?"

Julian looked away from the window. Randal had stopped reading some moments ago, and Julian was aware that he'd gone on staring out the window for some time after the secretary's interruption. The secretary stood in the doorway, as if she had no right to cross the threshold. "Dr. Preston," she said, "there was an emergency call for you." She held a slip of paper.

"Yes," Julian said. It was time. Anna was going. He felt relieved, and then ashamed. "Yes, all right."

Julian's mother-in-law had made the call from the hospice. She would collect Yvonne from school and Nick from day care and meet him.

As he drove out of town toward the hospice, the snow fell

thick and fast. It swirled in his headlights and sometimes blew in the same direction that he traveled. In his daze, it seemed that the car was standing still, that the wheels rolled and bumped but somehow didn't carry him forward. He took his foot from the accelerator again and again, tried his brights, though that was worse. He opened his eyes very wide and fought to stay awake and on the road.

There was no other traffic, and it was dark, astonishingly dark for the early afternoon. Why did the hospice have to be a dozen miles out of town? But he knew the answer to that. He understood.

He almost missed the turnoff. The lights of the hospice were just barely visible from the road. The parking lot had not been plowed, and Julian half drove, half sledded to the far corner of the lot, away from the other cars.

When he turned off his lights and killed the engine, the light outside seemed to shift. It was dark, but not too dark to see. There was a sort of blue-gray glow to the woods that surrounded the parking lot.

Now that he could release it, Julian felt how heavy the burden of staying alert and focused had been. He wanted to melt into his seat and keep on melting. Something gnawed in his stomach, and he realized that he was hungry. Famished. He couldn't remember eating breakfast—he'd been so busy getting the kids ready for school and day care. Had he eaten lunch?

They'd have something for him inside, if he asked. They were so good at this place, terribly good at noticing, terribly good at being concerned for everyone involved.

He closed his eyes. He should go in. They were waiting for him—his son, his daughter, his mother-in-law. He wondered about Anna, wondered if his wife had already . . .

But he'd know in a bit. He'd go in.

Right now, though, he wanted, for just a moment, to rest here, to let all the effort fall away. He could hear the snow falling, hissing gently, gently, a cottony sound. . . .

A bell jangled.

He opened his eyes. The window was open, and snow was blowing into the car.

The bell jangled again. He squinted into the darkness, and he could see that there was an old-fashioned telephone mounted on the tree next to his car. When the bell jangled a third time, he got out of the car to answer it.

"Yes?" he said. "Hello?"

"Julian?" said the tinny voice in the earpiece.

"Anna?"

"Julian?"

"Anna? Is it really you?"

"Julian?" she said, and there was no doubting that it was her.

"Anna! Anna, sweetheart!"

"Julian?"

"Yes, it's me!" he said. "Oh, God, Anna!" He felt weak with relief. He could hardly stand. "It's so good to hear you!"

"Julian?"

"Can't you hear me? I can hear you fine. Anna?"

"Julian?"

"Anna!" he shouted into the mouthpiece.

Only there wasn't any mouthpiece, just a knothole in the tree that he had wrapped his arms around.

An orange glow came and went, and a voice from behind Julian said, "Bad connection?"

He turned. He saw nothing but trees.

"Bad connections won't do you any good, you know," said the voice. "In this world, who you know is a big part of who you *are*." Then the orange glow returned, allowing Julian to make out an enormous caterpillar sitting on a tree branch and smoking a long hookah. The glow came from the tobacco burning in the bowl.

"And by the way," the Caterpillar went on, "who *are* you?"

When Julian didn't answer, the Caterpillar said, "Well, speak up!"

"I'm dreaming," Julian concluded.

"Yes, yes, of course you are," said the Caterpillar. "Or else someone is dreaming you. You can't tell until the very end! But in the meantime, you might be civil."

Julian pinched himself, or dreamed that he pinched himself. The pain felt real enough, and the Caterpillar was still there.

"I'm Julian Preston," he said, giving in. "Professor of English."

"Professor *in* English, you mean," said the Caterpillar.

"*Of* English."

"Don't be rude. I heard you, just a moment ago, profess to be Julian Preston, and you didn't do it in Latin."

"I mean that I teach poetry."

"I'm not surprised," said the Caterpillar. "Poetry has a thing or two to learn. It has more feet than I do and they're terribly difficult to keep track of. 'A was an archer, who shot at a frog; B was a butcher, and had a great dog.' When you say that one, you ought to beat your chest."

"Why?"

"It's written in Pectorals."

"That's not the right term."

"No?"

"No, but at the moment the correct term slips my mind."

"So *you* say. You've only professed *in English* to know poetry. I think you ought to repeat some. Know any Dickinson?"

"Of course," Julian said, and he recited:

> *Because I could not stop for Toast—*
> *Toast kindly stopped for me—*
> *And brought along a shapely Egg—*
> *And Jam and Juice and Tea.*

We chatted long—Toast knows so much
And speaks of all it knows,
Such matters as the Feat of Rhymes
And whether Verse has Toes—

Then round about began to dance
The Toast as it talked on
Of how each day gets started with
The Yeasting of the Sun—

Toast passed the Juice, then passed the Tea—
At last Toast passed the Milk—
The Toast went racing by them all
Until at last I spoke—

Said I—This is all interesting
Or would be if I knew
How it relates to Any Thing
I think or am or do—

But as I haven't dined as yet
And as you're toasted Bread—
Instead of puzzling out your Thoughts
I'll eat you up instead.

"That is not said right," said the Caterpillar.

"It does sound a *little* off," Julian admitted.

"It is wrong from beginning to end," said the Caterpillar decidedly, "and revealing, too. I expect you forgot to eat breakfast today."

"I may have. I feel as though there are a lot of things I'm forgetting. When I was speaking to my wife a little while ago, I was quite surprised to be hearing from her, but I don't remember *why*."

"Ah, *that,*" said the Caterpillar. "Well, it will be clear soon enough. Not that clarity helps."

"I don't follow you."

"I didn't ask you to, did I?" said the Caterpillar. It put the hookah into its mouth and began smoking again. Then it yawned, shook itself, got down from the branch and crawled away over the black carpet of fallen leaves. "You've got to go deeper in to get further out," it said. "That's the nature of the tulgey wood."

"The tulgey wood?"

"Where you *are*!"

"Where you are!" said another voice, as if in Julian's ear. He turned, but this time he was quite sure that there was nothing before him but the trees.

"And as long as you are," said another nearby voice, "you've got to be somewhere."

"Until you *aren't,*" said a third voice, "and sooner or later you won't be."

"Won't be what?" said Julian.

"Whatever you *are,*" said the first voice.

"Or anything else, for that matter," said the third.

Julian wasn't sure, but he thought it might be the trees themselves that were speaking to him. They seemed to sort of sway in time with the words.

"I wish I could see you," Julian said. "It's awfully dark."

"Awfully splendidly," said the first voice.

"Awfully wonderfully," said the second.

"Awfully terribly beautifully dark," said the third. "Too dark to see the stars!"

"No stars! How de*light*ful!" said the first.

Now Julian was positive—the voices were indeed coming from the trees, and they were swaying as they spoke. Not only did they sway from side to side, but the bare branches moved like arms. One branch bent down and pushed Julian backwards. Before he could protest, another was pushing him in the same direction.

"Careful!" he said. "I can't see where I'm going!"

But the trees showed no sign that they heard him. They kept pushing him toward a part of the forest that was, if anything, darker than where he already was. And as the branches shoved him, the tulgey wood sang in voices that varied as he moved past different trees:

Beautiful Dark in heaven so wide
Through thine emptiness we glide
How to escape you? There's nowhere to hide,
Dark of the nightfall, beautiful Dark!
Dark of the nightfall, beautiful Dark!

    Beau——ootiful Daa——aark!
    Beau——ootiful Daa——aark!
    Darkness of Nightfall,
    Beautiful, beautiful Dark!

Even in daylight thou seemst to say,
I'm in the shadows, come, come away.
Not long do we tarry, swift ends the day.
Dark of the nightfall, beautiful Dark!
Dark of the nightfall, beautiful Dark!

    Beau——ootiful Daa——aark!
    Beau——ootiful Daa——aark!
    Darkness of Nightfall,
    Beautiful, beautiful Dark!

Creep in about us, comforting gloom,
Without your predations, we'd run out of room,
We welcome you, welcome you, welcome you, doom.
Dark of the nightfall, beautiful Dark!
Dark of the nightfall, beautiful Dark!

Beau——ootiful Daa——aark!
Beau——ootiful Daa——aark!
Darkness of Nightfall,
Beautiful, beautiful Dark!

"Chorus again!" cried one of the voices, just as Julian found himself in absolute blackness. The branches stopped pushing. All the trees had just begun to repeat the chorus when a very different voice called out, "Time for the judging! He's needed for the judging!"

"Out, out, out, then!" said one of the tree voices while the rest continued to sing. Branches swept him forward again, but not, to Julian's dismay, back into the light. It was as dark as ever when the words faded into the distance:

Darkness of Nightfall,
Beautiful, beautiful Dark!

He realized, suddenly, that the branches were no longer urging him forward, though he'd kept on walking.

Julian stopped.

"You might go a little further," said a voice.

"Contrariwise, you might stop where you are," said a voice much like the first. "It hardly matters to us. *You* be the judge."

"He *is* the judge," said the first.

"I don't suppose," said Julian, "that you would have a light?"

"If you suppose we did, then we may not," said the first voice.

"Contrariwise," said the second, "if you supposed we didn't, we might yet. And if you didn't suppose at all, we could still. That's logic."

Suddenly, the sun was blazing overhead, and Julian found that he was standing on the edge of a cloud. If he only took a step to the left, he'd go plummeting toward the distant ground.

The speakers, not to Julian's surprise at all, turned out to be wearing identical outfits, and stood, each with an arm around the other's neck, a little higher up on the cloud. Julian could see "DUM" embroidered on one of the collars, and "DEE" on the other. Of course, round the back of each collar would be "TWEEDLE."

What did surprise Julian was that Tweedledum and Tweedledee were not fat. In fact, they were almost skeletal.

"Bring on the Ace!" said Tweedledum, and four playing cards entered through a door in the cloud. Two of the cards walked on either side of the Ace of Spades, who was struggling heroically against them.

The fourth card, walking behind, carried a large axe on his shoulder.

"I won't! I won't!" said the struggling Ace. "I positively refuse! Never! Never!"

"What's this about?" said Julian.

"It's about over," said Tweedledee.

The soldier cards dragged the struggling Ace behind a screen that was just short enough to show the axe rise a moment before it fell with a great CHOP!

Three cards emerged from behind the screen and exited.

"What do you think?" said Tweedledum.

"Ghastly!" Julian said.

"Quite," said Tweedledee.

"Contrariwise," said Tweedledum, "it was *heroic*. But is it the best?"

"The best?"

"That's right," said Tweedledee. "He's only seen one."

"The Deuce! The Deuce!" cried Tweedledum.

Four cards emerged from the door in the cloud. This time, the prisoner was the Deuce of Spades.

"He's not struggling," observed Julian.

"Why should I?" said the Deuce. "The thing to do is accept what's coming. There's nothing to be done, anyway."

The cards went behind the screen. The axe rose and fell with a CHOP!

As the surviving cards left, Tweedledum said, "Well?"

"Horrid!" Julian said.

"I was thinking *philosophical,*" said Tweedledee.

"Better than the first?" asked his brother of Julian.

"You're asking me to *compare* them?"

"He's right," said Tweedledee. "He has to see them all before he can decide."

Next was the Trey of Spades. He giggled as he was led toward the screen.

"What's funny about this?" Julian said.

"It won't really happen, you know," the card said. "This is a big cosmic joke. What happens next is an illusion. Nobody really dies. I'll be right back, you'll see."

The axe rose and fell.

"*Foolish,*" said Tweedledee. "There are some advantages to that one."

"They don't last long," observed Tweedledum. "Four's next." He called out, "The Four! The Four!"

The Four of Spades emerged and actually led the way to the screen. He tried to hold himself up, make himself a little taller than his guards. "I give myself willingly," he said. "Let there be a lesson in this. I permit, I invite it, so that you will all remember!"

"*Martyr's death,*" Tweedledee said as the axe fell.

"Well, I don't think I *will* forget it," Julian said, "or any of the others!"

"You can hardly call it outstanding, in that case," said Tweedledum, and he called for the Five.

The Five of Spades had to be dragged to the screen. He said nothing, looked at no one.

"*Morbid* sort," said Tweedledee a moment in advance of the CHOP!

"He has my sympathy," said Julian.

"But does he have your vote?" asked Tweedledum.

"Yes," said Tweedledee. "Which one wins?"

"I can hardly say that any of them won," said Julian.

"A tie!" said Tweedledum and Tweedledee together. Tweedledum added, "Wonderful!"

"Blue ribbons for all of them!" said Tweedledee, clapping his bony hands. "How democratic!"

"Well done! Well done!"

"And since we are done," said Julian, "how do we get down?"

"Well," said Tweedledum, "you could jump."

Julian looked over the edge of the cloud. The ground was a very long way down. "Jump?" he said. "That would be suicide."

"Contrariwise," said Tweedledee, "it could be homicide, with the proper encouragement." And he gave Julian a push, then jumped behind him. Tweedledum followed.

As they fell, Tweedledum said, "Jumping is to Suicide as Pushing is to Homicide."

"How about burning?" said Tweedledee.

"Firecide," said Tweedledum.

"Drowning?"

"Lakecide!"

"Oceancide!"

"Rivercide!"

"Pondcide!"

"Poolcide!"

"Sewercide!"

"Oh, that one's especially good," said Tweedledum.

"Then there's dying in your sleep," said Tweedledee. "That's bedcide."

"In an automobile: roadcide."

"By falling: cliffcide or mountaincide."

"It's not the falling that kills you," said Tweedledum. "It's the hasty stop at the end."

"Speaking of which," said Tweedledee, "how about leaping from a tall building?"

Tweedledum scratched his head with a skeletal finger. "Give me a hint."

"What are you likely to meet?"

"The Cidewalk!"

Until then, Julian had been too busy falling to take part in the conversation, but he noticed that although they seemed to be dropping like stones, the ground was not getting any closer. "I wonder," he said, "if perhaps we'll survive."

"We have so far," said Tweedledum.

"Contrariwise," said Tweedledee, "that's not always the best indication." Then he said, "We haven't asked if you like poetry."

"Some poetry," Julian said cautiously. "When there's time for it and my mind isn't quite so occupied with death."

"That's the very time!" said Tweedledum. "What shall we repeat to him? We barely have time for one before we hit, I think."

" 'The Tiger and the Engineer' is the longest," Tweedledee replied. "If we have time for just one, we should make it a long one." And he began to recite:

> The void was empty as a pail
>   Containing only air:
> Except the air was absent and
>   The pail, it wasn't there.
> How long this lasted none could say
>   As none was quite aware.
>
> The absence finally ceased to be,
>   It simply couldn't last,
> When Something suddenly arrived
>   From nowhere with no past.
> No one was there to measure it,
>   But it was Something vast.

The stars bunched into galaxies,
        The land cooled and congealed;
The sun shone bright and tartly
        Like a lemon that's been peeled,
When two came walking close at hand
        Across the cosmic field.

The Tiger and the Engineer,
        Who trod the new-made ground,
Saw absence in the Somethingness:
        "There's still not much around!"
They said, "If there were more to this,
        We'd find it more profound."

The Engineer, whose task it was
        To supplement Creation,
Began to work, though at his back,
        With equal application,
The Tiger stalked to bring his works
        To their annihilation.

Said he, "We need some mountains
        To enhance the flat horizon."
The Tiger said she quite agreed,
        So Engineer devised 'em.
Then with her massive sweeping tail
        The Tiger pulverized 'em.

"And if there were some trees about,
        Now wouldn't that be grand?"
So Engineer arranged for some
        To sprout out of the sand.
The Tiger gave each trunk a swat
        That no tree could withstand.

Then for a while the Tiger walked
    Most peaceably behind,
While Engineer was raising up
    Two things of every kind,
From fish to frogs to chimpanzees,
    And then, at last, mankind.

The Earthly population swelled;
    The Tiger was astounded.
"And now we'll dance a merry dance,"
    The Engineer expounded,
"To celebrate fecundity
    And all that we have founded."

Hand in paw and paw in hand
    They circled as they sang,
"Not long ago was nothing,
    Now we've got the whole shebang,
From shoes and ships and sealing wax
    To Finland and meringue!"

"The time has come," the Tiger said,
    "To focus our attention
On how this crowd will grow and grow
    Without some intervention."
The Engineer considered this
    With growing apprehension.

"Why not let them multiply
    And swell and grow forever?
These recent ones, the hairless apes,
    Are marvelously clever.
They'll entertain us endlessly:
    Just see how they endeavor!"

And it was true, these human things
    Were good at clever tricks.
They dressed themselves in ostrich skins,
    Built Taj Mahals with bricks;
They learned to ski and parachute
    And light cigars with Bics.

"I'm tempted some," the Tiger said,
    "To do as you suggest,
And let them cover all the globe,
    Key Largo to Trieste.
The counterargument is this:
    They're easy to digest."

With her great paw, the Tiger snatched
    A recent generation,
Chewed it up and swallowed it,
    And said with some elation,
"With claw and tooth I engineer
    Creation's cancellation."

Just what she meant to say by that
    Was in a moment clear,
For in a gulp she ate the anti-
    Podal hemisphere.
She ate the ground they stood upon;
    She ate the Engineer.

When she had swallowed all the Earth,
    She took a bite of Mars,
And when she finished chewing that
    She swallowed up the stars.
The Tiger then was singular,
    Which briefly felt bizarre.

> *"A Tiger ought to finish what*
> *A Tiger starts to do,"*
> *That's what she said, and bit her tail,*
> *And ate herself up, too.*
> *Thus begins a Universe,*
> *And thus it bids adieu.*

On that last word, Tweedledee disappeared, and with him Tweedledum. In their place was a man in black armor. He wore a helmet in the shape of a horse's head, and in his arms was a large bundle of rags.

"Well, here I am, to the rescue," he said.

"What's that?" said Julian, nodding at the bundle. "A parachute?"

"Perhaps rescue was the wrong word," said the Black Knight. "What I should have said is, 'Here I am, reliably.' "

"Oh," said Julian. "So that's who you are."

As they fell, the wind begun to unwind the rags, which weren't rags, really, but one piece of cloth. A shroud.

"Tell me," said Julian. "Tell me why."

"*Lots* of reasons," said the Knight. "There are poems and songs about it. *You* should know."

"I want your opinion," Julian said. "I want your version."

"Well," said the Knight, "there is a song that I'm particularly fond of. If you'd like to hear it."

"I asked, didn't I?"

"So you did," said the Knight. And he sang:

> *I met a sickly, sickly man*
> *Upon his bed a-lying:*
> *I tapped him with a two-by-four*
> *And asked why he was dying.*
> *"See here," I said, "I want to know*
> *What is your soul's intention?"*

I asked because it mattered, though
    I failed to pay attention.

He said, "I die because the whales
    Who swim the salty waters
Won't introduce me to their wives,
    Much less unto their daughters.
And so I die of loneliness
    for love I never knew,
The floaty whale-ish sort of love
    That might my life renew."

But I was thinking of a plan
    To dig a hole so deep
Insomniacs could hurtle down
    And safely fall asleep.
This hole would open at each end,
    A metaphor for living.
Distracted thus, I had to shout,
    "What answer were you giving?"

He coughed a bit, and then he wheezed,
    "I'll tell you if I must,
The likes of me is never pleased
    To linger here as dust.
I'm meant for finer things, you know,
    I'm made in God's own image.
I'll live on as a concept, say,
    A quark or line of scrimmage."

But I was puzzling out a means
    Of earning higher wages
By building artificial Queens
    For London's daily pages.

"See here!" I said, "You make me feel
I'm wasting all my breath!
Now tell me how it is you die,
And why life ends in death!"

He said, "The answer's plain enough,
You needn't holler so.
I'll tell you how it is we come
And why we have to go.
Life is a rope of broken pearls
That once was painted green,
It's carried by a pair of girls
Who stop sometimes to preen.

"The butter that they walk upon
Spews from eternal churns,
The pearls glow like the pages
Of a novel as it burns.
And so, you see, simplicity
Requires that our lot
Be that we exit, when we must,
With only what we brought."

For once I followed what he said,
Since I had finished thinking
About a poison that would cure
The ills of too much drinking.
I thanked him much for telling me
His insights into dying.
He said it was a piece of cake,
Then did it without trying.

"I suppose," Julian said, "that's as satisfactory an answer as I'm going to hear."

"I haven't heard any better," said the Knight, "and I've heard them all, believe me." The blowing shroud knocked his helmet slightly askew, but he didn't rearrange it. "Any time you're ready," said the Knight, "you can reach out and grab my hand."

"And if I'm not ready?"

"Then sooner or later," said the Knight, "I'll reach out and grab yours."

The shroud continued to unwind and at last ripped free in the wind. Anna's body, curled up like a baby's, rested in the Black Knight's arms; the fingers of his right hand twined with hers.

Julian reached out to stroke Anna's hair and tuck a flying strand behind her ear. He thought of the end of a different poem, a poem about another woman dying. He'd heard the first lines of it just recently. It ended like this:

> *We waited while She passed—*
> *It was a narrow time—*
> *Too jostled were Our Souls to speak*
> *At length the notice came.*
>
> *She mentioned, and forgot—*
> *Then lightly as a Reed*
> *Bent to the Water, struggled scarce—*
> *Consented, and was dead—*
>
> *And We—We placed the Hair—*
> *And drew the Head erect—*
> *And then an awful leisure was*
> *Belief to regulate—*

"That's a good one, too," said the Black Knight. Julian hadn't known he was speaking the lines aloud.

"Contrariwise," said Julian, "they're all good. It's not a question of which poems to say. It's a question of saying enough of them enough times."

The Knight was silent for a bit and then said, "I'm not sure I follow you."

"I didn't ask you to, did I?" said Julian.

"Didn't ask me what?" said Anna's mother. She had gotten up to tuck a strand of Anna's hair into place, then returned to her chair next to Yvonne.

Julian's leg tingled. It was falling asleep. He shifted Nick on his lap. "For something to drink," Julian said. "How about some juice? Nick, that sound good to you?"

Nick nodded with his whole body, head and shoulders going in opposite directions. "Apple juice!"

"Yvonne?"

His daughter sat very still in her chair, looking at her mother's lifeless face. She had known that her mother was dying. It had been explained to her many times. But it was clear that she didn't know what to do with the event now that it had arrived. She hadn't cried. She hadn't asked any questions.

"Yvonne? Some juice?"

"Okay," she said.

Anna's mother left the viewing room.

Julian took his daughter's hand in his. She didn't respond. Julian followed her gaze to the place where Anna lay.

Julian squeezed Yvonne's hand and sang a single note three times: "Mi, mi, mi."

Yvonne kept staring straight ahead. Julian withdrew his hand, bounced Nick on his knee and sang,

> *Ring around the rosie,*
> *Pockets full of posy,*
> *Ashes, ashes,*
> *We all fall down!*

Yvonne looked at him. Julian started the song over, and Nick struggled to get out of his lap. Julian set him down.

"Ashes, ashes," Julian sang, and Nick started to dance. He collapsed on cue, then said, "Do it again!"

"And again and again," Julian promised. And to his daughter, he said, "If you want to, you can help me sing."

Nick sang, "Rosie, rosie!"

Yvonne smiled a little, then stopped smiling.

"If you want," Julian said.

And then he repeated the song, singing it as if it were the song that Nick thought it was, a song about playing on the grass in a circle. But Yvonne was old enough, knew enough now, that she might be able to hear what was really in the words. It was in the words of so many songs. But not enough. New songs were needed all the time, and they needed singing again and again.

You've got to go deeper in, Julian thought, to get further out.

"Ashes, ashes," he sang, "We all fall down."

And on the next verse, his daughter joined in.

Cocoons

Robin Wayne Bailey

O n tiptoes, Tommy sneaked quietly, secretly down the long
tunnel of darkness. A distant, dim flicker of light beckoned him onward. He eyed it curiously, suspiciously, wondering what it could be, if it threatened him. No matter, whatever
the menace ahead, he would not turn back.

"Tommy! Tommy!"

Casting a fearful glance over his shoulder, Tommy quickened
his pace. Nothing behind him but darkness, yet out of that horrid
black his mother's voice came.

"Tommy, please come back!"

He began to run toward the light and away from that voice as
fast as he could go. Though his feet were bare, he could feel no
floor, and that vaguely troubled him; nor could he see any walls or
even a ceiling. Just a long tunnel of darkness and that small, wa-
vering light.

"Tommy, you come back here this instant, you hear me?"

His mother's scream rocketed down the tunnel after him,

smashed him in the back like a giant hand, and sent him toppling. Tommy screamed his own high-pitched scream of terror. Head over heels he tumbled through the blackness, out of control, scrambling for any handhold or foothold, finding none.

"Tommeeeeeeeeee!"

Covering his head protectively with his arms, he drew his legs up into a fetal ball, afraid to answer, afraid she might find him even here. Yet, he continued down that tunnel, no longer running, but falling—floating actually toward the little light, which he could see just over the tops of his bare knees.

His mother continued to call, but her voice faded and faded away. A sound like weeping almost caused him to look back again, but fear flooded his small heart, drowning that impulse. Stubbornly, screwing up his face, he pressed his palms against his ears to shut out the last quavering echoes of his name.

The distant light grew brighter, closer. It held a warm, yellow color, an inviting golden glow. He felt better, braver when he looked at it. "Pretty," he murmured so low he was sure no one could have heard him. He put out a hand toward it.

As if in response, the light reached for him, becoming brighter, warmer still. The darkness melted like wax, and Tommy gave a little gasp.

He wasn't falling at all. Instead, he found himself standing in a strange, but pleasant, room of overstuffed velvet chairs and tall, slender-legged tables, a huge old desk, and a big wooden cabinet. A thick purple carpet tickled the soles of his feet, and a smell like old pipe tobacco teased his nose. Shelves lined the walls, full of mysterious books, and a fire—the light that had beckoned him?—crackled merrily in an enormous fireplace.

Immediately, he dived behind a chair and crouched out of sight. For a long time he hid, holding his breath, trembling, afraid to look out. He listened for a sound, any clue that some grown-up was in the room with him. Finally, gathering a tiny measure of courage, he peeked over one of the chair's plushly upholstered arms. Slowly, he stood up.

"Alone," he whispered, wiping his brow with relief.

Walking to the fire, he hugged himself nervously. Fear gave way to a growing wonderment. It was a magnificent fireplace with a gleaming oak mantel and a huge mirror stretching above it to the ceiling. But gazing into the flames he wondered, who fed the fire?

Once again, fear seized him and he began to shiver. Someone had to be around. Someone must live here. They'd be mad to find him standing in the middle of their house. They'd think he broke in, that he'd done something wrong.

He'd better get out quick while he could!

But the room had no doors. No windows, either. Tommy whirled about nervously, clenching and unclenching his fists, his heart hammering. *I can't get out!* he thought, in a panic. *I can't get out!*

But then he thought, *No one can get in!*

He relaxed considerably. In fact, he began to feel quite safe and secure. Little by little, he started to explore the room. He sat in the velvet chairs, enjoying the lush cushions that sponged up against his bottom. He ran his fingers over the smoothly polished surfaces of the tables. He pulled several books from the lower shelves and ran his hands reverently over their cloth-bound spines and covers.

He turned his gaze upward toward the highest shelf. He would need a ladder to reach it. And every wall had shelves just like this, all full of books. Hundreds of books, thousands! "I may come to like this room very much," he whispered to himself, looking around. "If I don't starve."

He put a hand to his stomach. He was not hungry yet, but he thought he might be soon. Maybe he'd find some candy in one of the desk drawers or in that big cabinet.

The cabinet stood in one corner. It had two tall doors with gleaming brass handles that he could barely reach and a single narrow drawer at the bottom. Rising on tiptoe, he caught hold of the handles and flung the doors open.

It was not a cabinet, but a wardrobe, and a suit of clothes hung on the only hanger. They were peculiar clothes, though. The soft brown pants and jacket were made of velvet like the chairs, and the crisp white shirt had ruffles all around the neck and sleeves.

Pinned to the jacket's lapel, he found a handwritten note that said, *Wear me.*

"No way," he said, making a disgusted face. He knelt down in front of the drawer. Maybe he'd find some jeans and a T-shirt inside. Instead, opening it, he found some funny-looking slippers and a pair of silk stockings. Frowning, he glanced up at the suit on the hanger. "Maybe it's a Halloween costume," he said doubtfully.

On the inside of one of the doors was a narrow mirror. Standing up, he looked at himself, and his frown deepened. A dark bruise discolored one eye and the whole right side of his face from his jaw to the edge of his unruly blond hair. More bruises showed on his ribs and shoulders, and the scar of a cigarette burn glowed lividly on his left forearm.

For a moment he stared at the skinny nine-year-old boy in dirty underwear that he saw in the mirror. Then tears began to leak from his eyes, huge wet tears that streamed down his face and fell to the rich carpet. He didn't make a sound, not even a sob, though, and quickly he wiped the tears away.

His parents didn't like it when he cried. Bad things always resulted. And even if he was alone right now, it was better to stifle his crying.

He blew his nose and wiped his hand on the backside of his briefs. Abruptly, he noticed an unexpected wetness under his feet. He wiggled his toes. The carpet was soaked. A fine sheen of salty tears covered the entire floor!

Tommy watched wide-eyed as one of the velvet chairs, buoyed on the shallow pool of his tears, floated slowly by. He shot a glance toward the lowest bookshelves, relieved to discover the books were safe.

"I'd better put on those shoes after all," he murmured, shaking water from one foot as he lifted it. "And the rest of those weird clothes, too."

He wriggled into the shoes and the outfit, surprised to find how well it fit him. Still, brushing his hands over the ruffled collar around his throat, he thought, *I look like a geek. Who wears this stuff?*

The trousers fastened with little buttons around his knees. Frowning hopelessly, he adjusted the fastenings and tried to tug the hems lower. Without warning, the slick soles of his shoes slipped on the tear-drenched carpet, and he tumbled backward into the wardrobe. The doors slammed shut.

Tommy screamed in the darkness, panic filling his mind, his heart racing in terror. "Let me out!" he cried, banging his fists and heels on the old wood. "Daddy, let me out! Let me out!" He grew suddenly silent and hugged his knees to his chest. *Don't shut me in again*, he pleaded wordlessly.

One of the wardrobe's doors popped open a crack. The ribbon of light that shimmered on the edge had a new quality. Shivering, Tommy sat up, leaned forward, and put an eye to the opening. He pushed the door wider.

Sunlight streamed down through the leafy branches of sweeping trees to dapple the ground. The sky above was bluer than blue, and a pair of fluffy white clouds sailed on it like ships at sea.

A light, warm breeze blew on Tommy's face as he stepped out. He caught another glimpse of himself in the mirror. "Wow, this is more like it!" he exclaimed softly at his image. His weird clothes had changed into jeans and a white T-shirt, and on his feet were brand new Nike hi-tops.

But how had they changed? And how had the wardrobe come to this meadow? He backed up a few paces, puzzled. The wardrobe looked like it had been standing there for ages. In fact, it looked like someone had been using it for a house. A small white picket fence surrounded it, and a garden of flowers grew to one side. A mailbox even stood out front. Yet, it was plainly just a wardrobe.

Tommy backed suspiciously away; then turning, frightened again, he began to run blindly. Holding back his tears, he cried inside as he dodged past trees and jumped over bushes, and ducked under low-hanging limbs in reckless flight.

At last, breathless, he collapsed. Lying on his side in the grass, he pressed his face against his knees and squeezed his eyes tightly shut. Though he fought against crying, his small body shuddered with deep sobs.

After a while, he stopped. Maybe he slept a little. He wasn't sure. But an oddly pleasant smell wafted under his nose, and he had the feeling he wasn't quite alone. Carefully, he peeled one eye open, then the other. Unmoving, he scanned as far as his field of vision allowed.

A trio of white smoke rings rose languidly into the air from just above his head. Tommy craned his neck to scan quietly around some more. It appeared that he had collapsed in the shadow of some kind of giant mushroom. Another trio of smoke rings drifted by.

Fear gave way to curiosity. Tommy uncurled slowly and stood up. A tuft of blond hair, then his forehead, then his large brown eyes rose over the mushroom's edge.

A plump blue caterpillar, sitting up in an unlikely position, puffed nonchalantly on a hookah while it knitted away at a shimmering silver cloth with its lower hands. The needles flew at a rapid pace, and the cloth grew even as Tommy watched. He could not tell exactly where the thread came from.

"Oh, gross!" Tommy muttered to himself in amazement. "A smoking worm."

Turning huge eyes upon him, the caterpillar winked. "Quite unique, don't you agree?"

Tommy jumped back, surprised and a little frightened to find the creature could talk. "Who are you?" he asked in the barest of whispers.

"Why, whoever I want to be," it answered curtly. "It depends on my mood, and the direction the wind is blowing, and whether there was one ring around the moon last night, or two, or three." Pausing, it inhaled deeply from the hookah again. "Want some?" it offered politely.

Tommy shrugged and looked at his shoes. "I'm supposed to just say no." He swallowed nervously. "Can you tell me where I am?"

The caterpillar rolled its eyes left to right, up and down. "Here and there," it said. "Everywhere and nowhere. Where do you think you are?"

"I *was* in a hospital," Tommy murmured in a low voice, feeling confused and fearful once again as he remembered a word: "coma." He'd heard it as if through a thick curtain, from far away, just before he'd fled from his mother into that dark tunnel with the inviting light at the end. He didn't know what the word meant, yet it scared him. "But I can't be there and here at the same time. You must be a dream."

The caterpillar smiled thinly. "Perhaps it is you who are the dream," it suggested, waving the hookah in a grand gesture.

Tommy cringed, covering his head as the pipe swung his way.

The knitting needles stopped. The caterpillar leaned forward in concern. "My, you are a pretty sight," it said. "All black and blue. Almost as blue as me. It's rude of you to be prettier than me, you know."

Tommy blushed with embarrassment. The caterpillar hadn't tried to hit him with the pipe at all. Straightening, he put on a sheepish face. "But you're only a bug," he said.

"A bug?" The caterpillar bristled indignantly. Inhaling deeply from his hookah, he blew three smoke rings. They settled over Tommy's head and oscillated up and down his form before dissipating. "A bug, indeed! Well, I am a bug with a future!"

The knitting needles resumed their clacking. The caterpillar worked at a furious pace, and the silver cloth grew by several rows.

Feeling ignored, Tommy asked in his softest voice, "What are you knitting?"

The caterpillar gave him a stern look. "Speak up, young man. You must learn to speak up. If you don't speak up, how shall anyone know you are there?"

Tommy pushed out his lower lip at this scolding, and his voice became even softer, a bare murmur. "I don't want people to know I'm here," he answered. "I just want them to leave me alone."

The knitting needles stopped again. The caterpillar looked at Tommy for a long time before he spoke, and Tommy began to squirm.

"Except for the occasional passing girl or boy," it said finally, "or a dormouse or that damnable Cheshire Cat, I've been very much alone on this mushroom for a long time." It jabbed the hookah in Tommy's direction. "Believe you me, being alone is not all it's cracked up to be." It took another puff from the hookah and exhaled the fragrant smoke in a long stream. "If you really wanted to be alone, why, you'd have passed me right by without so much as a hello-how-are-you. So the question is, if you don't *really* want to be alone, what do you want?"

Tommy scratched his head, inwardly irritated with himself. He'd felt stupid before, but never in front of a caterpillar. "I know I don't want to go home," he said.

The caterpillar nodded. "Then stay right here just as long as you want—nobody will make you leave." Finishing off another row, it set the needles aside, broke the threads and tied them off. "Excuse me for a moment," it said suddenly. Several pairs of hands shook and fluffed the silver cloth. Then, with an adroit movement, the hands flipped the cloth high into the air.

Like a glimmering piece of gossamer, the cloth settled lazily down over the caterpillar, draping him completely. The hookah disappeared just under the cloth's edge, and gray smoke filtered from beneath. The caterpillar coughed. "Guess I'll have to give this up now," it said in a somewhat muffled voice.

"Wow!" Tommy exclaimed, staring at the gleaming shroud with a sudden realization. "Is that your cocoon? I thought you made it from spit, or something!"

"Please!" the caterpillar answered disdainfully, giving a little shiver under its blanket. "I am far too sophisticated and well bred a caterpillar to go spitting all over myself. And the proper term is not cocoon, but chrysalis."

Leaning on the mushroom, Tommy reached out and touched the cloth. It felt silky, cool against his fingers as he gently stroked it.

"Ooh, that's good!" the caterpillar said. "A little higher on the left. Yes!"

"How long are you going to be in there?" Tommy asked curiously as he continued to rub where directed.

"Until I'm ready to come out," the caterpillar answered matter-of-factly. "One should never emerge from one's cocoon until one is perfectly ready."

Tommy paused. "I thought you called it a chrysalis."

Inside the silver cloth, the caterpillar shrugged. "Cocoon, chrysalis, whatever. At a time like this, semantics lose their meaning." Another cloud of smoke seeped from beneath the cloth's edge, stinging Tommy's eyes. He backed a step away as the caterpillar sighed. "It is so warm and secure in here. Quite snug and comfy."

Tommy hung his head. Sitting down on the ground, he plucked a blade of grass and idly shredded it. "I wish I had such a nice cocoon," he said.

"But you do," the caterpillar laughed. "And you're in it now."

A strange commotion began under the silver blanket. The hookah suddenly slipped from under the edge, streaming a small thin trail of smoke from its lip.

"I don't understand," Tommy murmured as he watched.

"Everyone has a cocoon," the caterpillar replied. The silver blanket shivered and stirred and quivered as if some kind of wrestling match were going on beneath. "Some people have lots of cocoons."

Tommy scoffed and tore at another piece of grass. "You just think that because you're a caterpillar," he accused dispiritedly.

"Oh, my!" the caterpillar exclaimed. "Would you mind? Grab a corner there and give it a yank!"

Tommy rose to his feet and, grasping a corner of the silver cloth, he pulled the blanket away.

A wondrous, large-eyed butterfly perched on the mushroom, fanning wings of black and blue and gold and silver, where the caterpillar had been. "Not bad!" it said in the caterpillar's voice. "Not bad, if I do say so myself." It gave a longing look at the hookah lying nearby. "Again," it asked, looking from the pipe to Tommy, "would you mind? Just one last time—for auld lang syne, as they say."

Tommy noticed that the caterpillar's hands were gone, and the butterfly's legs could not grasp the pipe. Carefully, he raised it to the butterfly's lips.

"Thank you," the butterfly said. Inhaling for a final time, it blew three final smoke rings high into the air. Together, butterfly and boy watched as the rings sailed away like clouds into the blue sky. "And now we put aside old things to seek new wonders."

"Let me come with you!" Tommy cried, suddenly frightened at the thought of being left alone.

The butterfly winked one large eye. "You have no wings yet," it said, "But in time, perhaps. In time."

It sprang into the air suddenly. Testing its wings, it circled over Tommy and the mushroom. Then it climbed higher and fluttered away above the trees. Tommy watched, his mouth agape, and the butterfly's voice came back to him, singing:

Full leisurely we glide,
Our wings are open wide;
The beauty kept inside
Nevermore to hide—
Nevermore to hide!

Tommy listened until only an echo of the song remained in his head. For a moment, he stood expectantly watching the tree-tops, but the butterfly didn't return.

Alone again, he felt a too-familiar sense of abandonment. A single tear glittered on the lashes of one eye, but he brushed it away, stubbornly refusing to cry. After a while, he sat down on the grass and ripped up yet another blade of grass, and tried to think what he should do next.

Then his eyes fell upon the beautiful silver cloth lying upon the lawn. Gathering it, he hugged it against his chest and face and wrapped its silky smoothness around his shoulders. The sense of abandonment faded. The caterpillar—that is, the butterfly—had left him something.

Slowly, he got to his feet and stared at the mushroom. A sudden urge possessed him, and with a little effort, he climbed up on top of it and settled himself in a cross-legged position. *How different it all looks from up here!* he thought as he gazed about.

His hand brushed the hookah. A bit of smoke continued to seep from its lip. He looked nervously at the hookah, wondered what exactly it contained and if he dared to try it. "In time, perhaps," he said with the tiniest smile, doing his best to mimic the caterpillar's voice as he fingered the slender pipe. "In time."

He thought about the caterpillar—really such a shriveled, blue little thing—and how it had transformed. There was something to contemplate, and he would figure it all out in time. He wondered what it would be like to open his own cocoon someday and find a splendid pair of wings.

In time, perhaps he'd learn.

Dreaming of that, he drew the silver cloth closer about his shoulders and huddled down inside its folds. For now at least it was enough to feel warm and secure, snug and comfy, and to know that the butterfly was out there somewhere, waiting for him.

Hollywood Squares

Lawrence Schimel

⤳ ⤳

I noticed him the moment he walked in, and he saw me notice
him and smiled. It was one of those perfect smiles, the kind
you see on toothpaste commercials, teeth gleaming so white
it almost hurts. I wondered if he'd ever done toothpaste commercials. Probably. He wasn't so famous that I knew him by name or
felt like I'd seen him before, and most actors wound up doing
commercials when the movie work was slow.

I didn't smile back but I looked at him and then pointedly
looked away and began totaling up some of the checks on my pad.
He came over to the counter and spun one of the stools in front of
me before sitting down. "Be right with you," I said, without looking up at him. He knew I was making him wait on purpose, but
that was OK. We were both playing the game now, even though I'd
already decided to sleep with him the moment he walked in.

He was older than most of the men I usually go for, but I figured that just meant he'd had more time to establish connections
in Tinseltown. It was about time I found someone who was my

ticket out of this job and into the limelight. I was almost twenty-four, after all. I'd been waiting tables here at the Starboard Diner since I ran away from home at seventeen and came to Hollywood, all those years waiting tables and waiting to be discovered. Some men claimed they had connections, but after I went home with them it always turned out that they really didn't, or that they hadn't been interested in me for anything but sex anyway. Or even if they did have connections, what was the point in their using them, since they had already gotten me in bed? All men want to do is get their dicks wet. I had read that in *Seventeen* a few months ago, in this story by a girl named Wendy Rawlings, and I bothered to remember her name because that one line just really struck me as being so absolutely true. It just summed everything up perfectly.

But this guy had seemed different when he walked in. I looked up at him at last and smiled as I got a menu for him. He was probably a bit over fifty, I guessed, although he looked younger. Maybe it was the tan, or the half-unbuttoned shirt, or the way he simply exuded this animal magnetism. Balding, but in a sort of cute way.

"Alice!" he said suddenly, as if with a shock of recognition, staring at my chest. I had a nice figure and I knew men would always be looking at my breasts first, so that was where I hung my name tag—where they were sure to notice it. "I was in *Alice*, once."

He meant, of course, *Alice in Wonderland*. I got that all the time from customers. Happens with having so many actors and wanna-be actors all over the place. I resigned myself to the inevitable jokes, which men thought made cute pick-up lines. " 'Eat Me,' 'Drink Me,' and watch it grow." I had hoped he would be different. But men were all the same, weren't they? They just wanted to get their dicks wet. He kept one hand in his lap, I noticed, and he was moving it back and forth as if he were stroking himself under the counter. I was revolted. How could I have thought of going home with someone so slimy?

"I was the March Hare," he said, looking at me intently. "I

was always late picking up my cues." I nodded and half smiled in a too-polite way and flipped my pad to let him know I was just there to take his order. I was no longer interested in playing this script out. I could see where it was going, and I'd been down that dead end too many times before.

He looked down into his lap and lifted a cat up onto the counter. I hadn't seen him walk in with it, but I guess he'd had it tucked under his arm, what I had thought was a jacket.

"And this is Chesh," he continued, and smiled up at me. This was pushing the bounds of credibility just too far. The things men said to pick up a girl. But he did have a wonderful, heart-melting smile. "I got him while I was working on that film, and it just seemed natural to name him that."

We didn't allow pets in the Starboard, although no one had ever tried to bring a cat in before, not in the years I'd been working here. It seemed well behaved enough, but at least I would have an excuse to have him thrown out if he got out of hand.

I felt better that it was the cat he'd been stroking, and not himself, but it was still kind of weird. But in some way it also seemed tender, endearing. He probably just used the kitty as a device for that effect. But if it was genuine, it was charming. Or perhaps he was so rich or so spoiled that he felt he could waltz into anyplace he wanted with this cat and no one would have the balls to tell him no.

"Do you recommend the turkey club?" he asked.

I did.

"I'll try it, then. And what flavor ice creams do you have? Do you have maple walnut?" I nodded. "Good, then I'll have a dish of maple walnut. And a root beer float. With vanilla."

"You're not pregnant, are you?" I asked teasingly.

"What?"

"Sudden craving for ice cream. Turkey club comes with pickles." I smiled, and he laughed out loud as he suddenly got the joke. I turned to leave but he called me back.

"And if you could bring the maple walnut with the sandwich instead of at the end—"

Weird, but I wrote it down that way anyway.

The ice cream, I learned, was for the cat. Chesh sat on the counter and daintily polished off the entire sundae, except for the nuts and cherry, which he left in the bottom of the dish.

The man didn't say a word the entire time he ate. He didn't even look at me, either, though I purposefully walked past him three or four times, to see if he would. No big loss, I decided, but I went over and asked if he wanted anything else. He polished off the last of the pickle and drank down the last of his root beer float and shook his head. He laid a twenty on the counter, not even bothering for me to give him a check.

"I'm Henry," he said, as he stood up. "Henry Wilcox. I'll pick you up around six."

Not a doubt that I'd be going with him. I wanted to feel pissed off at him, but I was sort of pleased. He was completely sure of himself, and there was something I found very attractive about that. He picked Chesh off the counter and tucked him under one arm.

"I get off shift at seven."

He smiled at me, that blindingly white, heart-wrenching smile. "Seven, then," he said, and turned away. "We'll play Hollywood Squares."

At seven on the dot Henry was back and picked me up. Chesh was with him, too, and he led the three of us to the Walk of Fame. Hollywood Squares, I thought. Okay. Now what? I waited for some clue from Henry. He smiled at me and read off one of the Stars. "Veronica Fittel." He looked up at me expectantly, but I still had no idea what I was supposed to say or do.

"I have no idea who she was, or even how to play this."

"Off with her head!" Henry cried out suddenly, then walked forward to the next Square. "Timothy Rodgers."

I began to laugh at the absurdity of it all. Him, the cat, the game.

I shook my head. "Nope. No idea who he was."

"Off with his head!" Henry shouted, and walked to the next Square. "Janis Dorfinger."

He was looking up at me so expectantly, smiling that heart-melting smile of his, and so, quietly, I said, "Off with her head."

Henry let out a joyful whoop and walked on to the next Square. I began to smile as well. Something about his enjoyment of this all was infectious.

"Derek Tikney," he read, and with more enthusiasm and volume I declared, "Off with his head!" Soon we were nearly running down the street as we read the names of Stars and shouted "Off with their head!" at the top of our lungs. People were pointedly going out of their way to avoid us, and I didn't even care, I was having so much fun.

"Henry Wilcox."

"Off with his head!"

Henry stopped and looked at me, suddenly serious like when you step out into the snow to sober up. I felt awful, but the words had been out of my mouth before I realized what I was saying.

"That's the problem," he said quietly. "No one ever has."

He turned and began walking down the street. He looked wrecked. Utterly dejected. I cursed myself for not having remembered his name. Chesh suddenly darted from behind me and trotted to catch up to him, tail held high.

Suddenly I realized: He had a Star on the Walk of Fame! Didn't he understand what an achievement that was? Even if people didn't remember his name, he was a Star! It was exciting even to think that someone with his own Star was right here with me, and even more than that, found me attractive.

I followed after him, to try to cheer him up.

A wanna-be, a has-been, and his cat, I thought, hurrying back over the Stars we had just passed. What a group we made. You almost had to laugh and be happy. This was the kind of stuff they made movies about.

I didn't know what to say to him, especially since he was so obviously in a different mood than I, so I just put my arm around his waist and walked quietly along with him until he snapped out of his blue funk. I bought us ice cream sundaes at C.C. Brown's, even one for Chesh, and Henry couldn't help but start to smile again and revert back to his jovial self, teasing and cracking jokes. After finishing off his own sundae and half of my cherry vanilla, Chesh lay sprawled on the plastic seat between us, purring loudly as both Henry and I stroked his fur. Our fingers brushed against each other as he petted Chesh.

"That is one contented cat," I said. And that was how I felt, too. Contented like I hadn't felt in years. I wasn't even concerned about "making it" right now, even though that was why I'd decided to sleep with Henry in the first place. And, my God, he had his own Star! Even if he wasn't working anymore, he'd have contacts galore.

But none of that was important right then. I was so caught up in the moment of just being happy. It was nice.

"Let's go back to your place and watch old movies I was in, back when I was a young and dashing man."

I scooped a dollop of whipped cream and, leaning forward suddenly, plopped it onto his nose. "You silly," I said. "You're still young and dashing."

I felt embarrassed as Chesh walked through the apartment, sniffing at my clothes and furniture. Did I smell? I knew Henry must be watching wherever the cat was, inspecting my life simultaneously; he seemed to always know exactly where Chesh was, instinctively, for he never let you catch him looking for the cat. But Henry pretended not to notice anything about my tiny, somewhat dingy apartment as he sat on the couch chatting amiably about his adventures. I, in contrast, noticed half a dozen things that needed desperately to be cleaned, but I couldn't even hide them lest I draw attention to them. To further distract Henry, I leaned forward as he was in the middle of a story about meeting Katharine Hepburn and kissed him. His story quickly melted into a heavy petting session on the couch, until Chesh got jealous and came over, wanting to get in on the petting. We laughed and moved into the bedroom, where we made love for what seemed like hours. Henry was wonderful in bed, caring and attentive. I've always liked men named Henry, I realized; the name itself sounds so comforting, solid.

I had to work the next morning, so we didn't have much time for pillow talk. I gave Henry the unopened toothbrush I kept in the medicine cabinet, and almost asked him if he'd ever done toothpaste commercials as I handed it to him, but held my tongue. And I was glad that I had, for when I used the bathroom after he was done I noticed that he'd left a set of dentures on the sink. Dentures! Who'd have thought he was old enough to need them? I remembered the feel of his muscular body while we made love, and knew they weren't from old age. Perhaps he'd been in an accident, or had had false teeth put in for the sake of his acting career. They had certainly given him a gorgeous, eye-catching set!

I woke at five twenty-three, just moments before my alarm went off. I leaned out of bed to shut it off before it woke Henry. I wondered if I should call in sick today as I turned over in bed to snuggle up to Henry, imagining a day of sex and more adventures like our Hollywood Squares. The bed was empty. I was suddenly wide awake, and I sat up, looking about the room. He must've gone to take care of Chesh, I thought, as I pulled on a robe and walked into the living room.

Henry was definitely gone. And so were half my appliances.

"Shit. Shitshitshit."

How could I have been so stupid? I was such a fool sometimes. Such a trusting fool. And now I had gotten my fingers burned.

But who would've suspected a man with a cat of being a thief? Unless it was all a joke. Cat burglar.

Damn him!

There was nothing I could do about it now, so I stumbled into the bathroom to shower before I was late for work. There, on the sink, were his dentures, which he'd forgotten during the heist. I didn't know whether to laugh or to cry. This was just too much. I stared down at the teeth within my hand, the little curve of his beautiful smile. I felt I was cursed by my name, that this was all one great practical joke someone was playing on me, that I'd suddenly wake up and it would all have been a dream. But I had his teeth in my hands and a looted apartment at my back and cat hairs all over the sofa.

I didn't care so much about the lost stuff, although it would be expensive to replace. I felt hurt that I had fallen for him. That I had fallen in love so easily, so quickly. That's what hurt.

And the man who was responsible for it all had faded so fast out of my life; faded like that damned Cheshire Cat, until all that was left was the smile.

Another Alice Universe

Janet Asimov

☙ ☙

I suspected nothing when Aunt Alice gave me one of her down coats, not even after I put it on, glanced into the hall mirror, and immediately felt dizzy. I didn't report this to my aunt, who was standing by looking slightly anxious, because I was afraid she'd stop me from going out.

The coat was white, with tight-fitting sleeves that puffed at the shoulder seams. The top was molded to the chest, but from the waist down it descended stiffly outward, for the down padding had been sewn into bulging horizontal rings.

"Thank you," I said, to be polite. "I won't be cold now."

Aunt Alice nodded. "You Californians always arrive during a Manhattan winter wearing only thin raincoats bought, no doubt, for those years your rainy season lives up to its name. This coat is warm, and you are so young that it doesn't make you look like the White Queen. In fact, it's probable that the coat won't give some-one like you any trouble."

I didn't ask her to explain what she meant because Dad had

warned me that his oldest sister—who has always been a bit strange, especially since she was widowed—was given to odd remarks that create suspense, perhaps because she makes a living writing peculiar novels.

Besides, I assumed she meant that the coat was lightweight enough to be carried easily, which I found to be the case as I went through various museums.

I also found it hard to concentrate on the museums, for I kept thinking about Aunt Alice and her mention of the White Queen. My aunt's real name is Alicia, but no one's called her that since childhood, when she had long, straight blonde hair like the girl in Lewis Carroll's book. I was named after her, and I also have long, straight blonde hair. But there, I used to think, the resemblance ended.

I have always prided myself on being as logically rational as my dad. We don't read much fiction. For us, down-to-earth reality is enough, and we always keep our cool.

That is, I did until a couple of months ago when I heard that my ex-boyfriend had married someone else. I guess Mom and Dad got tired of seeing me mope around the house, suffering over the permanence of my loss, and not getting at applications for business school. When Aunt Alice suggested that I visit her, my parents handed me an airline ticket and wished me well.

The book arrived just before I was due to leave California. It was an old copy of *Alice in Wonderland,* bound in faded purple leather. Enclosed was a note from Aunt Alice saying, "Please read this book on the plane and be sure to take careful note of the plot of the second story."

I had never read it before, you see. She'd asked me that when we talked on the phone about my trip. She seemed both amused and dismayed when I said I'd only seen the movie.

So I read *Alice in Wonderland* during the plane trip, and I must say it was a lot more somber and peculiar than the movie. I fell asleep thinking that the second story, "Alice Through the

Looking-Glass," was darker and full of anticipatory sadness over loss. Not Alice's sadness, for she wasn't sad. The author's.

The plane was landing at La Guardia airport when I woke up, my mind churning with the book's last words—"Life, what is it but a dream?" Nonsense, I thought.

I was relieved when Aunt Alice didn't grill me about the book she'd sent, and permitted me to go right out sightseeing. And there I was at the Metropolitan Museum, not experiencing any "trouble" until I visited the ladies' room. While there, I put on the down coat and looked in the mirror.

Instantly I was dizzy, so dizzy that the mirror seemed to mist over and I thought I was going to faint—toward the mirror, which unaccountably terrified me. I turned around and ran out of the museum to get a taxi back to my aunt's apartment.

By the time I arrived, I was feeling perfectly well—until I opened Aunt Alice's front door and saw myself in her hall mirror. This, too, became misty and I experienced what seemed to be a mysterious pull upon my person.

I was about to call out to my aunt when I thought carefully and logically, as Dad trained me to do. The dizziness had occurred before, when I had the coat on indoors. The problem was merely that a Californian is unused to the cold outdoor temperatures and the high inside temperatures that New Yorkers somehow survive. I peeled off the down coat and immediately felt cooler and better.

I unpacked, gave *Alice in Wonderland* back to my aunt, and after dinner we talked. I told her what I'd seen at the museums and she listened, although, as Dad had predicted, she did glance occasionally at her computer with what may have been suppressed longing. Her computer, by the way, contains software only for word processing. Aunt Alice doesn't play video games and she can't even do spreadsheets!

At one point, I said, "Aunt Alice, Dad says you've been awfully down in the dumps, at least you were when he visited a year ago. What was the problem?"

Aunt Alice did not bridle at my intrusiveness, as any of my other relatives would have. She said, "To paraphrase Lewis Carroll, it had something to do with knowing that eventually all of us are but older children, fretting to find bedtime near."

"Are you dying?" I asked in horror.

"I'm quite well, but everyone does die, you know. Except the great authors. I'm now sure they live on. Tolkien's still there in Middle Earth; Kenneth Grahame messes about with boats under the willows; and Charles Dodgson will always be Lewis Carroll."

"You are speaking metaphorically, of course."

"Of course, dear niece. Do you know that for a while I even went through a nasty period of being envious of other people, particularly children with all their future ahead of them, but now I'm trying to achieve a moderately serene acceptance of things as they are, at least here. Can you, dear?"

"I hate accepting things as they are," I said, thinking of that louse, my ex-boyfriend. I could feel myself scowling. "It's too bad you can't change reality."

"That depends on what reality you're talking about," Aunt Alice said. "I hope you read *Alice*."

"Yes, but I'm afraid I'm not big on fantasy."

"It's a pity you are so much like your dear father," said my aunt. "Otherwise . . . but then it's a pity I haven't the courage to right my own wrongs."

I didn't have the faintest idea what she was talking about, and since I was very sleepy from tackling Manhattan so soon after leaving California, I went to bed early.

That night I dreamt, not about my ex-boyfriend for a change, but about going from one mirror to another, trying to see my reflection but never catching it before the mirror misted up.

When I woke, Aunt Alice was not in the apartment. Pinned to the bathroom door was a note saying she was out buying jam, croissants and eggs, and would return soon to make breakfast.

As I waited for her, I kept thinking about the dream, and finally I went to the hall mirror, the only one in the apartment that's full-length. No mist, no dizziness, and I saw myself clearly. My brow was distinctly clouded, my eyes tired, and I looked so woebegone it was no wonder Mom and Dad had sent me away. I was an insult to California.

There was no reason to put on the down coat because I wasn't going out in the Manhattan winter until after a warm breakfast, promised me by Aunt Alice. But I put it on.

The mirror promptly became blurry. I rubbed my eyes, but it stayed blurry, and I was soon so dizzy I keeled over toward the mirror. To keep from falling, I put my hand on the surface of the mirror—and went right through!

I wasn't frightened because, as a logical realist, I immediately assumed that I was ill, no doubt feverish, and having hallucinations based on that damned book.

I seemed to be walking through a forest composed of ancient trees and scanty underbrush, in the company of an old lady wearing an expression of featherbrained stupidity, a long garment very much like my down coat, a shawl around her shoulders, and a crown on her very messy white hair.

"It's jam every OTHER day: today isn't any OTHER day, you know," she said.

"I don't care. I'll eat eggs." I don't know why I said that. It just came out.

The White Queen—she could be no other—gasped and stopped so abruptly that pins cascaded from her shawl while a comb and brush fell out of her hair. She looked every bit of one hundred and one years, five months and a day.

Before I could remember whether or not that really was her age or merely a joke, she took a good look at me.

"Botheration. I've already believed six impossible things and I'm ready for breakfast, not for another impossibility."

"I'm sorry," I said, to make up for starting things off badly with eggs. Then, before I could stop myself, I asked, "Well, where's Carroll? Or Dodgson?"

A suddenly shrewd glint came from the faded blue eyes of the White Queen, and she whispered, "Here. Everywhere. An echo in memory, a holding fast in the nest of gladness, a shadow of a sigh. No matter what happens. Checkmate."

"Well, I hardly think.. . ."

"It's not your job to think, hardly or otherwise. It's your job to do something about the bad changes. Make a memorandum of it, and don't omit your feelings."

"What bad changes?" Then I remembered the book's plot. "The child Alice is supposed to be here before you. Where is she?"

"Little Alice, my White Pawn, had been doing well through the first two squares," the White Queen said with a melancholy bleat in her voice, "and she even kept up with the Red Queen's race. She's had amnesia and lost it; she's coped with the identical twins (all identical twins being mirror images of each other, you know), but now she's . . ."

The White Queen stopped and suddenly screamed as piercingly as the whistle of a steam engine.

"What's the matter?"

"Oh, oh, oh, oh! Mixed up! Still mixed up! Since that awful old Alice was here. Any moment now there'll be death and disaster . . ."

"Is that why you screamed? Over something that hasn't happened yet?"

"Well, of course," said the White Queen. "I'm the only one around here who can remember what's going to happen in all the Alice universes. I live backwards, so I remember backwards and forwards, real and unreal, young and old, light and dark, summer and winter, autumn and July, hither and yon, now and then . . ."

I interrupted, because it seemed as if she'd go on forever. "You haven't told me what the bad changes are."

"It was her fault. That old Alice, wearing my clothes just the way you are, implying that little Alice turns into me, which wasn't the case and shouldn't happen to a nice child. Pawns turn into Queens if they're lucky, but their own sort, not somebody else's."

"You don't make any sense," I said angrily. "My Aunt Alice gave me this coat and I can't help it being like yours. Anyway, you're merely part of a feverish hallucination and I'm not only not a chess piece, I'm not part of any fictional game."

"Fiction?" The White Queen plucked at her drooping shawl. "If it makes you happier to think that way, go ahead. But I do wish you could remedy the situation."

"What situation?"

"Little Alice never meeting the White Knight. It will break his heart. Your aunt should have been punished for her envy, but perhaps you're here as a substitute. You'll be the better for the punishment, I know."

"I don't intend to be punished."

"But you are. She sent you here, without a word of advice, and if you don't fix things I'm going to order that you won't get even jam during the next week of Tuesdays."

"I have nothing to do with any of this," I said, struggling to remind myself that I must be feverish. It seemed to be getting lighter in the wood, as if a cloud had passed, yet the light was sinister. Was something horrible coming? I looked around for a looking glass so I could get out, but there was nothing to be seen, just the loneliness of the place.

"There, there," said the White Queen, patting my head. "Don't go on like that. Perhaps you've been punished enough. Remember that you're a great girl and you must stop crying."

I was. Crying, that is. I couldn't stop. The tears just went on wetting my face and clogging up my nose. I felt lost in this alien place, and it was becoming more alien, for a dreadful shriek rang out, followed by a crash and then a hideous crunching noise. It wasn't the White Queen, for she was still talking.

". . . that's better. You've stopped crying. Be good and it's jam today, even semper iam. Remember it's the rule to try to consider things so you can manage to be glad."

"Glad?" I cried, "when there's a noise that sounds like death? What's happening?"

"Nothing can be done about that, but you can still fix the rest. Here's little Alice."

The child who ran down the path toward us was an eerie duplicate, not of Tenniel's pictures, but of a photo I'd seen of Aunt Alice as a child. Only this little Alice's eyes were wide with fright.

"The Jabberwock is loose! It came whiffling and burbling through the tulgey wood, its eyes all aflame, and it just ate Humpty Dumpty, leaving over some of the yolk—oh, its jaws are so messy! And now I think it's looking for me!"

"This is not in the book!" I exclaimed, forgetting to be careful.

The White Queen jabbed my side with her elbow—I could feel it even through the thick down—and said to little Alice, "Pay no attention to her. She's out of temper and in that state of mind where she wants to deny something."

"And I know what to deny!" I yelled triumphantly. "All of you! All of this!"

Little Alice was staring at me as if I were crazier than the White Queen. "Are there three of you, now?"

"I am not a White Queen," I said indignantly. "I am not from around here. I'm from California."

"Is that on the weird side of the Looking-Glass too?"

"Not exactly," I said slowly.

Little Alice looked up at me sadly. "You don't sound as if you know the way out, either. I'm not having fun since I met that sad lady like you, only old, and I want to go home before the Jabberwock eats me."

"Where is—that old lady?" I asked.

"Gone. She said she wanted to make her own universes. I

didn't know what she meant. She didn't like me, and she was so sad that it was catching. I do want to go home, because I'm getting older and older and older . . ."

"Now listen here, Alice," I said, choosing my words with care. "You're not old. You're not like us."

"Well, you're not terribly old," Alice said, studying me. "You look much more the way I'd like to be when I grow up."

"That's nice," I said, absurdly pleased. "But right now you're seven and a half exactly, and it doesn't matter about Humpty Dumpty because he would have smashed anyway and all the king's horses and all the king's men . . ."

"Get on with it," said the White Queen. "Leave out the Egg. All he did was argue about the Jabberwock—or was it with the Jabberwock? No matter, he's breakfast, so get on with it."

I gulped. "Remember, Alice, you're not old, and you'll get home safely. Right now you're going to go on having fun here, with lots of adventures because they are ways you have fun with your mind. You'll especially enjoy the White Knight."

I suddenly shivered, remembering that Charles Dodgson, Lewis Carroll and the White Knight were one.

"Will the White Knight keep the Jabberwock away?"

"Yes, Alice. Concentrate on the journey. That's the best part of the game."

Alice turned to the White Queen, who was fumblingly rearranging her shawl. "Is this Alice right?"

The White Queen winked at me and bestowed a foolish smile on little Alice. "Now you won't miss your White Knight."

"Is he mine?"

"Yours," I said quickly. "It's supposed to be that way, even if it can't and won't last." I shivered again, knowing the words were my aunt's, coming to me through the damned coat.

"Won't last?" Alice said, her voice quivering.

I could hear a deep bass burbling, far off in the wood but coming closer.

"Well, nothing does—no, that's not true."

The White Queen peered into the wood, looked back at me, and flapped her shawl. "Truth is not quite another impossible thing. Try again; draw a long breath, shut your eyes, and get to it."

I did take a deep breath, but I didn't shut my eyes, not with the Jabberwock out there. "Alice, don't worry. I promise you that you'll get to the end of the game, and you'll go home. But no matter how old you get or how much you forget, you'll always remember the White Knight."

Alice looked puzzled, but then she smiled and asked the White Queen (as if knowing that I didn't know), "Which way is the next move for me?"

The White Queen pointed to another bend in the path. "Now run along and have a good time, dear. After your tryst with the White Knight, cross the brook to the eighth square—that's where you'll get your crown. I'll meet you there."

Alice curtseyed to both of us and, with happy eyes, vanished into the shadows of the trees.

After the echo of her footsteps died away, I noticed that the wood was silent.

"Has the Jabberwock stopped?"

"Been stopped. By the White Knight. Didn't you say he'd take care of things?"

"Yes, but . . ."

"It's your Alice universe, now, you know. Through joining."

"Nothing you say makes sense and I want to go home!"

"Very well," said the White Queen, and pushed me hard.

I flew through the mirror mist, landing in the hall just as Aunt Alice came in. Without a pause she said, "I see that your coat gave you an interesting time."

"I undid some of whatever the hell you did, I suppose by mistake because you were so unhappy then . . . now wait a minute, Aunt Alice! It wasn't—it couldn't be real. I must have a fever and I've been hallucinating."

She felt my forehead. "I don't think so, dear."

"But fantasy universes can't exist in time and space!"

Aunt Alice began to laugh.

"I am not amused," I said.

"Don't worry, dear niece. I understand that time and space can be thought of as fantasies, too."

"But—Carroll's, I mean Dodgson's universe—I mean, it isn't real, is it?"

"Wasn't it?"

"Only when I was in it. And that nonsense about joining. That doesn't happen when I read a book."

"It does if you're lucky. You and the author join. It's like love."

I was embarrassed. People of her generation shouldn't talk about love. "Isn't it more logical that, symbolically speaking, each reader creates a new universe with the author . . ."

"I believe that's what I was saying, dear," said Aunt Alice.

And with Finesse

Janet Pack

⟳ ⟳

"*En garde!*"

The warning, followed by the clash and hiss of two steel blades, echoed in the vast dark hall. They flashed in quick-changing patterns, wielded by a lone pair of men in their early twenties. The two worked their broadswords under the glare of a white overhead spotlight that puddled in the middle of a sawdust-covered show ring. Except for the baleful red EXIT signs glaring from above every door, the spot was the only light in the cavernous place. Heavy breathing provided a softer counterpoint for the harsh notes of the fighters' swords. Straight thrust, parry. Side blow, parry. Up, down, lunge, and miss. One of the fighters finally signaled a break and stepped back to the edge of the ring of light, his sword point balanced on the toe of his black boot, his chest heaving.

"Not bad," panted Bryan Conley, better known as the Black Knight, to his opponent, Nick Thornfield. "You've got good speed. And you're better than the average new man here." Bryan's cobalt eyes sparkled, one side of his mouth quirked upward with the excitement of battle. His ghost-pale face was framed by long inky hair pulled back into a tail at the nape of his neck. Nick thought it looked more blue than black in the unforgiving white light.

"Again, man," Conley said, stepping forward.

"Great," Thornfield agreed, settling the protective fencing jacket more comfortably over his chest. He stood eye-to-eye with Bryan and was fast as well as tall, two attributes the Black Knight wasn't used to in rivals. Those qualities would also make Nick stand out in the arena during the show, just as Bryan did. Thornfield grinned, feeling more adrenaline pour into his system as he strode forward to meet Conley. This was a very special practice bout, one that set him one-on-one against the Black Knight, undefeated swordsman of Medieval Tournament. Whether he won or lost would help determine his ranking amid the dozen horsemen-fighters who worked at the dinner theater.

Nick almost couldn't believe his good luck. He'd been practicing with swords for years, on foot as well as horseback, and watching old swashbuckler movies dozens of times each to digest the fight scenes. He knew all the moves of Flynn, Rathbone, Fairbanks, and Fairbanks Junior by heart. His obsession with swords and fighting techniques had finally paid off in a job. A few days ago he'd been hired by Medieval Tournament, the premier dinner theater in the Chicago area that featured food, tourneys, and horsemanship in the style of the late Middle Ages.

Now he stood in the middle of the show ring against the Black Knight himself. Nick's fingers itched, his eyes burned glass-green in the severe light. The muscles across his shoulders and in his legs bunched smoothly. He felt good. Giving Conley a short nod, Nick lifted the tip of his reproduction Malden sword another inch, signaling his readiness.

"Right." Bryan settled his feet in the sawdust and lifted his own blade. *"En garde."*

Nick threw himself completely into the exercise, making

Conley defend himself strenuously. One of the Black Knight's eyebrows raised in surprise at Thornfield's excellent attack. Nick felt an instant of pleasure before his mind stopped it. For good reason. Bryan's expression might be a ruse. Thornfield knew from talking to the other fighters in the show that Conley was a wily opponent, capable of cheating to gain another victory.

To this point in the bout the two men seemed evenly matched. Nick blocked a side blow, riposted, and lunged forward suddenly underneath Conley's blade, halting his sword just before its dull point dove into Bryan's stomach.

"Good one, man," the Black Knight acknowledged, stepping back to breathe. "What say we make it best two out of three?"

"Fine." Nick sucked in lungfuls of dusty air and leaned his sword against his leg. He regathered his wild mane of shoulder-length amber hair back into its leather thong, tying it more securely before grasping the hilt of his weapon again. "Ready?"

Conley nodded, flexing his knees and bringing up his steel. Their swords swung together, glowing in the light like comets. Bryan lunged. Nick blocked and cut down quickly. The Black Knight stopped the sword aimed at his right leg and answered with a swift cut up. Thornfield avoided that and lunged in for a touch before Conley could get his sword repositioned.

"That's two," Nick panted.

"Give me a chance to get even." The black-haired fighter swung his sword into position, a determined line hardening the corners of his narrow lips. He attacked fast and viciously. Nick met every cut with his own unyielding blocks until, as if by consensus, both fighters stepped back to gasp and study one another.

"Again, man," Bryan said after they'd recuperated somewhat. They met in the middle of the light, eyes alert for the slightest movement that would telegraph the next motion.

Thornfield lunged suddenly, trying to regain the advantage but realizing too late he'd overextended himself and couldn't recover in time. "Touch for me," Bryan said softly, stopping his sword against the padding on Nick's chest. They squared off and began again. Long minutes passed as their grunts of effort sounded almost as loud as the concussions of their swords. Dust rose from the sawdust, golden in the spotlight. It stuck to their sweat, making their grimacing faces resemble those of mineral-streaked gargoyles perched on ancient cathedrals.

Nick suddenly knew that losing was what spurred Bryan. Conley fought differently when trying to save his reputation. Being a couple touches behind seemed to awaken his cunning as well as give him more speed. The Black Knight put neither his sword nor his feet wrong during a complicated pattern of strokes that had the amber-haired fighter defending himself at maximum. Thornfield suddenly found himself eyeing Bryan's dulled steel.

"Two for me," the Black Knight whispered. "We're even, man. One to go." Nick didn't bother to reply.

They engaged again, but this time Thornfield had mentally prepared himself for Conley's quick ferocity. Nick's will to win was every bit as great as Bryan's. Defeating him in single combat would send his own fledgling reputation soaring.

Beat, beat, gasp, parry, grunt, lunge. Thornfield was tiring, and he knew Conley must be also. His opponent showed no signs of flagging even though they'd been fighting steadily for about thirty-five minutes.

Suddenly Bryan's exhaustion did show in a tiny gap in his guard. Nick thrust his sword through. The Black Knight stopped with Thornfield's weapon threatening his throat.

"*Touché,*" Bryan whispered, smiling strangely. "You win. But no one will ever know." Whipping the hilt of his sword toward Nick's face as he dropped the point, Conley caught Thornfield on the jaw just in front of the left ear with the heavy metal ball on the pommel.

Pain flashed through Nick's skull. He tried to stay on his feet by sheer willpower, but his body wouldn't obey. It seemed rubbery and useless. Darkness enfolded him. His last impression was sinking downward through the sawdust, through the floor, and beyond.

Light stabbed his closed eyes and something tickled his nose. Nick turned his head, trying to escape the feathery touch and to find a more comfortable spot for the back of his aching head. The light continued to bore through his lids, and the delicate brushing sensation came and went at irregular intervals. There also seemed to be a substantial weight on his stomach. Nick sighed, choked on dust accumulated in his throat, and coughed lightly. He could not do more because of that millstone on his abdomen.

"Owww, my head," Nick groaned. "What happened?" He opened his eyes to blurred vision and a headache as wide as the world. The light pouring down on him seemed to be from a normal yellow sun, or at least from something warm and bright hanging above him. A forest of thick-boled trees with large leaves coming up from wide stems around the base of the trunks stood nearby. He lay under another kind of tree, very green with knobbly foliage crowning it. And the thing tickling his nose appeared to be a cat's tail, dark in color with subtle stripes, attached to nothing at all.

"What the heck?" The weight on his abdomen did not change, but the tickling did. It stopped. Nick found himself looking into the huge dagger-toothed grin of a very, very large cat. Thornfield raised his head a little, trying to peer behind its round head and down along its body. He could see nothing except the tail, emerging from empty space exactly in the place it should be, still arrhythmically scything the air.

"Uh—hello," Nick gasped. The cat's weight made inhaling difficult. It didn't move and continued grinning, its round golden eyes never moving from his own. "Excuse me for asking, but isn't there supposed to be more of you?"

Very slowly the round head tilted to one side. "I suppose so," the cat said slowly in a peculiar high purring voice. "If you insist."

"I'm not used to bodiless cats that talk," the fighter felt compelled to explain. "You're rather—ummmm, different."

"Of course," the cat replied with pride. Its body materialized, linking the head to the tail with a trunk of appropriate size. Its stippled fur appeared both short and soft. Thornfield wanted to soothe his aching head by laying it against the cat's lovely dark coat, but he stopped himself. There was no telling what else the disappearing beast could do.

"Are you some sort of unusual tabby?" asked the swordsman lamely.

The cat bristled, making it look twice its normal size. "Absolutely not! A tabby, of all the commonest of things to call one!"

"Then what are you?"

The feline elevated its nose and announced, "I'm the Cheshire Cat, of course."

Nick's brain tried to work in hyperdrive, but his headache slowed things down to a mere plod. The animal on his stomach which named itself a Cheshire Cat made little sense. He vaguely remembered a piece of literature from high school English where a little blonde girl found such a feline in an imaginary place. Thornfield looked around, his eyesight gradually clearing. Nothing else here made sense, either. The trees weren't right, even though the sky appeared to be the proper blue with marshmallow fluff clouds melting and merging under a comfortably warm, vibrantly yellow sun. Where was he? The last thing he remembered was having a one-on-one with Bryan Conley in the dark vault of the Medieval Tournament show arena, and winning. Then something had happened, he couldn't remember what.

Nick tried to shake his head. Pain blinded him and a knot of nausea claimed his stomach. He quit thinking about anything other than concentrating on bringing his hurts to manageable levels. Next he worked on attaining a more vertical position despite the stubborn cat. Several minutes passed until he could lever himself to his elbows without feeling sick. The Cheshire feline never moved or offered to help, just continued grinning into his face. By the time he'd elevated himself and the beast to sit almost upright, Thornfield had the impression that he was in trouble.

"Okay," he sighed. "I'm definitely not where I came from. What am I doing here?"

"Anything you want." The Cheshire Cat tilted its head to look into the sky as if watching for something. "But I think you're here to fight. That *is* what you do, isn't it?"

"Yes." Nick looked around again. "Where the hell is this place?"

"It's been called many things," the cat replied, "but never hell. No, I don't think that title could be applied at all."

"Okay," Thornfield said, this time choosing his words more carefully. "What's this place called?"

"It's the Looking-Glass world. I'm supposed to be on another side, too, but I come in here every once in a while. It's not hard if you know how. Everything here's a mirror image, you know."

"As if that's supposed to make sense," Nick grumbled. "Who am I supposed to fight?"

"What."

Nick reined his temper. "I asked you who it is I'm supposed to fight."

"You don't understand much, do you?" The cat sounded miffed. "It's not a who, it's a what." The feline's expression became serious despite the smile. " 'Beware the Jubjub bird, and shun/ The frumious Bandersnatch!' "

"What?" Now the fighter knew for certain he was in trouble. The appearance of the Cheshire Cat had been bad enough by itself, but now it told him he'd battle foes that sounded like gibberish to his ringing ears. The line, obviously from a poem, did sound vaguely familiar. It was probably from another piece he'd had to read several years ago during English class. One he'd promptly forgotten.

"And we mustn't forget the Jabberwock," the feline contin-ued. "He's the worst of all."

Thornfield sat bolt upright, sending the Cheshire Cat into a short slide. His action caused it to lance out its prodigious claws. They snagged on his shirt and jeans, punching holes through and shredding the fabric and skin beneath as the cat scooted down-ward.

"Ouch!" Nick slapped the feline off his legs. "You damned beast, that hurts!" He suddenly wondered why he didn't have on his padded fencing jacket. He distinctly remembered wearing it during his battle with Bryan. It certainly was not in evidence now, just when he needed it.

"Oh," the cat said with dignity, stepping out of reach and lying down in the grass. "I don't think so."

"But it hurts," Nick argued. "Look, you drew blood. I've had sword wounds that didn't sting as much."

Demurely the cat laid one paw over the other and grinned again. "Not that. I doubt I'm damned. Mad certainly, but hardly damned."

"All right," the swordsman grated, controlling his temper. He shifted over to lean against the bole of the odd tree, looking up. "What's this thing?"

"Why, it's the Tumtum tree, of course."

"Looks more like a huge broccoli." Nick surveyed the rest of the forest, his eyesight nearly returned to normal. "And those all look like some sort of nasty greens my mother used to try to force me to eat. Is this a dream about some of the vegetables I tried to hide under my plate during supper when I was a kid? Are they re-turning to haunt me?"

The cat drew back. "You were a goat at one time?"

"No, no, you don't understand. Forget it." He didn't feel like explaining the idiom. "And what's this?" He grabbed and raised something that had skittered along with him as he moved. It re-sembled a sword, but had a hook in the normally pointy end, was double-edged along its length, was humped on one side and con-cave on the opposite, and had a hilt with an unusual pistol grip. It also shone a deep shocking blue and muttered with a raspy little voice.

"It's your vorpal sword, of course. It follows you. You're sup-posed to be standing under the Tumtum tree anyway, you know, not sitting," the Cheshire informed him.

"Why?"

"Because it says so in the poem." It yawned, revealing the enormous pit of its throat. "I was supposed to warn you, and I have. Farewell." The cat began to disappear, tail first.

"Wait! What poem? Where are you going?"

"Away. Elsewhere. Back through the Looking-Glass to Other places." Its tail and body gone, only the head was left. That also vanished, except for the smile that hung in midair. Even that began fading from both sides toward the middle.

"Hey! Hold it!" Nick leaped to his feet, grabbing the trunk of the Tumtum tree for support when his head reeled and his knees refused to hold him upright. "What am I supposed to do?"

The cat's dirklike teeth gleamed. "You'll probably have to hunt the Bandersnatch. It likes fresh meat and jam tarts. The Jub-jub bird and the Jabberwock, however, are more likely to come hunting you." The grin abruptly departed, leaving Thornfield very alone.

"Great. I'm standing under a broccoli tree next to a peculiar forest of greens, supposed to fight some sort of bird with a weird blue sword." Nick grasped the hilt and stabbed the weapon's hook into the earth in frustration. The blue blade protested with a thin whine, and the deep grass around the depression made by its entry surged back on all sides with tiny squeaks of distress. Hastily he pulled it out. "Sorry." Slowly, pausing every third moment to spy out danger, the suspicious stems returned to their accustomed places and rerooted themselves, grumbling.

The sun's light blanked for a moment, then returned to normal force. "Must be another cloud," Nick muttered. "I guess I'd better find some way out of this crazy place."

He stepped from under the tree and began walking across the small meadow, heading for the forest, the absurd vorpal sword in hand. Air rushing across huge pinions brought Nick around to stare straight into the silent scream of a bird larger than any he had ever imagined. He dropped flat on his face, the sword in his right hand ready for battle. The bird passed entirely too close overhead, shrieking its distress at missing prey.

"Jubjub," it cried, banking for another pass. "Jubjub!"

"Now I'm beginning to understand," Thornfield muttered to himself, beginning to feel fear. "That's one of the things I'm supposed to fight. But how am I supposed to get rid of a huge thing like that?"

The bird answered his question. It flew lower this time, snatching Nick in its claws in a sudden last-moment reach. The Jubjub wasn't used to such small quarry—its talons couldn't close completely around the fighter's narrow body. Thornfield's fear turned to jubilation. He whooped at his good luck, startling the bird with his noise, and began climbing.

First he shinnied along the scales on its legs. Carrying the sword in one hand forced him to climb with only one hand and both his legs, but he had no belt to hook it to, nor any string or thongs with which to tie it across his back. The route became easier when he attained the feathered portion of the body and could work his way beneath the plumage. Nick felt like a flea trying an assault on an animal a hundred times his own size. He didn't let that dissuade him. As he gained elevation, he planned.

There was no way he could stab the vorpal sword into the Jubjub's chest and expect it to come close to the great bird's heart; the weapon just wasn't long enough. And it would take too long for the creature to die if he punctured the lungs. He needed to reach its narrow neck. A good slice into that delicate part of its anatomy should bring the bird down to earth, where he could easily finish it off.

Snatching a new handhold as soon as he relinquished the old one, Nick tried to climb at a steady rate. Not having to deal with the slipstream flowing by helped greatly, but the bird's body heat soon became almost more than he could stand.

A sudden hard lurch dislodged the fighter's hold. He managed to grab a small feather and hang on until the odd turbulence stopped. "Feels like we crossed some sort of barrier," Thornfield mumbled aloud.

Sweating and tired, Nick finally poked his head out between feathers to one side of the bird's throat. Carefully he raised the vorpal sword until it touched his target. It clinked.

"Damn. Armored feathers." That meant more climbing, to a place where he could work the sword under the Jubjub's protective covering. It took him less time than he thought to angle his body to where he could force the blue metal beneath the bird's protection. Thornfield wrapped his legs around the largest feather he could find, hooked the curved end of his blade under the metallic layer at a likely-looking place, and hauled back with all his strength.

The bird dived with a horrible shriek, blood spattering from its throat. Nick wiped the hot viscous stuff from his eyes and surveyed his situation. The Jubjub was in control of its descent, at least for the moment. The fighter ducked back beneath the feathers, cleaned the murmuring vorpal sword on plumage, and made his way to the area between the beast's wings. That might be the safest place to ride out a rough landing.

When it came, that landing was more like a crash. By the time the Jubjub and his passenger neared the ground, the bird had lost a great deal of blood. Nearly unconscious, it hit the earth without benefit of backwinging and tumbled across a greensward. It came to rest upside down, dying.

Almost numb after hanging on tightly to the roots of feathers during the bumpy ride, Nick worked himself out from beneath the Jubjub. He heard voices as he did so. Standing, Thornfield saw an irregular green field full of wandering flamingos and skittering hedgehogs. He also came eye-to-eye with a playing card topped by a sour face surmounted by an elaborate diadem.

"The Queen of Hearts," Nick exclaimed, unwilling to believe his eyes.

"You killed my—my bird, whatever it is," she yelled in his face.

"*Your* bird?" Thornfield asked. "It's a Jubjub."

"Of course it's mine. It crashed in my realm, didn't it? Therefore it, and everything else within the borders of my queendom, belongs to me. Not only that, it's ruining my croquet. I assume you're the cause of this Jubjub's demise. And you're filthy dirty as well." She whirled to her attendants. "Off with his head!"

Cards of lower designations began running toward them from all over the lumpy field. Without thinking Nick raised his weapon of eye-searing blue.

"He's got a sword!" The Queen of Hearts staggered back into the approaching King and sent him tumbling backward down a hillock. "Attack, attack, hurry!"

The military cards surged toward Nick. Suddenly they sagged back, spun around, and ran into their advancing confederates. The din and confusion were amazing.

Nick felt a timid touch on his arm. He turned to face the King of Hearts, who smiled weakly. "The frumious Bandersnatch is here. You're pardoned. Good luck." The King whirled and ran across the playing field straight through the herd of flamingos. Squawking loudly, the pink birds milled about. One, more irate than the rest, tried to trample a squealing hedgehog beneath its long toes. The little spiny beast finally escaped his tormentor and ran for the shelter of the nearest hedge, squeaking at full volume the entire way.

Thornfield heard a peculiar snuffle-snort-grumble coming

from behind the Jubjub. He didn't really want to investigate the sound, since everything in this world had proved to be so very peculiar, but something in his mind rebelled at being maimed or killed by an enemy he couldn't see. Using the hook of the vorpal sword to help him climb the Jubjub's feathers like a slippery ladder, Nick labored partway up the bird's body to view the new arrival as it swung around the tail of the dead bird.

"So that's a frumious Bandersnatch," he said softly. The beast was already busy, driving its dark brown snout into the bird's feathers and pulling them out by mouthfuls so it could get to the meat beneath. Nick had seen grizzly bears at the Brookfield Zoo in Chicago, and pictures of a wolverine and a Tasmanian devil on television. This creature seemed to be a combination of all three, and also had the flappy ears and hollow snorting of a pig. It ripped a gout of flesh from the bird's body, tossed it into the air, opened its huge jaws, and bolted down the morsel without bothering to chew. Washing a pale pink tongue over the thick ivory needles ringing the inside of its mouth, the Bandersnatch glanced to both sides, its nose working furiously as a new scent caught its attention. Snuffling and grunting, it followed the savory smell to a table where a platter of the Queen's jam tarts sat. Levering itself to its hindquarters, the Bandersnatch rested its broad forepaws rather delicately on both sides of the tray and began licking up the treats three at a time.

With the Bandersnatch involved in eating, Nick saw his chance to get away. He tried to ease down the feathers, but that proved impossible. Either he got buried beneath them or he slipped too quickly over their surfaces. He wished for a rope instead of the sword.

An idea struck—Thornfield could use the hook in the vorpal sword to help, much as he had used it climbing. After he learned to apply it properly by digging it into the feathers and working it from one to the next as he descended, his plunge slowed and proved easier to control. When he reached the grass, Nick turned from the Jubjub and found himself facing a jam-covered Bander-snatch that stood only twenty-five yards away.

The two stared at each other for long seconds. Nick discovered paralysis brought on by fear for the first time in his life. He had no idea how fast the Bandersnatch could run. His own muscular legs would take him a short distance at a good pace if he could persuade them to work, but was he speedy enough to escape his toothy opponent?

The Bandersnatch licked sticky sweetness from its muzzle and snorted, seemingly giving itself the impetus to check out the puny thing standing between it and its main course. It pushed itself into a lumbering run, gaining a velocity impressive for such a large being.

Nick's mind finally propelled him to action. The beast's speed convinced him the only way to go was up. He swarmed over the Jubjub's feathers until he gained a perch atop the body. From there he gazed down at his adversary. The Bandersnatch articulated its short thick neck upward, looking back at Nick from calculating black currant eyes.

"Now what?" the fighter asked himself aloud. "How can I get rid of that thing?"

"Swordsman, the Queen wants to know what that beastly thing is," Thornfield heard the King of Hearts shout from a safe distance away.

Nick replied through a megaphone of his hands after setting down the vorpal sword. He kept one boot on it so the weapon wouldn't slip out of his reach. "It's the frumious Bandersnatch."

"Such rudeness," the Queen shouted. "That Bandersnatch is ruining my croquet. How did it get here, anyway? Off with its head!"

Several things slammed together in Nick's mind. "It must have come through the barrier between here and the Looking-Glass world, as I did," he thought aloud. "Maybe that division caused the strange turbulence I went through during the last part of the Jubjub's flight." The fighter looked down at the Bander-snatch, who was again pulling mouthfuls of feathers from the bird. "And there seems only one way to take care of this guy."

Dropping on him from above was not Nick's idea of fun. His aim would have to be perfect, his hold on the creature's back secure, and his killing stroke quick and strong. One slip and he'd join the Queen's jam tarts sliding down the thing's gullet.

"No time like the present," Thornfield said, turning outward on the bird's body. "Ready, vorpal?" The weapon whined in response. "I'll take that as a yes."

Nick slid down the Jubjub's feathers, launching himself into the air from the middle. He came down with an unexpected breath-expelling *whump* on the Bandersnatch's back. Unfortunately the creature had changed position, and the fighter's head faced the beast's short tail.

Digging both hands into the coarse fur and finding purchase with his boots around the thing's neck, Nick endeavored to hang on while the surprised Bandersnatch reared, hollered, and pawed the air. Its antics gave Thornfield no chance to turn around.

Suddenly the Bandersnatch dropped to all fours, sniffed deeply, and took off at full speed across the croquet field. Its gait mixed the forward-and-back motions of a camel rising from its knees and the springy pounce of a weasel. After making certain his hands were buried deep in fur, Nick risked a quick look over his shoulder. It aimed straight for the gallery of onlookers. Knowing he could do nothing to guide the creature, Thornfield concentrated on keeping his chin out of the way of the beast's pumping hindquarters and clung more tightly than ever.

The entourage of the Queen and King of Hearts scattered in every direction, running for their lives. Swerving suddenly, almost tearing Nick's grip from its fur, the Bandersnatch angled in pursuit of an individual. A horrible scream rent the air as the beast caught up with the card and knocked his legs out from under him with one huge paw. The animal stopped abruptly as soon as the entity went down.

Despite his secure hold, Nick became airborne and arrowed over the creature's head. He landed hard in the grass, the sword flying from his open hand. As soon as it came to rest, the weapon began making its way back toward the fighter. When he found he could breathe again, Thornfield forced himself to his feet, picked up the blue sword, and cautiously approached the Bandersnatch and its victim.

"Please, please, get it away, get it off me," pleaded the Knave of Hearts. The Bandersnatch was nosing intently around the card's midsection, snuffling and grunting, plainly not interested in killing the trembling being. It paid no attention to Nick as he approached, not even when he stood beside it.

The fighter studied the animal. It obviously wanted something from the Knave. "Have you got anything in your pockets?" he asked.

"Not much, just some string and a stone, and—"

"Anything edible?"

"Well, uhm, ah, yes, actually."

"Give it to the Bandersnatch," Nick ordered.

The Knave hesitated. "But—well, I—"

"Do you want the beast to rip whatever he wants out of your pockets instead? Give it to him now. I'll try to get his attention for a moment." Thornfield grabbed one of the Bandersnatch's floppy ears and pulled.

The creature swung his head toward Nick and looked at him mournfully before returning his attention to the Knave. During those seconds the card sat up and began fishing a profusion of comestibles from his pockets, everything from hard glossy candies to taffy in twists of paper, and from bits of savory spiced breads to heart-shaped jam tarts.

"Those are my jam tarts!" the Queen exclaimed, edging closer. "So the Knave did steal them after all. Off with his head!"

"Not now, my dear," the King soothed. "Let the swordsman kill the horrid beast first."

"I've got an idea," called Nick, waving the royals closer. "How would you like an addition to your zoo?"

"Zoo?" The King turned to the Queen. "We don't have a zoo."

"Then start one," Nick suggested. "Exotic animals in very large cages, and a park all around it. People would come from all over to see this Bandersnatch. He's famous, you know. And you can keep him calm by feeding him jam tarts." Thornfield watched as the animal licked up the last of the tart crumbs, then lipped in the taffy, paper and all. The great savage beast trying to chew the sticky stuff and spit out bits of tasteless paper looked so silly the fighter had to laugh before he could speak again. "And taffy. With some meat for the main course."

"I still want the Knave's head," stormed the Queen.

"No, Your Majesty, that's not the answer," said Nick. "Make the Knave the Bandersnatch's keeper. You know, the person who feeds the animal and cleans the cage." The Knave of Hearts wrinkled up his face in distaste, but the Queen's expression changed from angry to interested. "Can you think of a better punishment?"

"That's a thought. Good gracious, that's really a great thought. You and you," she turned to her underlings. "Go start building a zoo. When you finish, take the Bandersnatch and the Knave of Hearts there. Put them both in. And I'll teach the Knave how to make jam tarts so he can keep the creature happy. Fetch more tarts, right now."

The King sidled up to Nick. "My boy, capturing the Bander-snatch, designing the zoo, and making the Queen happy deserves a reward. Not a large one, mind you, but something small, perhaps even something interesting."

"No thanks, I really don't want—"

"But I insist. Here." The royal card pushed a hard bit into the swordsman's hand, then wandered off toward the sound of his wife's strident summons. "Coming, dear."

Thornfield opened his hand and looked at the object. It was a rounded and polished stone the size of his little fingernail, completely clear except for what looked like part of the aurora borealis trapped inside.

"That is interesting." He shoved it deep into the pocket of his jeans, intending to look at it later.

The Queen of Hearts led the Bandersnatch from the croquet field, holding out tarts one at a time in front of its nose to make it follow. The rest of her retinue trailed after at what they thought a safe distance from the beast. Nick was left alone with the Jubjub's body amid the placid flamingos and an occasional hedgehog.

"That's two beasts out of three," he sighed. "Now how do I get out of here?"

"You don't. Not yet, at least." The Cheshire Cat appeared in its entirety, seated on the table in the midst of the platter where the tarts had been. Its grin was as huge as ever; its dark tail lashed the air.

"Why not? I'm tired of this place," Nick grumbled.

"There's still the Jabberwock to fight." The cat's tail popped suddenly out of sight, then reappeared.

"All right." Nick sat down in the grass and laid the vorpal sword beside him. The blade moved to where its pommel touched him, and emitted what sounded like a metallic sigh.

Thornfield ignored it. "What can you tell me about the Jabberwock?" he asked the cat.

"Only that it has eyes of flame. And it whiffles."

"Flaming eyes," Nick said thoughtfully. "And whatever that other thing is. Doesn't tell me much."

The cat nodded knowingly. "You can't mistake that sound. But you have to fight the Jabberwock near the woods."

"What woods? The ones I started near?"

"No, no. Those were the Looking-Glass woods. You have to pass through again and find the tulgey wood."

"Oh." Thornfield felt suddenly tired. His stomach rumbled. "I have to have something to eat first. I didn't even get any of those jam tarts before the Bandersnatch gulped them all down. First I fought Bryan the Black Knight, then I wounded the Jubjub bird and rode it to Wonderland, and now I've taken care of the Bandersnatch." He shook his head. "All that on an empty stomach. Hey, wait a minute!"

The Cheshire Cat had started disappearing, this time from the middle outward toward both ends. "Find the tulgey wood, and the other Tumtum tree, and you'll soon discover the rest." As usual, the toothy grin vanished last.

"Nothing like having a guide service that just suddenly disappears," Nick complained. He searched the horizon, noting an odd blur in the middle of a grassland that he thought might be the barrier. "And if I'm wrong, hopefully that cat will come back and tell me." He set off in the direction of what he hoped was the tulgey wood and the second Tumtum tree, a happy vorpal sword in his hand. "Or would those things just be reflections? I don't know. It's all very confusing."

Nick had walked most of the way to the blurry place when he heard tiny voices. He paused, looking about. They seemed to come from within the knee-high grass ahead of and around him. He squatted on his heels and parted the stems. A crowd of small creatures such as rabbits, mice, voles, and a few excited birds milled there. They appeared to be watching caterpillars of several colors flexing their way through tunnels in the grass.

"What's going on?" asked the swordsman.

One of the voles turned to him and snorted derisively. "Don't you big ones know anything? This is the Great Caterpillar Race. The race of the year!"

"Now I've heard everything," Nick thought, hiding a grin.

Aloud he requested, "Can you tell me the direction of the Looking-Glass barrier and the tulgey wood?"

A chorus answered him. "That way." "That way." "No, *that* way." All the creatures pointed different directions with impatient paws or claws.

Thornfield pondered their answers. "Are you trying to tell me that no matter what direction I take, I'll still get there?"

"Right." "Correct." "Absolutely." "Hey, this big person understands better than others." The animals never took their eyes off the green, brown, and striped caterpillars arcing madly along the racecourse.

"Thank you." Nick began walking again, careful not to step on any part of the race. He continued striding through the rolling countryside of Wonderland, looking for the barrier that would return him to the Looking-Glass world. He found it within a house.

It rose from the rolling grassland from the top of a small hill, looking entirely out of place. The red brick and white-painted wood facade clashed with its surroundings. It had no path to the front door, no fence, no outbuildings, and no signs of habitation. Thornfield approached it cautiously.

"Hello?" he called, hoping for an answer. None came. He stepped onto the porch, made his way cat-footed to the closed front door, and knocked. "Anyone here?" Still no answer. The swordsman pushed open the portal gently, sword held ready. Inside the house, stillness held sway. The room he slunk into was comfortably furnished with overstuffed chintz chairs clustered around a fireplace. That feature drew Nick's attention. He stepped toward it to investigate.

The mantel had been crafted from carved wood, a vine and rose pattern that swept up the sides and gamboled across the top to the arch crowning the middle. It was darkened with smoke, but no wood lay waiting for the touch of flame in its firebox. The ashes had been cleaned out and the grate swept.

"Hey, cat," Nick called softly. "What do I do now?" He

waited for a long moment, but the grinning feline did not manifest itself. "Guess this one's up to me. All right. It's got to be the mirror."

Thornfield investigated the large glass set in a wooden frame that matched the mantel above the fireplace. There was a difference in the reflection. It showed images subtly doubled around the edges, similar to those in a bad looking glass, yet not quite the same. Nick climbed up on the wide-lipped mantel, balancing on his knees, studying the glass. "Now how do I get through?"

He pushed his fingers hard against the mirror. They rebounded, forcefully enough to almost throw him backward onto the hearth rug. Nick clutched the frame of the glass to help stabilize himself. "Okay. If quick movements bounce off, maybe slow movements will do it." Pressing the barrier gently this time, his fingers disappeared. He felt a peculiar tingle.

"Good-bye Wonderland, hello Looking-Glass world where I started." Vorpal sword held first, the fighter oozed through the mirror, coming out on a mantel ledge in a room exactly like the one he'd left. Jumping down, Nick strode to the door, opened it and stepped out onto the porch. He looked out over a grassland very similar to the one he'd just left, searching for the tulgey wood.

"Maybe that's it." A haze in the distance might be trees. He raised his voice. "Is it?"

No reply came from the Cheshire Cat. "It's as good a direction as any." Nick stepped off the porch of the brick house and started forward at a distance-eating walk.

He reached the tulgey wood somewhat sooner than he expected. As he approached, it rose majestically above him, looking like almost any forest from his world except for the occasional purplish vine snaking up a bole and winding through branches. Thornfield finally located the Tumtum tree in a clearing beneath a mass of vines that cascaded from its top on all sides. The growth formed a gazebo in the forest.

"This stuff looks kinda like kudzu, except it's purple," Nick muttered, inspecting the vines. His uncle in Atlanta had told him about the imported ornamental vine when the fighter had gone there to look at some replica swords. The stuff suffocated gardens and forests, and resisted the city's efforts to eradicate it. Using the vorpal sword, he hacked through a couple vines. They fell to the grass beneath the tree, weeping pinkish liquid. "That's definitely not kudzu," Nick said aloud.

A peculiar sound from above caught his ear. Thornfield peered upward from under a sunshade hand. He could see nothing in the glare. The call sounded again much closer, a whispery yet rasping "whiffle, whiffle" vibrating through the sky over the trees.

"The Jabberwock!" Nick was suddenly bowled over by the tip of a huge glossy bronze wing. He clutched the vorpal sword and rolled as the backwash swept over him. Completing the roll, Thornfield leaped to his feet and tried to get a look at the mighty bird.

It was huge, every bit the size of the Jubjub but with more wingspan, a longer tail, and a neck that resembled a feathered dragon. Metallic colors of bronze, brass, bright gold, and antique gold scintillated over its body. It banked around for another pass, giving the swordsman a view of its front. The head stuck out from the end of the long neck and looked too small for the rest of the bird. Its eyes were peculiar and spaced high on each side of the head, set above a cruel raptor beak hooked like a huge Nepalese kukris fighting knife. A horny bronze-colored plate swept back along the summit of its face and over the Jabberwock's crown, outlined with dark feathers. Longer tufts protruded from its cheeks and a beard of them, much like that of a wild turkey, graced its chest. Its wing tips grazed the trees as it swooped by. He could hear its grumbling soft voice.

"Stupid, standing out there in plain sight," Nick chastised himself. "How am I going to kill this thing? I doubt jam tarts would tempt it even if I had some." He studied the bird as it climbed the air. "I don't think I want to risk going up those claws.

Especially since it looks like they articulate better than the Jub-jub's did."

The Jabberwock banked and dove, angling for a pass between the Tumtum tree and the woods. The area was too small. With a snort of frustration, the dragon-bird made a tight turn and back-winged. Thornfield dashed for shelter under the Tumtum. The beast landed on top of the tree, neck outstretched, watching below.

Its tremendous weight made everything from the bulging crown to the end of the thick trunk creak and crack alarmingly. Convinced the Tumtum was going to fall, Nick headed for the cur-taining vines on the opposite side, hoping he could get to the for-est before the dragon-bird turned and saw him.

The beast's long neck catapulted the savage, tearing beak downward, coming within two feet of the fighter. Nick had a good look into its hot red-orange eyes before he sprang back to pant be-hind the bole of the tree.

"Eyes of flame." He controlled a shiver of dread. "The cat was right." The lack of adrenaline allowed fear to take over. He could see only one way out of this situation that didn't end with his own death. If he could get the bird to strike twice in approximately the same place, Thornfield could gauge his stroke from the first thrust. Perhaps he could stab a vital area with the vorpal sword during the second. It meant revealing himself to the Jabberwock again. Nick quelled another surge of fear and lifted his sword.

"No time like now." Adrenaline again poured into his system as he assessed his position, that of his enemy, and calculated where the strikes would land. Carefully he stepped toward the vines.

The giant bird's beak thudded into the grass again, aiming at Nick's movement inside the vines. The fighter sprang backward, then forward again as the head lifted.

"C'mon back, you," Thornfield screamed, holding his brightly colored sword ready.

The Jabberwock's head lanced down, coming within inches of

where it had struck previously. This time the swordsman controlled his inclination to leap to safety and brought down his blade.

He missed. The steel bounced off the side of the bird's beak and kicked into the air. Knowing he only had one more slight chance, Thornfield dug his feet into the loam beneath the tree, putting all his body weight against the hilt of the sword to drive it into the dragon-bird's neck before it twisted out of range.

It almost didn't work. The vorpal sword's hook caught the beast just behind the head. Nick put everything he had into one final lunge and managed to bury half the deadly length in the Jabberwock's neck.

Dark blood fountained. The beast howled, whipping its injured neck back and forth. Nick lost his hold on the vorpal sword and rolled into the shade, past the Tumtum's trunk, and out into the sunlight beyond the curtain of vines.

Thornfield forced himself to his shaky knees, realizing he was unarmed. "Guess it's hand-to-beak fighting now," he said grimly as the Jabberwock crashed to the ground from the top of the tree. "I wonder if the Cheshire Cat will bury me."

The bird thrashed and whiffled mightily in distress, its wing-beats cracking a few trunks in the tulgey wood. Nick watched, tensed to run if the beast suddenly regained its senses and aimed its fearsome beak at him. A peculiar sound, one he'd heard before, tickled his ear. The swordsman listened harder.

Still buried in the beast's neck, the vorpal sword appeared to be sawing back and forth across the fleshy conduit, whining a cheerful song to itself as it did. New blood surged from the wound onto the ground.

"I don't believe this. My sword's going to finish the job." He grinned hopefully. "Hey, assistance is appreciated."

A long time passed before the Jabberwock gave in to death. Its writhings became feeble and its head finally dropped to the ground, making a squishy sound as it thudded into the blood-soaked grass. The body stilled except for occasional twitches. The blue blade fell with the head. Remaining in place, it finished severing the final bit of muscle. Whining, it slipped through the muck to where Nick stood.

"You're a very strange sword, but I kinda like you." Thornfield picked it up by the slippery hilt and carried it to a hummock of long grass. He cleaned away the last vestiges of Jabberwock slime, the stems grumbling in high, squeaky voices as blood smeared them. "You've been a good friend," Nick said to the sword. It groaned with pleasure.

The swordsman had an irresistible urge to walk over and pick up the dragon-bird's head. He had no idea what to do with the heavy thing. Turning, he searched for something to lead him.

"You're supposed to go galumphing back." The Cheshire Cat appeared on the limb of a nearby tree. Nick whirled to face it, sword lifted.

"Where were you when I needed you?" he growled.

"I was where I was," stated the feline.

"And that wasn't here. Or there." He gestured with the sword's hook. "Back on the other side of the mirror."

"But you did get through, and you killed the Jabberwock. Now you can go galumphing back, we can all have a frabjous day, and there'll be a big party."

"To where am I supposed to go back?"

"Anywhere you want." The cat looked at him with its large golden eyes.

"But I don't know where I want to be—wait. Wait a minute!"

The cat had begun disappearing. More than that, the entire scene—forest, vine-covered Tumtum tree, the Jabberwock's body—was becoming blurry and fading. The last thing Nick heard was the howling protest of the vorpal sword as his hand left its hilt. The last thing Nick saw was the grin of the Cheshire Cat hanging disembodied in the tree at the border of the tulgey wood.

"He's coming around. Nick, earth to Nick. Wake up, man."

"Hmmm? What?" Thornfield opened his eyes to light that stabbed like a knife through the orbits of his eyes clear to the back of his brain. He turned his head and winced. "Head hurts."

"Careful, don't move much. You've had a bad fall or something."

"What happened?" Nick closed his eyes, tried opening them again. The pain was becoming manageable now. He recognized Mark and Thom, his friends and fellow fighters at Medieval Tournament, standing in the pale blue-and-white room that housed emergency services for the dinner theater.

"Bryan told us you were fighting him, then you slipped and fell," Thom said. "Although how you got that ugly bruise on one side of your jaw is beyond me. And I don't remember you coming in this noon with a sunburn on your forehead, either."

"Part of what he told you is right," Nick replied, trying to remember. "I did fight Bryan. And I was doing well."

"Did you win?" Mark asked, excitement replacing his concern.

"He sure did." Craig, another fighter, appeared in the doorway, a big grin that reminded Nick of the Cheshire Cat's on his craggy face. "The Black Knight's been vanquished. And I've got it right here on tape." He held up a videocassette. "Bryan cheated. Clipped Nick on the jaw with his sword pommel as soon as he won. That's why he's got that bruise."

Mark turned to Nick. "Hail, Green Knight, our new leader. Way to go, man. Bryan's been needing a taking down for some time."

"C'mon," Thom urged. "Nick needs to sleep off his headache, and the rest of us need to practice." He grinned at his bruised friend. "Just keep quiet on that cot for a while, and I'll be back later. Okay?"

"Sure," Thornfield replied. "Thanks."

"Hey," Mark said. "Think you'll feel good enough later to come to my apartment? We can all watch that video of your fight."

"Great," agreed Nick.

"Good. See you later." Nick's buddies filed out of the room.

"Yeah. Later."

It was too quiet in the med area after Mark, Thom, and Craig tramped away down the corridor. Thornfield pushed himself slowly to a sitting position on the cot, holding his aching and burned head gently in his hands with his elbows on his knees. He remembered.

"It all seems so real. The blood from the Jubjub bird flew against my face and that's where I got the burn. Then I tamed the Bandersnatch, tried to talk to the Cheshire Cat, and killed the Jabberwock. I would have liked to keep that vorpal sword. Turned out to be a pretty good weapon after I learned to use it." The sword's song whined faintly through his memory.

Kicking his fencing vest out of the way, Nick set a hand against the cot, ever so slowly working himself off the edge until he stood, bent forward at the waist. "Gotta find some aspirin. Get rid of this headache. Then I'll—ouch!"

Something pulled and burned across his stomach and groin as he straightened. He looked down, green eyes widening as he recognized the slashes in his shirt. The same slashes that had been made in the Looking-Glass world by the Cheshire Cat.

"What the—" Suddenly remembering the other object, Nick dug a hand into the pocket of his jeans. He pulled it out. On his palm gleamed a clear oblong polished stone, rounded on top, that appeared to have part of the aurora borealis captured inside.

"The gift from the King of Hearts for taming the frumious Bandersnatch," he muttered, gently shaking his head. "The rest of my friends will never believe this." He took a deep breath. "I don't think I believe it, either."

But there lay the shimmering stone. Nick reburied it in his pocket. Forgetting the aspirin, he exited the med room and walked slowly through the hallway toward the arena.

In his mind the whining call of the vorpal sword got louder.

Alice's Adventures in the Underground Railroad

Tobin Larson

ᗧᗧ

*T*he Cheshire Cat chewed mournfully on a stub of cigar as it gazed down at the ruin of its tail, which had been shortened to a mere quarter of its original length. "This," it sighed, "is what comes from being a freedom fighter." Then it brightened a minuscule amount. "Still, I suppose that liberating even a small part of myself is better than none of me at all."

The Cat's five companions, Alice, the Gryphon, and the Dodo, each dressed in khaki military uniforms similar to that which the Cat was wearing, and the Mad Hatter and the March Hare, who were still wearing white hospital attire, all moved from where they were seated round a rough-hewn table to where the Cat stood. They gave it gentle pats upon its furry back and offered it encouragement in a friendly manner and agreed that even a little liberation was a good thing.

"Yes!" said the Mad Hatter. "A little libation!" With these words he took an empty bottle down from a shelf in the corner of the dimly lit hut and poured its contents into a glass. "This," said the Hatter, handing it to the Cheshire Cat, "shall make you feel better and perhaps dull the pain of your shortened appendage."

"What is it?" asked the Cat as it eyed the glass suspiciously, a lone olive rolling around the bottom.

"Why, a *very* dry martini, of course," said the Hatter.

The Cheshire Cat explained that it had thought that it was a martini, but wished to be sure, and wondered whether it was a gin martini or a vodka martini. The Mad Hatter looked at the bottle but found that it had no label. "It is neither," he said, "but it is decidedly a non-alcoholic drink."

The Cat sipped the drink gingerly at first, slipping its tongue over the lip of the glass to scoop up a mouthful then drawing it into its mouth, as cats do. Then, as it found the drink to its liking, it quickly lapped up the entire contents of the glass (of which, of course, there was none). Feeling the drink go straight to its head, the Cat began to speak more bravely than it had been before, and soon it was telling the tale of its tail.

The Tale of the Cheshire Cat's Tail
and What Became of It

"Well," began the Cat, lowering its voice and squinting its eyes to make itself seem very serious indeed, "as you all know, I had been involved in a very important mission of military intelligence."

"A contradiction!" shouted the March Hare from the dark corner where it had been seated quietly, gnawing at the thick laces of its straightjacket until it could wriggle free enough to shout. "A contradiction!"

"Be quiet, sweet creature," said Alice as she walked over to the Hare and knelt beside it, patting it on its head, "and allow Cheshire Puss to finish his story." With a grunt Alice tugged hard on the straightjacket's laces until the Hare was quite bound up tight again. "Do go on with your story," Alice said.

"Thank you," the Cat replied. "As I was saying, I was attempting to do some information gathering in the throne room. I wished to find out what new plans the Duchess has up her sleeve, and to find out in which direction the Army of Cards is marching. I had seated myself under the Duchess's throne, all curled-up-comfortable, as cats do, quite faded away, of course, and I pricked up my ears and listened."

"And?" asked the Gryphon.

"And," said the Cat, "in a very short time I heard the answers to all of my unasked questions."

"Wonderful!" said Alice.

"Wonderful!" said the Mad Hatter.

"Wonderful!" said the Dodo.

"Not quite so wonderful," said the Cheshire Cat. "You see, finding out my information so quickly and so easily, I couldn't help feeling smug and proud. I gave a little grin."

"You didn't," said Alice with a gasp.

"I did," contradicted the Cat. "I couldn't help myself. The next thing I knew the Cook was shouting at the Duchess and asking her how she expected to eat her dinner, leaving her dentures under her chair. Next thing after that, hands were grabbing for me. I bolted towards the door, which was, thankfully, open. But the Royal Executioner, having been so busy of late, was standing at attention near the door, waiting for his next assignment. With a quick stride he stepped into my path. I raced through his legs, but not before he brought his axe down.

"You know the rest," he finished.

Alice examined the Cat's tail and clucked her tongue sadly. "I am sorry, brave puss, for the loss of your noble tail. I'm afraid that there is nothing to be done but to perform a bit of minor surgery."

"We are all over twenty-one here," said the Dodo, looking around at the faces of his friends.

"But we *are* all underground, we are," said the Gryphon. "Mayhaps that might qualify us."

At these words Alice laughed in her own charming way, and when she was finished she explained that what she meant was a small, and not very dangerous, bit of surgery. "But," she said, pointing at the tail, "it will need some sewing up, and I have plenty of thread, but no needle."

"I shall remedy that." With these words the Mad Hatter jabbed the Cheshire Cat in the ribs with an elbow and began to sing in a high, thin voice:

> *If an axe was as quick,*
> *as the wit of a Hatter,*
> *and the Cat had stayed sat,*
> *or had been a bit fatter,*
> *then the blade would have caught 'im*
> *and cut 'im in two.*
> *And the hymns that I taught 'im,*
> *would no longer do,*
> *for vital "organs" destroyed,*
> *by an axe with a lurch,*
> *can not be deployed,*
> *to play hymns in the church.*

"That is a needle," said Alice when the Hatter had finished, "but not a very sharp one, I'm afraid."

"It's the best I can come up with on such short notice," said the Hatter with a grumble, as he bowed to the others in the room.

"Then it shall have to do," said Alice. She took up the needle and threaded it and began to suture up the wound in the Cat's tail. As she sewed, she thought back, a few months past, to the incident which had brought her to this hut in the woods and among this odd assortment of creatures:

The whole of the afternoon had been full of dark clouds and

pealing thunder, and late in the evening, as Alice drove home from her menial job as a secretary for an insurance company, rain still pattered the blacktop highway. The road was slick and the headlights shone barely a dozen yards ahead of the car. Alice was driving her father's car, her own car being laid up in the repair shop. The car was a new Olds (which confused her no end) and she was not very much used to it. She had fumbled for the lights and for the windshield wipers as she had left the parking lot and now was trying to feel comfortable as she strained to see the road ahead.

Exactly how it happened, Alice could not be sure, but suddenly she found herself stomping on the brakes with all her might. You see, a small white object had darted out in front of the car. There was a "ker-thump" as the front of the car bumped up over a small lump of something or other. The rear of the car made a great "whooshing" sound and spun about on the road, finally coming to rest in a shallow ditch.

Of course the first thing one does after running over something is to get out of the car and see if anyone has been hurt. Alice did just that, calling out, "Hello!" and "Are you all right?" as she did so. At first she heard no reply and could see nothing in the road. Then, after a moment, she spied something glittering near the ditch. On closer look, she saw it was a silver pocket watch, the crystal smashed and the hands pointing to an impossible time.

Alice followed a trail of ripped, torn, and broken objects that led off the road and down a few feet of faded path. At the end of the trail was a large rabbit hole, and curled near the hole was the crumpled body of a large white rabbit wearing a vest and a waistcoat.

Alice ran to the hurt creature. As she got near she saw that both of its large rear legs were broken. "Oh! You poor little thing!" Alice cried as she fell beside it. The rabbit slowly turned its head towards her.

And with his dying breath told her the most amazing story:

Through the rabbit hole next to them, he told her, was a foreign land populated by mythical creatures, talking animals, and living game pieces. The Queen and King of Hearts had ruled the land for as long as anyone could remember, but the Duchess had recently gained the support of the Army of Cards and staged a military coup d'état. The Royal Family had been beheaded and now the Duchess was ruling the land with an iron hand, holding its citizens in virtual slavery. A few of the inhabitants had fought back but most of them who had, had been imprisoned.

The White Rabbit had escaped, hoping to find someone to help free the people, but he didn't know about highways and automobiles. And he found out too late.

Alice was sorry that the rabbit had died, but she recalled a saying she had learned in school, "You can't make an omelet without breaking a few legs," and it had been the dying rabbit who had persuaded her to climb down the hole and form an underground movement there, to free the Duchess's prisoners and lead them above ground to safety and freedom.

As Alice put the last stitch in the Cheshire Cat's tail, her thoughts returned to the present where the Gryphon and the Cat were arguing.

"And what be it that you learned while curled under the Duchess's throne?" the Gryphon said. "What were the information to make you smile as you did?"

"I'm afraid I don't know," the Cat replied.

"How can it be," said the Gryphon, "that you don't know?"

"I can't recall it. It is gone from my mind," said the Cat sadly.

"Oh, dear," said Alice. "You can't remember it? At all?"

"It is gone from my mind," the Cat repeated. "I have lost the end of my tale."

"So you have," Alice said as she studied her surgery.

"Then it don't be doing us no good," the Gryphon said. "You getting yourself all chopped up for nothing."

"Well," said the Dodo, "there's nothing to be done about it."

"True. What's done, be done," the Gryphon said. "But the Cat's brawny back and paws would been of use in the fight we were boldly engaged in while he were napping under the Duchess's rump."

The Cheshire Cat suddenly perked up. "What's this about a fight?"

"Aye, you should have been there. 'Twas a grand brawl," boasted the Gryphon. "It happened there in the noggin infirmary."

"It was where?"

"He means the State Asylum for the Sane," the Dodo explained. "Where the Hatter and March Hare were being kept."

The Mad Hatter stood up indignantly. "Excuse me," he said, "but I wish it be put on record that the Hare and I were political prisoners. We were tossed into that horrid place by the Duchess for speaking out against her. Why"—he paused for emphasis, pointing at the March Hare—"we're no more sane than the rest of you."

The Gryphon nodded. "However it happened, 'tis lucky indeed that we be here today. You should have seen us, Cat." The Gryphon puffed with pride and began swinging his fists in an imaginary fight. "We had grabbed the Hatter and the Hare and were hightailing it out of the scullery."

The Hatter said, "We had been forced to slave in the kitchen. It was such humiliation."

"Anyways," the Gryphon continued, "I hears someone shout, 'Look! There be someone escaping!' And quick as a wink we be surrounded by cooks, and chefs, and scullery maids. So, we start in to swinging. Somehow we escaped all intact."

"You must have shown great bravery," the Cheshire Cat said.

The Gryphon looked down at his feet. "Well, perhaps I did. Perhaps I did, indeed." Then he looked up with a gleam in his eye, and pointed at Alice. "But you should have seen Alice in action. She fought like a trapped vixen, she did. Taking on the kitchen help, both man and woman alike!"[*]

[*]Further details of this incident may be found in the volume *Alice Threw the Cooking Lass.*

Alice, who had studied judo in a woman's self-defense class, could only blush at the Gryphon's boast.

After an embarrassing silence, the Dodo spoke up. "We need to be moving on," he said. "We must get to the rabbit hole and climb to freedom before the Duchess and her army catch up to us."

"Come," said Alice. "Let us gather our few things and be off."

The creatures all did so, and very soon they were treading along the dusty path. As they walked along they began to hear a strange jumble of sounds. First a crash of metal, then a "tooting," soon a "blat," then finally the "buzz" that reminded Alice of the sound a horsehair bow makes when it is being drawn across the strings of a cello. "Why, it's the sound of an orchestra tuning up!" she said.

Music began to play, following them as they walked. It was the sound of a brass band and it was loud and it was bouncy. "That music is so very familiar. But what is it?" Alice asked.

"Sousa!" the March Hare (who had managed to untie himself again) shouted. "Sousa!" The March Hare was correct. It was indeed a march by John Philip Sousa.

"Look at him," said Alice of the wriggling March Hare, as she tied him up again. "He seems to be in ecstasy."

"It's because it's his favorite music," said the Mad Hatter.

"Really?" said Alice.

"Of course. He is the *March* Hare, you know," said the Hatter. "What I want to know is where the music is coming from."

"I'm sure I don't know," said Alice. "There is so much that I don't understand about this place. But the music is exciting. It makes a simple thing such as walking so much more interesting. Like background music does on T.V."

"What's Tee Vee?" asked the Dodo.

"I know," said the Hatter. "It's a small laugh."

"No," said the Cheshire Cat. "That's a 'tee hee.' Tee Vee is a score in a football game."

"No," said the Gryphon. "That's a 'T.D.' Tee Vee is the beginning of a soliloquy."

"No," said the Hatter. "That's 'To be.' Tee Vee is something one uses in the toilet."

"No," said the Dodo. "That's 'T.P.' Tee Vee is a disease."

"No," said Alice, laughing. "That's 'T.B.' T.V. isn't a disease. It's the most wonderful thing. It's a great box which sits in the parlor at the center of attention; although it clashes with the rest of the furniture and decor. It shows beautiful colored pictures. People sit and look at it all day and night while it tells people what they should think. And what is beautiful. And what is ugly. It is such a wonderful thing that people watch it until they no longer remember how to communicate with each other, and they don't know how to read anymore, and they lose all their ambition, and they grow fat and all of their muscles stop working.

"So you see, it's not a disease at all. It's just the most marvelous invention!"

"And shall we be able to see a Tee Vee when we are above ground?" asked the Dodo.

"Of course you shall," said Alice. "You may watch all you like. It's just about the only thing people do up there."

The Gryphon said, "It sounds a grand thing. We shan't need to think for ourselves no more. It is such a difficult thing: to think for oneself."

Alice patted the Gryphon tenderly. "Then you shall be truly happy where we are going. Hardly anyone thinks for themselves up there."

"Oh, look!" said the Cheshire Cat. It stopped and pointed to a spot no more than a hundred yards ahead. The grassy ground at which it pointed was encircled by a great bright light. Alice and her companions turned their heads up. They could see that the light was created by sunbeams streaming down an earthen shaft fixed above the ground.

"It is the rabbit hole," said Alice as she began to run towards it.

At this moment, somehow or other, they found themselves surrounded by the Army of Cards.

Thinking about it later, Alice and her friends realized that the cards had been hiding flat in the long grass where they could not be seen. Now they were up and quickly approaching, swinging clubs and spades with dangerous intent as they advanced.

"Don't worry, now," said Alice as the others gathered, cowering, behind her. "I shall deal with this pack of horrid things." Alice reached into the pocket of her army fatigues and pulled out a small, round cake. The words "Eat Me" were written in frosting across the top.

Alice popped the pastry into her mouth. After a moment's wait she found herself growing and stretching until her head bumped the loose earth around the rabbit hole. "Here, you naughty thing," she said, picking up the Ten of Spades, "this will fix you!" Using her gigantic fingers, Alice bent an edge of the card until the "10" could be viewed from either side.

"Oh, I am ruined!" said the card, twisting his neck over his shoulder to see the damage. "In fact, the whole deck is ruined."

And of course, it was true. When you can tell the suit and number of even *one* lone card from the back, the *entire* deck is useless.

Defeated, the cards surrendered, their cardboard bodies bent with sadness. They shuffled away, leaving Alice and her friends to escape up the rabbit hole.

It was a long, hard climb up, but mostly uneventful. Although, once, the March Hare did get most ways out of his straightjacket, and there was some difficulty in capturing him again as he bounded from ledge to ledge. But soon they climbed out of the hole and stood blinking in the bright sunlight.

Alice was listening to the roar and buzz of the traffic and cautioning her companions not to walk in the direction of the highway, when large, thick human hands grabbed them and lifted them up. Alice looked up to see a clean-shaven face, the eyes hidden by mirrored sunglasses. She and her companions were carried, kicking and screaming, to a waiting van, the windows of the van covered with metal bars. Then Alice read the inscription on the man's uniform: U.S. IMMIGRATION SERVICE.

As they were tossed into the van, Alice cried out to her friends, "Don't worry! We'll apply for political asylum!"

"Another asylum!" shouted the March Hare, who had managed to undo himself again. "Another asylum!"

Muchness

Jody Lynn Nye

∞ ∞

*V*alerie Hodges looked at the shimmering wall of force between the transformer pillars in the center of the Electromagnetics Lab, and glanced up at her fellow scientists with dismay.

"Why me?" she asked. "Why don't one of you big, muscular mooses go first?"

"Conservation of mass," one of them replied almost too quickly. "You're the smallest and lightest person in the lab. Therefore if something goes wrong, we can pull you back more easily."

"I don't like it." She ran a hand through her short blonde hair, and sensed that her fingers were trembling. "I'm a power technician, not a test pilot."

"You did volunteer," Clyde Sawyer reminded her.

"Well, that was before I *saw* it." She stared at the insubstantial metallic field, painted on the air and quivering as if seen through heat haze. "You've been very secretive about how the transference

159

system functions. This is the first time I've been allowed in this chamber for six months."

"By necessity," Professor Connor Fitzhugh said, smiling down from his height of six foot three. "We couldn't risk data leaks. No offense, Hodges. I know we could trust you, but we had to omit all or none. We didn't want some other university stealing a march on us. Think of it! If this works, you'll step out of the field into the receiver station four thousand miles away!"

"You're about to make history," Clyde said.

"I don't want to *be* history," Valerie said crossly.

Connor dropped the theatrical air that was his everyday manner of lecturing and became serious. He loomed paternally toward her.

"Val, we can't order you to do this. It's not as if we're asking you simply to stay overtime. We're cognizant of the danger involved. The retrieval system isn't perfect yet, but we can't wait any longer to pass a human through so we can have a sentient report on the transference process. The rats survive, the ones that come back. You've seen them. They're not even too disoriented. Yet we still do not know how the process appears to the human mind. That's vital before we attempt longer transferences, say to the Moon, or to Mars. We need your help."

His appeal made, he withdrew to a carefully measured psychological distance to let her think. He needn't have been so considerate. Val realized she had already made up her mind to go. The adventuresome streak in her personality was what had pushed her into the sciences in the first place, and the native stubbornness had kept her going through her necessary A-levels and university education even when she'd been actively discouraged, first by her parents, then by the males in her classes and her first jobs who felt threatened by women advancing into their field. Here they were now, asking for her help—as a guinea pig, mind you—but still *asking* her as if she and they were equals. This could work to her advantage. She could demand concessions later on, if she survived.

At the moment, she didn't care. The silvery haze drew her. It felt unreal, torn from some other Creation. Its other side was not merely beyond the pillars, but entirely elsewhere in the world.

"How will I know I'm in the right place?" It seemed to Val that Connor exhaled gustily. He was afraid she might back out! She looked him up and down, eyeing the weight that had accumulated on his long frame over the years. *He* wouldn't have to go, unless the notion of less mass was a load of antiquated shoemakers.

"We've postulated that there will be the greatest saturation, the greatest concentration of the field which will draw you in, and form an energy carrier around you. That will disperse on contact with the receiver station, which is synched to the frequency of this one, and deposit you at your destination. This theory seems to be upheld by eyewitness accounts at the far end, in Chicago. It certainly has been upheld in trials here in this facility. You should have awareness of the field. In fact, you may be able to help yourself reach the terminus point."

Val nodded. "What's the field like that I'm searching for? Does it look like anything? Can I hear it? Will it broadcast any particular frequency?"

The man shook his head. "It does, but it isn't perceptible within the system. Whatever we have tapped into is beyond, or between, our normal ability to sense it. I don't know. Any of the scopes we've sent through with the rats have failed to register any readings whatsoever. The videotapes have all been blank. Whatever we're dealing with here is not something we've yet learned how to make a monitor to detect. That's why we need an eyewitness."

Clyde spoke up, fixing her with his intent, shortsighted gaze. "I've been working by feel. When we sent rats on the short hops between here and the other room, all I can tell you is on the receiving end just before they appeared it *felt* like more." The brown eyes opened up wider, and his pupils dilated. "*More.*"

161

"More what?" Valerie demanded. "More power?" The man shook his head. "More light? Heat?"

"More. That's all. A sense of *much* rather than *little*. Go towards it, and you'll come out the other end, no worries."

"Brilliant," Valerie said, laughing hollowly. "My life will depend on my being able to distinguish muchness."

"It's not that bad," he said. "The energy carrier will do all the work. I want to warn you that the frequency we are using is not unique. Don't let the carrier disperse. You may end up trapped somewhere other than where you want to be."

"You're going to shotgun me toward the field, and count on the right receiver to attract me, although you don't know exactly how it does it."

"That's about the size of the shoe. Will you wear it?"

Valerie studied their faces. They hoped, and they were scared, too.

"I suppose so," she said slowly. "Ever since I was a little girl listening to my mother read storybooks, I've wondered what much of a muchness was. I see I won't find out unless I go and experience it for myself. None of you seem to know what it is."

They accepted her agreement with the solemnity of graduates being conferred the degree of Doctor of Medicine by the Chancellor of the University. At once she was a goddess, offered any favor within their power lest she withdraw her blessing from them.

"D'you want a chair, Val?" "How about a drink?" "I'll feed your cats tonight. Do you want me to stay over with them?"

That question caught her attention as she was reaching for the proffered lab beaker full of orange soda. "How long am I going to be gone?"

Connor cleared his throat. "If this was a textbook trial, perhaps a matter of minutes. But no one has written the textbook yet."

"Real science." Clyde straightened his glasses on his short, upturned nose and leered at her. Connor ignored his subordinate's levity.

"The transference will be instantaneous, but our counterparts in Chicago are to run a full medical examination on you and complete a debriefing, which may take several hours. Should all go as planned, they'll send you back here at once. Any questions?"

She glanced at Douglas Viernes, her coworker at the power console. He nodded as if to say that he would take care of their department. Valerie shook her head.

Suddenly, instruments appeared, and the scientists poked, prodded, measured, weighed, estimated, and noted. "Aren't you going to get out calipers and measure my fingernails?" Val asked.

Startled, Fitzhugh turned, about to issue an order, then aimed his fishy gaze at her. "Young lady, that's not funny."

Valerie shrugged.

"It may be the last joke I tell."

"No graveyard humor here, please." Clyde bustled his narrow form through the crowd of technicians around her, and threw a heavy white cloth over her head.

"Wear this, and keep it cinched. The panels are made of Kevlar and treated with a coating of high-grade reflector, in case you run into anything. At the speeds you'll be traveling, all purely theoretical of course, contact with even a minute piece of matter could result in, er, damage. This should protect you; if it doesn't, nothing can."

"It's a pinafore," Valerie said, spreading her hands downward over the long, white skirts. No wonder the men were so eager to have her go instead of one of them. They'd look complete fools in what to her was a mere encumbrance. The straps settled heavily on her shoulders, and she felt the weight of armor for a short time until the garment was adjusted to spread the mass evenly over her torso. She yanked on the sleeves of her lab tunic to keep them from bunching up underneath. "A combat pinny. My gran would approve. She was a fierce old one."

Fitzhugh straightened the straps and patted her on the shoulder. "In the absence of normal sensation, you'll be subject to random neural firings during the transition. One of the reasons we have chosen you is that your psychological profile suggests you can handle sensory deprivation. You have a strong grasp of identity."

Valerie gulped, nodded, and waited. Connor smiled. "Just remember all you can, even if it doesn't make sense. Our counterparts in Chicago will debrief you, and then send you straight back to us."

"With luck," Clyde said. "Thank you, lass. Good luck."

The heavy hum felt hypnotic, drawing Valerie in as she moved closer to the shining field. She could see herself reflected perfectly in its silver surface, as in a looking glass. Compared with the others' images behind her, she was tiny, almost childlike. The heavy white skirts that hung below her knees made her seem smaller still. For a moment, she felt vulnerable. Then the sense of helplessness made her so angry with herself it propelled her forward. As the sweep second hand on the lab clock passed six P.M. precisely, Clyde nodded to her. She stepped through the looking glass.

The static electricity that enfolded her body as she passed through the barrier crushed down tight, constricting her breathing. She knew she was getting smaller and smaller and smaller . . .

Consciousness returned with the same drowsy feeling she had when waking up from a vivid dream. Her eyelids weighed heavy when she blinked them. She focused her eyes to make sense out of the grayness that surrounded her. It didn't coalesce into anything, but remained a deceiving, free-form mass. She covered one eye. No, altering her depth perception didn't help.

"Well, I'm sitting on *something*," Valerie said out loud. If this was an elaborate joke played by the fellows in the lab, using ether and a sensory deprivation tank, she was determined not to let them get a laugh on her. She disentangled her hands from the folds of her "combat pinny" and felt the surface under her. Rubbery but not slick, flexible but not pliable, it was made of the same stuff as the air, but thicker. It moved by itself, too, changing in texture and topography. As she tried to get to her knees to stand, she toppled over into a shallow pit that hadn't been under her left hip the moment before. Gasping, Valerie rolled onto her belly. The gray formlessness changed into swirls of color and raised up high beneath her feet, precipitating her down a slope that ended sharply in a low protrusion like a garden wall. She fell forward, catching herself on her spread palms. Sparks flew out from beneath her hands, and she noticed a faint glow around her fingers. Her whole body was enveloped in a second skin made of light. Valerie's heart began to pound. No, the experience wasn't a joke; it was real. Connor Fitzhugh didn't have the budget to create an environment like this. She was on the other side of the door, the first human being to follow the lab rats to oblivion, or to Chicago, if she could find her way there.

She forced herself to calm down. Swiftly, before the terrain could change again, she clambered to her knees, and thence to her feet. Standing on one foot was easier for keeping her balance at first, until she thought of keeping her heels very close together. This usually unstable position perversely permitted less chance of losing her balance than a legs-apart stance. And now that she was standing, where should she go? Connor Fitzhugh said that she would find herself instantaneously in Chicago. Since that was palpably untrue, she had to find her own way to the receiver site. She scanned the panchromatic landscape. But would she have to walk all the way to Chicago?

Muchness. She thought of Clyde's shamefaced grin as he tried to describe to her a sensation that involved none of the normal five senses. What did he say? More. Where was *more*? Which way should she go? She tried to open herself to any input, any direction, where something made her feel different from the other ways, and, closing her eyes, spun in a slow circle.

Suddenly, she knew. There it was—as if a light breeze brushed against her skin, but on the *inside*. The muchness was at a great distance off to her left. Leaping off the slowly gathering mound underneath her feet, she strode swiftly off toward the light touch with a surge of joy, knowing she was heading the right way. The landscape seemed to share her elation, forming a series of mounds like stepping stones that reached up one at a time to meet her feet.

She felt a rush through her body each time she swung her leg forward, as if each step encompassed miles. Within the protective bubble of energy, her body kept changing shape. Sometimes she had dozens of legs, all wanting to go in different directions.

I'm making history, she kept telling herself. *I am about to do a new thing no one else has ever done before.*

As a technician, Valerie wondered about the source of the light. Within a singularity traveling thousands of miles per second, she shouldn't be able to see, yet the area around her was lit in some way. Everything was suffused with a neutral light. She cast no shadow, not between her fingers or under the hem of her skirts, not even underfoot.

Ahead of her, now to the left, now to the rear, was a node of the matter that made up the terrain, but it felt different to her from the rest. The skin of light around her brightened in intensity, but even without that clue, Valerie knew that here was muchness. She moved toward it, excited. What should she say to the scientists in Chicago? Would she have to grow larger again? The terrain parted into a kind of trough, leading her down toward a wall, where the light inner touch called to her joyfully.

Something did not feel quite right. Valerie knew it even as she passed through the grayness.

One foot set down more forcefully than she intended upon a polished length of wood. To her right and left were dozens and dozens of bottles. She had come in through the mirror over the rear bar of a tavern of some kind, though not English. By the unmistak-

166

able noise of traffic coming in the open door, the urban styles of dress and the depressed expressions of most of the patrons sitting on stools around the room, she guessed she must be in New York City.

The humming carrier around her was still intact, but it felt as if it might dissolve at any moment. Whatever had generated the feeling of muchness had pulled her here by mistake. Perhaps this was the destination of some of the lab rats that had never come back to Oxford.

A man looked up from his glass as the bartender leaned over to pour. His eyes widened as he saw the small blonde scientist in her protective pinafore, and he blanched.

"Never mind. I've had enough," he said, pushing the glass away with haste. He threw a few bills onto the bar and hurried out the door into the midday hubbub.

Valerie took a moment to get her bearings, and plunged back into the field. It closed around her again, almost nipping at her heels.

That experience was worrying. Valerie wondered what would happen if she stepped out of the field in the wrong place and let the static dissipate. Would the resulting inequality tear her apart? The swirls obligingly showed gaping red and white and rotted brown. She felt ill, but her stomach was somewhere above her head and behind her about six yards. At such a remove, it didn't interfere greatly with her thought processes.

She remembered something else Fitzhugh had said just before she went in. In the absence of normal sensation, her brain would play out images to have something upon which to focus. In other words, she'd see what she expected to see, or wanted to see. Could she create her own scenery, to amuse herself while trying to find the correct receiver? She homed in on the next feeling of muchness, then, drawing on childhood memories of a family holiday in the New Forest, filled the empty spaces around her with the images of a pleasant beech and oak forest, with a hard-packed dirt path underneath her feet winding its way amidst the trees toward her destination.

For the first time, distinct sounds arose around her: birdsong, the rustle of deer in the neighboring undergrowth, the creaking of old fences, the light whistle of wind, the snap of twigs and leaves. Valerie enjoyed her make-believe world, sustaining it as best she could, pummeling her memory for details of the long walks she and her father had taken. She populated her forest with shy deer, the odd fox, a wild sow and her piglets. A pair of equestrians paced her on a parallel path at her left hand, posting up and down on their tiny saddles, tightly braided steeds trotting along at a businesslike pace. They soon crossed in front of her, and departed to the right. Their hoofbeats resounded hollowly, and faded away to a distant sound like heartbeats. Valerie waded the shallow water of a ford, hearing the pum-pum, pum-pum, pum-pum long after they were out of sight.

The noise persisted, taking on a haunting quality. Valerie wondered if the horsemen were returning, but it no longer sounded precisely like hoofbeats. The forest closed overhead, forming an arch of long, thin fingers of black. Valerie started to fancy she could see red eyes aglow in the underbrush. Her heart began to beat with the rhythmic pounding. Suddenly terrified, she broke into a run. Branches opened and closed, steering her into paths that were ever narrower and darker. Her world was closing around her, driving her at its will, away from the muchness, away from sanity and safety. Twigs tore at her hair and white dress. She crossed her arms tightly and bent her head to protect her face as she ran. A lonely howl rose from the woods, and she shrieked in terror.

Her own shout made her come to her senses. Valerie skidded to a halt, and forcefully put aside the fairy-tale fear. It had crept up from her subconscious with the good memories, and she would banish it.

"This is *my* reality!" Valerie shouted. One by one, the pairs of red eyes blinked out like lights switching off. The black branches receded, melting away into the usual grayness. Her beautiful, green forest opened at the top like curtains drawing back, falling away, dissolving, until she stood there alone, a small, determined figure in white.

"There," she said firmly, planting satisfied fists on her hips. Connor said they'd chosen her because she was sane, didn't he? She'd cleared away all the holiday folderol, and nothing remained but the gray terrain. Pinpointing the muchness afresh, she strode forward.

No more pretty pictures, no more imaginary wolves, Valerie vowed. *I am in charge. I will get my job done, and get it over with.*

But something was not quite right.

"If I am in full control of this reality," she said out loud, staring at the humpbacked path before her, "then why can't I make those footprints go away, too?"

The trail led away from her. Huge, dark, triangular pads, with five, no, eight toes on each foot. Small, three-cornered depressions in the plastic ground at the front of each toe suggested long, sharp claws. What on Earth was out there? Fitzhugh certainly didn't say anything about the space in between the fields being inhabited by anything. For all the scientists knew, it was nothing more than a postulatum, a pause between disappearing into one mirror and coming out of the next. She knew now that that theory wasn't true, but certainly there had never been evidence of other *beings*, with huge feet and long claws. She measured her foot against one of the prints, and found it barely covered one of the toe-marks. The creature must be enormous! She wished she knew anything about tracking, to tell whether the beast ahead of her went on four feet, or two, and whether its walking upright was a good thing or not.

To her dismay, Valerie realized the track was going in the same direction she was headed. She saw no reason to court danger. She veered away to the left at approximately thirty degrees to the muchness and trotted forward through the polychromatic hummocks and hillocks, keeping an eye open.

To her horror, the steps came around to meet her—not the tracks, but new footprints. They formed one after another, their pace matching her heartbeat. She skidded to a stop as the gray terrain buckled under her feet, then sent a hill hurtling upward between her and the invisible menace. The prints pattered across what would have been her path and trotted away. The landscape itself had saved her from encountering whatever it was.

As soon as the invisible beast had created enough distance between them, Valerie slipped around the convenient hummock and trotted in the opposite direction, but not before patting her rescuer gratefully.

"Thanks." Was it just her imagination, or did the hummock rear against her palm like a friendly cat?

Her equilibrium began to restore itself. Valerie cast about for the feeling of muchness. The sensation of saturation manifested itself not in her eyes or nose or ears, but somewhere between them inside her head. The receiver site was close. Another dozen paces or so, and she would be in Chicago.

As she neared her exit point, she understood exactly what Clyde meant by a sensation of "more." The glow suffusing her body intensified, crackling with an opalescent St. Elmo's fire. Valerie sustained a similar elation, her mood improving with every step.

Suddenly, she slammed into an invisible obstruction. She was propelled five paces back and flat onto her rump. Valerie sprang up, fists balled by her sides, ready to defend herself.

Before her, something began to take shape. It was only a transparent outline at first, but swiftly limned in details like a chalk picture or a piece of computer art composed of hideous green and brown scales. Not only did it have four legs, as she had at first suspected, but it walked upright, too. *Six* limbs. And wings. And thousands upon thousands of fangs, *rows* of them. It snarled fearsomely, lowering its deadly jaws within inches of Valerie's face. She cringed, spun on her heel, and began to run. One of its long arms stretched so that a claw headed her off. She revolved three quarters of a turn, saw only ugliness most of the way round, then dashed toward the only opening, which was fast closing because another claw had entered the picture from the other side.

The ground, which had been her friend before, lowered her swiftly out of the circle of the beast's arms, but the monster stuck down an eight-clawed foot, catching Valerie under her bottom just before she sank out of reach and propelling her upward. The beast caught her against its scaly chest and snorted in her face. She struggled against the steel-strong muscles, too angry to be terrified. Its breath smelled of decayed fish and sour coffee grounds. She wrinkled her nose.

"Wh—what do you want?" she gasped. It growled again, looming toward her, sniffing and snorting. It didn't seem eager to kill her, so perhaps it was intelligent.

"What do you want?" she demanded, louder, throwing her head back so all of gray creation could hear her. "I insist that this reality make it possible for you to understand me!" The atmosphere around her changed, ever so slightly. The beast grunted out some slimy polysyllables. The gray air altered again, and Valerie felt herself change. She grew a little taller, and she had to spit out excess saliva that flooded her mouth.

"You're not going to make me like you!" she sputtered. She pictured herself as she had last seen her reflection in the lab: human, smooth-skinned, and far less juicy. The beast could dry up; she wouldn't.

They vied for dominance in a strange battle of wills, until the beast's eyes narrowed. It hissed, "Enough!"

Valerie didn't know if it spoke English or she suddenly understood Monster, but they were communicating at last.

"What do you want?"

"Completion," it growled. "Conclusion. Symmetry. You are unbalance. Fix!"

"How can I give you conclusions?" Valerie asked. "Do you want scientific theories? Logic problems?"

The beast regarded her greedily. "Energy. Must start and finish—like your life."

"If you let me finish my mission, you'll have a conclusion. A complete arc of energy."

"Not see beginning or realize end. Want experience of symmetry, here, *now*. You conclude, I drink. Otherwise, I conclude you." It moved closer, sniffing its wedge-shaped nose up one of her arms and down the other. No escape. She was going to die. Valerie surreptitiously wiped the damp mucus off her skin with a fold of her skirts. The beast raised its head suddenly and roared in her face. Valerie jumped backward, then braced herself as a thought occurred to her.

"What if I tell you a story?"

"Eh?"

"A story. An experience; um, does it matter if it's real or not?"

"If begin at the beginning, and end at the end, then stop, no difference."

"So a fictional account is all right? It will do?"

It nodded greedily.

Valerie clawed at her memory for a fairy tale, or any kind of a story she could remember from beginning to end. Her nerves were interfering with her concentration. Not surprisingly, her mind was blank. At her hesitation, the beast moved closer to her, with saliva gleaming on its fangs and dripping down out of the corners of its complicated jaws. She blurted out the first thing that came into her mind, an echo from the distant years of childhood.

"Once upon a time, there were three bears." While she recounted the adventures of the ungrateful Goldilocks ransacking the home of three nonoffensive ursines, Valerie had the growing urge to burst out into hysterical laughter. The last thing she'd have imagined on the way to work this morning was telling bedtime stories to a scaly monster.

Goldilocks was routed, and the bears had their home again. Valerie shakily stated, "The End."

The monster nodded its huge head. It seemed pleased but not at all satisfied. Its moist, rubbery lips spread back, revealing rows of sharpened molars that went almost all the way to the back of its skull. Hastily, Valerie snatched another tale from memory, Andersen's "Little Match Girl."

That didn't really have a conclusion, at any rate not a satisfying one, to her or to the monster. The beast became displeased, and threw back its head in a howl that made the flesh crawl on her body. The muchness seemed to get farther away. Valerie knew instinctively the portal would recede until it was out of her reach forever, and the beast would pick its teeth with her bones. There would be an end. The monster could feed on her conclusion. Fitzhugh and the others in the lab would never know what became of her. She didn't want to die.

She flung story after anecdote after fable at her captor. Each recitation was consumed or discarded, but none of them seemed to be what the beast wanted. Every moment she felt herself being drawn closer and closer to an inexorable doom.

" 'T—'twas brillig,' " she began, her voice weak with fear. The beast neared her, baring rows upon rows of multicolored fangs that seemed longer and more terrifying than ever. It looked like the illustration of the Jabberwock in *Alice*.

Yes, that's what it resembled: a Jabberwock. Perhaps she had given the beast its form when she perceived it.

In that case, the nonsense poem by Lewis Carroll should serve well.

" 'Did gyre and gimble in the wabe. All mimsy—' "

Valerie's mind raced ahead of her tongue. It concluded in the same fashion that it began, with the same stanza of nonsense rhyme. The symmetry pleased the mind and the ear—she'd never thought of it in that way before. Energy begins, energy builds, peaks, dies away, ends. A complete and functional circuit, described in poetry. The beast fed on physics!

The thought gave her strength. When she came to the verses that described the battle, she flung herself back. Surprised, the beast let her go. Valerie flailed one arm like the vorpal sword, slashing and stabbing at the imaginary Jabberwock, while the real one watched her with growing delight. Its tiny eyes glittered, and an endless flood of drool ran down its jowls. A tongue, a heretofore unimagined color that was a murky blend of red, gray, and brown, emerged and swabbed the corners of the beast's mouth. It was feeding. It was enjoying the meal. Valerie darted in and out, taking both parts of the duel, both hero and foe. Her body changed back and forth between her two roles, drawing her up and out like clawed putty or compressing her into a taut mass that focused on the right hand wielding the sword. In a moment, it was over. Her Jabberwock staggered and fell, vanquished.

Exhausted, Valerie halted her war dance and took a few steps forward, dropping her imaginary weapon.

" ' "And hast thou slain the Jabberwock? Come to my arms, my beamish boy! Oh frabjous day! Callooh! Callay!" he chortled in his joy.' "

Trying to reproduce the same tones she had used, she recited the last verse. She watched the monster warily, wondering if it would pounce as soon as she was done.

" '. . . All mimsy were the borogoves, and the mome raths outgrabe.' "

As the last word rang on the cold, gray air, the beast dislimned, fading away into insubstantiality, leaving behind only an awful smell and a half-heard phrase.

"Balance of open and close!" it hissed.

Valerie closed her eyes and breathed a silent prayer of thanksgiving. As if in answer, she felt the muchness approach. It floated toward her, enveloping her. With certainty she knew that the match was right this time. Before she could properly explore the sensation, she felt herself growing bigger. Bright lights glared in her eyes, and voices burst upon her ears like exploding skyrockets.

"Ms. Hodges! Right on time!" A rangy, red-haired man, almost the opposite number to Connor Fitzhugh, grabbed her arm and helped guide her through the portal. He had to be Dr. Ewing. She had made it to the other side of the mirror at last. The room had a high ceiling lined with a blinding array of fluorescent rods, humming in tune with the silver field behind her. A clock on the wall read fourteen seconds after twelve.

"Welcome to Chicago!" "Boy, right on the tick. We just hung up with Professor Fitzhugh." "How do you feel?" A handful of men and women clustered around her, patting her shoulders and shaking her hand.

"My God," exclaimed a woman wearing a white lab coat and an alarmed expression. She looked Valerie up and down. "How'd you gouge the Kevlar like that?"

Valerie looked down at her shredded pinafore and burst into laughter. "Beware the Jabberwock, my son! The jaws that bite, the claws that catch!"

"Huh?"

"Pay no attention to her," one of the men said, with a grin. "She's just been through a lot."

"More than you'd ever imagine," Valerie said, throwing up her hands helplessly. "I can't think where to begin."

"Tell us all about it," Ewing said, smiling broadly. He gestured her toward a bench. The woman in the white coat put on a stethoscope and pushed it down the back of Valerie's pinafore. "We want to know everything."

"It's quite a story," Valerie said, settling back with her white skirts around her knees. "I'd better begin at the beginning. All good stories and circuits work that way. Travelers through that portal"—she pointed at the shimmering, featureless mirror—"would do well to keep that in mind."

Transformation and the Postmodern Identity Crisis

Lisa Mason

෮ ෮

I want to thank you all *very* much for inviting me here tonight to this, the anniversary of my Fall into Wonderland. I would never have come if this Dodo hadn't promised there would be a fat speaker's fee in it for me—oh, I *beg* your pardon. I don't mean to offend. Of *course* it's not as though you have kept in touch. It's not as though you have given me a jingle just to say, "How's tricks, Alice?" It's not as though you *give* a—oh, I *beg* your pardon. It's not as though you have any notion of what I've been through all these years.

What ever happened to Alice, you want to know. She was, after all, such a strange little girl. Had an attitude. Of *course* I became a writer as my sister encouraged me to do. You should see how much money I owe *her*. My books include *The Shapeshifters*, *Down and Out in Berkeley and Boston*, and a journalistic piece, *Tart-Gate: the Swindle and the Tea-tray*. Thank you, thank you *very* much. You applaud, you congratulate me. How glamorous, Alice. How exciting. What an adventure.

Have you any notion how the publishing business works? One slaves on a book for two years, seriously compromising health, sanity, and financial security. One's editor pays an advance that will last two months, not counting food and Lotto tickets. One's book gets noticed for one week; *Publishers Weekly* is snide. And after plant costs, printing, paper, binding, marketing expenses, and general overhead, one never makes a red cent, while one's editor implores one to get off that lazy duff and write ten more before the year end.

Who would ever aspire to a literary career? One would have to be raving mad.

I should have gone to law school.

But you don't care. That's on me, you say. Get a job. You don't want to hear about it. You don't *give* a—oh, I *beg* your pardon, you don't want to know about my troubles. My trials and tribulations. The bouts of depression. The drinking and smoking. All the drugs, all the anonymous sex. The arrests for disorderly conduct. You're an Artist, Alice, you say. Drowning in one's own sorrow. It's in the cards.

You want to romanticize the Fall. You want to hear how *terrific* it was. What a profound influence Falling into Wonderland had on my life. How the experience uplifted me, enriched me, inspired me. Informed my very identity with a unique and distinctive stamp. How Wonderland transformed me. Transformed us all.

Have you any notion what happened to the White Rabbit? *He* always had a cushy situation. Nice house, domestic help, fine clothes. He had every advantage. Got admitted to Stanford Law School. Graduated cum laude. Joined the blue-chip law firm of O'Hare & Leporiday. Made partner in five years. White-collar crime and commodities fraud his specialty. I suppose we should have seen it coming when the White Rabbit finally came out of the closet. Moved to San Francisco, the Castro district. Dances every night at the End Up. Joined Queer Nation. Marches down Market Street every year on Gay Freedom Day in a ruffled dress, satin bow, and full makeup. Tooting, I should add, a trumpet. Gives speeches 'round the country in support of cruelty-free AIDS research since he tested HIV positive.

His poor old mother, whom you *never* hear about, nearly had a stroke. She calls *me* though I hardly knew him. "Where did I go wrong?" she says. "He had every advantage." "Exactly, mum," I tell her. "It's postmodern life. Life after Wonderland. None of us know who we are anymore."

You're silent now. Not exactly chuckling, are you? Do I imply—you wonder—that the White Rabbit's youthful experience underground had something to do with his coming out later in life? Do I imply that Wonderland was an aberration, an incitement to explore the dangerous depths of the subconscious mind? An inducement to abandon the moral structures and conventions that society, our families, and our peers struggle so mightily and with the best of intentions to imprint upon us? In exchange for *what*? Illicit—perhaps even deranged—freedom?

Uncommon nonsense, you say? Ridiculous? Paranoid?

Well. Not that I have any opinion about the White Rabbit's sexual preference, though he lost his position at the law firm. He's suing. And his mum won't speak to him. And he *still* goes to the bathhouses. You may draw your own conclusions.

But that's the White Rabbit, you say. The White Rabbit is a shining example of the Dr. Spock generation. Those coddled Boomer kids. Give 'em whatever they want, *when* they want it. They've had every advantage. And see how they turn out?

Yes, and have you any notion what happened to the Mock Turtle? There's another casualty. Diagnosed a schizophrenic with delusions of bovinity, as any simpleton could plainly see. But since when has mental illness ever interfered with superstardom? Since when has delusion impeded huge fame? Oh, those big brown eyes, that throbbing tenor. The sighs, the sobs. That disingenuous self-pity, the sudden sulking silences. Those maudlin dance tunes! What tabloid on the grocery store checkout stand hasn't told the story of how he became the idol of millions overnight? The Mock Turtle: the King of Sop.

But Wonderland left its mark on the Mock Turtle, too. I only became aware of how deeply he was damaged when we began to date, oh, years later. The Mock Turtle is not exactly a fella to introduce to your grandmother. I should know. But we met on the beach. I always was such a sucker for his Poor Me act. He took me to a Miami Dolphins game. We stood up for the pledge of allegiance to the flag, and what do you suppose he said?

> *A wedge of lemon in my glass*
> *of salt-rimmed tequila;*
> *And with my french fries dipped in lard:*
> *One burger,*
> *In a bun,*
> *With mustard and relish for all.*

Eating disorder, nothing. *Obsessed* with food, he was. Always crooning about soup and fish sticks. A foodaholic, a gourmand *in extremis*. A fat man struggling to get out of that shell. Food fetishes? Try ketchup on cottage cheese, venison pizza, peanut butter with bacon. Oh, my goodness. Couldn't get through the day without a box of Ritz crackers. No wonder he packed on the pounds. When the shell wouldn't fit anymore, he had a bigger one custom-made. Let me tell you, tortoiseshell just doesn't have the same sex appeal on a butterball. Heart attack material, that's what he became. And that's what finally did him in right in the middle of a gig at Las Vegas. That's the truth—it was a coronary. Not the drugs, the booze, the smoking, the young girls.

But you don't *give* a—oh, I *beg* your pardon. I don't mean to offend. Yes, I *am* just the tiniest bit dying of thirst. What's this? A tall vodka and tonic? Thank you, thank you *very* much. Of *course* you all know I'm in Alcoholics Anonymous. It's no secret I'm struggling to stay sober. One day at a time. And this Dodo hands me a vodka and tonic?

Never could resist a drink . . . cheers.

Oh, that's good. Yes, and the consumption of mood-altering substances was commonplace in Wonderland. Rampant; ubiquitous. The drinks, the cakes, the mushrooms. Do you want to say the mushroom really altered the body—like steroids? Or merely altered the mind—like ludes, downers, acid, speed? Of *course* plenty of body altering there. Take one's liver, for starters. Never mind the brain cells. But *oh so good*, as the song says. Can you imagine the rat race without a drink after work? A number, a hit? No wonder so many of us in postmodern society still seek inspiration, elucidation, consolation in a bottle, a pill, a smoke. Can you blame us?

The Caterpillar took full advantage of his status as a drug-culture hero. Featured in the Jefferson Airplane song that hit number one on the charts? You can't *buy* publicity like that. What an image! The cerulean skin, the elegant drooping sleeves. That mushroom! That hookah! The Socratic patter: "Explain yourself" and "Who are *you*?" and "I *don't* know." An instant celebrity with the Hollywood navel-gazing crowd. Guru Blue they called him. They adored him! The more abusive, the better. Big names threw money at him, starlets their bodies. He bought a house in Malibu. Founded his "religion" on the ingestion of psilocybin. Who are *you*? Do you *know*? Got busted four times, but he never did time. The Caterpillar just up and booked a flight on Lufthansa with nothing but a sleeping bag. Several devotees committed suicide. I think he did what all . . . caterpillars . . . do . . .

What about the Knave of Hearts, you ask? He never did time, either. As I suggest in my book *TartGate*, the suit against him was frivolous. Temper tantrum of an older woman spurned. Of *course* I mean the Queen. Of *course* I mean they were doing it. Of *course* she was paying his bills. Fancy cars, clothes, hotel rooms for their rendezvous, vacations. But it wasn't enough for the Knave. He had met the Queen of Diamonds. Is *she* loaded. That didn't last, either.

With the Knave of Hearts, what relationship does? Oh, his long blond hair, that suave little mustache, the condescending stance. The Knave could attract the attention of many a young girl. I should know. Never mind the rosacea, so he drinks. But the Knave cares nothing for youth and beauty. First he looks at the purse. Won't touch 'em if their net worth is under a million. Goes to Reno, hangs out at the bar. Pillaging the Medicare crowd. You'll find him there to this very day.

And the King and Queen of Hearts? They haven't changed; as heartless as ever. The King as dense as double-weave polyester. Never noticed the Queen's *affaire d'amour*. With her face? That rosacea, so she drinks. They retired to San Diego. You should see their pad. A villa with grounds. The King hired a new pack of gardeners. Tremendous fellows, keep the gardens immaculate. Never a slipup. Of *course* all from Mexico. Zip across the border in the dead of night. No green cards for those folks. The Queen pays them a buck fifty an hour under the table. They're happy to get it. Trouble is, she and the King are card-carrying members of the white supremacist group, Caucasian Nation. Big supporters of Proposition 187, the California legislation that takes away welfare benefits, medical care, and schooling from illegals. Yet the King and Queen are one of the biggest employers of gardeners in southern California.

Uncommon nonsense? What do you expect from denizens of Wonderland?

Take the March Hare, the Mad Hatter, and the Dormouse. Take them, please. They just can't let go. Made the pilgrimage to Haight-Ashbury in 1967. Love, love, love. Live there to this very day. Sign fake names on the lease, never pay one cent of rent. Move from one cheap apartment to the next when the landlord finally catches up with them. Living in such squalor one cannot imagine. Never change their clothes. That rumpled hair. Those secondhand hats. Haven't done the dishes in twenty-seven years. Keep picking up the young girls, though. Fur bedspreads, jugs of wine, sourdough bread, and Cheez Whiz. Of *course* the tea. A never-ending party. And clever repartee? Jokes, riddles, innuendos? "Come to our tea party, little girl, heh, heh, heh." What a line. I should know.

And do you give a—oh, I *beg* your pardon. I don't mean to offend. Yes, I *am* just the tiniest bit famished. What is this? A generous slice of chocolate sour cream cake? Thank you, thank you *very* much. Of *course* you all know I'm in Weight Watchers. Any simpleton can plainly see I'm seventy pounds overweight. Ten seconds on the lips, ten pounds on the hips. And this Dodo hands me a slice of chocolate sour cream cake?

Never could resist cake . . . yum.

Speaking of frivolous lawsuits, I'm sure you all know the case against the Duchess was finally dismissed. Lack of evidence. Testimony of the kids unreliable. Three years in court, who knows what *that's* costing us taxpayers. Of *course* I'm talking about the People versus Peppertree Day Care Center. Charges against the Duchess made the front page. Dreadfully savage: how she beat them, tossed them up and down, flung kitchen utensils at them, called them insulting names, fed them nothing but Doritos Ranch Flavor, made them listen to Spanky and Our Gang over and over. Her own kid in therapy for twenty years after what she did to him. He can't quite get on his own two feet. Wallowing in his own misery. But the plaintiffs never could show bruises. Every kid still had its nose *and* its tail *and* its hooves. No one knew the words to "I Love the Flower Girl." And if the Duchess *had* made ritualistic animal sacrifices, where were the bones? Case dismissed. But the Duchess had to get out of town. Public sentiment against her. With her face? That rosacea; of *course* she drinks. Moved to Bakersfield, opened up another Peppertree Day Care Center. A fresh herd of kids. Doing a bang-up business, I've heard.

So. Does the case of the Duchess *prove*—you ask me—that not everyone who spent time underground has wound up confused, schizophrenic, or dead? Perhaps Wonderland had *some* beneficent influence? Yielded *some* spark of inspiration? Produced *some* extra edge? Induced *something* of the marvelous that encouraged ultimate success?

I suppose it *would* be churlish of me not to mention the Gryphon. Remarkable how a scruffy beach bum could have made out so good. Of *course* he went to New York City. The rude approach, the lack of sympathy. The crude discourse, the demystifying stance. New York suited his temperament to a T. Hadn't an ounce of talent. Started constructing these tortured burlap and concrete scaffolds dappled with bits of butcher-shop blood, gobbets of rotting flesh. Called them sculptures. Absolutely hideous, but who knew the difference? Have you seen what passes for art these days? The Gryphon became all the rage with the international interior decorator crowd. Full-length features in every artsy rag you can think of. Exhibitions in Los Angeles, New York, Paris. Hailed as the father of a new movement. Pundits called it Uglification. A big star now. Made the cover of *People*. With his face?

And of *course* the cook has done well, too. With her face? With her temper? Wrote *Backlash: The Cookbook (How Health Food Took the Fun Out of Eating)*. Sixty-five weeks on the *New York Times* bestseller list. I should write a cookbook. Retro cooking, that's what the cook calls her technique. Heavy on lard, butter, salt, refined sugar, sour cream, bacon, rum, and, need I say it, pepper. I bet you used her recipe for this chocolate sour cream cake. Four hundred calories a tiny slice.

Thank you, I *will* have another.

And then there's all of you: the participants of the Caucus-race. The Mouse, the Crabs, the Lory, the Eaglet. Look at the silver beehive hairdo on the Magpie. This Dodo tells me you're the country club set now. Look at the sparkling diamonds on every claw. Voted for Reagan *and* Bush. Organized your club—the Caucus-race Club—to bring in speakers like Ollie North, Jesse Helms, Nancy. Your conscience is clear, if empty. All you need to do is stick in the race, you say, and—then—everybody wins! Never mind the chaos.

Never mind some of you have had every advantage. Never mind that the rules change, the deadline is never the same, and your Uncle Sam decided to raise interest rates again. Pull yourself up by your own bootstraps. Put your nose to the grindstone. Love it or leave it. Get a job. And you too can have a house in the suburbs, two cars in the garage. A TV in every room, a chicken in every microwave—oh, I *beg* your pardon. I don't mean to offend. I quite forgot some of you have feathers. I wouldn't want to ruffle them. I really do need that speaker's fee.

I just can't quite get over Wonderland.

All right. You want me to concede that Wonderland *was* terrific. That the Fall was an experience not to be missed. That life is change, transformation is as inevitable as death. That the postmodern identity crisis is a symptom of wellness in a sick society. That we took away something special: the willingness to take risks, to be irreverent, to be oneself, to question authority. Not to mention the art of changing the words to well-known tunes and rhymes to suit one's special purpose. Safeway—Nobody Does It Better; the Office Depot—Taking Care of Business. Did I mention Bill the lizard went into advertising?

The real star of Wonderland went on to real stardom. I suppose that's the final validation of Wonderland. Of *course* I mean the Cheshire Cat—who doesn't love him? Even felinophobes get a chuckle. The disappearing act—who could top it? Those big eyes, that toothy grin. Star quality. Right from the start, the Cheshire Cat had star quality in spades. Of *course* he went on into stage magic. Disappearing acts his specialty. Himself; a Ferrari; a Lear jet; a Pullman railroad car; the Statue of Liberty. Pulls in fifty-five million dollars a year. Dates a blonde supermodel. Stars in a CBS special on TV every season. "Alice," the Cheshire Cat once said to me, "all you've got to do is smile."

If you were making fifty-five million a year, wouldn't you?

Teapot

Jane M. Lindskold

T hey were stuffing me into the teapot again.

I'd been sleeping, which I feel is the only reasonable way to get through an eternal tea party. Now, without a proper pause to come around, I was struggling to keep my nose out of the tea, my paws sliding on the soggy mash at the bottom of the china pot. My struggles did me no good.

With a resounding "Heave! Ho!" the Mad Hatter and the March Hare popped my haunches in through the opening and I heard the lid rattle into place.

My head went completely under but I managed to twist until the tip of my nose poked enough above the surface that I could breathe. Then I heard the Hatter speaking to the Hare.

"May I have some more tea?"

"Of course," he grunted as he raised the teapot, heavier by one soaked dormouse.

The teapot tilted and though I scrabbled with my paws

against the slick china, I was poured out through the spout, landing indecorously on my haunches on something hard.

Someone screamed—a high, shrill noise that curled my wet whiskers.

I blinked tea from my eyes. The tea table had vanished. Instead of having poured out amid the clutter of cups, saucers, and bread and butter plates, I was sitting on a blue-and-white tiled floor, surrounded by all manner of polished cabinets. A large fireplace with a kettle on the hob dominated one wall.

Three large faces, each nearly as large as my entire body, were staring down at me. One face was dominated by a large red "O" that I realized, as an afterthought, was a mouth.

"Good heavens, Elsie," said one. "What is that!"

"I don't know, Lacie," Elsie replied. "Do you know, Tillie?"

"I most certainly do not." Tillie—who was apparently the screamer—leaned forward. "It looks rather like a rat, but it's too fat. Perhaps it is a rabbit."

"No, it cannot be a rabbit," Lacie interrupted bossily. "It doesn't have long enough ears. Could it be a guinea pig?"

"Can't be," Tillie shot back. "It has a tail. Guinea pigs don't have tails."

I yawned mightily. I couldn't think of the last time I had been awake for this long.

"I am a dormouse," I started to explain, but Tillie was screaming again.

"Look at those horrible teeth!" she shrieked, backing away, crashing into Lacie, and bringing them both to the floor.

Elsie darted over to help them to their feet. Viewing the chaos critically, I decided to take my leave without completing my introduction.

Everything in the room seemed to be on an unnecessarily large scale, but a big door is as good as a small one when it comes to making an exit. Once through the door, I found myself in a completely different area. The white and blue tiles had vanished along with the tall counters and gleaming brass and chrome fixtures. In their place were grassy lawns and towering trees. The sun blazed overhead, indecently bright.

I scurried off to the shade of a nearby oak. I desperately wanted a nap, but more urgent than my desire for sleep was my fear that I was stranded in this strange realm. I knew how these things worked. Logically, as I had come here by being poured from a teapot, so I needed a teapot to return. I had seen a teapot on the hob in the room I had vacated, so I needed to get back to it. While I worried over how I was going to manage this, sleep claimed me.

I awoke to a dreadful shock. The sun had moved. When I had fallen asleep, it had been directly overhead. Now it was midway on the western horizon. However, this place of horrors was not through shaking my sanity. When I looked back to where the door had been, I now saw a towering structure replete with towers, porches, gables, and lace-curtained windows. It was bordered with bright flower beds.

My door was still there, but from this vantage it was much smaller than I recalled. I wondered if I could get through it again.

As I contemplated the scene, Elsie, Tillie, and Lacie came out through the door. Each bore a pad of paper, a metal pencil box, and a fat cushion. They marched across the lawn and set their cushions in a row between me and the door. When they were seated, they busied themselves opening boxes and turning pages.

"I hate drawing lessons," Lacie said and pouted, sharpening a pencil.

"We live well, and a lady must learn to draw," Elsie replied sanctimoniously, her pencil already busy.

"But houses?" Lacie retorted. "I'd like to draw something rare—a moonrise or a mountain. Maybe even a monarch."

I started slowly walking across the lawn, heading towards the door. I hoped that the three girls wouldn't see me, but a shrill scream from Tillie banished that hope.

"The rat! The rat!"

"It can't be a rat," Elsie scolded. "Rats are gray. This creature has brown fur, rather pretty brown fur at that. It reminds me of the trim on Mama's best gloves."

My heart softened towards her, but I didn't wait around to see if she would pat me. With an almost athletic leap, I hid in some shrubs, creeping away under their rather thorny protection. But as I crept, sleep crept up on me. The last thing I heard as I drowsed off was Elsie rattling in her pencil box.

"Would either of you like some treacle? I have a jar here and some bread."

"No, thank you," Tillie answered. "I have some Turkish Delight."

"Treacle?" Lacie said. "Well . . ."

When I awoke, the sun had vanished, leaving the world a dull gray. The grass was damp and the girls were gone. The door, sadly, was closed. I hurried up to it, but it grew larger as I came closer. Although a dormouse is a much more statuesque creature than a house mouse, I still could not reach the latch.

Elsie, Tillie, and Lacie were inside. When I pressed my ear to the door, I could hear them arguing about someone named Millie. I looked around the dooryard, but no useful mushrooms or cakes presented themselves. At a loss as to how to get through this door, I decided to make my way around the house and try to find another entry.

Moonlight and houselight cast disconcerting shadows, distorting the decorative greenery around the house into dancing monsters. The roses I saw illuminated by the scattered light were neither red nor white, but unnatural shades such as yellow and pink. The lot were rudely uncommunicative. I tried a polite "Good afternoon" but not one answered.

An eerie "too-whoo" that made my fur stand on end stopped my attempts at civility. Then a silent monster with a hooked beak and glowing golden eyes swept down on me. I dove beneath a shrub with a speed that surprised me, but my troubles were not ended.

A large ginger cat, wicked and unsmiling, sprang from ambush. I hauled my tail from beneath her paw and rolled out into the open, the cat toying with me before closing for the kill. I jogged across the weirdly dappled lawn, barely ahead of her, my every breath aching in my sides, my feet protesting such ungenteel exertion. I was near collapse when the owl glided in for another attack.

I froze in pure terror. The cat could not stop as quickly. Her momentum carried her up and over my huddled mass. Then a shrill caterwaul rent the darkness as the owl's claws bit into the cat's shoulder. Still trembling, I hurried back to the shelter of the house, hardly believing my good fortune. A shower of fur and feathers dusted the dappled greenery in my wake.

I didn't feel more than the least bit sleepy as I continued my search. The house's basement windows were locked securely, but at last I found a hole gnawed in the wood. It was a bit smaller than I would have liked, but I gamely poked a paw inside. A sharp snap and a sharper burst of pain at my paw tip rewarded my effort. Drawing my injured member out, I found a mousetrap securely clamped around two of my toes. Pressing down on the release with my uninjured paw, I freed myself and hurried on—leaving the trap buried in some loose dirt so that its evil could work no more.

Sucking on my injured digits, I rounded a corner of the house. A large porch decorated with pots of geraniums dominated this side. Nodding a greeting to the flowers, I mounted the stair and found another door. Alas, this one was on the same titanic scale as the first, and I was near to weeping when I noticed a smaller door set within the first. The legend above it read "Mail" in curling script. Not seeing one labeled "Mouse," I supposed that this must do.

Stretching to the tips of my hind paws, I lifted the bronze shutter with my uninjured paw and bent to squeeze myself through. Nose and front paws fit without much difficulty, but my

191

torso was well rounded from too much bread and butter or perhaps from taking cream and sugar in my tea.

Undaunted, I kicked and pulled and squirmed, my abused tail reminding me that the cat might come a-hunting at any moment. Nor was I particularly enchanted by the prospect of Elsie, Tillie, or Lacie finding me. Thus far, the other side of the mail slot was a dull, dark place. However, I had no desire to be pitched out into the owl-and-cat-infested wilds by irate young ladies.

With a final heroic kick, I pushed my way through the slot. The shutter snapped shut with a parting pinch to my tail tip as I was propelled into the darkness. I fell for what seemed like an extraordinary distance, given that outside I had been able to reach the mail slot merely by stretching.

I landed with a clatter. No one screamed. No one yelled. The only sound, other than my labored breathing, was a familiar voice humming, "Twinkle, twinkle, little bat! How I wonder what you're at!" Hardly daring to look, I opened my eyes the smallest bit, than wider.

Just down the table, the Mad Hatter and the March Hare were methodically smearing butter into the works of the Hatter's watch. The sun beamed beneficently from the west, marking six o'clock—tea time—just as it should. As the scene fell into further order, I realized that I was upended amid a heap of disarrayed crockery, my feet over my head, the whole of me leaning up against a very familiar teapot.

I thought about moving, but sleep seemed so much more attractive. As I dozed off, the teapot warm at my back and my feet shading my face from the sun, I heard the Hatter and the Hare arguing as to whether a bit of cold tea might rinse the crumbs from the watch-works.

I smiled sleepily, glad to be back home where everything was so very normal.

Who Killed Humpty Dumpty?

Mickey Zucker Reichert

*T*he icehouse was every bit as cold as its name, and Alice shivered as she walked amid the boxes, straw, and ice blocks, lighting the way with her candle and using her hand mirror to reflect the dark corners where monsters might lurk. "One can't be too careful," she told herself, scuffling through sawdust to make certain nothing horrible lay sleeping beneath it. "Of course, if a monster slept there, then I would have awakened it and I would much rather share an icehouse with a sleeping monster than a wide-awake one." Alice moved more cautiously now to the big wooden crate that held the eggs. She reached inside to brush straw aside when suddenly one egg leapt from the others and stood staring at her, tiny hands on the roundness where a human would have hips. But an egg could not have hips, you know.

"Oh, dear," Alice said, unable to think of anything more clever in her startlement.

"It is very insulting," said the tiny egglike creature, "to be called a deer when you look nothing like one. Very insulting indeed."

Another jumped up beside the first. "Contrariwise, if you were a deer, it would not be insulting at all."

Alice looked around nervously, quite expecting more to join these two, an egg army with eyes, noses, mouths, legs, arms, shoes, and cravats—certainly not the sort of thing one usually expects in an icehouse. "I wasn't calling you a deer, I just said, 'Oh, dear,' because you frightened me."

"Some people," said the first, tipping back his head to look at her over his nose. Since he stood so much smaller than she did, this required him to turn his eyes crosswise and to stare only at her shoes. "Some people call others names when they get frightened."

"Contrariwise," said the second, "she could just as easily have called you a cow."

"And sounded just as stupid," said the first.

Alice stomped her foot indignantly, forgetting about the monsters she might awaken in the straw. "You sound almost just like these two boys I know called Tweedledum and Tweedledee." (Truly, she had only met them once—during her adventures through the Looking-Glass). "Only ruder. And you look like Humpty Dumpty himself."

"Almost or just like," said the second egg. "You can't have it both ways."

"Our mentors and our father," replied the first, without giving Alice a chance to explain.

"Contrariwise," said the second, "our fathers and our mentor. But that wouldn't be right, of course."

At that, the first gave the second a kick that knocked him onto his bottom in the crate. Alice cringed, concerned that he might break, but he rocked back and forth a few beats, then picked himself up without so much as a glare at his companion, as if they did just this on a regular basis.

"I am Hum, and he is Dum," said the first with nary a look at his companion.

Alice thought the second name particularly apt, but she was too polite to say so. "Well, I would say Tweedledee trained Hum and Tweedledum trained Dum."

"Then you would say wrong," said Hum. "And that would little surprise me. What more could you expect from a girl who chatters to herself about monsters?"

Alice ignored the insults, not wishing to drag out the conversation. The coldness of the icehouse was creeping into her fingers, toes, and nose.

"If Dum trained me," said Dum, "we would forever be calling ourselves by each other's name. That would get too confusing. I might wind up raising him, and that just wouldn't do."

Alice didn't see how anyone could make such a mistake. Besides, Dum had the same irritating habit as Tweedledee of shouting "contrariwise" all the time.

"Our father was killed, you see."

"Someone pushed him off a wall."

"The king sent all his horses and all his men, as he promised."

"But they couldn't put him back together."

Alice looked at each as they spoke in turn, though it made her quite dizzy. She remembered the incident both from the poem and from the single time she met the giant egglike being who had been their father.

"They said he was too scrambled."

"Beaten."

"Fate played him a cruel yolk."

Not to be left out, Alice added a pun of her own. "At least it brought him out of his shell."

Angry stares met this proclamation. Hum's tone went as icy as the house, and he spoke directly to his brother as if Alice no longer existed. "Spiteful, isn't she?"

"I bet she *is* the one who did it."

"Did what?" Alice enquired, hating to be left out of anything.

But the egg brothers did not answer, only looked sadly at one another. "Come with us," Dum finally said. He leapt for Alice's hand mirror with a suddenness that made her drop the candle and nearly the mirror as well. She cringed, expecting him to shatter himself on the surface, but he passed right on through it. The candle's wick fizzled out, trailing a thin plume of smoke.

"Go on," Hum said.

Alice looked at the mirror. Her face reflected back, a perfect opposite.

"You are a slow little girl," Hum remarked. "Hurry up, now. Go on through."

Alice was not sure she could go through the mirror, even if she wanted to do so. (She had had such fun the last time she entered the Looking-Glass, but she had met some very strange creatures, too.) She touched the mirror with a finger, and it had the same smooth feel as always.

"Go on through. Go on through," Hum badgered her.

Alice pushed harder, but it was no use. The mirror remained too solid for her to enter it. "I can't," she lamented, just as Dum reappeared from the egg crate.

"I said to come along."

"I can't," Alice repeated.

"Well, certainly not with that attitude," Hum said.

"Here, eat this." Dum handed Alice a wedge of cheese.

Dutifully, Alice nibbled at it, recalling how foods had altered her size the day she fell down the Rabbit's hole.

"Delicious, isn't it?" Dum asked.

"Yes," Alice agreed as she waited for the world to grow around her. But nothing changed.

"Go through. Go through," Hum said, shoving at Alice's shoe, a wasted motion as he was so much smaller she scarcely noticed.

Alice tried again, still without success. "Why aren't I changing?"

"I don't know," Dum replied. "Do you usually?"

"Not from moment to moment," Alice admitted. "But I do grow over time."

"Well don't be growing here," Dum shot back. "That certainly isn't going to help."

Alice stared at the second egg brother, who seemed less intelligent but not nearly so nasty. "I thought that cheese might help me go through."

"Does cheese usually make you go through things?" Dum stared back at Alice, and Hum shook his head as if he found her too silly for comment.

"No," Alice said.

"But you have to admit, it was delicious," Dum finished.

"I don't have to admit anything." The cold had begun to make Alice irritable, and the odd conversation was not helping her mood.

"Contrariwise," said Dum, "not admitting something doesn't make it any less so."

"Come on." Hum jumped onto a box and placed one tiny hand on Alice's huge fingers. Dum followed, pinching the thumb of her other hand into his gloved palm.

The icehouse disappeared around Alice, replaced by a room filled with creatures of myriad shapes and sizes. Some were animals, some cards, and some chess pieces. Either she had grown smaller or Hum and Dum bigger, for they stood at her either hand as large as she. Larger, for their shape made them the size of very round people indeed.

Alice recognized many of the creatures she saw. On a cluster of thrones were seated the red and black kings and queens she had met when she followed the White Rabbit down his hole, as well as the black and white royalty she had gotten to know on her adventures through the Looking-Glass. The Gryphon sat on a chair, wearing a monocle and a white wig. "The judge," Alice guessed aloud, and several of the animals glanced toward her as she spoke. The kings and queens numbered twelve in all. "The jury," Alice guessed, proud of her understanding.

The white king's Messengers, Haigha and Hatta, stood stiffly by a door. As Alice and the egg brothers had appeared in the middle of the room without actually entering, the Messengers seemed quite agitated. They whispered back and forth all the while. At least, their voices had the hissing quality of whispers, though they spoke quite loudly; and some of their sentences reached Alice's ears over the chattering of the crowd. "Really, how rude. How do they expect us to announce them when they won't use the door like well-bred people?"

The conversation nearest to Alice and her escorts died, the ring widening as more of the guests noticed her. Soon, the only sound was that of the Queen of Hearts pacing wildly before the other pairs of royalty shouting, "Off with her head! Off with her head!"

"Not yet, my dear," the King of Hearts soothed softly, though, as he was the only one speaking, his words reached the assemblage quite plainly. "She must get a fair trial first."

"Very well," agreed the Queen. "A fair trial. *Then* off with her head!"

Alice winced, glancing around, feeling very sorry for the victim of the Queen's verbal attack. What use was a fair trial if the punishment remained the same?

Dressed in a tabard and a regal air, the White Rabbit blew a shrill blast on his trumpet. It sounded more like a scream than music, but it drew the attention of all in the room, including the Queen of Hearts, who finally went quiet and took her place among the others.

The creatures filed to various corners, leaving Alice and her eggy escort in the center.

"Begin!" hollered the Gryphon judge.

The Rabbit cleared his throat, searching frantically about his person. Finally, he looked at the judge and confessed, "I cannot find my paper."

"Here, use mine." The Mad Hatter stepped from among the assemblage and plucked a piece of parchment from his hat band.

The Rabbit raised his head and read loudly, "Style 28. Four pounds. Eight shillings."

Alice glanced about, bewildered. She had not seen so many creatures assembled since the day she had become a queen in the Looking-Glass land.

"That's not right!" shouted the Queen of Spades.

"It is, too," returned the Hatter. "I set the price myself."

"Well, un-set it," shouted the King of Spades, "and get a different paper."

"My turn! My turn!" shouted Tweedledee, whom Alice now noticed standing amid the others. He handed a crumpled bit of paper to the Rabbit. "I do so love poetry. I'd give you something longer, but I don't know how to write."

"Then how could he put even a short poem on paper?" Alice whispered, truly interested.

"Sssh," said Hum.

"Contrariwise, ssh," Dum added.

Alice went quiet as the Rabbit read:

My girl, Charlotte, is always there
A smile on her beautiful face.
Wherever I am, that's where she is
In a long dress bedecked with fine lace.

Charlotte's favorite dinner is steak;
She won't settle for anything less.
She takes my arm when we walk the street.
It makes me feel strange, I confess.

Charlotte is sweet, with impeccable taste.

Her wardrobe is really quite pretty.
What I can't understand, in my human haste:
Why can't Char be a regular kitty?

The Queen of Hearts sprang from her throne again. "Why that has nothing to do with anything! Off with his head."

To Alice the poem made as much sense as anything else in this place. But, before she could say as much, guards started racing from all directions. The White Rabbit covered his eyes with his ears, as if this might hide him. But, before the guards could carry out the Queen's awful decree, the Gryphon banged his gavel so hard his wig slipped over his beak. He shoved it back into place too hard, and it flopped backward onto one wing. Apparently, he did not notice this as he left it in place, shouting, "Order! I'll have order in my court!"

Obediently, the guards ran about, slamming into each other repeatedly and knocking one another down on a regular basis. Eventually, they separated themselves out and lined up numerically, from two to ten. By that time, the other queens and kings had coaxed the Queen of Hearts back into her proper position, her command quite forgotten.

"Very well now," said the Gryphon. He looked over at the White Rabbit, who still stood in place with his eyes covered. "What our court announcer was trying to say is that we have all gathered to try this girl Alice . . ." He waved a wing in her direction, which sent the wig flying. It landed on a pig, who cocked his head this way and that trying to see. ". . . for the murder of Humpty Dumpty."

Well, Alice was more than a little frightened and surprised by this. "But I didn't kill anyone!"

"Contrariwise," said Dum, " 'anyone' wasn't murdered. Our father was."

"Silence in the court!" the Gryphon bellowed, so loudly he sent the lined-up cards toppling like dominoes. Everyone obeyed, even the kings and queens, though they looked ruffled and un-used to having others order them about. "As the first witness, I would like to call the Hatter."

The Mad Hatter strode to the center of the floor, snatching back his paper from the White Rabbit and replacing it in his hat-band. The Rabbit had finally peeked from beneath one ear, the Hatter's sudden movement startling him into hiding again. The Hatter cleared his throat, then looked directly at Alice.

"Do you know this girl?" the Gryphon asked.

"I know her pourly," said the Hatter. "We had tea. She poured. It was six o'clock." He shook his watch, which had stopped years ago and, Alice remembered, only showed the day of the month anymore.

"That watch doesn't tell him the time," Alice felt obliged to remark.

"No," the Hatter admitted sadly. "It doesn't tell me. I have to look at it."

"Go on," the Gryphon encouraged.

"Well." The Hatter scratched at his head, only, since the hat got in the way, he scratched at it instead. "She couldn't tell me how a raven is like a writing desk."

"But, it was a riddle," Alice said. "And I didn't know the right answer."

"See," said the Hatter. "Insults. She called me 'butt,' you heard. It seems to me that a girl who can't tell a raven from a writ-ing desk could prove very dangerous. Very dangerous indeed."

"I didn't insult anyone!" Alice defended. "I said 'but,' with only one 't'."

"Yes," the Hatter acknowledged. "We had only one tea. More with a murderer would have been the pity."

"I'm not a murderer. And the question wasn't about the dif-ferences—"

"Off with her head!" shouted the Queen of Hearts again, and by the time all the others had shushed her, the Gryphon had dismissed the Hatter and coaxed Tweedledum and Tweedledee to the stand.

The two stood perfectly still beside one another, each with an arm across the other's back. Though Alice had met them previously, she could not tell them apart now except that Tweedledee had "DEE" embroidered across his collar while Tweedledum had "DUM" on his. "I told her the poem about the 'Walrus and the Carpenter,'" Tweedledee explained. "Shall I recite it here again for the court?"

"No!" everyone shouted at once so that it sounded ear-splitting, like thunder.

"Well," Tweedledee said among the echoes, clearly put off by the forcefulness of their answer. "Then you'll just have to remember that the two tricked hundreds of innocent oysters to the shore, then ate them every one."

"Cruel creatures," said a plaintive voice from the corner. Before Alice could identify the speaker, another said, "Sick creatures." This last seemed to come from a clam perched near the jury.

"She said she liked the Walrus." Tweedledee pointed an accusing finger at Alice with his free hand.

"Contrariwise," added Tweedledum, "she said she liked the Carpenter best as well."

Alice had to think back to remember exactly what she *had* said. It was not until the judge dismissed the brothers that she remembered calling both of the characters unpleasant, favoring the Walrus only because he seemed to feel a little remorse, then favoring the Carpenter because Tweedledee told her he had eaten fewer of the oysters.

Alice had no time to sort out these details before the court erupted into shouted hisses and boos, all directed at her!

The Gryphon spoke over the crowd with a question for Alice. "Young girl, how old did you say you were?"

Humpty Dumpty had once tricked her with that same inquiry.

Not to be fooled twice, Alice answered, "I didn't say. But I'm eight—"

"She ate too!" Tweedledee shouted. "No wonder she liked the Walrus *and* the Carpenter best."

"No! No!" Alice said. "Stop interrupting! It's rude."

"So is murder," said Hum. "And *we* haven't yelled at *you* for that."

"But I didn't kill anyone!" Alice shouted.

"Order! Order!" demanded the Gryphon, and quiet returned to the courtroom. "I would like to call the White King as a witness."

"Then do so," the White King returned.

"Very well." The Gryphon looked at the Rabbit, who had finally returned his ears to their proper position.

"Calling the White King as a witness!" bellowed the Rabbit rather more loudly than was necessary.

The White King wove through the jury grouping and into the center of the room. Alice knew enough about courts to feel certain it was not proper for a juror to serve as a witness, too. But, she liked the White King and hoped he would prove fairer in his judgments of her than those who came before him.

The Gryphon addressed the King. "I understand you were nearby when Humpty Dumpty fell from the wall."

"Pushed by this murderer," Hum added loudly.

"Alleged murder," Alice said, proud of her knowledge of such a long word, though still a bit frightened by the proceedings.

"Ah ha!" shouted Hum. "A-ledged she was. She admits she was up there with him."

"Silence!" shouted the Gryphon with such intensity that all sound disappeared completely. "Except you, Your Majesty." The Gryphon bowed, waving a talon at the White King. "You may answer, Sire."

"Yes." The King responded as if none of the interruptions had occurred. Even Alice had already forgotten the Gryphon's question. "I was near. And I sent all my horses and men, as I promised. Exactly four thousand two hundred and seven." He paused a moment in thought. "Well, since I am in a court of law, I should say that actually two of the horses didn't go because the Queen needed them for the games and my two Messengers went to town. But otherwise all my horses and men went."

"And you saw this girl there?" the Gryphon persisted, refusing to be sidetracked.

The White King peered at Alice, as if noticing her in the courtroom for the first time. "Yes, oh yes. Hello! She came by just after the Great Fall, you know. Very pleasant company."

The Gryphon glanced about the courtroom, as if challenging all those assembled to cause a commotion again. But, this time, no one spoke. "Was there anyone else nearby? Anyone else who might have been responsible for Humpty Dumpty's fall?"

"No," the King said sadly. "No others about . . ." He paused, face lost in a pile of thoughtful wrinkles. Then his eyes and nose reemerged from the creases. "I did ask her to look for my Messenger on the road, and she said she saw Nobody on the road." The King sighed. "I remember envying her vision, that she could see Nobody when I had a hard enough time seeing real people in the twilight." He glanced at his Messengers near the door. Haigha nodded thoughtfully, and Hatta studied his shoes as if he planned to do a painting of them.

The Gryphon winked at Alice, then leaned forward to question the White King further. "Which direction was this Nobody person going?"

"Well." The King laced his fingers through his beard. "Well, since I didn't actually see him, I had assumed him to be coming toward us. But, then, Haigha said he had passed Nobody on his way to us. And Nobody never arrived, so I'd now have to guess that Nobody was actually going away from us."

"And away from Humpty Dumpty," the Gryphon finished.

"Yes, quite so," said the King. "And he didn't stop to pay his respects, which is impolite if not illegal, so he must have been avoiding us."

"Which means," finished the Gryphon as every creature in the courtroom stared in fascination, "that he must have had something to hide."

"So Nobody killed Humpty Dumpty!" the White King hollered, voice deafening in the quiet room.

"Nobody?"

"Nobody!"

"Nobody?"

"NOBODY!" The word was whispered, shouted, squeaked, barked, quacked, and screamed around the courtroom until it all became a painful clamor that ached through Alice's ears.

"Therefore," the Gryphon called over the others, "if Nobody killed Humpty Dumpty, then I have to rule his death a suicide. Case dismissed." The bang of the gavel disappeared beneath the hubbub.

The courtroom doors banged open as creatures of every description poured outside. The noise grew softer as more and more hopped, walked, or slithered from the courtroom, leaving Alice alone in a silence that felt comfortable in her ears. She had just turned to leave herself when she heard a gentle, familiar voice. "Hello." Alice turned to face a huge, pointy-toothed grin hovering over the judge's table. This, she felt certain, belonged to the Cheshire Cat she had met during her visit down the Rabbit's hole. She knew of no one else who could perform this trick; but, then again, she had known of no one at all who could until she met this Cheshire Cat.

Now, Alice breathed a sigh of relief. She had always found the Cheshire Cat more sensible than the others here, though it named itself mad. At least, it acknowledged its strangeness while all the other creatures seemed to assume themselves normal. She waited patiently while the Cat's other features appeared in appropriate positions around the smile: first the eyes, then the nose and whiskers, the head, and finally the body and tail. "Oh!" said Alice, impressed with the Cheshire Cat's grooming. "Your coat shines today."

"There are things one can eat to put a sheen to one's fur," the Cat said, winking. "In a way, you might say Humpty Dumpty bequeathed me my good grooming."

The only outfit of Humpty Dumpty's that Alice recalled was a cravat that his strange build had caused her to mistake for a belt. Nevertheless, it seemed respectful to speak kindly of the dead, especially after having been found innocent of his murder. "He had good taste."

"I would say," said the Cheshire Cat, grin widening and voice rumbling like a purr, "he was a creature of egg-ceptionally good taste. Egg-ceptionally good, indeed."

Not wishing to contradict, Alice simply nodded.

"For fur, there is nothing like a hefty meal of raw egg."

"I should think," Alice said, "that a bath and a good grooming would be better."

"I didn't say there was nothing better. Only that there was nothing like it." The Cat started to fade.

Only then understanding dawned. "Wait! *You* ate Humpty Dumpty?" Before Alice could question the Cat further, it melted into the background, teeth lingering the longest. "Come back! Come back!" yelled Alice to the empty air. She flailed wildly at the place where the cat had hovered.

And found herself shaking two eggs in the icehouse. The very eggs she had gone to fetch. Alice looked from one to the other. "Hum and Dum," she whispered, then placed them back in the box and chose different ones in their places. After all, she would not be responsible for murder.

Wonderland Express

Connie Hirsch

∽ ∽

"I shouldn't have eaten that mushroom," Alice said, stumbling toward what she hoped was a road. It helped to speak aloud, to convince herself that the thoughts were her own—after all, they were spoken by her voice, were they not?

The taste came back to her, filling her mouth and mind like an expanding bitter balloon. Cramps rumbled in her stomach, making her bend over so abruptly she feared she would shut like a telescope. She saw herself as from a height, dressed in a pinafore, her golden curled hair straggling around her face, on her hands and knees. "I wasn't always like this," she said, which comforted her.

The road was blacktop asphalt, a white stripe down its middle. "Which way should I go?" Alice said. There were no signs posted, just the road in both directions, featureless. Alice folded her arms, a gesture her governess used when Alice could not make up her mind. "It is too *vexing* that I haven't an idea. Perhaps I should give myself a stiff scolding!" But an approaching car spared her that task.

The bright green T-Bird had a broad nose and mean little headlight eyes, and tail fins that rose to ridiculous heights. Its top was down, and the inhabitants' hair blew in the breeze. Alice stepped back from the shoulder as the car careened past. Within but a short distance its brakes squealed and it pulled off to the side of the road in a cloud of dust.

"Perhaps they know which way to go?" Alice said. They were two men—more or less—and scarcely had the car stopped but they had vaulted over its sides and sprinted to the bushes, where they tore off whole branches of leaves and carried them back.

Alice approached slowly, puzzling over a correct greeting. They were a strange pair, even taking into account her befuddled state of mind. The more normal one had a weak chin, with a baseball hat that read "In This Style 10/6," its bill aggressively jutting over his huge nose. He was dressed in jeans and a denim work shirt with "Hatta" lettered neatly above the pocket.

The other was quite strange—Alice was not sure if he was a man who looked like a rabbit, or a huge rabbit who looked a bit like a man. Certainly, his white ears were strangely shaped, set high but flopping down to his shoulders. His nose seemed to grow into his mouth, with a split in his upper lip, and it twitched as he scurried back and forth with his armloads. He wore the same outfit as Hatta, only his embroidery read "Haigha."

Alice hung back, watching, but she did not go unobserved. "You there," said Hatta. His pupils were not the same size, and his hands wavered as if they had a will of their own. "Carry these!"

His tone was commanding, but Alice decided that helping was only the polite thing to do. "Certainly," she said, turning and plucking her own armload of scratchy brush. The pair were heaping greenery in a circle around their car, piling it higher than she would have thought possible. "Hurry, oh do hurry," said Haigha nervously. "*They* shall be here any minute."

"Who are *they*?" Alice asked, genuinely puzzled.

"You'll find out soon enough if you don't continue," snapped the hat-wearer. "Already you can hear the siren! Faster!"

There was a siren, Alice noticed for the first time, loud and getting louder. It spurred her companions to greater effort, and they rushed past in a blur of blue and white and trailing ears.

She had added three armfuls of camouflage to the tall heap when the rabbit-man grabbed her by the arm. "This way!" he cried, and dragged her into the brushy enclosure. He pulled the brush together behind them, so they were inside a circular wall.

"If you lie flat, you can see," whispered Hatta, already on his hands and knees. Alice daintily placed herself on the ground—it was all dirt—and saw that she could just see out from underneath, a fine view of the road. The siren was louder than ever, and she fancied that her ears might well burst, though she held her hands over them.

Down the road came a most strange vehicle, so wonderfully narrow that Alice could hardly see it from a distance. Even up close, all that could be seen was a narrow windshield, a whiplike antenna, and a single flashing light. The obnoxious siren stopped just as the vehicle pulled in.

Piling out of the vehicle were the strangest police Alice could ever imagine—as thin as cards from the side, their arms and legs at the corners of their squarish bodies. Their backs were blue, and on their heads they sported peaked caps with badges. They bent over sinuously, their flat bodies making upside-down U's and sideways S's, examining the tracks that the car had made.

"What are they looking for?" Alice whispered. "Will they find us?"

"Shhh," said Haigha, handing her a large silver revolver from his pocket—he had another in front of him. Alice took it, surprised by its size and weight. She quite needed two hands to keep it upright, let alone point it. "Now think like a bush, as our lives depend on it!"

This command quite stymied Alice, for how did a bush think,

after all? "I should *dread* pruning shears," she whispered to herself, "and have ambitions—perhaps a position as a privet hedge or a career as an ornamental shrubbery."

They were quite close to the impromptu hedge now. Though the tracks led plainly to the heaped branches and leaves—even Alice could see this from where she lay—*they* did not seem inclined to push through the greenery. Beside her, Hatta was murmuring "Bush, bush, bush" and on the other side, Haigha quite clearly said, "Shrubbery. Shrubbery."

Alice closed her eyes and thought quite strongly of topiary. When she opened them, the police had gotten rather flatly into their car—like a pack of cards being boxed up at the end of a game, she thought—and were driving off, the siren reversing its progression from loud to soft to inaudible.

"Shrubbery, shrubbery," Haigha repeated, his eyes still closed. Alice looked over to Hatta with his chin pillowed on his palm. He twitched an eyebrow at her. "I do hate to disturb him, but he *will* get an idea in his head," he said apologetically. He got up, came round the car from the other side, and gave Haigha a good kick to the ribs. "Enough with the shrubbery, already!" he roared, and the poor rabbit-man jumped straight up into the air, coming down on his feet with his gun pointed at his companion.

"What did you want to do that for?" he demanded querulously, the barrel not quite six inches from his friend's large nose. Alice sat up cautiously, lifting her own gun into her lap.

Hatta merely grabbed Haigha's gun by its barrel and pointed it down at the ground. "*They've* gone," he said. "There's no use being a bush! 'Shrubbery today, gone tomorrow,' as my grandmother used to say."

The rabbit-man seemed to take it in stride. "And *gun* we must be," he said, tucking the gun in the back of his jeans waistband. He hopped into the driver's seat in one smooth move, fishing out the keys. They dangled from a keychain decorated with a stylized rabbit's head, ears and all. Hatta went around and clambered into the passenger seat as Haigha turned the engine on with a roar.

Alice sat on the ground, unsure of what to do, when Hatta stuck his head over the side. "Well, are you coming?" he said.

It didn't so much decide Alice as it gave her something to do, so she put the gun in her apron pocket and climbed into the back of the T-Bird, brushing fast-food wrappers and old newspapers off the seat. There were some rather strange leather straps back there, but nothing that functioned as a seat belt so far as she could see.

"All settled?" said Haigha, his ears flapping. Previously they had hung like wilted celery stalks but now they moved about vaguely, like antennae in search of radar. "All ready to go? All raring for the road? All raving for the speed?"

"I'll rave you," said Hatta, cuffing his friend's head. "Drive already!"

The rabbit-man pulled a fearsome-looking lever—it had an eagle's head with ruby-red gems for eyes—and the car leaped forward, demolishing the brush wall and slamming Alice back into her seat.

As the car bounced along, Alice slid to the floor, almost buried among the trash, but eventually she climbed up. It was an enormous backseat, all shiny pink vinyl, which seemed larger all the time. She leaned forward, holding on to the passenger seat that Hatta rode in.

"Pardon me," she said, "but we haven't been introduced."

Hatta turned from the radio controls he had been fiddling with, and looked back at her. His irises were so pale they were scarcely darker than the whites of his eyes, but the pupil of one was huge, gazing off into the middle distance. "Haven't been introduced?" he repeated after her. "Well! I suppose we shall do that at some time or another, shan't we?" He turned back to the radio, twisting dials and poking buttons, or sometimes vice versa.

"Pardon me," Alice said again. "But aren't you the least bit curious as to who I am?"

"Curious?" said Hatta. "Well, I *am* curious, or so I have been told." He put his hand over his heart, closed his eyes and recited: "Curious, adjective—rousing interest because of novelty or strangeness. See: curiosity." His eyes popped open and he leaned close to Alice. "And you know what my grandmother would say: 'Curiosity thrilled the bat.'"

"That's not what I meant," said Alice. "What I meant—"

"She's mean," said Haigha, his eyes on the road. "Will mean, has meant, has been meaning." His ears, though, twitched toward Alice quite independent of the breeze.

Alice regarded him with puzzlement. "Don't you wonder—" she began.

"Of course, I wonder," Hatta said. "We're in Wonderland, are we not—is that not to wonder?"

"And wander, too," put in Haigha.

"Really," said Alice, blinking.

Hatta smiled broadly. "Oh, *reality*," he said dismissively. "A poor sort of substitute for wonder, no?"

Alice almost said "Really" again, as it was quite her favorite word for "Oh, please, I cannot put up with much more of this," but caught herself before the *R* started down her tongue. Instead she said, "This is going nowhere!"

Hatta smiled beatifically, and Alice realized what she had said. "Don't you dare answer that," she said with a withering glare, and he blew her a kiss.

"Why, I think she apprehends our direction, dear Hatta," said Haigha. "Better than the cops, no?"

"I," said Alice, slowly and deliberately, "am Alice. You"—she pointed at Hatta's nose, so close that he crossed his eyes, or tried, to see it—"are Hatta."

"Well, whyever didn't you say so earlier?" said Hatta. "It would have cleared things up so well, don't you think?"

Alice stuck her tongue out at him. "And you," she said to the rabbit-man, "are Hay—Hayg—Hayg-ha?"

"Haigha," said Haigha. "Rhymes with 'burgomeister.'" He smiled at her—he had the most spectacular buck teeth Alice had ever seen.

"Why, it rhymes with 'mayor,'" she said.

"Same difference," said Haigha. He had not taken his gaze away. "And it rhymes with 'mayo,' sideways, though only condimentally."

"You mustn't mind him, dear," Hatta whispered in Alice's ear. "He's Anglo-Saxon."

"I suppose that explains the 'burgomeister,'" Alice replied. Haigha was still gazing at her, and for the first time she looked down the road beyond him. There was a truck ahead of them, the first vehicle she had seen since they started driving, so huge that it took up almost the entire road—and it was headed straight at them! "Oh, my!" she cried. "Oh, do turn!"

What happened next Alice didn't exactly know, though she certainly *felt* a great deal. She was sure that Haigha had grabbed the wheel and given it a sharp wrench, but she lost her grip on the seat back and was flung to the floor. "At least it is well cushioned," she thought, looking up at the sky spinning overhead in such a strange way, with such a squealing of tires. By the time she had climbed up to the seat, the truck was far behind them.

"Keep your eyes on the road!" she said sharply.

Hatta turned around in his seat, adjusting the brim of his hat—somehow it had gotten turned around, too. "Do you really think he should keep his eyes on the road?" he inquired. "How ever will he see? Wouldn't it be better if he kept his wheels on the road?"

"Really," Alice said, and put her hand to her mouth.

"Not *that* again," sighed Hatta. "I shall let it pass, though. You're obviously new around here."

"Do you think so?" Alice said quickly. "I haven't the slightest idea how I got here or where here is." She was quite eager for information.

"Oh, I'm sure you got here in the usual way," said Hatta, nodding. "But as for where here is—" He reached into the glove compartment and pulled out a map, and began unfolding it.

And unfolded it.

And unfolded it.

And unfolded it, until it filled his hands, his lap, the footwell, and the top waved in the breeze over his head. It came apart in great sheets, and he began to pass Alice handfuls of paper. She put it in her lap, on the seat beside her, on the floor among the trash. "But all it says," she wailed, "is 'You Are Not Here' over and over again!"

Hatta stopped unfolding, and turned in his seat so he regarded Alice over the back. Bits of map were blowing away along the road, but he paid it no mind. "But that's perfectly accurate," he said. "Quite logical."

"No, it isn't—or is," said Alice uncertainly. "I suppose there must be one place on this map where I am—but how would the mapmaker know it?"

"Why he doesn't," said Hatta. "Obviously, you have to be in the right place for the map to be of use."

"But that's—" Alice started to say, but Haigha interrupted her.

"Harumph, I say," he said. "You can't be *on* the map at all. Unless, of course, you were *quite* small."

With that, Hatta threw the rest of the map out of the car, excepting the bits Alice caught as they flew past. She struggled to fold it up neatly, and she had to settle for stuffing the more recalcitrant parts between her skirt and the seat. It made a rather large wad of paper that took two hands to hold. "I know it was smaller when it started," she said.

"Oh, they always get larger when you *look at* them," said Hatta. He was still hanging over the back of his seat, chin atop the headrest. "Can't observe something without changing it, you see." He held out his hand for the map, and Alice passed it forward. He pounded it against the back of the seat, like beating the air from rising bread, until he got it small enough to put back in the glove compartment.

"But why keep a map at all, if it's no use?" Alice said, thinking aloud.

Hatta just looked back at her and smiled. "Not so much where you've been, but where you're going," he said, and Haigha chimed in, "Not so much where you're going as where you've been." They both laughed until the car began to swerve across the road.

"Oh, do be careful!" cried Alice. This time she was better prepared, and braced herself with her foot against the back of Hatta's seat.

"Care, dare, fare," sang Haigha, his ears rising to their full height. "How I care to dare, for the fare is so delicious!"

"He's mad, you know," whispered Hatta, finger next to his nose. He turned around in his seat (he hadn't been shifted, even with all the swerving) and said to his companion, "Find us a place to stop, for I am quite in need of some fare."

Alice thought she might enjoy stopping. They had traveled some distance, she wasn't sure how much, past rolling hills and bare plains, the road always perfectly straight with its white line bisecting the blacktop out to infinity. In the distance now, she could see a building with a sign on top.

"That will do quite nicely, I think," said Hatta, pointing. He turned back to Alice. "They call it a 'diner,' you know, because you can 'dine here.'"

"Are you sure—" Alice said, but they were pulling into the parking lot and she misplaced her thought. The building had glass windows, with booths with tiny curtains. Over the door was painted a little crown, and the sign—almost as big as the roof of the building—said "Duchess's."

Haigha turned off the car and twirled the keychain around his fingers. "Shall we, then?" he said to Hatta, who nodded, and vaulted out of the car. Alice got out more cautiously—a stray bit of map blew away in the breeze.

There was one other car in the lot, a Volkswagen with huge puffy black tires and a foxtail hanging from the antenna. "I wonder who that could belong to?" Alice said to herself. Her companions were already halfway to the door, and she crunched across the gravel after them.

With his hand on the handle, Hatta paused, saying, "I almost forgot the Dormouse!" Haigha bowed and tossed him the keys, and Hatta went back past Alice to open the trunk.

Hatta lifted out a small brown man. He was most securely tied up, his arms bound with many strong ropes, and a gag in his mouth. He had a face that was almost all nose and no chin, sleepy dull brown eyes, and tiny round ears set high on his head. Taking hold of him firmly by the back of his jacket, Hatta marched him over to the diner.

Alice, raised always to be polite, opened the door for them. "Has he been in the trunk the whole time?" she said. "Why, I never!"

Hatta smiled at her. "Never?" he said. "If you like it, you can ride there too—the Dormouse here won't mind, will you my good fellow?" With his free hand, Hatta tilted the brown man's head up and down, though his prisoner's gaze was dull and fearful.

Alice blinked and let her eyes adjust to the dimness of the interior. It was all plastic and linoleum and chrome, in shades of blue and white and silver, with crowns embossed on the tiny jukeboxes in each booth, and a coat of arms on the wall next to the menu. Alice stopped at the sight of a sales counter. It was stacked with bottles neatly labeled "Drink Me," and packages marked "Eat Me," and cigarette packs blazoned with "Smoke Me." *No doubt what one is supposed to do with those*, she thought.

Haigha had taken a chair at the far end of the counter; Hatta had joined him there, placing the Dormouse next to him, so that

Alice must take the next seat over. Of the proprietor there was no sign, save for a clattering noise from behind a swinging door.

At the opposite end of the counter, a man—well, more of a rabbit than even Haigha—sat, nervously regarding the newcomers with very pink eyes. His skin was pale almost to whiteness, and his suit was even whiter. His white bow tie bobbled as he checked his pocket watch, and his nose twitched every once in a while.

"Service! I will have service!" cried Hatta, pounding the counter with his open palm. He seemed quite cheerful, thought Alice. She dutifully regarded the counter before her, which was littered with the remnants of someone's meal and after-dinner coffee—most unappetizing.

"Coming!" cried a voice from the storage room, and shortly thereafter a woman dressed in a waitress's uniform appeared. Her face was remarkable for a large nose and sharp chin. *You could hone razors on that chin*, Alice thought. Her name tag read "Duchess" and she wore a tiara underneath her hairnet. She put her hands on her hips, regarding them. "What shall it be?" she said, her voice an alto rumble. "The menu's on the wall, and I'm your waitress, don't confuse the two."

"How could you confuse one with the other?" Alice said aloud to herself. Duchess turned, putting a hand to her hip.

"You can order a menu, but you have to *ask* a waitress," she said, her eyes boring into Alice, who blinked. "What will you be having, then?"

"Tea," said Hatta, his nose in the air. "Tea for me and my friends." He bowed slightly to Haigha, who nodded back.

"Crumpets and cress sandwiches," said the rabbit-man, thumping the Dormouse on the back, "with their crusts cut off, and digestive biscuit."

"Scones and clotted cream," said Hatta, wrapping his arms about himself—it kept his hands from shaking, Alice noticed. He got up and came down the counter to sit next to her, abandoning his former seat. "We shall have tea, proper tea, wonderful tea!" he sang to the waitress.

Duchess crossed her arms over her chest regally. "Tea," she said, in freezing accents. "With or without caffeine?"

Hatta flapped his hand, which gesture was somewhat spoiled by palsy, Alice thought. "With, my dear woman," he said.

Duchess regarded him for another second before she busied herself with the kitchen equipment behind the counter. There was a great deal of it, most of which Alice could not identify. Some of it gleamed, some of it was rusty or discolored, and it had knobs, spigots, containers, and levers beyond counting. There was even a kitchen sink—which Alice thought was appropriate under the circumstances. She had never before seen one with eyes, a mouth, and a worried expression. *It seems depressed,* she thought.

The proprietress moved swiftly, twisting something here, pouring something there, venting a great hiss of steam from some infernal device at odd intervals. Alice wondered if making tea was always this complicated.

Haigha got up and moved down next to Hatta, without a word. This left only one place between him and the rabbit, who looked more nervous all the time—his nose was twitching faster and faster, until Alice began to wonder if it might fall off. He checked his watch again.

"Nice weather we've been having," Alice said. She had been taught to introduce innocuous subjects when the conversation lagged, but as the Duchess chose that moment to let out a particularly large billow of steam, the effect was quite ruined.

"Pardon me," the rabbit said. "Did you say something?"

Hatta looked over at him, moving his head slowly, in a way Alice thought must seem threatening. "The weather," Alice said. "It's been quite nice, has it not?"

Haigha grinned back at his companion, showing off his buck teeth again. "Nice *and* not, it's been whether," he said.

"Tea!" cried the Duchess, slamming saucers and cups down

on the counter with such enthusiasm that Alice thought they must crack, but they didn't. "Tea is served!"

Each of them got their own teapot: Hatta's in the shape of a hat, Haigha's like a rabbit, the Dormouse's like a log, and Alice's—well, she examined it closely. It seemed to be a grinning cat—at least she thought it was grinning. It might be showing its teeth instead.

There was one thing wrong with these teapots: they didn't have spouts, and Alice had to pour her tea by taking off the lid and pouring over the side. Haigha and Hatta cursed as they dribbled and dropped and generally made a mess of the counter.

The Dormouse, of course, was tied up, so Alice poured for him. His moist brown eyes were *so* grateful, but then she realized the gag would prevent him from drinking easily. "Shall I loosen his gag?" she said as she turned toward Hatta, but found he had moved to the remaining chair, next to the nervous rabbit, whose meal he was in the process of appropriating.

"I say, sir," sputtered the rabbit. "Have you not your own food and your own place, sir?"

Hatta threw his head back and laughed, then held the rabbit close to him by the neck. "My place is where I choose it," he said. "My place is where I make it, and none other." The palsy of his hands did not seem to affect his grip.

"Unhand me, sir," sputtered the rabbit faintly.

"We could definitely unhand you," said Hatta, and nodded to his companion. Haigha hopped down from his chair and went around the counter, picking up a fearsomely large knife, which he tested with his thumb. Hatta forced his victim's arm down on the counter.

"Here now," said Duchess, her eyes flashing. Alice looked to her gratefully. "We'll have none of this here," she said. "Take him outside."

Haigha pointed the knife at her. "And if we don't?" he said, displaying his buck teeth in a broad grin. "What will you do then?"

219

Duchess rolled her eyes imperiously and grabbed a container off the counter. "This, you impertinent little man!" she shouted, and threw its contents at him—a shaker full of pepper!

Such a black cloud it made!—and it filled the diner. Alice sneezed, and sneezed again. She could hardly see. From within the cloud, she could hear Hatta cursing and Haigha stumbling about, the whimpering of the rabbit and the Duchess's comment that she was going to get more pepper. "Oh, there could be no *more* pepper than this," thought Alice, and went out the door of the diner.

After the darkness, the light was quite startling, and even more worrisome was the siren noise approaching. "Oh, my goodness," said Alice. Behind her, Hatta stumbled out the door, with Haigha close on his heels, both of them choking and coughing. Alice realized they had left the Dormouse inside, but all things considered it was probably for the best.

"Quickly, to the car, my dear," Hatta said to Alice, tossing her the keys. So rattled was she that Alice had gotten all the way into the driver's seat before she realized what she was doing.

There was a bewildering array of controls on the dashboard. "Hurry, do!" cried Hatta, tumbling himself upside down into the backseat, so that his feet projected over the side. Haigha, who had gotten the worst of the pepper, merely wheezed in the passenger seat beside her, his eyes streaming.

Alice knew that the key must be in the ignition, and that the lever must be depressed, but beyond that she had only sketchy ideas. "Oh, I shall just have to learn as I go along," she said, and turned the key.

The engine roared into life, and she was so startled that her hand pulled down on the lever. The car leaped forward, and it was only good luck that it had been pointed in the direction of the road. There seemed to be an amazing profusion of pedals on the floor, so Alice stepped on two or three, in the hope of getting one right.

By dint of wiggling the steering wheel back and forth, and

tromping on the pedals once in a while, Alice got the car straightened out. But the sirens were as loud as before, and Alice wrestled the rearview mirror (it had the sweetest little face, which stuck its tongue out at her as she moved it) so she could see the rear.

In the distance, the strange narrow little police car was visible. Hatta knelt on the seat so he could see over the back. "They're gaining on us, my dear," he said. "You'll have to drive faster."

Alice gripped the steering wheel tighter than before. "But I don't know how!" she said in a small voice.

"Haigha," said Hatta, buffeting his friend on the back of the head. It made Haigha's ears curl.

"Very well," he said, and gave a final sneeze. "Better brace yourselves," he said. He took off one shoe (his big toe stuck out a hole in his red and white striped sock), and, wedging himself down in his seat, he reached out with that foot and pressed a button that Alice hadn't noticed before—strange, because it said "Press Me."

But she didn't have much chance to wonder because as Haigha's foot pushed the button, the green T-Bird took off with such force that it was all Alice could do to hold on to the wheel. Countryside whizzed past, and the breeze was so loud that Alice couldn't have heard the sirens fading as they must be. She concentrated on keeping the car on the road.

Alice drove for some time, until she decided to stop. The T-Bird had not slowed from its excessive speed, and her arms were getting tired. Because she did not know which of the many pedals (and she could swear the engine had grown a few more) was the brake, she despaired of stopping until she remembered the key. She cut the engine, and the T-Bird coasted to a silent stop.

At first all was quiet in the car, then Haigha let out a whoop that almost sent poor Alice tumbling to the floor underneath the steering wheel. His ears pointing straight up, he leaped from the car, capering and dancing on the blacktop. Hatta joined him, and they linked hands and spun round in a circle.

Alice got out of the car on shaky legs, and leaned against the hood watching them, until they spun near and grabbed her by the hands into the dance, swirling and twirling until they all fell down, panting.

"Alice, dear," said Hatta. She rolled over and propped her head up on her palm. He smiled at her, beneath his big nose. "Do ride with us forever?"

"Four evers," said Haigha, "I say, four evers and a day, and not a minute less."

"Four evers, and a day, then," Alice said. "Truly."

"*Really?*" said Hatta.

"'No substitute for wonder,'" said Alice, and Hatta flung his baseball hat into the air. "Where to, now?" she said, getting up and brushing herself off.

"The road!" sang Hatta, sliding into the driver's seat. Haigha clambered into the back, which left the passenger's seat for Alice. "The open road, raring for the road, all raving for the speed!" He took off his hat and put it on Alice's head, backwards, and she admired herself in the mirror.

He started the car, and they drove off along the endless Wonderland road. Alice leaned back, the wind streaming out her golden curls. Up ahead, she suspected, there was a roadblock, with more police, more obstacles, but for right now, the journey was enough.

Waiting for the Elevator

Kevin T. Stein

℘ ℘

"O sir, we quarrel in print: by the book, as you have books for good manners: I will name you the degrees. The first, the retort courteous; the second, the quip modest: the third, the reply churlish; the fourth, the reproof valiant; the fifth, the countercheck quarrelsome; the sixth, the lie with circumstance; the seventh, the lie direct. All those you may avoid, but the lie direct; and you may avoid that too, with an if."

"What?" Alice asked.

Harlequin adjusted his cuffs, though he had none to adjust. It was an affectation that was beginning to annoy Alice, though this was the first time she had seen it. She just knew that adjusting his cuffs was something Harlequin did often, and would do again. She braced herself in advance.

"With an 'if,' I said," Harlequin replied. "With an 'if.' I knew when seven justices could not take up a quarrel; but when the parties were met themselves, one of them thought but of an 'if,' as 'if you said so, then I said so'; and they shook hands and swore brothers."

"What are you talking about?" asked Alice.

"Your 'if' is the only peacemaker; much virtue in 'if,'" Harlequin answered, as if he had not heard Alice's protestations. He ended his speech with a bow and a sweep of his hat, another accoutrement he did not have.

Alice crossed her arms and leaned against the wall, feeling vexed. She didn't know why this buffoon was trying to entertain her, and understood less why she had an incredible craving for chocolate-covered apricots.

Harlequin gestured absently and turned his head politely away. "Adjust your skirt."

Glancing down, Alice saw that her skirt, indeed, needed adjusting. She reluctantly dropped her arms and pulled down on the hem of her leather mini.

"I must say," Harlequin said when he was sure Alice had done the appropriate adjusting. "Black is certainly your color."

"It was either that, or go as that young schoolgirl Carroll loved so much," Alice replied somewhat harshly. She was more angry at herself for bringing up Carroll's preference of dress than at Harlequin for prompting her to say something she did not necessarily want revealed.

Harlequin appeared incredulous, though if he had a face, it was covered by a perfectly featureless mask, the right side white, the left black. It was more the magnitude of his reaction, the way his head drew back, his body twisted, as if from something venomous, and he guarded himself with a raised right arm. It was all these things that gave the appearance of being incredulous, though Alice thought she might be wrong.

He asked, "You mean to tell me that you are . . . that Carroll . . ."

"Think what you want," Alice said, dismissing her companion's gesture with one of her own. "Everyone's got to make a living."

"Oh, this is too, too much," Harlequin said, wrist to forehead. He continued, muttering to himself, "Too, too much."

"Yeah, whatever. How much longer do you think we're going to have to wait?"

Harlequin continued his tirade, which slowly devolved to silence. Alice glanced at the elevator's floor indicator, which seemed to have risen a level or two, though she couldn't be sure because the boredom of waiting had the strange effect of making her memories race to fill the time. Unfortunately, she couldn't quite remember the things she was remembering.

The rest of the waiting area was reasonably forgettable, with the kind of paint Alice was sure she had seen as a young girl in some old school somewhere, or perhaps in a dream of an old school, the same kind of dream that she wished had been the dream of somewhere nicer, somewhere where she wore better shoes.

Alice stared pointedly at Harlequin and waited till she was sure that he was done talking to himself. Of course, from what she heard before, she guessed that he did very little else but talk to himself, even when others were inclined to answer.

"How much longer do you think we're going to have to wait?" Alice asked again.

"What?"

"How much longer—"

"I heard you, I heard you," Harlequin replied somewhat testily. Alice wondered why, of all the people she had known, and of all the people she had wanted to run into at some time in her life, Jim Morrison, perhaps, or Picasso, she had to be stuck with a guy wearing a skintight outfit of black and white diamonds and no face. At least if he had a face, she could take some pleasure in eventually slapping it, as she knew she eventually would.

"Well?"

"Well what?"

"Well, how much longer?"

"Oh, that old question," Harlequin answered with a wave. "That's the same question everyone asks me. Why don't you ask me something interesting?"

Alice looked askance. "Like what?"

Throwing his hands up, Harlequin said, "And that's always the other question." Leaning against the wall, he added, "You're an intelligent girl. Well traveled, and well connected, I might add."

Harlequin bobbed his head, and if he had eyes, Alice knew he'd be winking, or perhaps leering. She'd had her fill of both, and was tired of getting implications when all she wanted were straight answers.

"What do you mean by that?" she demanded.

"Instead of asking me that question, why don't you ask me about what I said?"

"When?"

"First."

"First when?" Alice asked.

"When we first started, of course," Harlequin replied, adding a gesture with his thumb over his shoulder.

"Oh, then," Alice said, nodding. "I hardly remember that at all."

Gesturing around the dull waiting area, Harlequin said, "Must be the decor." Before Alice could say anything, Harlequin strutted in a two-foot area, a hand behind his back and one gesturing in the air like a schoolteacher. Alice had very little schooling except for what she had learned as a girl, and everything since then she had taken to be the gifts of fate. Not that she wasn't learned: she knew that she knew more than most girls her age, or even women; she just realized that she didn't like to be lectured at, especially not by someone obviously too ready to lecture. If she had a motto, she guessed it might be something like "Never trust anyone over thirty," though she wasn't sure such a definite age break applied to someone like Harlequin, whom she guessed to be either much older or far, far younger.

"As I was saying before you stopped paying attention," Harlequin said, leaning close to Alice for emphasis, "it's what we hear when we first start that is most important."

Alice crossed her arms again. "To be honest, I didn't understand a thing you said."

"And that, my girl, is because I haven't told you."

"I'm not your girl."

"Then whose girl are you?"

"Nobody's," Alice said, hugging her arms tighter in what she realized was quite a silly gesture. She dropped her arms, then crossed them again, not wanting to seem defensive even as the gesture gave her away. "All I want is to get on this damn elevator and go up."

"So that's what this is all about?" Harlequin inquired archly, gesturing grandly around the room. "Waiting for Godot?"

"Who?"

"Sorry," Harlequin said, shrinking back. He gestured grandly again and said, "So that's what this is all about? Waiting for the elevator?"

"I certainly think so," Alice replied. "Why else would I be standing here talking to you if I wasn't waiting for the elevator?"

"Take the stairs, then," Harlequin said, pointing to the door with the truly useful sign painted on it that read "STAIRS."

"I don't want to take the stairs. I want to take the elevator," Alice said through gritted teeth.

"Which brings us back to the beginning, and what I said in the beginning," Harlequin answered loudly and with a grandiose sweep of both arms in a circle. "Do you remember now?"

Alice thought a moment. She remembered little, still. "A quote?"

"Not just any quote, mind you, but a quote from Shakespeare, from Touchstone."

"Don't they make movies?" Alice asked, not in the least intrigued.

Harlequin leaned in conspiratorially. "Shakespeare would not have a thing to do with movies. You can blame everything bad on the actors."

Alice took a brush out of her square leather purse, black to match her outfit, and ran it through her straight, blonde hair. The brush was perfectly clean, without a strand of her hair caught in its stiff, plastic bristles, and for the life of her she couldn't remember cleaning it, or even buying it. The lack of hair, the lack of relative dirtiness disturbed her greatly, as if the cleanliness of the elevator waiting area had somehow crept into the chaos that she knew was part of her purse, and all other purses like it. She glanced inside it, attempting to be surreptitious, but closed it quickly when Harlequin attempted to peek inside as well.

"You wouldn't happen to have any chocolate-covered apricots in there, would you?" he asked.

"No."

"Pity," Harlequin said.

"I know what you mean," Alice replied.

"Oh, in that case, do tell me about the quote."

Alice rolled her eyes. "The Shakespeare quote?"

"Just so."

Alice drew in what she hoped was a nonchalant breath. "It has something to do with the reason I'm still waiting for this damn elevator, and I'm sure that no matter how close I come to the true answer, you'll tell me I'm not right. Right?"

Harlequin seemed disappointed, as if she had spoiled his joke. He leaned against the elevator door and rubbed his chin, though his lack of a beard or other facial components made the gesture seem out of place. She suddenly regretted being so smart with him.

"Well, I guess you're right," he said.

Alice was no longer as regretful.

Before either could add to the response, the elevator's tone suddenly rang.

Alice stood anxiously, the moment building, growing longer as the sound of the elevator grew louder as the car came closer, the distance decreasing. Alice thought a moment about this irony, but the sight of Harlequin leaning against the elevator's doorframe, arms crossed across his chest, left leg crossed in front of the right, gave her pause. "And just what is that look for?" she asked, thinking that he must be giving her some kind of "look."

"This look," Harlequin replied, "is what we in the theater would call a 'knowing look.' I'd give you the number but I can't think of it."

"Number?" Alice asked.

"Well, yes. All looks have numbers."

Alice tore her gaze away from the seemingly eternally unopening elevator doors and replied, "That's the most ridiculous thing I've ever heard. Looks with numbers."

"Oh," Harlequin replied in turn, standing straight and bringing a hand to his diamond-patterned chest. "Really? And how long have you been in the theater?"

Alice bluffed. "Long enough to know that looks don't have numbers. In the theater. Only in modeling, and there aren't that many numbers, at that."

"Ha!" was Harlequin's only reply.

"Ha?"

"Yes. Ha!"

And that's when the elevator doors opened, when Alice wasn't at all ready for them, and certainly not ready for what, or rather who, was inside.

"Going down?"

Alice turned at the sound, at first curious about who was inside, then second excited to find that the doors had finally opened, and third, and most slowly of the three, furious at the question.

"What the hell do you mean, 'Going down'?" she demanded, the fury she felt finding fuel in her frustration. "And just who the hell are you?"

The woman in the elevator put her finger on what Alice knew must be the "HOLD DOORS" button. With her other hand, she brushed away a curtain of silken hair from her face, revealing the features of nobility that Alice always wanted but knew she could never have. At least not without a lot of money. But at a good salon, maybe just the hair . . .

"You are the Alice, are you not?" the woman inquired lightly, with a voice that Alice also always wanted and knew she could never get, even with a lot of money. Of course, she did know that she could change her voice if she smoked enough, but her voice probably wouldn't change in the direction she desired.

However, these thoughts were quickly vanquished by others more pertinent and immediate as she asked, "How did you know my name? And what do you mean, 'the Alice'?"

Harlequin stepped forward before the woman could utter a word and took up her free hand in his own and touched it to the place where his lips would have been, had he been a normal man. His manner was most gracious, ingratiating to Alice, as he said, "My lady. You are truly of a noble birth, and may I be the first to welcome you to this, most humble of elevator waiting places."

He's off his nut, Alice thought to herself. Alice guessed that her normal poker face must have slipped, as she noticed the woman in the elevator smirk in her direction when Harlequin had finally withdrawn himself to a safe distance.

To Alice the woman said, "I am Guenevere, of the castle of Camelot, and I bring you a message."

"A message. For *her*, no less," Harlequin grumbled under his breath, crossing his arms and looking away with what passed for disdain. Alice waited for him to adjust his nonexistent cuffs, but he was spared the ignominy of being slapped. She figured it served him right for being such a buffoon.

"*Guenevere?*" Alice asked in disbelief. "Queen Guenevere. From the castle Camelot. With King Arthur, and Lancelot, and all that? Where's Merlin?"

"I assure you, this is a ladies-only elevator," the queen replied, brushing back another wave of golden hair, which seemed golden even in the elevator's bad fluorescent lighting. "Are you ready for the message?"

Alice shrugged. She didn't know what message the lady might have, since she wasn't expecting anything, nor did she know anyone at the top. She replied, "Sure."

Guenevere switched her hands, so the other one was holding the "HOLD DOORS" button, then pushed back her hair again. Alice changed her mind about wanting the hair. Guenevere said, "There are two sides to the road less traveled, and what you desire most comes to those who wait."

"Excuse me," Harlequin said, stepping forward and holding up an index finger by way of interruption. "I know a great deal of just about everything, and I must say I haven't a clue as to what you just said."

"Maybe you're not quite as smart as you think," Alice said aloud. To herself she hoped that Guenevere was talking about chocolate-covered apricots.

"Maybe you're not quite as smart as you think," Harlequin mimicked, bobbing his head back and forth at Alice. "Well, if you're so smart—"

"Yes?" Alice challenged.

"If you're so smart—"

"Yes?"

Harlequin paused in the face of Alice's challenge. After a moment, he said, "Well, if you're so smart, why don't you take the stairs instead of waiting for this damn elevator?"

"He does have a point," Queen Guenevere said before Alice could reply. Alice was slightly miffed by the interjection, figuring that the queen would naturally side with her. They had both been, after all, en-buffooned by Harlequin, if that was the proper term. Unfortunately, this interjection, and Harlequin's actual statement, made Alice pause, losing the argumentative momentum she felt and forcing her off the track, as it were. She wondered why she didn't take the stairs, and to hell with this damn elevator.

Alice turned to the lady and asked, "This elevator's going down?"

"Yes," the queen replied, switching hands again.

"And there's no way for it to go back up before it goes down?"

"Not that I'm aware of."

"I'm waiting for the elevator because that is what I've chosen to do," Alice finally answered, her mouth fueled by the annoyance of knowing that the elevator would be traveling down an uncertain number of floors before it would travel back up an equally uncertain number of floors. She stood her ground and waited for either of her companions to challenge her.

Which, of course, Harlequin did by saying, "So your decision is an intellectual one."

"Yes."

"Because you've waited this long, you might as well wait longer?"

"Yes."

"Sort of"—he physically sought the words—"'vengeance betting,' as it were, against the time already spent. Like the Jews of old, or the Christians thereafter, waiting again for the savior to come, while—"

"Sir!" Queen Guenevere commanded, cutting off Harlequin's long-winded analysis.

He stopped in mid-gesture and turned to the woman. "Yes?"

"You'll iv-gay aught away," the queen spoke cryptically.

"Did I say too much?"

Alice watched this interchange with interest, not really knowing what was going on since she was actually thinking about what Harlequin had said about vengeance betting against time. When she had been in Vegas (merely as a detached observer among a number of less detached observers, all of whom became detached from their life's savings), she had heard the term used to describe

232

betting new money to get lost money back. At the time she had thought it merely stubborn and petty behavior, but now, at the moment, she could understand the theory. At the moment, she didn't mind being petty. But she knew there was something more to her waiting. She just couldn't give it a name.

"Well, I've got to be going now," Queen Guenevere said, pulling her hand back away from the "HOLD DOORS" button. She shook the feeling back into her fingers, clutching the air. She waved to Alice with the other.

"Wait!" Alice cried, stepping forward, then pulling down the hem of her black mini with embarrassment. The doors closed as she asked, "Who gave you the message?"

"It was mff im mff-mff," the queen replied through the closed doors. Alice heard the car begin its downward motion, and soon, that too, was gone.

"I wonder who that could be?" Harlequin asked the air, holding his chin with his right hand, his face tilted up thoughtfully.

"Who?" Alice asked in a huff.

"Mff im mff-mff, of course," her companion replied.

"O sir, we quarrel in print: by the book, as you have—"

"Shut up," Alice huffed, still waiting for the elevator to come back up. Again, she did not know how long she had been waiting, and her memory had grown foggy once more, or perhaps muzzy, she could not be sure. In fact, she was sure of very little except for the annoying sense that Harlequin knew more than he was telling and in not telling her the things he knew was deliberately trying to do . . . something. It was the identity, the face of that something that she found most annoying.

"You are easily the most rude of all the Alices I have ever met."

"Thank you very much," Alice replied with a polite nod of her head. Since her time studying with Carroll, when she had been both sweet and innocent, she had taken it upon herself to run with a bad crowd, the kind that would scrape both "sweet" and "inno-cent" off the bottom of their shoes with a stick. Unfortunately, the only bad crowd Alice had found had been a small group of Rasta-farians at a Bruce Lee film festival, and they had left after her tub of popcorn had run out. So as it was, anyone who told Alice she was "rude" outside of the influence of the bad crowd she never found was paying her a compliment.

"Thank you very much," Harlequin nodded and mimicked in return. "You definitely always seem to want to be like someone else. Don't you?"

"And you always act like you have all the answers!"

"What answers?"

"The answers to everything!"

"Which everything?"

"Don't play word games with me!" Alice shrieked, suddenly turning and pounding on the elevator doors. "Why the hell won't these damn doors open?"

"Because the elevator's not—"

"Shut up!" Alice ran her hands through her hair and asked, "What do you mean, I always want to be like someone else?"

Harlequin said nothing, then shrugged. "I don't know. I just wanted to get your attention."

"That was a cheap shot."

"Yes, it was, but now that I have your attention, I would like to point your attention to the elevator floor . . . thing." Harle-quin gestured vaguely at the thing that told what floor the eleva-tor was on.

The thing showed that the elevator was above the current floor level, astounding Alice for the briefest instant until she real-ized that she was obviously somewhere truly remarkable, despite the fact that it looked like a drab, unremarkable elevator waiting area.

"You're probably wondering how all this can happen," Harle-quin began, initiating the same pacing program that he had already used, hand behind back, other hand in the air, finger pointed up-ward. "That, of course, is not important."

"It isn't?" Alice asked, leaning against the elevator's door-frame.

"It isn't," Harlequin answered, continuing his pacing. "What is important is why you continue to stand in this remarkable yet obviously boring place instead of taking the stairs."

At least I got that part right, Alice thought to herself. She con-tinued thinking to herself and thought about the query. Why don't I take the stairs and get all this over with? But before she could go any further, the elevator doors opened, revealing another beautiful woman that Alice wanted to be, but this one had dark hair. She wouldn't have to go quite as far.

"Marion," Alice said.

The woman in the elevator put her hand to her throat; the other was already on the "HOLD DOORS" button. "Yes?"

"That's your name."

"Lucky guess," Harlequin muttered.

"Maid Marion. Robin and his merry men, and all that," Alice said, glaring out the corner of her eye at her bothersome compan-ion.

The woman in the elevator frowned beautifully. "Ah, no. Sorry," she replied. "I'm the other Marion."

Alice was definitely confused. She thought she had this whole waiting for the elevator thing pegged. "Really?"

"No, just kidding," the woman replied. "Got to keep you on your toes."

"Thanks for thinking of me," Alice grumbled, pulling at the hem of her skirt.

Harlequin pushed himself forward past Alice and bowed, bumping his backside into her and nudging her out of the way. Be-fore she could protest, he made a grand, sweeping gesture with the hat he did not have and said, "Welcome to this most humble and uninteresting of elevator waiting places, Lady Marion. May I just say that—"

Marion jabbed a finger into Harlequin's chest, cutting him off as he gave a painful "eep" sort of sound that Alice thought only came from those cheap rubber squeaky toys she never bought for the pet she never had.

"Back off, cocky," the woman interjected harshly. "The young lady and I have business." Marion continued to jab with her finger, pushing Harlequin back from the elevator.

"I get ten percent," he whispered at Alice from the corner of his mouth.

"You'll get nothing and like it," Alice replied.

Marion reached inside a small pouch at her waist and glanced across at Harlequin, who had taken it upon himself to turn away from the two who so obviously did not desire his company. Actually, it wasn't that Alice did not want his company, it was just that she did not want the company that he was currently willing to give. If he had been more restrained, or perhaps even charming, or if he could tell a joke . . . then his company would have been just fine.

Whispering, Marion said, "Here," slipping something into Alice's hand.

The something was soft on the outside, firm on the inside. Light, flat, warmish, roundish, and, Alice knew by looking, delish.

"Just what I've been waiting for," she said to herself. She quickly unwrapped the something and popped it in her mouth.

An explosion of flavor made her wince.

"Straight from the confectioneries of the realm," Marion said. "Simply the finest chocolate-covered apricots the world has ever known."

Alice tried to agree with her mouth, but she couldn't stop chewing, the candy was so large. All she could do was continue chewing, nod, and continue chewing. It was somewhat difficult to chew and keep her mouth closed at the same time. But Marion seemed to be one of the girls, and she didn't turn away in embar-rassment.

Alice continued to chew. Marion asked, "Been waiting for this long?"

"Hmm-hmm," Alice agreed.

"Think it's a great reward?"

"Hmm-hmm."

"A great reward though you weren't doing anything to deserve a reward?"

"Hmm-mmh?"

Reward without deserving? Reward without action? Alice questioning herself, finally swallowing. She felt the chocolate on her teeth, gritty but sweet, and cleaned them off with her tongue, then a most ill-mannered finger.

"That's an odd thing to expect," she finally said.

Marion nodded. "Sure is."

"No, I mean *really*," Alice said, finding herself somewhat alarmed that she should think *so* odd a thing. "I've never thought that way before. At least not that way before I came here—"

"However that was," Harlequin muttered a short distance away, barely heard, still turned.

"There are as many sides to you, as many ways you might be represented in a poem, or a story, or a book, as there are ways to quarrel. Everyone changes, some stay the same. It's all part of the answer you're looking for," Marion said. With a gesture, she added, "If you forget that, you can look at the wrapper."

Alice followed the motion down, looked at the wrapper that had kept the chocolate of the superlative apricot from cracking off or melting away, and saw that the words that Marion had just spo-ken were printed in nine-point type, Palatino, with a three line drop-cap in some Chancery face or another, on the wrapper.

Alice shrugged. "Interesting, but what does it *mean*?"

Marion returned the shrug. "It means as much as you can make use of. As much as anybody can make use of."

"There you go, talking about anybody again," Harlequin interjected, finally returning from his place against the wall. "On matters of anybody, I should definitely be consulted."

"I thought you were everybody," Alice returned, angry that she was not being given the chance to sort out her thoughts, or Marion's words.

"Yes, him too," Harlequin said with a broad sweep. "Everybody, anybody . . ."

Alice rolled her eyes and muttered, "Big deal." To Marion, as much as herself, she said, "So if I were, say, Sherlock Holmes, I would deduce that this wrapper and your final words are the message that you are supposed to give me."

"Yes," Marion agreed.

"And if I were, say, Sherlock Holmes, I would also deduce that this elevator is going down, and not up."

"Yes, that too," Marion agreed.

"Yes. Well. Damn," Alice said.

"Before I go, I'll give you some help," Marion said. "You're waiting for the elevator. You're waiting in the middle. There was probably a beginning. There is always an end."

Incredulous again, Alice asked, "That's it?"

Harlequin stepped up even further and asked, "That's not enough?"

"Got to be going now," Marion said without answering. Alice stood agape as the doors to the elevator closed slowly, the new visitor gone.

"Oh, well," Harlequin said. "What shall we talk about next?"

Alice spun on her heel and pointed angrily at Harlequin's not-face.

And that's when she saw the answer.

She was finally able to put a face to the question.

The annoying sense that Harlequin knew more than he was telling was true, but in not telling her he was deliberately trying to make her *understand for herself*. The identity, the face of that something that he was not telling, had a face.

Faith. Faith was the face of the thing that kept her waiting by the elevator. It wasn't necessarily faith in something like God, or the God of any religion. It was just faith that for her, things would sometime be better. And it all started with a trip up the elevator. Or maybe it was the trip itself. She decided not to think about that until the next story.

"So all this," Alice began, piecing her words together like a simple, but huge, puzzle, "is my middle. Of this story, as it were. What's the beginning? Where's the end?"

Harlequin made a gesture so grand that it spun him around on his toes. "Who said you'd be lucky enough to have a beginning, middle, and end? Most people are lucky just to have a middle. I ought to know, since I'm everybody."

"Or so you think."

"Or so to say. But that doesn't change that you are the Alice, in all its knowledge and glory. You are everything, if not analogous to my first words here, as multivaried and metaphorical as ever a character was. In literature. And you have to choose whether to take the stairs or wait for the elevator."

Alice thought about it for a moment, then finally remembered everything she had forgotten previously. It was the middle of which Marion spoke, and Alice was lucky to have hers. She looked to the sign marked "STAIRS," and back to the elevator lights, and realized that she was actually in no particular hurry. She was willing to wait for the elevator if that meant she had a longer life, or at least one more fulfilling than taking the quick way to understanding.

Oh. Before Harlequin knew what hit him, Alice stepped up, raised her hand, and slapped him across the face. It's not every day that someone gets to slap the face of God.

Or someone who looks like him.

Conundrums to Guess

Peter Crowther

⟳ ⟲

Sheila didn't see the box, not at first.

In fact, the only reason she saw it at all was thanks to the spider's decision to run across the floorboards toward her bag, an interesting-looking (for spiders, she presumed later) tote affair sporting rope handles and a patchwork exterior. The spider looked like those hairy arachnid monstrosities you always saw on cheap horror movies or television documentaries about sad individuals with acne and a bad case of stuttering who kept pet tarantulas called Cecil or Cedric.

"Ohmygod!" Sheila screeched, leaping to her feet and smacking the bag away from her to her right. The spider—which, in truth, did have a colossal leg-span—stopped dead in its tracks, thought about the situation for a moment (which was possibly an entire sabbatical in spider terms) and then took a sharp left turn onto the carpet, whereupon it raced beneath the table, seemingly in a crouched position ("and with its eyes closed and neck tensed," Sheila would tell William later, mimicking the movement across the floor of the pub) towards the open door and the stairs beyond.

"What is it, dear?" Mrs. Braithwaite's concerned voice was accompanied by an equally concerned-sounding clatter of feet coming up the stairs. Sheila half-expected to hear a loud squelch as the rotund landlady placed a well-meaning orthopedic shoe on the hapless and confused beast, but the woman's face appeared around the doorjamb without any further sound. "What on *earth* is the matter, dear?" she said, slightly out of breath and looking around the room.

"A spider," Sheila explained, suddenly feeling ever so slightly silly and wimpish. "It was a spider."

Mrs. Braithwaite nodded sagely. "Well, dear, there'll be a few of those up here, I'd imagine. There's one thing, though," she added conspiratorially. "If there's spiders, there's nothing else."

"It's a good job," Sheila said as she bent down to retrieve her bag. As she did so, she saw that it had pushed aside part of the thin boarding of the interior wall. "Oh, the wall. Did I do that?"

Mrs. Braithwaite leaned forward and squinted at the damage. "Oh, don't you go worrying about that, my dear. There's not much hurt you can do up here." She reached out her hand and pushed the board testily. It gave a little and then twanged backwards as though springing out of position. "Oh!"

Sheila stepped backwards, expecting a whole stream of many-legged things to come pouring from behind the wall, but the board shuddered twice and then fell backwards to rest against the roof beams behind it. It was then that she saw the box.

"There's something behind there," she said.

"Behind where, dear?" Mrs. Braithwaite turned around to face the door.

"No . . ." Sheila took hold of the old woman's arm and turned her back to the wall. "Behind *there*." She pointed to the board and to a small, white object nestled half in shadow just to the right of the gap. "Look."

"Oh, yes, so there is." Mrs. Braithwaite crouched down and pushed the board hard, seemingly ignorant of the horrific things that could be waiting in the musty darkness beyond, waiting to tear her limb from limb. "It's a box."

"What kind of box?"

Mrs. Braithwaite grunted as she reached in and lifted the object out into the light. "It looks like a shoebox."

Sheila nodded. It did, in fact, look exactly like a shoebox, although, unlike most shoeboxes she had seen, it featured no illustrations or information—such as that relating to size or color—on its narrow ends. Rather, it seemed singularly devoid of any markings at all. Sheila shook her head, as if waking from a nap, and looked again at the box. Markings such as what? she thought. Then, a small voice whispered deep in her head: *Such as a warning,* it said.

"Preposterous!" Sheila thought, suddenly realizing that she had spoken the word aloud.

"What, dear?" Mrs. Braithwaite paused in her close scrutiny of the box's exterior and turned to Sheila. "What's preposterous, dear?"

"What . . . oh, the box—putting a box behind a wall. I mean, whatever for? And who could have put it there?"

"I'm sure I have no idea," Mrs. Braithwaite said. And, so saying, she gently eased up the box lid.

Sheila thought about grabbing the box, about preventing the woman from lifting the lid and, most important, about leaving the box's contents where they were. But by the time the thought had occurred to Sheila, Mrs. Braithwaite had removed the lid and was peering inside. Almost against her better judgment, Sheila leaned closer to get a better look for herself.

The box was draped down the sides with wisps of dust and cobweb. Mrs. Braithwaite had disturbed much of it by removing the lid, and now several strands had dropped over the lip and across the contents. Mildew had formed on one of the sides—the one that had been nearest the outer wall, Sheila guessed—and on the top envelope in what appeared to be a thick bundle, at one time held together by an elastic band, which had rotted and adhered itself across a carefully written address that she could not make out.

On each side of the pile of envelopes was a jumble of screwed-up tissue paper, bundled up as though in haste—Sheila presumed the tissues had been placed in the box in order to prevent the envelopes bouncing around. Nestled on the top of one of these was a small bottle containing, she guessed, some kind of perfume or scent. The bottle bore no label that she could see.

"My, oh my," Mrs. Braithwaite trilled, "treasures rich and rare." She placed the lid under her arm and then lifted the bottle out of the box, shaking it gently and staring myopically at the liquid that sloshed around inside.

Sheila squinted. "What is it?"

"What is it, indeed, dear?" Mrs. Braithwaite laid the box carefully on the floor and tried to unscrew the bottle's metal cap. "Umph . . . it's stuck," she said after several attempts.

Sheila reached for it. "Here, let me try."

Mrs. Braithwaite handed over the bottle and lifted out the stack of envelopes. As Sheila twisted and turned the cap, thinking she might have felt it move a little, Mrs. Braithwaite said, "Verity Lansdale . . . well, would you credit that!"

"What?"

The old woman half-turned, split indecisively between confronting her new tenant or some dusty old memories. "The Lansdales, Verity Lansdale. Well, I never."

Sheila was growing impatient. "What about them? Who were they?"

"Well, as I remember it—but I wasn't around then, mind: wasn't even born then!" She laughed and shook her head.

Sheila gave up on the bottle and set it back in the box.

"Anyway," Mrs. Braithwaite continued, "the story went that

the Lansdales had a daughter, Verity. They had two sons as well, but I'm blowed if I can remember their names. Anyway, she disappeared."

"Disappeared? When?"

"Oh, it would have been . . ." She removed her glasses and squinted down at them as she rubbed the lenses with her apron. "It would have been before the turn of the century. I was born in nineteen oh-seven, and I don't suppose as how I can have heard about it until I was a youngster." She replaced the glasses and smiled at Sheila. "Eighteen ninety something . . . maybe eighteen eighty something, I couldn't really say. It was common talk among the children. You know, a mystery."

Sheila took the envelope from Mrs. Braithwaite's hand and looked at the writing, dimmed by age but still flowing in beautiful copperplate scroll. "There's a letter inside."

Mrs. Braithwaite chuckled. "There'll be a letter inside every one of them, I'm sure, dear. She took up with that—what do they call them? Oh, fantastic writers."

"A great writer?"

"No, well, yes: he was famous. But he wrote that book about—fantasy, that's it. He was a fantasy writer. Isn't that what you call them? Now, what was his—"

"Tolkien?"

"Who, dear? Dolkin? No, I don't think it was him. I've never heard of *him*. No, the one as wrote that *Alice in Wonderland* book. Now, what—"

"Lewis Carroll?"

"Yes, that's the chap. Lewis Carroll." She straightened out her apron and chuckled again. "*Alice in Wonderland* indeed! *Phuh!*" She shook her head at the very thought of such errant nonsense. "And those must be some of her letters."

"Looks to me like *all* of her letters. There's a whole pile of the things." Sheila bent down and removed a stack of the envelopes, flicking through them slowly. "Yes, they're all addressed to Verity Lansdale. And all in the same writing." She grasped the bundle tightly and turned to the landlady. "I want to read one of them. Do you think she'd mind?"

"Mind? Good lord, dear, she'll be long past minding now, indeed she will. You go ahead and take a look."

Sheila lifted the flap of one of the envelopes and removed a carefully folded piece of writing paper. She unfolded the paper.

"It's signed by C. L. Dodgson. Who's he?"

Mrs. Braithwaite shrugged.

"The Chestnuts, Guildford—Guildford! Why, it's from here. Where's The Chestnuts?"

"I'm sure I've no idea, no idea at all."

Sheila grunted and looked back at the letter. "Right, then: it's dated January the . . ." She leaned closer to the paper, ignoring the vague perfumey-musty smell, to get a better look at the faded writing. "January the sixteenth, eighteen eighty-one. 'My dear Vetty,' it begins. 'Alas, alack! Verily Verity, I write with the sincerest of regrets (Have you ever seen an insincere regret, I wonder? I did, just the one time, and it was indeed a singularly wretched creature, thinner at each end than it was at the other.'" Sheila looked up from the letter and frowned. "Thinner at each end than it was at the other? This is gibberish."

"It'll be him, dear. It'll be that Lewis Carroll writing under a pseudo-name or some such."

"'But I digress.),' it continues. 'This most brief example of the absolutely briefest variety of note merely conveys my regret (*very* sincere!) that I fear I shall be unable to keep our appointment tomorrow. I have a young lady by the name of Agnes Hull paying me a visit and I must give her my fullest attention. Perhaps we may arrange a new time and date for your sitting. Your loving friend, C. L. Dodgson.'"

"Hmmm," said Mrs. Braithwaite enigmatically.

Sheila refolded the letter and returned it to the envelope. "I wonder what he meant by sitting."

Mrs. Braithwaite picked up the box and returned its lid. "If it *is* that Lewis Carroll fellow, then I seem to recall he rather liked to paint young girls, or some suchlike. Not natural." She placed the shoebox on the bed and dusted her hands on her apron front.

Sheila had picked up another envelope from which she removed a small square of paper. "This one's written in a circle," she said, turning the paper round and round as she read it. " 'They roused him with muffins—they roused him with ice—they roused him with mustard and cress—they roused him with jam and judicious advice—they set him conundrums to guess.' This one is signed by Lewis Carroll . . . and it's the same writing."

Mrs. Braithwaite grunted, clearly unimpressed. "Doesn't make much sense, does it, dear? *Who* did they raise? And who are *they*? It doesn't make any sense at all. I couldn't see it if it did."

"It's got 'The Hunting of the Snark' in brackets at the bottom of the page. I've *heard* of that," Sheila said.

"Well, that's enough excitement for me." The old woman began to shuffle to the door. "Time to put the kettle on, I'm thinking. Have a nice cup of tea before you settle in."

"What did you mean by a mystery?"

Mrs. Braithwaite had already started down the stairs. "Mystery?"

"You said that the girl—Verity—had disappeared and that it was a mystery."

"I did, didn't I? Let's get ourselves a cup of tea and I'll tell you all about it." Reaching the bottom of the stairs, the old woman turned around and looked back up at Sheila. "I take it you'll be taking the room, then?"

"Oh, yes. I love it here."

"Good, dear," Mrs. Braithwaite said. "That's good." She shuffled along the hall and disappeared into the kitchen, humming quietly.

Sheila breathed in deeply and held the breath, a deep feeling of contentment and satisfaction welling inside her. She stepped back into the room and spun around once, hugging herself. Then she slid the shoebox into her bedside cabinet and went downstairs.

"And if it hadn't been for the spider . . ." Sheila's voice trailed off as she put down her glass and got to her feet. "I'm not kidding, its legs were *this* big"—she held her two index fingers out about four inches apart—"but I think it was even more scared of me than I was of it. When it ran off, it seemed to be crouched down—almost running on its knees, if spiders have knees—and with its eyes closed and neck tensed. Like this . . ." She hunched up her shoulders and ran across the pub with her knees bowed.

Henry and Marianne laughed out loud.

"They must be worth an absolute fortune," William said as he rummaged through the envelopes on the pub table.

Sheila returned to the table, ignoring the strange looks she was getting from the people at the bar. "You weren't watching," she said petulantly.

"Oh, sorry. It's just . . ." He shook his head and gestured with his hands at the spread-out envelopes. "It's just *these*. I mean, they're a part of history."

"How'd you come to find the place, anyway?" Marianne said as she fished the piece of lemon out of her tonic water.

"My mother. She saw an ad in the local Guildford free paper. She's had a friend sending copies for . . . God, years it seems like."

"Mummy dudn't vanna lickule girl to get—Oww!" Henry rubbed his arm where Sheila had punched him. "That hurt."

Sheila smiled. "Good."

"What are you going to do with them?"

Sheila frowned at William. "Do with them?"

"Yeah, you know. Are you going to sell them?"

"They're not mine to sell. Mrs. Braithwaite doesn't even know I've taken them out of the house."

Henry loudly drained the last remnants of beer from his glass and set it on the table, partly covering one of the envelopes. "She didn't even know they existed before this afternoon."

Marianne nodded enthusiastically. "Yes, and she doesn't know how many there are. She wouldn't miss a couple."

Sheila looked amazed. "I can't believe I'm hearing this." She scrabbled the envelopes together. "Oh, God, you've made a mark on this one," she said to Henry, pointing at a beery ring that partly obliterated Verity Lansdale's name on one of the envelopes.

William watched her stack the envelopes neatly and place them in her shoulder bag. "So, these other things. What are they like?"

"Oh, just a bottle and a few pieces of paper all scrumpled up. Nothing much."

Henry pulled on his jacket and zipped it up. "What's in the bottle? If it's booze, then maybe you should ask us round for a housewarming."

"If it's booze, then it wouldn't have got the spider drunk," Sheila said. "Anyway, I haven't been able to open it."

Henry slapped his knees with his hands. "We off?"

"Yeah, I'm ready," William said.

Marianne said, "So what was the mystery?"

"Oh, yes," Sheila said, enjoying being the center of attention. "The mystery."

Henry scowled. "This is getting to sound more and more like an Enid Blyton book."

Marianne sniggered. "Yeah, *Five Get Literary in Guildford*."

They all laughed.

"Well," Sheila began, "it turns out that the Lansdales stopped little Verity from seeing Dodgson any more. Seems he had a thing for seeing her without her clothes on."

"Dodgson: that's Lewis Carroll, right?"

Sheila nodded to Henry.

"How old was Verity?" William asked.

"About eight years old, Mrs. Braithwaite says. Apparently he had her sit for him without any clothes on, and fed her cake and lemonade while he photographed her. Anyway, one day, they caught him at it."

"At it? You mean—"

"No, Henry, not *at* it. There was never any suggestion of anything . . . well, anything *wrong* happening. They just weren't comfortable with having their daughter pose for him in the nude."

" 'They' being Verity's parents?"

"Right," said Sheila. "So, they stopped him from seeing her. The story then gets a bit hazy. It seems that Dodgson called around at the house a few times when he was up in Guildford: he also spent a lot of time by the coast, at Eastbourne, and at Oxford of course. He told them that he hadn't finished."

Marianne frowned. "The photograph? How could he do a photograph in stages?"

Sheila shrugged. "He told them that they didn't understand. He told them that Verity was special—well, of course, she was special to her parents, which is why they stopped him from seeing her. Then she disappeared."

It was William who broke the silence that followed. "He had already had problems before that, you know."

The others turned to William, mocking amazement at his sudden display of knowledge.

"Yeah, I read up on him years ago—for 'A' levels. I was doing an essay on nonsense-writing. Turns out that Dodgson wanted to marry Alice."

Marianne looked astonished. "She really existed?"

William nodded. "Alice Liddell. He asked her parents—and get this: her father was dean of one of the Oxford colleges, no less. He asked them if he could marry her when she got older. He was in his early thirties then, and Alice was about twenty years younger. Needless to say, they didn't go a bundle on the idea and he was banned from seeing her again. This was . . . in the eighteen sixties, I think."

"Was there any suggestion of . . ."

"No, at least I don't think so. You have to remember that photographing children in the nude was a very Victorian thing."

They waited for more, but William had settled back in his chair.

Henry turned to Sheila and said, "*I* remember some of this."

Marianne laughed. "You! But . . . well, you're a boffin—smoking test tubes and everything."

"Yeah, I know, I know. But I studied applied mathematics, and Dodgson wrote a very influential book on logic—*Symbolic Logic*, I think it was called. It's still referred to today. He had this whim, I remember. Something about Christ Church—"

"That was the college where Alice's father was dean," William suddenly interrupted.

"Right. That's right," Henry said. "Well, Dodgson said that it took the sun five minutes to move from Greenwich, where world time was measured, to Oxford. Therefore the cathedral clock would say nine-oh-five when your watch said nine o'clock."

"Fascinating," Marianne said as she reached over and lifted Henry's hair from his ears. "I'm just checking to see if they're pointed."

Henry smoothed his hair back. "There *is* a logic there. I read a book once, *An Eternal Golden Braid* by Douglas R. Hofstadter—it was discussing the mathematical background to the work of Gödel, Escher and Bach; its tag line was 'A metaphorical fugue on minds and machines in the spirit of Lewis Carroll.' And—"

"Well, this is all more than I can take," Marianne said, standing up. "I'm definitely going."

As they left the pub, Sheila felt the first gnawing pangs of apprehension, though she had no idea why.

*   *   *

Charles Dickens declared Guildford's High Street to be the most beautiful in the kingdom.

Even now, more than a century after Dickens's death, Sheila sensed the history of the narrow pavements and gently cambered tarmac. She felt a wave of strangeness mingled with security, a race-memory perhaps of the way things truly were once upon a time. Maybe this was why High Street was frequently referred to as the Street of a Thousand Years. Or maybe it was just the night making her feel so thoughtful, cold and autumnal, sending leaves from age-old copses scudding along beneath the still-lighted shop windows like discarded sweet-papers.

She stood watching the taillights of William's old VW Beetle disappear around the far corner onto Stag Hill and listened patiently for the soft soughing of the gentle wind to drown out the fading motor. Then she was alone.

Alone with the street.

All of Guildford's ancient places clustered around High Street, rolling up and down like Time itself. Sheila drank them in like the finest wine, savoring their musty aftertaste of nostalgia and mystery.

At the top stood the fine 16th century grammar school, the 16th century hospital and the 18th century church. Halfway down, the 16th century clock of one of the quaintest guildhalls left in England hung out, elongated above the street like a precision-made gargoyle, silently watching for someone to pass beneath. Beyond it, the Saxon tower of St. Mary's and, at the bottom, the 19th century tower of St. Nicolas. Up above, on a hill on each side of the river Wey, sadly invisible in the late-night air, stood Guildford's ruined walls, the great walls of the castle and the small walls of St. Catherine's Chapel, each looking down on the Hog's Back stretching out to Farnham, with Pewley Hill and the old semaphore tower, and the great height crowned by St. Martha's Chapel on the Pilgrim's Way.

The chapel's fine red brick turrets and charming chimneys

had an almost guilty look about them, as though they were poised, caught red-handed in the act of reaching their gnarled and weatherworn countenances for the gray clouds that sped playfully across the moon's face.

Sheila pulled her jacket tight and set off along Dalby Walk, leaving the reassuring glare of commerce behind her and striding ever deeper into the history of the town. When she reached Mrs. Braithwaite's house, she stopped. Save for the flickering glow of the fire, there were no lights showing from the windows.

She frowned and checked her watch: a little after ten o'clock, surely too early even for Mrs. Braithwaite to retire to bed. But then, she was an old lady. Sheila started to walk again. But wouldn't she have left a light shining for her new tenant? She paused again, across the road from the house, and stared into the gloom. Had she seen something in the downstairs window, a shadow standing behind the window facing onto the street?

Staring only made the darkness darker, in much the same way as straining to hear a faint sound magnifies the silence that surrounds it. She shivered and blinked twice, trying to scare away the tiny spicules of light-dust that seemed to waft in front of her eyes. She thrust her hand into her jeans pocket and pulled out the key fastened to an old, worn cotton-bobbin. It felt good to get it out of her pocket.

Sheila checked the empty street, giving a quick glance behind, and started across. As she reached the door, the wind picked up and blew her hair around her face like a veil. She inserted the key gently into the lock and turned, marveling at the heavy sound of tumblers turning like those—she imagined—of an ancient castle dungeon.

The door opened easily without any sound, and she stepped inside to the warmth and the lingering smell of old toast and old people, a potpourri of heat and mothballs. As she pushed the door shut behind her, Sheila heard a sound. She held the door a few inches from the jamb and listened.

It sounded like someone giggling, tiny whispers and sharp intakes of breath.

She cocked her head to one side. The sound was coming from the living-room door at the foot of the stairs that led to her room. Mrs. Braithwaite. It must be. But who did she have with her at this time? And why were they in the dark?

Sheila tiptoed to the door, placed her head against the wood and listened. It was definitely whispering that she could hear, though by whom she could not make out. She looked down at the door handle, silently dreading it turning suddenly and someone stepping out into the hallway. As she looked, she saw the faintest of flickers coming through the keyhole. Sheila bent down and put her eye to the keyhole and then stood up again sharply.

Mrs. Braithwaite was standing just in front of the door and to the right of the fire's tired glow, which etched her in dull oranges and ruddy pinks. Her face was smiling at the keyhole, as though she knew that Sheila was watching, and she had something in her hand. Sheila could make it out perfectly: it was the big spider she had seen run across the upstairs floor, lying on its bulbous, furry back, kicking its seemingly myriad legs in the air in gay abandon as the old woman tickled its belly with a spindly, crooked finger. Rising from the lower part of the spider was a barbed appendage that seemed to be quivering, while, from the sides of the old woman's hand, Sheila could see blackness dripping in long, gossamer strings.

Sheila backed away from the door towards the staircase, kicking an old, metal umbrella stand on the way. She stopped immediately and looked down at what had caused the knock, noting as she did—in the very same way that they often did in the films—the umbrella-stand spiraling round and round on its base, seemingly in slow motion, its revolutions widening as its neck toppled further over, reaching for the polished floor that ran beside the hall carpet, getting nearer as she thought about reaching down, quickly, and steadying it, until, suddenly, it flipped over and clattered against the floorboards and the baseboard that traveled along the foot of all the walls in the house.

It sounded like a clarion call, the loudest burglar alarm she had ever heard, cutting through the stillness like a rusty knife, leaving thin traces of itself in the echoing silence that followed it.

Sheila lifted her hand to her throat and waited.

There was a sound of movement in the living room, the sound of something coming to the door. She thought, as the door handle began to turn, that she heard a dull thud and a faint *yelp!*—followed by a hissed instruction—but she could have been wrong. And then, amid the bright glare of electric light, Mrs. Braithwaite appeared in the hallway, rubbing her hands on her apron. When she took her hands away, a black stain remained, glistening in the light.

"Hello? Is that you, dear?" the old woman said.

"Ye—yes," Sheila replied, trying to keep the front door near to her. She couldn't help staring at the mark on the old woman's apron, though, for some reason she could not explain, it made her heart ache to do so.

Mrs. Braithwaite reached up her hand to the hallway light switch and flicked it on, bathing the hall in a comforting whiteness that stretched all the way to the distant kitchen which lay beyond the dining-room and cellar doors at the far end of the hall. Propped up against the kitchen door was a large axe.

"Well, I declare! Asleep. Sound asleep like a baby I was," she said. "And here you are wanting a nice cup of tea." Mrs. Braithwaite started towards Sheila, smiling widely. As she reached her, Sheila stepped to the side and towards the bottom of the stairs.

"Whatever's the matter, dear?" The old woman reached out and lifted two keys from a hook on the wall beside the door. One of the keys was like the one that Sheila had; the other, a large and cumbersome key the likes of which would usually be expected to open a garden shed, was not. Mrs. Braithwaite slipped the keys into two locks and turned them energetically. Then, smiling at

255

Sheila, she removed them and dropped them into the pouchlike front pocket of her wraparound apron. "Don't tell me you're the worse for drink."

"N—no," Sheila stammered, wondering why she had not noticed the second lock when Mrs. Braithwaite had given her a personal key just a few hours earlier. "I just kicked the—"

"Bucket? Did you kick the bucket, dear?" The smile broadened into something resembling a grimace and then faltered. Around a throaty chuckle, Mrs. Braithwaite said, "Surely not . . . not yet, anyway, eh, dear? You're only a *child*." The final word dripped with venom.

Sheila turned around and started up the stairs. "I'm going to turn in," she said, trying to sound as though she was tired.

"Would you like me to bring you up a nice cup of tea?"

"No. No, thank you. I'm going to turn in."

"As you wish, dear. Goodnight."

" 'Night."

Sheila reached the top of the stairs, opened her door and slipped into the room. As she started to close the door, the downstairs hall light clicked off and the darkness returned.

Sheila closed her door fully and, turning around, slumped against it. There had been something strange about the old landlady, something that Sheila found quite disturbing but which she could not quite put her finger on. She flicked on the light and stared around the room.

She had half-expected the place to be different . . . ransacked maybe, as though the old woman had been up here while she had been out, but everything looked the way it had been before she left for the pub. Sheila stepped away from the door and dropped her bag onto the bed. Then she flopped onto a nearby chair and rubbed her face with both hands.

What *was* the matter with her?

Sheila got to her feet and shrugged off her jacket. As she did so, she noticed that the piece of wood she had dislodged earlier had been jammed back into place. So Mrs. Braithwaite *had* been up here while she was out. But then, why shouldn't she? After all, this was her house. And Sheila had broken the wall, so why shouldn't the old woman take advantage of her guest's absence to restore the wall to its former glory?

No reason. In fact, it made eminent good sense.

She knelt down by the replaced boarding and tapped it gently. It seemed firm enough. Then, as she was running her finger along where the board met the rest of the wall, the board slipped down slightly before dropping to the floor with a dull clunk. Sheila looked inside.

The space behind the wall seemed to stretch back a long way, though quite how far she couldn't tell. It was pitch black in there. She needed light.

Sheila stood up and walked across to the bed. She unplugged the small lamp on the bedside table and carried it across to the exposed hole in the wall. At first she thought it had all been in vain and that there was no nearby socket, but then she spied the telltale switch pad on the woodwork beside the door, only a couple of feet away. She inserted the plug and switched on the lamp.

The light shone bright, even though the bulb was undoubtedly of a low wattage. It lit the floor directly inside the wall immediately, even without Sheila planting the lamp into the hole. She stared at the floor beyond the wall and frowned. That was the spot where they had found the box. Sheila continued to stare at it, moving her eyes slowly across the floorboards . . . the *dusty* floorboards, and something gnawed at her: where was the dust-free space that marked where the box had lain?

She leaned closer, almost into the hole, holding the lamp near. There *was* no dust-free area. That meant . . . What *did* that mean? Trying to think, Sheila turned slightly to her left and saw a shoe lying on its side.

Behind the shoe was a stockinged foot. She recognized it almost immediately.

"Mrs. . . . Braithwaite?"

Sheila spoke the words quietly, as though to speak too loudly might disturb the old woman. But what was she doing here, behind the wall, lying so still?

Sheila brought the lamp closer, its light aura spreading into the crawl space behind the wall, a crawl space, she saw now, that seemed to extend into the immeasurable distance, littered with pieces of brick and small lumps of hardened cement, far beyond where the outer wall of the house should be.

She reached in and took hold of the foot, feeling the coldness of it, and shook it gently. "Mrs. Braithwaite?"

"She can't hear you."

The voice sounded tiny, as though it were coming from somewhere far away, carried on a friendly wind into the darkness behind Sheila's room wall. Sheila pulled her hand back and shuffled away from the hole.

"She can't hear you because she's dead," the voice went on. "The Queen killed her."

She heard a shuffling sound, a sound of small movement—a mouse, she thought at first. A talking *mouse*? The truth was, perhaps, even stranger.

A tiny figure stood up from behind a piece of brick just a few feet into the darkness.

Sheila shook her head.

"I know, I know. It can't be happening to you. But it is." The man stepped fully into the light.

He was no more than six inches high but otherwise looked entirely normal. He wore a frilly shirt, tight leggings—they looked like ski pants but, somehow, Sheila knew they weren't—and buckled shoes.

"Who . . . who *are* you?"

The little man held his hand out towards Sheila and smiled. "I'm Emmett," he said, "Emmett Dodgson."

"Dodgson? Like—"

"He was my father."

Sheila sat backwards with a thud. "I think . . . I think I'm—"

The man dropped his extended arm to his side with a shrug and stepped over the wooden rim of the wall, slapping his trousers to send small flurries of dust wafting into the light. "No, you're not going mad. Listen . . ."

And the little man told Sheila a story.

"There are worlds within worlds," he began, in a voice that was just slower than an insect's hum but faster and higher in pitch than regular speech. "And worlds within even *those* worlds. The world of Wonderland—as well as those of Heaven and Neverland and Valhalla and El Dorado and Narnia and—" (he mentioned many more that Sheila had not even heard of) "—they all exist just off the shores of your own plane, like floating islands filled with alternatives. They're not necessarily better or even worse than your world," the little man went on, "only different."

Quite *why* Sheila listened, she could not have said. The man's story and his way of telling it filled her head and spilled out of her ears into the room itself, washing up to the walls in waves of words and sound, lapping gently at the edges of her skepticism and slowly eroding it away. She was suddenly aware of the fragile sanctity of her room, and of the shadows leaning in towards her as though listening along with her to the small man's tale.

He told her of his father's fanaticism with mathematics and of how, using a particularly pure brand of quantum mechanics, he proved—at least on paper—the existence of these secondary realities. He told her of how, after many failed attempts, his father had determined that the only way in was through innocence. Thus had he embarked on his controversial secondary career of photographing young girls.

At first, this too had failed to open the way. And yet, the equations—whole walls of them surrounding his books and meager accommodations at Oxford—were indisputable. His subjects were entirely free of corruption, even the most minuscule and infinitesimal transgressions: thus the answer had to be in the clothes. "Perhaps it was their flounces of cotton and lace," the little man said, pretending he was his own father, stroking his chin with feigned consideration as he waved his other arm expansively. "Of wool made from sheep's coats and shoes made from cattle . . . perhaps all of these were clouding the portals of beyond."

And so it was that the late Mr. Dodgson had suggested that his "models" remove their outer garments.

"The result was by no means immediate," Emmett Dodgson said. "But, after a while, and with all the patience that a true scientist may bring to bear, a breakthrough was achieved."

"Was this . . ." Sheila's voice sounded very loud after the gentle timbre of her guest, and she lowered her voice to a whisper. "Was this the rabbit hole?"

"What? Oh, no. It was a piece of loose slate beside a rain barrel in Oxford. But my father wrote it up as the rabbit hole."

"Was Alice there, the *real* Alice?"

The man nodded. "But she did not know or, at least, she did not remember. In every woman there is a gateway. Picture it as a weed-festooned gate, an overgrown path leading to unlimited beauty beyond. The way through from the other side is clear, and those who live there may travel relatively freely into your world."

"You mean, like . . . fairies?"

He nodded, hoisting himself onto the board rim and crossing his legs. "Fairies and shades . . . and children."

"Children? I don't—"

"Babies. That's where babies really come from. That's what I meant by every woman having a gateway. Babies and children are the only magic that exists in your world, and even those are—how would you say? Imported?" He waved his hand dismissively. "Anyway, it's very complicated and we don't have the time to go into it here. Suffice to say that my father discovered the way through from your side, and he discovered it in Alice Liddell."

"But then he was prevented from seeing her."

"Correct. One could not fault the decision made by Alice's parents but, nevertheless, it set him back considerably in his work. But then he found another."

Sheila's brain was beginning to creak under the pressure of what she was hearing . . . what she was *thinking*. "Was that . . ." The shadows seemed to lean in closer to hear the words so softly spoken. "Was that Verity Lansdale?"

Emmett Dodgson nodded. "My mother," he said.

"But how could that be? Verity Lansdale disappeared in eighteen eighty-something while Dodgson—your father, you say—died here on—" She considered saying "Earth" but then thought better of it and simply repeated "here."

"Yes. That is true. My father died of pneumonia here, in Guildford, in 1898. That's when he passed over."

"Passed over?"

"To the other side. I told you that all the alternative worlds exist there. It's a simple matter to move from one to another. The only difficulty is moving from here to there. The one, shall we say "tried and trusted," method is to die. But my father discovered another way, the way into Wonderland." He paused for a moment. "There are other routes, so I am told: a doorway in a wardrobe and riding a tornado-wind are but two of them."

"And your father's way . . . how was that achieved? Was it simply by photographing little girls without any clothes on?"

"It's far too complex for me to attempt a full explanation here. But, yes, the gateway opened through a mixture of innocence and technology . . . of ignorance and knowledge: the unspoiled child and the camera—contrary to some popular beliefs, the camera *will* record things that the human eye can miss."

Sheila considered all that the little man had said and, as she did so, she realized that he had said very little. Why did she feel so calm? She gave out a nervous chuckle. "There's a dead body in my—wait a minute. If that's Mrs. Braithwaite in there, then who is it downstairs?"

261

"That, I am afraid to say, is the Queen."

"The Queen? The Queen of where? Of Wonderland?"

"Of Hearts," he answered.

Sheila frowned and then leaned into the hole in the boarding. She could make out the full length of the body as it lay crumpled against the boards to her left. She suddenly realized that she could see the woman's—Mrs. Braithwaite's—legs, and her torso all the way up to her shoulders but then, where its head should be, the body was jammed against the wood.

"Oh, God!"

"Stay calm," said the little man.

Sheila jerked her head back and knocked it against the wood above her. "Oh, God . . . her head is—"

"The Queen took it."

"Why?"

Emmett Dodgson shrugged. "She likes heads. They contain feelings and thoughts and ideas. She has none of these. She merely reacts to situations, she never considers alternative paths or solutions. The Queen of Hearts is . . ." His voice trailed off as he searched for the right words. "She's quite mad, I'm afraid."

"None of this makes any sense."

"Sense, nonsense; right, wrong; who can say what is what? It simply is, that's all. The Queen is here. She set up the box of letters for you to find—you or somebody like you."

"Why me?"

He shrugged.

"Will you stop shrugging all the time and give me a straight answer?" Sheila snapped.

"There *are* no straight answers. The Queen has been searching for the pathway into your world for a long time. The pathway fluctuates with the sun and the stars and the seasons. It has more than one route but it is only one path, and—"

"For goodness—"

"*And* it will always be near to this house . . . my *mother*'s house." The man's voice cracked a little.

Sheila watched his face and saw Emmett Dodgson's eyes mist over. "Your mother's house. Then, how did the Queen—"

"She killed my mother. She stole her heart and her head and fished out all the knowledge and the information with a black, three-pronged spoon she keeps in her pants. Then she found the way and crawled across the dividers into the barren no-man's-land that surrounds your world and separates it from all the others. She left the box of my mother's letters and sent one of her slaves ahead to cause you to find them."

"Her slaves? Was that the spider?"

"It was a *hatojan* spider. His name is D'Rango and he is her mate."

"What's *hatojan* mean?"

"Hatred. The *hatojan* spiders live on the very edges of Wonderland, forever listening to the waves of the Blue Sea of Aspiration wash on the Beach of Blissful Realisation. They live in the crusty rocks that lie between the two, doomed to be aware of hope and of achievement but never to experience either. It makes them the bitterest creatures in the universe."

Sheila shook her head slowly side to side without even realizing she was doing it. "I saw its . . ." Sheila felt herself blush. "I saw its, you know . . . its penis."

"When?"

"When I came home. I sneaked a look through the keyhole and she was tickling the thing's tummy. The . . . the appendage was sticking up in the air like a flagpole."

"You probably interrupted her hatemaking."

"Hatemaking?"

"Yes. Where humans make love, the Queen and her spider-slave make hatred. The sperm of the *hatojan* spiders is a black emptiness. It has long been cast by the Queen into the void between our worlds. Most of it drifts on the winds and settles on your plane like fine dust. Some of it collects far out in space. You have a word for it: despair."

"I saw it on her apron. It made me sad to look at it."

The little man said nothing.

"But, if the spider is her mate, what of the King?"

"The King died many years ago. That was after he interfered and protected Alice Liddell from her. He told her that Alice was only a child."

Sheila remembered the venomous way the old woman had referred to *her* as being only a child. "She killed her own husband?" Sheila asked, shuddering.

"Not really," Dodgson answered. "She removed his skin and pulled out all of his intestines without severing them in any way. Then she kept him on a silver salver covered by a bell jar for all to see what might befall them if they betrayed her. The King lived for several years before simply giving up."

"And this woman is *here, downstairs?*"

Emmett Dodgson nodded apologetically. "I'm sorry," he said. "This is one occasion when something *very* nasty has crawled out of the woodwork."

"What does she want?"

As the little man began to answer, Sheila heard a soft creak from somewhere beyond her door. Someone was coming up the stairs. "She wants to feed on your goodness," he said, glancing across at the door. "And here she comes now."

"What do we do?" Sheila whispered.

Emmett Dodgson jumped from the boarding. "Where is the box? The box containing my mother's letters?"

Sheila got to her feet quietly and moved across the room to the little cabinet beside her bed. She opened the door—grimacing at the sharp click of the ball-bearing latch—and stared inside. For a second, she thought that Mrs. Braithwaite (should she still be referring to the thing downstairs as Mrs. Braithwaite?) might have removed it but, no, it was still there, pushed to the back where she had left it.

"Here," she said, turning around.

Emmett Dodgson ran soundlessly across the room. "Open it!" he hissed, looking over his shoulder toward the door.

Sheila removed the lid. Everything was still there: the letters—save for the few she had taken with her to the pub—and the bottle and the crumpled paper. "Now what?"

"Put it down on the floor."

Sheila did as she was told.

There was the unmistakable sound of movement, a presence, outside her door. "Are you asleep, dear?" the old woman said, her voice drifting into the room like an icy draught, accompanied by the faraway cracking of icicles that Sheila knew in an instant was the sound of her fingernails running across the panels in the door.

The little man pulled himself over the rim of the box and, balancing his armpits on the edge, rummaged in the crumpled paper. After a few seconds he pulled something out of the mess and slid back onto the floor.

"What on earth is it?" Sheila asked, staring at what looked for all the world like a piece of moldy biscuit.

"A biscuit," he replied, his voice quivering with wonder. "It's still here." He held the piece aloft as though it were some magnificent relic of a bygone race, and then, slowly, brought it down and held it out towards Sheila. "Eat it," he said.

"*Eat* it? You have got to be—"

The handle on the door started to creak.

"Eat it," he said again, thrusting the biscuit forward.

Sheila reached down and lifted the biscuit from his hands. "Then what happens?"

Emmett Dodgson had already turned away and was running back to the hole in the wall. "You grow," he said.

Sheila glanced at the door and saw it slowly begin to open.

She shook her head and, lifting the biscuit to her mouth, took a small bite.

The door suddenly burst open and the old woman stepped triumphantly into the room. On her head, she wore a battered red-and-yellow pillbox hat, and her dress was the frayed edges of a playing card, splattered with heart-shapes, the back of which rose up, creased and buckled, behind her. In her hands she carried the long-handled axe.

For a second—though it seemed like an hour, an endless time during which the woman stared at the empty bed and then at Sheila—nothing seemed to happen. Then Sheila felt her stomach rumble and the old woman seemed to start shrinking, stepping back towards the door.

But the woman wasn't shrinking; Sheila was *growing*.

Just a little at first and then, step by step, she felt herself beginning to bulge. She dropped to her knees by the side of the bed and clutched her stomach, horrified to see that her hands covered her entire torso from her neck to her groin. Then, a sharp pain in her midriff, and her stomach distended, ripping the beige blouse— the one that her mother had given her for her eighteenth birthday—right down the middle. "Oh . . . oh, God . . . it *hurts*!" she shouted, the words deafening her.

The old woman stepped back, knocking the door closed behind her, as Sheila slumped forward. A sudden brief pain in her feet subsided when the shoes she was wearing split apart.

She threw out her hand and cracked the wall plaster across the room (suddenly so much closer . . .) with her clenched fist, groaning in agony. "Oh, make it stop!"

Soon her backside touched the exposed beams of the old ceiling, pressing against them so hard that Sheila felt splinters of wood pierce her bottom and the backs of her thighs.

The strap of her brassiere snapped, twanging painfully against her side as her breasts bulged outwards; her jeans ripped along the seams, falling apart in wide flaps, while the zipper crunched and the metal fastener clattered against the chest of drawers at the side of the room as though it had been shot out of a gun.

Sheila was filling the whole room now, buckling over as more and more of her body touched different walls, forcing them outwards into the cold night and the reality that she dimly believed still existed beyond Mrs. Braithwaite's house. Somewhere far away, she could hear the sound of glass breaking.

"For Christ's sake, make it *stop*," Sheila screamed, her face only inches from the old woman. She lunged forward again as another wave of pain assaulted her chest, placing her right hand just in front of the old woman.

Seizing the opportunity, the woman jumped onto Sheila's hand and, swinging back with both hands, brought the axe down into the knuckles.

"Oh—" Sheila pulled the hand back in pain and promptly fell forward with her head against the door. The old woman fell to the floor in a heap. "My . . . my hand."

"Off with it," the old woman hissed. It was a cross between hatred and laughter. She pulled herself into a sitting position and then started to lift herself from the floor, the axe still dangling from her hand.

Sheila twisted herself around so that she could move her left arm, which was pinned against the boarding at the side of the room.

"H . . . here!" A little voice, smaller than a mouse's squeak, brayed urgently beside Sheila's ear. She turned her head slightly and saw Emmett Dodgson staggering towards her carrying the bottle from the shoebox. It was slightly less than half of his own size and he was clearly having great difficulty in handling the thing. Sheila pulled her left arm forward so that the hand lay open in front of the man.

"What do I do with it?" she said.

The old woman, having staggered to her feet, was immediately bowled over just as she was hefting the axe to take another strike at Sheila's damaged right hand.

Dodgson dropped the bottle into her hand and stood up, puffing. "Feed it to her," he said.

Sheila moved her head slightly to see what the woman was doing.

She was lying crumpled against the door, one leg trapped between the door frame and Sheila's right shoulder. Sheila dragged her left hand, still holding the bottle, up to her mouth and inserted the bottle cap between her teeth. Then she twisted the bottle.

It opened immediately.

Sheila twisted frantically until the cap was completely free and then she spat it onto the floor. Seconds later, amid much grunting and sighing, she had somehow managed to transfer the bottle to her right hand. As the old woman started to get to her feet again, Sheila jammed her left arm up under her own chest and took hold of the woman's head.

"Don't you *dare* touch me," she shouted. "How *dare* you touch me!"

"*Feed* it to her!" Emmett Dodgson shouted.

Sheila pressed the woman's head—now some three or four times smaller than her own hand—against the floor and jammed her index finger into her mouth.

"Horchh*dare*youuch—"

"*Now!*" screamed the little man.

Sheila thrust her left hand forward, wincing at the sharp pain in her shoulder, and tipped the bottle into the old woman's open mouth. She watched the liquid run out, a thick linctus that rolled along the bottle's side and dripped in congealed lumps around her index finger, now the size of a medium-width tree trunk. The woman gagged, coughed once and then swallowed, shaking her head desperately. Sheila withdrew her finger and pulled back her hand.

Almost immediately, the woman's head seemed to implode

like a waxwork effigy, the skin drawing in upon itself. Now coughing harshly, she spat repeatedly, trying to disgorge as much of the
liquid as possible. But it was too late.

Even as she watched, Sheila felt a sudden movement by her
left hip and a sharp stab of pain in her thigh. She twisted her head
around as well as she could and looked along her left side. She was
now completely filling the room, cramped against the walls and
ceiling, with her left foot—she now saw—protruding from the
smashed window behind her bed.

She looked back and saw Emmett Dodgson standing beside
the withering form of the Queen of Hearts, who was now visibly
shrinking into her clothes, twisting and turning as though in great
pain. A cracking sound made Dodgson look up as parts of the
cracked roof rained down around Sheila's head.

"Drink the rest of the potion," he said. "Quickly."

Sheila tried to lift the bottle to her mouth, but her hand was
now bent double at the wrist against the room door, which, in turn,
was buckling out onto the staircase beyond. "I . . . I can't reach it
to—"

"You *must*," he said. "Try!"

Sheila forced her head against the floor, her nose jammed into
the old woman's clothes, which, aside from a slight twitching lump
in the center, lay still and flattened. She opened her mouth and
flicked the bottle over against her bottom lip. Then she tongued
the bottle neck into place, grasped it between both lips, and
tipped her head back. The bottle was the size of a thimble to her
now, and the contents—if there were any—were indiscernible
amid the taste and texture of her own saliva. But still she drew on
the liquid, sucking for all she was worth.

The floor gave out a large crack and lurched sideways, towards the window behind her, and the bottle fell from her mouth
and smashed onto the floor beside the old woman's clothes.

Suddenly, Sheila felt herself slipping and falling. It was a
strange and not entirely unpleasant sensation, a mixture of drifting

off to sleep and of waking up refreshed. There was no other way that she might explain it.

In a dreamlike haze, she saw Emmett Dodgson run across the old woman's now empty clothes back to the gaping hole in the woodwork. Behind him, a small pink thing, that seemed to mewl like a kitten, scurried from beneath the hem of the old woman's apron and followed as fast as its tiny legs could carry it. Then, also from beneath the apron, a black ball ran out and followed the pink thing. As it, too, disappeared into the crawl space, Sheila saw a shiny, black object resting amid the folds of the old woman's apron.

As she reached and grasped it, the walls of the room buckled in towards her, everything growing bigger quickly, rafters and beams falling as though in slow motion amid showers of mortar and brick and stone. A thick cloud of dust and rock fragments roiled out of the crawl space . . . along with one other object that tumbled over and over upon itself towards her: Mrs. Braithwaite's head. Then Sheila was through the window, shards of glass scraping at her arms and legs, and falling, falling endlessly through space until—

pain
sound
It was all around her; pain and sound.
Someone was shaking her shoulders, speaking to her.
Sheila opened her eyes.
"There you are! We thought we'd lost you, miss."
The policeman's smiling face was bathed in what seemed to be a stroboscopic red light. She shifted her head to the side and moaned in pain.
"Take it easy, take it easy," he said, placing a large but gentle hand beneath the side of her face.
She was lying in the street. Next to her, a police car's spinning red light sent its scarlet beam scudding across the houses opposite. She saw three or four people standing by the side of the road,

watching her. She turned her head slowly the other way and stared at the heap of rubble that was once Mrs. Braithwaite's cottage.

"The—the Queen . . ." Sheila tried to move, but the pain in her legs was too bad. "Mrs. Braithwaite . . ."

The policeman held her shoulders and made soothing noises, soft whispers. "The old woman didn't make it, miss," he said. "Looks like a piece of boarding took her . . . well, let's just say she didn't make it."

"Didn't make it?"

"There, you take it easy now. Ambulance'll be along in a minute. Best you don't try to move until it gets here."

"What . . . what happened?" Sheila asked.

The policeman knelt down beside her and placed a blanket beneath her head. Sheila suddenly noticed that another blanket had been wrapped around her body.

"Old property," he said, shrugging, as though that explained everything that had happened.

An explosion sounded amid the wreckage and a ball of flame erupted, quickly catching on the woodwork and spreading across the fallen masonry and torn beams.

The policeman shielded Sheila from the light by lying between her and what remained of the house. "That'll be the gas supply," he said, the words sounding almost casual.

Somewhere in the distance, Sheila heard the cawing sirens of fire engines and ambulances.

"I . . . I have to go back inside," Sheila said. "I have to—" She stopped. There was something in her hand.

"You won't be going anywhere, miss. Not for a while." He pushed back his helmet with his free hand. "Nothing to go back in there *for*, anyway. It's all gone."

Sheila lifted her hand from beneath the blanket and stared at the spoon, marveling at its sharp, polished tines. "The runcible spoon," she said.

"Miss?"

She closed her hand around the spoon and shook her head. "Nothing," she said.

Sheila watched the fire lick the remains of the house and remembered sitting with her grandmother all those years—a lifetime?—ago, staring into the dying embers of her grandparents' ever-present coal fire. Her grandmother, all white hair and pink skin that smelled of lavender, would point to the flames and tell her they were the fairies in the fire.

Where do they go, Sheila would ask, *when the fire dies away?*

Why, to fairyland, her grandmother would explain, *to rest until they're needed again.*

Will they come back?

"Miss?" The policeman shook her. "Miss?"

Sheila opened her eyes and smiled at him. "They always come when you most need them," she said, remembering her grandmother's words.

The policeman turned to watch the ambulance pull up with a squeal of tires. "That they do, miss," he said. "That they do."

> *The pictures, with their ruddy light,*
> *Are changed to dust and ashes white,*
> *And I am left alone with night.*

From *Faces in the Fire*
Lewis Carroll, January 1860

FOR HANNAH BOWLING, 1892–1960

A Pig's Tale

Esther M. Friesner

⤫ ⤫

After he escaped from Alice's clutches, the first thing the piglet did was to rub that annoying baby bonnet off his head against the bole of a tree. Free at last, he clipped through the dark woodland as fast as four trim little trotters would carry him. He was not a very big piglet at first, but the Wonderland wood was as full of acorns and beech mast as any other, and the piglet had an inherent knack for knowing which mushrooms were good to eat and which were someone's idea of a joke.

Time means nothing to a pig, as the old rouser goes, so it was no wonder (even for Wonderland) that for this little piggie the years did not pass but the meals did. At length there came a time when acorns were at a premium, and the woodland did not seem either so dark or so cozy. This was disquieting, to be sure. The misshapen birds and uncanny cats who haunted the leaf-strewn forest alleyways seemed—to a pig's perception, at least—to be fewer and farther between and occasionally beside themselves. Not good.

It was all rather sad, really. Pigs are as subject to free-floating anxiety attacks as humans, and since this pig had been human once (or as human as one could get, considering his environment) one fine afternoon he found himself plunged into the murkiest depths of Byronic *angst* and melancholia.

Byron really should have been a pig. (Lady Caroline Lamb said that he was, the minx.) It would have perked him up no end. For pigs possess a certain native intelligence and common sense by and large missing from our greater poets. When despair lays its clammy paws across their fevered porcine brows, they do not slump about composing sonnets; they take action.

The only action the pig could think of taking was to go home and see about things.

It was the first time in years he'd thought of Home and Hearth and Mother. He recalled the sounds of crashing crockery and clanging pots, the voices of women raised in strident quarrel. Pigs lack the proper dentition to pronounce the word "dysfunctional," so he went home anyhow.

Home was gone.

The pig stood in a little clearing, gazing at the ruins of what must have been a fairly pleasant little cottage in its day. He snorted and stamped his hoof, much put out by the thoughtless nature of Circumstance, which had so dared to discommode him. Then he decided to investigate more closely. Snuffling and rooting around the ruins filled his snout with the lingering odor of woodsmoke. Charred timbers protruding from a mishmash mess of broken furniture and other domestic effects were another surefire (indeed) indication that someone had not closed cover before striking.

Accidents happen. The pig was not unhappy, merely disappointed. It would have been nice to see his mother again, he fancied, for *nice* belonged to the same class of words as *interesting* and *we'll be in touch* and *your child has great potential*. It carries little meaning other than the vague sense that no one is going to be hit with anything heavy.

There being nothing else to do, he turned himself back into a boy.

It was in this state that the Mad Hatter found him. Or rather, he found the Hatter, who was, as ever, ensconced at the tea table. "Have some tea!" that worthy cried when the boy stepped out of the bushes.

The pig in boy's form—if not boy's clothing—said, "I'd rather have some britches."

It was a good thing that the Mad Hatter also dealt in miscellaneous haberdashery on the side. This revelation might have boggled Alice, but the pig accepted it as Q.E. very D. How else to explain the neatly tailored accoutrements of Wonderland's ill-sorted mob of zanies, beast and human? It wants a job of custom tailoring to fit a rabbit with a waistcoat or a frog with footman's livery. Accidents happen; clothing does not. Some people just don't stop to *think*; they're too busy swallowing nightmares whole.

Before long, the Hatter had the pig turned out in a dapper schoolboy style that would be the envy of any Eton scholar. "There!" he said, tying the lad's tie. "Now you're ready to leave."

"Leave?" the pig echoed. "But I just got here."

"Then it's past time you got out," the Hatter replied. "Save yourself, lad! It's too late for me, but save yourself while you can."

"Save myself from what?" the pig asked. A vase sailed across the sitting room of his memory and smashed against the far wall.

"Times," said the Hatter ponderously, "change."

"Am I to save myself from times or from change?" the pig inquired.

"Neither," the Hatter replied. "Both. Though always keeping a bit of change on hand to buy the *Times* is never a bad notion, Oh, bother it, lad, don't you see? They're *here*."

The pig glanced up and down the length of the Hatter's tea

table, taking in a panorama of stale cakes, crumbled crumpets, a shambles of old scones. "Roaches?" he suggested. "Ants?"

The Hatter clucked his tongue. "Don't waste your time talking, but *listen*." He then lapsed into silence.

No one practices patience better than a pig, but even so there are limits to the length of time one can sit at a cluttered tea table in company with an attested loony and listen to nothing. Pigs could not care less about Zen. The question needs must at last arise: "Listen to *what*?"

"To me, of course," said the Hatter.

"But you haven't said anything," the pig objected.

"Of course I've said *something*," the Hatter countered.

The pig sighed and picked up the largest cake knife he could get his hands on. He held this to the Hatter's throat and said, "Mother used to complain about you. If this is going to turn into another one of those word-swaps where you go on to say that you have, in the past, said something, I'm not the one to put up with it."

"Children today," the Hatter grumbled. But he eyed the cake knife askance and added, "Fine. I'll speak plainly. But it's not going to endear either one of us to generations of children yet to come."

The pig merely snorted. Then he snorted again, put out no end to learn that a boy's nose is physically unable to produce as loud and satisfying a snort as a pig's snout.

"You said *they're* here," said the pig. "Tell me who *they* are and you won't have to whistle through your windpipe."

"Analysts," said the Hatter.

"What?" The cake knife insistently pressed the wattled skin just above the Hatter's high collar and cravat.

"Analysts," the Hatter repeated. "Diggers after *meaning*, blast them all to an eternity of moldy jam and rancid butter. D'you remember Alice?"

"We met," the pig admitted.

"Well, she woke up, told tales out of school, bent the ear of a *mathematician*, no less. A nice young man, scared witless of women. He was devoted to the girl; most girls, until they reached the age of imperilment. Next thing anyone knew"—the Hatter shuddered—"text."

"I don't understand," said the pig, but he was courteous enough to set aside the cake knife and pour the Hatter a fresh cup of tea.

"I am a poet," the Hatter said, pressing a hand to his well-starched shirt bosom. "I don't get out much, nor keep up with any books other than the slim volume of verse I am even as we speak preparing for the printer's. But some folks rush their scribblings into print with indecent haste, as if they were brides already eight months gone with child. Alice's adventures were common fodder long before you took it into your head to walk on two legs again."

"You know who I am?" The pig cast a weather eye behind him, as best he was able, to see if perhaps his transformation had been incomplete. No corkscrew tail distorted the seat of his trousers. All was well.

It was the Hatter's turn to snort, and very well he did, too, even lacking a snout. "Of course I know, you clod! How could I avoid knowing?" He reached under a pile of dusty Banbury tarts and excavated a floury copy of Mr. Carroll's most beloved work. "It's all in the book."

The pig helped himself to the relic, paging through Alice's dream with the proper mixture of reverence and resentment that he had not merited longer mention. While he consulted the text, the Hatter grumbled on.

"The havoc he's wrought! The simple, homespun pandemonium! Oh, it was fine, at first—a book for children, harmless, charming. But then—*meddlers*! Not enough to occupy them, turning over every rock in their heads to see what hideous crawlies haunt the undersides, no! They must invade the nursery bookshelf and read, and read *into* everything they find."

The pig looked up from the book. He didn't understand much of what the Hatter was saying, but he dismissed it as madness. After all—! No need to have recourse to the cake knife. "Scone?" he suggested, passing the plate and pronouncing the word to almost rhyme with *done*.

"Yes, it is," said the Hatter, glancing at the plate. "Although I prefer to pronounce it so it rhymes more nearly with *alone*, which is what I have been ever since *they* invaded." He helped himself to sugar.

"The hare was the first to go," he told the swirling depths of his tea. "They called him a rampant pagan fertility symbol and he never got over it. So much to live up to, and he a Methodist bachelor! The dormouse, on the other hand, was a dream of the womb. How clearly I recall his words of farewell: 'When they can't tell Assam tea from amniotic fluid, it's time to move on,' he said."

"Have they all gone, then?" asked the pig. His gaze weighed the all-surrounding woodland. At the Hatter's words it seemed to have put on the bleak aspect of a deserted house, dust on the oak leaves, cobwebs veiling the bark of the walnut trees.

"The Queen of Hearts is still around," the Hatter said. "I see her sometimes when she stops by to drop off a platter of tarts and to ask me whether I've yet been able to find out what, precisely, a symbol of Woman as Castrating Bitch (capital w, capital c, capital b, no less) is supposed to *do* all day. *Noblesse oblige* and all that. She feels the responsibility. Responsibility for *what* remains the question. The King tells her it was just an idle compliment, but she's a stickler. The distraction has sweetened her temper no end. She's no fun anymore."

"At least it doesn't seem to have affected you," the pig offered by way of consolation.

"That's because I may be mad, but I'm not a weathercock. I've steadfastly refused to let them make me *mean* anything at all. Oh, they tried to have at me, lad, don't doubt it for a moment!" He waved a teaspoon in the pig's face. "I've been called everything from an icon of the ultimate tragedy of the Industrial Revolution to a fragment of embedded Masonic code. Do you know what you get when you rearrange the letters in the words *Mad Hatter*?"

"Nnnnno," the pig admitted with some reluctance.

"You get *Rhatemtad*, which some idiot decided was the name of a heretical Egyptian pharaoh of the Old Kingdom who did odd, un-Christian things with trowels and whose monuments were therefor suppressed." The Hatter's head fell forward heavily. "Get out, boy. There's nothing left for anyone here. They've stripped the flesh from the bones, sucked the blood and licked out the marrow."

"But where shall I get out *to*?" the pig asked.

"Their world. What else is there?" The Hatter sipped his tea morosely, then suddenly demanded, "Why is a raven like a writing desk?"

"Who cares?" the pig replied. "How do I get there from here?"

"With an answer like that, you're halfway there," said the Hatter. "Although the usual method of transportation is to wake up."

"Wake up? But I'm not even asleep," the pig said, pinching himself to make sure.

"Then *fall* asleep, you tollywug," the Hatter snapped. "And wake up in a better world than this. That's how the rest of 'em did it."

The pig thanked the Hatter and took his leave. "And whatever you do," the Hatter shouted after him, "don't mean more than you are!" He backed up this advice by flinging a teacup at the pig's head. This caused the pig to feel the prickle of nostalgic tears in the corner of one eye (the left one) and the rise of a lump in his throat that turned out to be a poorly chewed piece of scone (pronounced however you damn well like). He returned to the forest, retreated to the shade of an ancient sycamore, curled up at the roots, and went to sleep.

He awoke in the shade of an ancient sycamore, but that was as far as Coincidence was willing to carry him without a supplemental fare being paid. Wonderland had vanished. He was on the grounds of an impressive, imposing, implicitly British boys' school. Instead of the tender hand of an older sister to brush away the leaves that had fallen on his face while he drowsed, he met the stern gaze of a Master who instructed him to get his lazy carcase into chapel for Evensong or expect six of the best across his backside afterwards.

The years that followed there—and at Cambridge after—are of little interest to the general reader and less to the pig. No one on the faculty, staff, or student body at his first school ever re-marked upon the fact that there was an extra mouth to feed, a new bed to be made up, a fresh face to be recognized. The bills were paid in timely fashion; that sufficed.

The pig went home with his friends during the school holi-days, where he was duly presented to this or that brace of beaming parents as the son of a duchess. (True enough.) On the school records, he rejoiced in the name of Anthony Piperade, Lord DuCoeur. He grew up straight and tall and honest, with a healthy pink complexion and an appetite that made fond mothers admon-ish their own chicks to emulate him.

He did not get fat. He did not see anything wrong with eating bacon.

When he attained his majority, he was summoned to the Inns of Court where he was solemnly invested with full control over his inheritance. Documents were pushed back and forth across the table. Thus did young Lord Anthony learn that the Mad Hatter's mercury-induced insanity had not left him blind to the advantages of investing (heavily) in textile interests. A sealed letter was placed in the pig's hands. *It's too late for me, my boy*, it read. *They have brought up the big guns. By the time this reaches you, I will have suc-cumbed to being an Orphic archetype. Madness and poetry supposedly sleep in one bed. Fools that they are, they willfully overlook the fact that* some *poets manage to earn a living at it. Adieu and toodles. Destroy this before reading.*

"There was also this," said the man of law, giving the pig a small pasteboard box. It held the fragments of a broken teacup.

The pig looked up. "Why is a raven like a writing desk?" he asked.

The man of law chuckled and said that his lordship was pleased to be jocular.

Now that the mystery had been removed from his finances, he was his own pig. It was a very good feeling. He read Law at Cambridge and came to be a barrister with rooms in town and a fine place in the country. He continued to keep up his public school and university friendships. He traveled abroad and was enriched without becoming unduly aesthetic.

One drizzly day he encountered his mother in a Paris sidewalk cafe. The Duchess was sipping absinthe and reading a copy of Virginia Woolf's *Orlando*. (Time had passed. It will, given half the chance.) "Mother?" the pig inquired.

The Duchess looked up from her reading. "Oh, it's you," she said in an affable manner. "Join me, won't you?"

The pig was rather nonplussed by his mother's casual attitude. After all, he'd thought her dead, and what she'd thought *his* fate had been—

Or had she given that matter any thought at all? Women who thrust their infants into the care of other children—total strangers— cannot possibly have more on their minds than whether they've left themselves enough time to get good seats at the theater.

So the pig ordered a glass of gin-and-bitters when the waiter came, and made small talk until the drink was brought, and in general made himself as agreeable a companion as his social reputation always painted him. ("Good old Tony! He's a safe guest to make up your dinner party, Mavis. Pleasant-looking, wellborn, rich, nowhere near as witty as me, eats what's put in front of him, and he goes with any decor.")

But eventually the demon of Meaning would have his day, and the pig heard himself telling the Duchess that she was looking quite well for someone who had ostensibly burned to death in a conflagration lo, these many years agone.

"Oh, that," said the Duchess. She snapped her fingers and the waiter brought her another absinthe, although the fashion for the drink of Decadents has passed with the turning of the century and the introduction of mustard gas victims to polite society.

"Yes, that," said the pig as his mother imbibed. "I found the ruins. What happened?"

"Dejaneira set fire to the place," the Duchess informed him. She drank more absinthe.

"I see." He nursed his gin. "And who is or was or might be Dejaneira?"

"Why, the Cook, of course!" The Duchess regarded her son as if he had dropped out from beneath the tail of a pig rather than merely being one. "What else could she do? We were the embodiment of a fiery Sapphic romance gone awry under the merciless strictures of Victorian society. Her servile status was a galling reminder that even though she was the dominant partner, I would still have to be the one giving the orders. No wonder she threw things. As for the pepper—"

"*Must* I know?" the pig pleaded.

"It's all part and parcel, and you *did* ask," the Duchess reminded him. "Considering the shape of the peppercorn, my darling Dejaneira was grinding up the withered testicles of our enemies every time she employed that condiment. I don't even want to think about what significance the pepper mill's shape conveys." She smiled happily and patted the pig's hand. "My dear boy, it's been *eons* since anyone's asked to know all that. You can't imagine what a treat it's been to be able to get it out in the open one more time."

The pig shifted in his chair. "Where *is* Cook?" he asked. "She's not—she won't—will she be joining us?"

The Duchess's smile collapsed upon itself. She sighed. "She won't. It's over between us. I blame this post-War morality. Raise the hems and anything can happen. Everyone's gone all Sapphic now, even in the best homes, the finest families. Even in print, no less!" She waggled *Orlando* high, which the waiter took to mean an order for more drinks. "One can't *épater le bourgeoisie* if *les bourgeois* are looking at you over their milk-white shoulders and waiting for you to catch up. Some days I don't know what to do with myself."

The pig rose from his seat and laid a hand on his mother's shoulder. "Whatever you are, don't do more than you mean," he told her. It was advice given with the kindest of intentions. It was also the last time he saw the Duchess under those circumstances.

The Depression left him undepressed and as happily bereft of meaning as ever. During the bombardment of London by the Nazi forces he opened the doors of his country seat, *Gadara*, to several shipments of East End youth. Nothing was filched or broken or made to smell worse than before, and the experience left him curiously attracted to the thought of fatherhood.

Unfortunately, the practicalities intruded. Every morning he studied his reflection in the mirror and tacitly accepted the fact that he had aged, but nowhere near enough to account for all the years he'd seen pass by. To marry implied the inclusion of a more observant, less objective witness than the looking glass. From what he knew of women, not one of them would not consider it a privilege to be wed to a partner whose looks remained essentially unchanged while her own were diligently nibbled away by the mice of the minutes, the weasels of the weeks, the stoats of the seasons, and so on, until he ran out of measures of time and metaphoric animals with which to couple them.

Therefore he himself remained uncoupled, although he did engage in love affairs. Knowing himself to be what he was, he took pains to please his partners. When the dawn of the Women's Movement found him, no lady could point the finger at him and justly name him swine. (For the same reason, he had avoided a career in law enforcement when he came to the States in the '60s.) He remained in the States until all his old school chums were tidily dead or so senile they assumed he was his own grandson. Here he safely built up and improved upon the Hatter's textile empire.

A century had come and gone since the first publication of *Alice's Adventures Underground*. There had been some moments of dread, among the fluttering years, when he came dangerously close to meaning something. For a time he feared that *they* might view his slow, almost imperceptible aging process as symbolic of Man's Dream of Eternal Youth. Then he read about the Peter Pan syndrome and breathed easier. That slot was already occupied by Barrie's bonnie flying boy. His own peculiar loitering on the shady side of forty meant nothing, in and of itself. It was merely the halo effect of having first seen the light in an immortal work of fiction, a Chernobyl of the spirit.

The pig sat behind his desk and gazed out over the towers of Manhattan. The polished rosewood surface was only broken by the leatherette ticket folder his secretary had handed him a minute since. A one-way passage, First Class, would convey him back to Britain in three days' time. It would be good to see the old homestead—now a tourist mecca famous for its topiary display, damn the Inland Revenue to hell.

His telephone buzzed. He pushed a button and asked his secretary what she desired.

The woman was weeping. He could hear the great, shuddery sobs, could imagine how they must be shaking her slender body. Had she lost a loved one? Received some discouraging medical report? Merciful heavens, it sounded like the end of the world!

Which it was. Someone else had chosen to push a button not too long before the pig had taken similar action. The news was blaring through the streets even as the missiles were shrieking through the sky. He was able to cast one last, fond lingering look over his ticket-folder before the bowl of heaven shattered like a teacup against a wall of light.

For a time afterwards, he clung to life by threads of pain that twisted themselves into hawsers before finally fraying and letting him plummet into a pit of oblivion (as viewed from Survivor's Point). The panorama, like most, was breathtaking. This was unfortunate, since want of breath precludes a wail of heartsick pity getting any farther than the teeth.

Not blinded by the blast, the pig was forced to see what had become of other beings and all their scattered toys. For a time he did, until his intelligence told him he had the option of will—that basic I-don't-give-a-shit-about-you-I'm-doing-this-*my*-way attitude that is the principle of all survival outside of beehives and ant colonies and certain family reunions. He did not *have* to look at the devastation surrounding him if that was not his—wrong word, but still—pleasure. And if he did look, he did not have to *see*. As the few miserable remnants of humankind (How kind? How human? How dangerously close to the forced extraction of *meaning* it is to hold a word accountable for its syllables!) straggled their way back onto the burnt and gutted stage, the pig kept to himself and pretended they were not there.

In part, this was the meat and not the intellect at work. Even in human form, even with his flesh frizzled by the bomb, he knew he was still edible. Prudence preached retirement, both for the purposes of healing and survival. No matter what the speculative bards had sung about the tedium of immortality, the pig knew they plucked their tunes from a lute strung with sour grapevines. What the hell was wrong with living forever? Losing your loved ones all the time? It was just an Army brat's life writ large. You'd adjust. You'd make new friends, dear. If you're bored, you must be boring. Snap out of it.

The pig wanted to live. Maybe not like this, he thought, casting a wary look over yet another scorched cityscape, but things would get better. Or if they didn't, he'd get used to them. He wanted to live.

And whether it was his faith or his philosophy or just the fact that the world grew weary of supporting so much evidence that her top-of-the-foodchain children couldn't be left alone for two cosmic blinks without someone clobbering someone else (*Don't make Me stop this universe, kids, I'm warning you!*), the Earth kissed the nuclear boo-boo and made it all better.

Trees returned. Rough chunks of pavement not scavenged for cottage walls were worn away by the roots of new green things. The cockroaches decided to try for a better press this time around and evolved shimmery, iridescent wings and a lilting song that left the flash-fried nightingale spinning in her sepulchre.

And there were children. Babies were born hale and well, with the old-fashioned number of fingers and toes. The pig didn't see too many of them all at once, but he had lived through a time of not seeing too many automobiles, either. He saw his first when he left his hovel and went down to the riverbank to fetch some water.

The child was not dirty or scabby, nor did it look like a hunted animal. Its long yellow hair was clubbed back and there was a distinct pong of sweat and grease wafting from it, but the pig knew he was no bed of vanished roses either. He had some food with him—a dry but filling cake he made from acorns—and he offered it as a lure. The child carried mushrooms in a pouch and declined the lure in favor of a trade.

They did not speak the same language, but gestures helped and pigs learn fast. It also helped that they did not have much to talk about, which let them come to grasp the basics of each other's tongues. The pig still spoke English as he recalled it, the child an evolved offshoot of the same. It was a language linked to the mother tongue in the same way English was blood-kin to the lingo of *Beowulf*. It also helped that the pig was willing to play the fool to win a child's heart and that the child still knew laughter.

So the pig returned into a world that had recaptured its laughter and its joy in childhood and its sense that occasionally there would be times of no sense (which is as different from *non*sense as chalk from most kinds of cheese except Romano). He had gone gray by this time, and wrinkly, although he still had most of his hair and teeth and a peeling leatherette case that held crisp, crumbly yellow scraps of magic. And he knew where to find the best acorns.

The tribe took him in and sat him down with the other old men and told them to keep an eye on the children. The children tumbled around in the sun when it shone and sopped up the rain when it fell and loudly told one another that the real meaning of life was that they were to keep an eye on the old men.

The pig heard the M-word and shuddered. *Even here?* he thought. *Even now?* And he touched his leatherette ticket-folder and dreamed of topiary clipped into the shape of March Hares and Mad Hatters, of frogs in footman's livery and strident queens.

And one day, he began to talk of such things in his sleep—a sleep that is an old man's dozing compromise between slumber and death. He murmured of riverbanks and rabbit holes, of luckless lizards named Bill and flamingos coerced into service as croquet mallets. Asleep, awake, eyes open or closed, he spoke of these solemn matters, and like a tribe of wary dormice the children crept near to listen.

He knew the story, start to end. How could he not? It was his essence more than any double helix or stately manor now drowned beneath the waves that had devoured distant England. He spoke it slowly, neglecting not a word, and the children who did not speak the language of his tale still gathered close and cocked their heads and listened to the melodies of enchantment.

Most of what he told them was a barrage of names like autumn leaves, fluttering about wildly, detached from the objects they had once defined. It had been ages since anyone touched a teacup, let alone tea. But how much of Alice's world ever did follow her back up the rabbit hole, and for how long did it linger in the rolling world of daylight, leisure suits, and bombs? Her story did not deal in artifacts, but in wonders. In lands where men of law never wore wigs and climes where Cheshire Cats were never seen except as supper, Alice endured.

There are always miracles where there are children, and fascination for any tale that opens their eyes to marvels, whether or not they are sensible marvels. Even a pig knows that.

Soon the children were speaking a language closer to his own, and repeating long selections of the story. Soon the other old men waxed envious of the pig's ascendancy and dredged up other tales their own grandsires had told them when age made ancients babble nonsense: sweet nonsense of wolves who dressed up in granny's clothing, and maidens whose taste for pomegranate seeds deprived the world of spring, and babies whose birth brought winged beings down from the heavens, riding the tail of a splendid star.

And no one ever thought to tack a shred of *meaning* to a single one of those tales. Not one of all.

When the pig saw that the yellow-haired child he'd first met by the river had grown to have children of her own, he knew the time had come for him to go his ways. The old men's corner hummed with tales of many tellings, the old women joining in with stories of their own in the wintertimes. Some of the striplings had taken to the road with only a burden of stories on their backs and returned with tales garnered and traded and fresh-made from among the other peoples they encountered in their wanderings. The world-heart beat strong with the blood of *Once upon a time*.

Yes, it was time to go.

He made a last batch of acorn cake and crumbled the last of the first class airline tickets into the mix. "Well," he said, "I'm going." The other old men nodded. Sometimes a man preferred to meet his death where the leaves would look after his burial.

He was on his way out of the settlement when he heard a trip-trip-trip behind him, like the ghost of a piglet long gone but never dead. He turned and saw that he was being followed by the daughter of his first child-friend. Her name was nothing like Alice.

"What is it, my dear?" he asked as she caught up to him and solemnly took his hand. "You should go back. Your mother will be worried."

"You never told," she said.

"Told what?"

"Why *is* a raven like a writing desk?"

He smiled. "Have you ever seen a raven, child? Or a writing desk?"

To his surprise she replied, "Yes, I have."

"What? But where—?"

"Over there," she said, pointing with one hand as she used the other to smooth the wrinkles from her pinafore. "By the riverbank." She took his hand and said, "This way. Hurry. We're late."

He was dragged after her as easily as if he were made of paper. Leaves were falling from the trees, riffling across his eyes, bewildering him with their flittering pips of black and red, diamonds and clubs, hearts and spades. A church bell sounded somewhere far away. The child ran faster, so fast that he cried out for her to have a care, she'd tear her stockings on the brambles shielding the mouth of the rabbit hole. She ducked her golden head and pulled him through. His pouch of traveler's fare spilled in the root-hung darkness. She waited impatiently for him to gather up the fallen acorn cakes while she tapped her paw and frequently consulted a large gold pocketwatch. The last cake he retrieved was adorned with the words "EAT ME" picked out in currants.

"No time!" she cried, clapping a furry paw on his forearm. "She'll be furious! We're late!"

Past roses white and dripping red they ran, past the Queen, who flailed at her hedgehog-ball with her flamingo-mallet, past an ocean of human tears where all manner of curiouser and curiouser creatures ran heedlessly round and round in circles on the strand. It meant everything. It meant nothing. The pig went stumbling on, after a white-furred dream-child.

He hardly recognized the clearing. The Hatter and the mad March Hare laughed and sang and hailed him merrily. He drank a cup of tea that tasted suspiciously of dormouse and reached for a crumpet that filled his mouth with memory.

"Ah, no!" the Hatter cautioned, raising a finger. "Don't you start that old business all over again, my lad. It's only a story, you know. The troubles come when they try to make it mean things."

"Doesn't it?" asked the pig. "Does none of it mean anything?"

"It's a story," said the Hare. "It's a dream."

"You know, speaking of that dream, if you rearrange the letters in the words *Mad Hatter*, you do get something sensible," the pig said.

"And what do you do with that sensible thing after you've got it?" the Hatter asked. "Stick it in your writing desk? Leave it out for the ravens?"

The dormouse popped out of the teapot. "Whatever you mean," he said sleepily, "don't be more than you do."

"Here," said the Hatter. "This one should fit you." He pulled a tiny, white embroidered baby bonnet from his sleeve and tied it around the pig's head. It fit precisely.

The infant in his cradle screwed up his red, wrinkled face and cried. His mother picked him up herself and began to rock him, singing a lullaby while thunder scoured the heavens with a sound like kitchenware and crockery being flung by an irate Cook.

Some of *them* would say it was all a dream. Some of *them* would insist his crying meant an anguish for the womb's Wonderland lost.

Some of them might have the presence of mind to check his diaper and see if what they found in there *meant* anything.

Only an eternal story. Only a glimmering dream.

Only a child.

And for some, through all the ages of uncounted lives that yearn for wonder more than meaning, that would always mean enough.